James Philip

A Line in the Sand

[The Gulf War of 1964: Part I]

Timeline 10/27/62 – BOOK SEVEN

Cover concept by James Philip
Graphic Design by Beastleigh Web Design

Main Series

Book 1: Operation Anadyr
Book 2: Love is Strange
Book 3: The Pillars of Hercules
Book 4: Red Dawn
Book 5: The Burning Time
Book 6: Tales of Brave Ulysses
Book 7: A Line in the Sand
Book 8: The Mountains of the Moon
Book 9: All Along the Watchtower
Book 10: Crow on the Cradle
Book 11: 1966 & All That
Book 12: Only in America
Book 13: Warsaw Concerto
Book 14: Eight Miles High
Book 15: Won't Get Fooled Again

The War in the South Atlantic

Stumbling Towards the Edge
Book 16: Armadas
Book 17: Smoke on the Water
Book 18: Cassandra's Song

USA Series

Book 1: Aftermath
Book 2: California Dreaming
Book 3: The Great Society
Book 4: Ask Not of Your Country
Book 5: The American Dream

Australia Series

Book 1: Cricket on the Beach
Book 2: Operation Manna

A Timeline 10/27/62 Novel

Football in The Ruins – The World Cup of 1966

Timeline 10/27/62 Stories

A Kelper's Tale*
Cuba Libre
La Argentina*
Puerto Argentino*
The House on Haight Street
The Lost Fleet

*Available in a single volume as 'The Malvinas Trilogy'

For the latest news and author blogs about the
Timeline 10/27/62 Series check out
www.thetimelinesaga.com

Chapter 1

Monday 13th April 1964
RAF Faldingworth, Lincolnshire, England

After a wet and dreary, almost wintery weekend when dawn broke over Lincolnshire the sky was clear and the first rays of the morning Sun brightly illuminated the low-loaders queuing along the perimeter road. Several of the ugly vehicles were hauled by big Scammell tank transporters, including several of World War II vintage which had been recovered from half-forgotten mothball depots after the October War.

The light of the new day fell across the fresh camouflage paint on the slab sides of the big tractors; and as each periodically fired up its engine clouds of acrid yellow grey smoke belched from their exhaust stacks, hazing the still Lincolnshire air.

The slow, methodical business of moving nuclear bomb components from dispersed sites across the old airfield to the assembly bunkers had continued unabated while the big transporters came and went for over a hundred hours now. Shifts of ordnance technicians and changes of the guard – eight hours on, eight hours off – succeeded one after the other until to the men and women of 92 Maintenance Unit, Faldingworth Nuclear Bomb Store (Permanent Ammunition Depot), night and day slowly merged into an unbroken, meaningless continuum. At regular intervals technical teams were escorted out to the concrete 'hutches' – small above ground 'hardened' structures where the fissile cores of individual weapons were stored – and returned to the big 'Special Munitions' assembly bunkers with their heavily shielded loads. Every hour, sometimes one, or perhaps, two warning alarms would sound, the great steel blast doors of the complex would roll open, and another bomb, or pair of bombs, would be unhurriedly, carefully trundled out to be gently hoisted onto the low-loader that had been summoned forward to bear it away to its designated 'Forward Permanent Ammunition Dump'.

Most of the high-yield weapons were being sent to the FPADs – in former years, the modified 'bomb dumps' – at the RAF V-Bomber stations at Coningsby, Scampton and Wyton; while eleven low-yield, Hiroshima size bombs, were scheduled to be transported to the Royal Naval 'Special Weapons Depot' at Fort Nelson near Portsmouth for future deployment on board the aircraft carriers HMS Ark Royal (currently in dockyard hands), HMS Eagle and HMS Hermes (both based in the Mediterranean).

At the gates to RAF Faldingworth each departing transporter picked up an escort of machine-gun armed Land Rovers, Ferret armoured cars and at least one truck load of heavily armed infantrymen before setting off for its final destination. Striking out ahead of each convoy RAF Regiment detachments cleared *all* the roads, and units of the 4th Infantry Division, based in Lincolnshire continuously patrolled and 'secured' the countryside around *all* the routes between Faldingworth and the V-Bomber stations awaiting the deadly cargoes. Different security arrangements were being developed to transport the 'Navy's eggs' south to Portsmouth in either a single large, or two smaller fighting columns.

RAF Faldingworth was in the eye of the approaching storm.

A State of Emergency had been declared within hours of the atrocities at RAF Brize Norton and at RAF Cheltenham a week ago; and one hundred and seven hours ago the United Kingdom of Great Britain and Northern Ireland had unilaterally declared war on the Soviet Union.

RAF Faldingworth had come into existence as a decoy airfield called Toft Grange in July 1942. On completion it had become a Bomber Command satellite station of RAF Lindholme; between August 1943 and February 1944 hosting 1667 Heavy Conversion Unit. Then in the spring of 1944 the Lancasters of No. 300 (Polish) Squadron had taken up residence at Faldingworth, staying until the official disbandment of the Free Polish Air Force in 1946.

Although the old wartime airfield was unsuitable for the operation of the new generation of post-war fast jets, Faldingworth had survived the disposal programs and various rationalizations of the late 1940s and 1950s as Bomber Command was re-shaped ahead of the formation of the V-Bomber Force.

Soon after No. 92 Maintenance Unit had started operating at Faldingworth in 1948, the RAF had determined to concentrate its ordnance in a small number of strategically located depots - under a 1950 plan codenamed 'Galloper' - rather than in literally scores of local sites as had been the historic practice. The new 'Permanent Ammunition Depots' or PADs, would accommodate purpose-built bunkers, assembly and handling facilities. It was initially envisaged that the new PADs would be at Binbrook, Coningsby, Waddington, Scampton, Hemswell and Faldingworth. However, it was one thing making a decision; another entirely implementing it. Between the original 'staff decision' in 1950 and the planned opening of Faldingworth and the other PADs, Great Britain had acquired nuclear weapons and it was belatedly appreciated that storing thousands of tons of conventional bombs on the same sites as the new 'special weapons' posed very obvious, and possibly insuperable problems.

Safely storing and handling the new 'special weapons' like *Blue Danube*, the RAF's first 'homemade' atomic bomb, required wholly different and vastly more complex skills and procedures than those appropriate to managing even the most advanced conventional munitions. Secrecy and security were paramount; and after much treasure had been wasted and large areas of countryside had been dug up to bury unnecessary and redundant concrete bomb dumps, plans for most of the Permanent Ammunition Depots were scaled back or quietly abandoned.

In the end the RAF had constructed only two 'special weapons' PADs; Faldingworth and a twin facility, located at Thetford Heath in Suffolk, known as RAF Barnham. The two PADs had 'opened for business' in 1957 and 1956 respectively. While Barnham had survived the October War physically intact, over half its personnel had died on the night of the war off base and many of the survivors of the nearby Soviet air burst strike over what was otherwise rural East Anglia, had subsequently died of radiation sickness. In February, March and April last year Bomber Command had mounted a salvage operation to remove all remaining 'nuclear stores' from Barnham to Faldingworth, and to the pre-existing secure 'on station special weapons bomb dump' at RAF Scampton.

For most of the last year Faldingworth had accommodated a mixed inventory of *Blue Danube* and *Red Beard* tactical – Hiroshima-type free fall devices – and *Yellow Snow* city-killer bombs. In the dreadful jargon of these things, *Blue Danube* and *Red Beard* came in various 'flavours' with 15-kiloton and 25-kiloton warheads; and *Yellow Sun* in variants with a tested 400-500 kiloton, and an untested 1.1 megaton capacity. Until two months ago several American dual key bombs and missile warheads previously held at V-Bomber bases, had been stockpiled at Faldingworth but these had all been handed over to the US Air Force Radiological Materials Recovery Task Force based at Greenham Common near Newbury, under the terms of the 'US-UK Mutual Assistance Treaty' initialled in Washington in January.

Until the end of March 1964, No. 92 Maintenance Unit had been systematically recovering, making safe and storing the bomb casings, the physics packages and the fissile elements of over eighty percent of the United Kingdom's entire nuclear arsenal. A major part of its work recently had been processing the consignment of over thirty warheads secretly brought back to England from the officially unacknowledged 'special storage facility' at Singapore in the holds of two modified merchant ships, and in the air-conditioned 'special magazine compartments' of the Ark Royal and the Hermes under cover of Operation Manna the previous autumn.

Just a week ago Faldingworth had been implementing plans to operate on a 'long-term' secure 'care and maintenance' level, involving the mothballing of one of the two assembly bunkers. Ironically, only days before the outrage at Tehran, and notwithstanding Red Dawn's nuclear strikes in the Mediterranean in early February, Margaret Thatcher's government had issued revised 'special weapons' policy guidance directives to the RAF based on the assumption that another 'all out' nuclear exchange was 'unlikely in the foreseeable future'. Therefore, henceforward the reduced V-Bomber Force and the Royal Navy's ongoing nuclear 'throw' should be reduced to and to be maintained at a 'prudent minimum deterrence level' rather than a 'first strike level'.

In practice this had meant that by mid-summer less than forty free fall weapons would be available for deployment at any one time; of which only ten *Read Beard* Mark I 15-kiloton, and ten *Yellow Sun* bombs with 400-kiloton *Green Grass* warheads should be immediately available to RAF bomber squadrons based in the United Kingdom. Moreover, under the new arrangements all Royal Navy-held nuclear weapons would be brought ashore to the two 'secure depots' at Fort Nelson in Hampshire and Rosyth in Scotland pending transfer to Faldingworth.

However, a week was a very long time in this brave new post-October War World. Now Faldingworth's row upon row of squat, ugly fissile 'Hutches' were being methodically emptied, and its bomb assembly shops were working non-stop to enable the RAF and the Royal Navy's Fleet Air Arm to wage all-out nuclear war at the press of a button.

Chapter 2

Monday 13th April 1964
Arabian American Oil Company (Aramco) Headquarters, Dhahran,
Saudi Arabia

Although Tehran was over six hundred and fifty miles away as the crow might fly from Dhahran, fifty-four-year-old Thomas Barger, the Chief Executive Officer of the Arabian American Oil Company (Aramco), sensed the seismic shift beneath his feet as he stood looking out of the windows of his second-floor office across Half Moon Bay towards Al Khobar – half lost in the mid-day heat haze – where he had first set foot in Arabia some twenty-six years ago.

The Cuban Missiles War had not directly touched Arabia; there had been no radioactive fallout clouds and bizarrely, in the first weeks and months after the cataclysm things had seemed oddly unchanged. However, lately the aftershocks had been arriving almost daily. One by one all the old assumptions about the nature and reach of American power had been subtly undermined in Arabia in ways he feared had been largely discounted or dismissed out of hand back in the United States.

Now the unthinkable had happened; the Soviets – whom the 'best and the brightest' in America had declared vanquished – had destroyed Tehran and had invested the mountains of Northern Iran. Whether the Red Army poured through the passes of the Zagros Mountains, out onto the plains below the headwaters of the Tigris and the Euphrates, or drove south across the great rocky plateau of central Iran mattered not one jot. In either case the oilfields of Kurdistan in northern Iraq, and the biggest refinery complex on the planet at Abadan in the south, and everything in between lay at the mercy of the Russians. Even if the Soviets *only* – and *even* this was an incalculably nightmarish 'if' – planned to capture the Iraqi and Iranian shores of the Persian Gulf, American hegemony and what little remained of European influence in the Middle East was about to disappear in a huge oily cloud of smoke.

Nobody had really known what was going on until the last twenty-four hours. And then the scale of the impending disaster had suddenly been writ plain in impossibly and frighteningly massive letters. The news was so bad that Barger had started to bypass the conversations he had been having with *his* people at the US Embassy in Riyadh and *his* contacts at the Consulate in Dhahran, and was getting his news exclusively from the BBC's recently re-instituted World Service and Aramco's internal wire service.

Red Army airborne troops had seized the Shah of Iran; put the bastard up against a wall with several terrified members of his harem – all young European women – and machine gunned him, and the unfortunate young women to pieces. Copies of the movie of this atrocity and of the nuking of Tehran had been sent to every foreign ministry in the Middle East! Subsequently, Soviet tanks had besieged Tabriz, and driven south as far as Bonab and Malekan; simultaneously airborne forces had taken the city of Urmia without a fight ensuring that the invaders controlled both the western and eastern banks of Lake Urmia. There was nothing to stop the invaders over-running the key city of Qoshachay on the Zarriné River; and thereafter the whole of Azerbaijani Iran opposite the old Turkish border and the - probably virtually undefended - north eastern border of Iraqi Kurdistan would soon be in Russian hands; from that impregnable mountainous bastion the Red Army could turn back into Iran, or fall upon Iraq, a sad country sliding into an inevitable sectarian civil war.

The fate of Tehran had – predictably – totally unhinged the regime in Baghdad whose first irrational response to the news from Iran had been to probe across the Iranian border north of Khorramshahr with elements of three armoured brigades, looking for advantage from the old enemy's misfortune. After forty-eight hours of inconclusive fighting with a much smaller Iranian force a handful of British Army tanks sent north from Abadan had fallen on the flank of the leading Iraqi brigade, prompting the local Iranian defenders to mount an immediate counter attack. Within hours the Iraqi invasion force had been routed, and was retreating in pell-mell confusion and panic, the survivors abandoning at least half their tanks on the eastern, Iranian side of the Arvand River as they melted back into the suburbs of Basra on the west bank. By all accounts there had since been widespread rioting and civil disorder in the city.

Farther north nobody actually knew for sure what was going on in Baghdad; other that was, than in the wake of the 'disaster' in the south there had been some sort of 'palace coup' and that there was sporadic fighting in the streets involving competing units of the Iraqi Army.

Thomas Barger would have despaired if he had believed it would have helped; but he was not that sort of man. Among his countrymen he was a rare animal, an authentic Middle East 'expert', a man who had devoted much of his adult life to developing an affinity with, and an understanding off, that most ephemeral of things; the 'Arab mind'. There was of course, no such thing as the 'Arab mind', any more than there was any such thing as an 'American' or a 'British' mind; what there was in reality was a regional culture that to most westerners, was as ancient as it was unfathomable. Therein lay the root cause of the majority of 'western' misconceptions about Arabia and the Middle East.

The Middle East was a jigsaw of feudal emirates, countries invented by the reckless – and criminally lazy - pens of European diplomats, religious hatreds, ethnic bigotry; and an unholy farrago of proxies of past and present colonial overlords. The region had been a powder keg in Ottoman times; and then after the greater part of the World's known easily extractable oil reserves had been discovered under its deserts and rocky fastnesses in the first half of the twentieth century, East and West had ruthlessly vied for the upper hand, weaponry had poured into the region, unspeakable despots had been propped up, and the region's multiple fracture lines papered over. It was a miracle the whole Middle East had not imploded after the October War; the trouble was that anybody with eyes in his head could see that the day of reckoning had not been averted, merely delayed.

Today it was beginning to look as if judgment day had not been delayed overlong.

Barger was an oil man, a businessman and he understood that at times like this, diplomats were no better than flimflam men. The World had gone to Hell in a hand basket in the last week. The news from Malta had been bad enough – very nearly disastrous, in fact – but at least the British had held on until the Seventh Cavalry, in the shape of the US Navy had belatedly saved the day.

The repulse of the Soviet invasion force at Malta was the last of the good news. Hard on its heels had followed the reports of the atrocities perpetrated by the Irish Republican Army in England. After that who could blame the British for reacting as they had? Worse, in the Middle East the United States' former clients had noted - with no little alarm and growing despondency - the feebleness and indecision with which the Kennedy Administration had responded and drawn their own lessons; none of which boded well for the future of Arab-US relations. The irresolution of the American response – bordering on 'disinterest' – was in stark contrast to the uncompromisingly belligerent line that the British had adopted following the Soviets' 'unilateral employment of a nuclear weapon against a civilian population' in Tehran.

Every thirty minutes the BBC World Service broke into its normal programming to broadcast an unequivocal statement of intend that began: 'The Soviet leadership is hereby given notice that any further use of nuclear weapons by it, its allies or its proxies will result in an all-out strike by the United Kingdom against the forces of the Soviet Union and any surviving concentrations of population or industry within the former territories of the Soviet Union, or in any territories deemed to now be under Soviet control.'

The ninety second statement went on in a relentlessly similar vein and concluded: 'RAF bombers stand ready at the end of their runways at four minutes notice to go to war. Other RAF bombers are airborne at this time ready to strike within minutes of the receipt of the order to attack!'

It went without saying that there had been no such unambiguous statement of intent from the Kennedy Administration.

The arrival of two 'bombed up' RAF Avro Vulcan V-Bombers and three transport aircraft carrying their spares and service crews at Dhahran yesterday afternoon had sent the Saudi government exactly the sort of signal that it had been waiting in vain for the Kennedy Administration to send it for much of the last week.

The Chief Executive Officer of the Arabian American Oil Company sighed and looked to his companion; whom he knew to be a gifted, westernized example of the Kingdom of Saudi Arabia's *new* generation of technocrats who understood exactly what the catastrophic events unfolding over six hundred miles to the north portended.

"So," the younger man remarked dryly in Arabic, subconsciously brushing his immaculately trimmed goatee with his right forefinger, "it seems that the World turns again, my friend?"

The first thing Thomas Barger had done after he jumped onto that rotting, dilapidated pier at Al Khobar in 1937 to set foot in what was then an impoverished, tribal backwater populated with still warring desert tribes, was to attempt to familiarise himself with the terrain and the basic customs of Arabia. The second thing he had done was to set about becoming fluent in Arabic; which over the last quarter of a century he had learned to speak like a native. This was no idle affectation; the Kingdom was his home; four of his children had been born in Saudi Arabia and many of his closest friends and practically all his most trusted lieutenants were Saudis.

"I think we must wait and see, your Excellency."

The younger man nodded politely.

Ahmed Zaki Yamani, the thirty-three-year-old Minister of Petroleum and Mineral Resources whom westerners with no understanding of the Kingdom and little respect for its ancient mores and traditions, casually referred to as 'Sheik' Yamani, nodded thoughtfully. Like the older man he understood that regardless of their business, personal, or political agendas – which inevitably were radically divergent – the situation in Iran and Iraq was profoundly dangerous to absolutely everything they *both* held dear.

There was a knock at the door and two young men – Saudis on Thomas Barger's staff entered and placed a coffee jug and cups and saucers on a low table set away from the Aramco CEO's broad desk.

Presently, Barger and Yamani were alone again.

Today the quietness seemed somehow oppressive with shadows looming over their heads. It was a signature of the times that two such powerful men could feel so insecure on account of unforeseen events over which they had no control taking place many hundreds of miles away.

In retrospect recent events in Iran now came into sharp perspective; it was nothing less than the unmistakable *end game* of a brilliantly conceived and executed Soviet campaign to wrest back the geopolitical strategic initiative from the *victors* of the Cuban Missiles War.

First there had been the deeply troubling events in the Mediterranean in December: the hostilities between the British and the Spanish which threatened to close the Straits of Gibraltar and to de-stabilize the North African coast; immediately followed by – bizarrely – the American bombing of Malta just before the rebellion which had left half of Washington DC in ruins. Next there had been the nightmare of a Red Dawn horde over running the Anatolian littoral of Turkey, infesting and defiling the Aegean and plunging the Balkans into bloody turmoil. The British had been driven off Cyprus, the Royal Navy had been attacked with Hiroshima-size nuclear weapons while attempting to recover the pre-October War cache of thermonuclear warheads stored on Cyprus, and in this and other operations in the Eastern Mediterranean; a cruiser had been sunk, an aircraft carrier crippled and several smaller warships lost or badly damaged.

As if this was not bad enough, on the morning of 7th February the most powerful ship ever to have steamed upon any ocean, the brand new nuclear-powered super carrier the USS Enterprise had been badly damaged by the airburst of one of two very large – low megaton range warheads – which had 'missed' their intended target, Malta, after being launched from deep within the Soviet Union. In that attack the Enterprise's consort, the fifteen thousand tone nuclear-powered guided missile cruiser Long Beach and one of the two American ships' flotilla of escorting British destroyers, HMS Aisne, had been destroyed by the same airburst, and only the courageous fire-fighting assistance of two other small Royal Navy ships, HMS Scorpion and HMS Talavera had, after many hours enabled Enterprise's crew to contain and extinguish her fires.

One ICBM launched in the same salvo had over-flown Cairo before detonating relatively harmlessly several miles beyond the Great Pyramids of Giza, but a second had obliterated Ismailia in Egypt, this latter strike blocking the Suez Canal with several sunken merchantmen and an Egyptian Navy frigate. Thomas Barger was not alone in thinking that in the light of the Soviet invasion of Iran – and in due course, probably Iraq – that the probably coincidental obstruction of the Suez Canal making it impossible to transfer heavy forces quickly from the Mediterranean to either the Arabian Peninsula or to the Persian Gulf, was the cruellest of the unintended consequences of those February nuclear strikes. There were no roads or railways across the deserts of Sinai, Arabia, Jordan or Iraq connecting the Gulf to the Mediterranean; no way to expeditiously transport tanks, vehicles, artillery, ammunition or the thousand and one spares and supplies a modern army required to fight a war from the United Kingdom, America, or anywhere in the Mediterranean other than by sending ships the 'long way' around the Cape of Good Hope. Dhahran was over twelve-and-a-half thousand miles from the United Kingdom or Malta by sea around the Cape; forty to sixty days steaming even if reinforcements could somehow, against the odds, be scraped together within the next few days which nobody thought was very likely.

Mistakenly, the British and the Americans had believed that February's paroxysm of violence had burnt itself out when there had been no further attacks; in hindsight it was obvious that this had been just so much wishful thinking. The British had been preoccupied with retaking Cyprus, and with containing what seemed to be a waning Red Dawn menace in the Aegean and the Eastern Mediterranean, and with the arrival of several US Navy nuclear submarines in the theatre to 'police' the seaways in retrospect, a somewhat surreal – lull before the storm - *calm* had settled across the Eastern Mediterranean.

It was hardly surprising that when the storm struck it had been with utterly unexpected sudden violence which had come within an inch of carrying all before it.

At the very moment that Malta – the most strategically important Anglo-American base in the whole Mediterranean was virtually undefended, with practically the whole British Fleet deployed over a thousand miles away to retake Cyprus from the Red Dawn horde – an audacious Soviet combined sea and air assault on the Maltese Archipelago had come within an ace of overwhelming the under strength British garrison. But for the heroic action of the men of two small, hopelessly out-gunned and out-numbered Royal Navy warships; HMS Yarmouth and HMS Talavera, the great fortress of Malta might have fallen to the Soviets in an afternoon.

Maskirovska!

It had all been a smokescreen.

Smoke and mirrors!

The Russian martial art of convincing one's foe to fixate on one hand while plotting to land a knockout blow with the other.

In the great scale of things, it did not matter that Malta had resisted the invaders; what mattered was that the West's gaze had been dragged back into the Central Mediterranean at the very moment two Soviet tank armies were crashing into the mountains of Iraq, and that Tehran ceased to exist.

When Thomas Barger had joined Aramco, the company had still been the *Standard Oil Company of California*; and much of the 'real' information he had thus far received about the crisis back home and elsewhere had been in cables sent from Aramco's California offices, over two-and-a-half thousand miles away from the politicking in Philadelphia. That events in the mountains of Iran could so swiftly lead to a potentially irrevocably rift with the United Kingdom, supposedly the US's oldest and closest ally, spoke eloquently to the ongoing tragedy of the age. It also confirmed to Thomas Barger what he had suspected at the time; that the Kennedy Administration had never actually intended to honour its side of the US-UK Mutual Defence Treaty negotiated in January. Beyond, that is, in areas it perceived to be of immediate vital national interest to the United States.

The 'Treaty' had served its purpose, now it could be consigned to the dustbin of history. Back in December last year avoiding a war with the 'old country' had been the number one priority of the Administration in the aftermath of the Battle of Washington, the Administration had needed a fig leaf behind which to hide when it dramatically reversed 1963's 'peace dividend' cuts to the military. Back home the reversal of the cuts had already begun to re-energise the flagging American industrial machine, and given President Kennedy a shot at re-election in the fall. Cynics were already whispering that sending the US Navy to the Mediterranean in the interim had been a price worth paying to retain a foothold in Europe, ahead of the mammoth task of reconstruction, which stateside, it was assumed would sooner or later inevitably enrich the World's only superpower beyond the dreams of Croesus...

Barger snapped out of the darkling cycle of his thoughts.

The Saudi Minister of Petroleum and Mineral Resources had been placidly studying the face of the man who was at once the single greatest obstacle to the Kingdom regaining control of its own massive oilfields; and the single most tangible symbol of American imperial might and therefore, until recently the ex officio guarantor of Saudi Arabian territorial integrity. The October War had created a new World order. It was now self-evident that in the aftermath of the Cuban Missiles War the Kingdom had made a series of bad decisions, several of which were now coming home to roost.

"What do you think is going on in the Philadelphia White House?" He asked softly.

The oilman shrugged.

Thomas Barger had been born in Minneapolis, Minnesota and grown up in Linton, North Dakota. After graduating from the University of North Dakota at Grand Forks with a degree in mining and metallurgy in 1931 he had spent several years in Canada and the American North West working as a surveyor, an engineer, assayer and as an under manager at a radium mine. Later he had taught at the University of North Dakota for a spell before joining the Anaconda Copper Mining Company. It was only when collapsing metal prices and the great Depression finally caught up with this last concern, coincidentally at the time he was contemplating marriage, that Barger had been compelled to seek work wherever he could find it.

Thus, had commenced the true odyssey of his life; within weeks of marrying Kathleen Elizabeth Ray, he had journeyed to Saudi Arabia as a surveyor and geologist on the payroll of the Standard Oil Company of California and the rest, as they say, was history. Barger and a handful of other American geologists, escorted across the fastnesses of Arabia by Bedouins of the Ajman clan had been responsible for, in a few short years, the discovery and mapping of the great – then as now the biggest in the World – oilfields of the Kingdom known to its disparate tribes as al-Mamlakah al-Arabiyyah as-Suʿūdiyyah.

Over the years all of Barger's fellow geologists and surveyors from those heady days of discovery and exploration had moved on to other things but he had remained, captivated and enthralled by Arabia. By the time the oilfields started to come into full production in the late 1940s he was Aramco's – the company's name had changed to the 'Arabian American Oil Company' on 31st January 1944 – key link with the Saudi authorities. For many years he was Aramco's Director of Local Government Relations and by the 1950s the right-hand man of the corporation's cavalier go-getting CEO, Norman 'Cy' Hardy, whom he had eventually succeeded in 1961.

Barger was aware of the uncomfortable silence. He shrugged an apology to his guest and forced his mind to consider the unpalatable practicalities of the unfolding crisis. Latterly, his thought processes turned like those of so many of his Arab friends; and when he went home, he often found his countrymen rude, crass, clumsily over-direct and impatient when simple common courtesy demanded circumlocution rather than a stab at the heart of a thing.

"I don't think you had any dealings with my old boss, Cy Hardy?" He asked Yamani, wholly rhetorically. "Cy was the ultimate 'one page' man. He believed that nothing was so complicated that it needed to be written on more than one page. If you didn't say what you needed to say on the first page you were wasting his time. I wonder how Cy would have coped with things the way they are now?"

The Minister of Petroleum and Mineral resources considered this unhurriedly, understanding exactly what the American was trying to tell him between the lines. In many ways the Chief Executive Officer of Aramco, superficially very much an American 'company man' operating in a supposedly alien environment, was infinitely more intuitively attuned to the Arab mind than he was to those of any of his stockholders back in the United States. He had lived so long in the desert beneath the great tent of the Kingdom that he saw things very differently from his fellows 'back home'.

How could it be otherwise?

Ahmed Zaki Yamani was of that generation of privileged young Saudis whom necessity had decreed should be educated abroad. In that way they might be exposed to the ways of the modern milieu and to the temptations of the West. While within the Kingdom Islamic orthodoxy - Sunni Wahhabism, in his own tongue *ad-Da'wa al-Wahhābiya* - admitted of no fault, no room for accommodation and compromise with the infidel; pragmatically, it was widely recognized that *peacefully* asserting control over its own oil and gas fields was going to demand a certain sleight of hand. Consequently, many young men like Yamani, of distinguished, but not invariably noble lineages had been sent abroad to learn what they might about the ways of the World.

Yamani, the son of a Qadi – a respected judge and scholar of Islamic law – who was currently the Grand Mufti of Indonesia and Malaysia, was one of the first of the new generation to rise to prominence in the Kingdom. Having earned a law degree at King Fouad I University in Cairo, his government had sent him to the Comparative Law Institute at New York University, where in 1955 he had earned a master's degree in Comparative Jurisprudence. Yamani, the son of a Qadi and the grandson of the Grand Mufti of Turkey had married Laila, an Iraqi woman in Brooklyn. Thereafter he had moved on to Harvard Law School where he had won a second master's degree.

Returning to the Kingdom he had become an advisor to the government during the 'troubled' period when Kind Saud and Prince Faisal were vying for power; demonstrating a priceless quality in any politician, that of adroitly not burning his boats with either of the competing factions. It had only been when Faisal became Crown Prince that Yamani – still in his early thirties - had replaced Abdullah

Tariki, the fiery nationalist long-time Oil Minister and founding light of the Organisation of Petroleum Exporting Countries (OPEC), as the new Minister of Petroleum and Mineral Resources.

"Forgive me, my friend," the younger man grimaced, "it seems to me that you and I must prepare ourselves and our principals for the shape of things to come."

Two decades ago, Roosevelt and Churchill had carved up the oil fields of the Middle and Near East like two ruthless Conquistadors of old. The United States got Arabia; the British Iran and a large slice of Iraq. After the Abadan Crisis of the early 1950s when Iran attempted to nationalise its oil fields and refineries the Eisenhower Administration had – via a CIA sponsored coup d'état had put the Shah back on the Peacock Throne in Tehran – and in a cynical *quid pro quo* 'bought into' the British 'concession' at Abadan. This latter 'investment' took the form participation in a so-called 'Consortium for Iran', a cartel set up *at the bidding* of the State Department comprising the World's seven largest oil conglomerates.

Under Eisenhower's Presidency the State Department concerned itself with practical 'Realpolitik' as opposed to the tenth-grade version the Kennedy Administration had pursued up to, during and after the October War.

The 'Seven Sisters' had formalised and organised the World's oil markets for the benefit of American, and by default, western industrial society. US Presidents rarely permit moral scruples to impinge on major foreign policy decisions; it was a lesson the British ought to have remembered before they allowed themselves to be suckered by the Kennedy Administration back in January.

Or perhaps, the British had not been 'suckered' at all, perhaps they had just wanted to avoid another war so badly they had not worried overmuch that they were being set up for another fall further down the line?

Now even the days of the 'Seven Sisters' were numbered. The 'Seven Sisters' – Anglo-Persian Oil, Gulf Oil, Aramco, Texaco, Royal Dutch Shell, Standard Oil of New Jersey, and the Standard Oil Company of New York - still controlled ninety percent of the World's somewhat diminished post-October war oil industry; although for how much longer was a moot point. It was one thing for the Kennedy Administration to carry on behaving as if Arabian oil was *American oil*; here in Dhahran the facts on the ground spoke to the increasing ambivalence of the Saudis towards their former overlords.

Having risen in rebellion against the dead hand of the Ottomans and later shrugged off the attentions of a waning British Empire, the Kingdom had never been at ease sheltering in the long shadow of the new American Imperium. After the October War the Kennedy Administration had mistakenly taken the allegiance of the Kingdom as a given. Who else was going to buy the Saudis' oil? Who else was capable of guaranteeing the territorial integrity of Arabia? Hell, in the new post-war World the United States did not even have to base significant military forces – or any forces at all – in the Region; it was sufficient just for Saudi Arabia's neighbours to know that the World's last nuclear superpower stood behind the Kingdom. The air bases had been mothballed, three massive emergency war stores depots stocked to overflowing at nearby Dammam and in the desert at Jeddah, and outside Riyadh– just in case of need – and all bar a couple of hundred logistics troops, military 'caretakers', had gone home.

Six months ago, the deal had perfectly suited the Saudi ruling family and the bean counters at the Pentagon.   However, what the 'masterminds' back in Washington had not told the Saudis was that when the USS Independence – the US Navy's 'guard ship' in the Indian Ocean - went back to Norfolk, Virginia for a twelve-month refit and overhaul, she would be taking her powerful escorting task force with her and she was *not* coming back.   To the Saudis, who viewed the presence of a powerful American naval presence in the Indian Ocean as incontrovertible evidence of the US's ongoing commitment to the region's security, the discover that within weeks of redefining its pact with the Kennedy Administration that the US Government had in effect, reneged, on its contract with the Kingdom was so extraordinary that men like Yamani could still hardly believe it.

American soldiers and airmen on the ground in the Kingdom had been both an irritant and a unifying force.   Many Saudis had viewed the 'foreign troops' as infidel interlopers but contrarily, felt safer for having them around.   In their absence the tribal tensions and religious fault lines within Saudi society had begun again to seek expression, sorely exacerbated by the fact there was no longer an insatiable market for seven-tenths of the oil the Kingdom now had to export the 'long way' around the Cape of Good Hope to the Americas, or across the Southern Ocean to Australasia.

The American and European post-1945 boom had been fuelled by Saudi and Iranian oil but now there was no longer an ever thirstier, European economic miracle guzzling hydro-carbons like there was no tomorrow.   Over fifty percent of the whole global oil market had disappeared overnight in late October 1962, and the price of crude at the well head was stubbornly stuck at significantly below one-third of its pre-war level.   America now slaked between eighty and ninety percent of its domestic thirst for oil from its own resources and those of nearby client states like Venezuela. The British, lacking credit lines within the Kingdom now relied wholly on the bottomless well of Abadan to feed their recovering industries and to heat their hearths. Last year the shortage of tankers and Nasser's closure of the Suez Canal had, for several months stopped them assuaging their thirst for Mesopotamian black gold.   Now that the British had completed their epic Operation Manna *exercise* – bringing every United Kingdom registered ship back under Royal Navy control and requisitioning and seizing every 'stateless' cargo ship on the high seas – the conveyor belt of tankers linking the British Isles to the oilfields of Persia via the Cape had been restored, further depressing the price of Saudi oil on the open market.

Where previously it had threatened to flood in; western gold now only dripped and trickled into Arabia. The Kingdom's long-term dream of being the World's banker, of building a great new modern Caliphate to rival that of the Safavids, of being once again the beating heart of a re-born Islamic empire now seemed vaingloriously hollow.

Thomas Barger was not a man who readily embraced apocalyptic notions of change and the resulting chaos; but he could not but be painfully aware of how tenuous his position and that of his company might become in the next few days and weeks. The mantra that applied was that *nothing lasts forever*, and in the words of John Maynard Keynes, 'in the long run we are all dead'. In many ways he was astonished that the pre-October War status quo had survived so long; and that even now the post-1945 settlement under which the British and the Americans had carved up the oil fields of Arabia, Mesopotamia and the Near East remained, albeit not for much longer, in force. True, there had been hiccups a plenty in the last few years.

"It goes without saying," Yamani decided, "that in the current situation the Kingdom must seek certain assurances from President Kennedy. If that is, the current relationship between our countries is to continue. But," again he was a little apologetic, "clearly, if the United States is unable or unwilling to guarantee the sovereignty and the inviolability of our territorial borders, then I am sure you will understand that the Kingdom may be forced to explore other options?"

The Chief Executive Officer of Aramco nodded.

He understood Yamani's threat perfectly.

The younger man had gone out of his way not to remind him that the only significant 'foreign' military forces 'on the ground' in the region were British and Australian, based mainly in Aden, Oman and at Abadan. It was common knowledge – probably because the British wanted it to be so – that the garrisons at Abadan and elsewhere had recently been reinforced by units withdrawn from Borneo, and armoured vehicles, including an unknown number of the latest Mark II version of the formidable Centurion tank, destined at the time of the October War for delivery to India, and at least two full strength Australian mechanised infantry battalions. In addition, the Royal Navy maintained a presence of at least two destroyers or frigates in the Persian Gulf and a force of smaller ships, mainly minesweepers and patrol boats at Aden and elsewhere around the Arabian Peninsula. At Abadan the RAF had stationed a squadron of Hawker Hunter jet fighters and a flight of 'nuclear capable' Canberra bombers. It was also known that the refinery complex on Abadan Island was now protected by sophisticated Bristol Bloodhound long-range surface-to-air missiles. Moreover, British troops had been actively combating communist insurgents in Oman and the Yemen, patrolling the southern Kuwaiti borders with the Kingdom, and had based 'tripwire' contingents in camps in and around Basra in Iraq.

The biggest British force was always at or around Abadan; and at its southern analogue, Aden. In the absence of US forces, the Royal Saudi Army and Air Force, equipped with small quantities of modern American and British equipment but still in the main reliant on outdated 'hand me downs', were probably a match for the relatively small British and Commonwealth forces in the area but, and it was an unquantifiable 'but', since the October War the Saudi regime had tacitly recognised that if the British ever felt that their vital Abadan oil lifeline was under threat it was inevitable that there would be another, very one-sided, nuclear war.

Yamani sucked his teeth thoughtfully.

Whereas, the Kennedy Administration had offered its 'friends in the Middle East' words of comfort; the British had sent two V-Bombers and unofficially re-opened 'military channels' of communication with the Kingdom. It had been a thing easily done; one of the numerous side effects - advantages - of so many minor sons of the Saudi ruling elite having been educated at English public schools and having trained at Sandhurst. Friendships had been forged that were now worth ten times more than the 'supportive' words of an American President who had behaved as if the Kingdom did not exist for the last eighteen months.

"It is a matter of trust," Yamani said, breaking the silence which had descended.

Thomas Barger was a man schooled by a life in the desert, and long acquaintance with unforgiving Bedouin logic.

"This I understand," he acknowledged. "I give you my word that I will attempt *again* to communicate the sincere *concerns* of Crown Prince Faisal and of course, of Kind Saud, to my *people* in America."

Chapter 3

Monday 13th April 1964
Corpus Christi College, Oxford, England

Margaret Thatcher had been working through her papers since six o'clock that morning. Just because the country was at war there was no excuse to ignore the normal 'documentary traffic' which came through her private office. Nor was she about to excuse herself in any way from carrying out her duties on account of the ongoing pain from the injuries she had suffered a week ago at Brize Norton.

While she sat at her desk, she had eased her left arm out of its clumsy sling, less inconvenienced by the nagging ache in her shoulder than she was by the constant, stabbing, jarring fingers of flame that periodically exploded from her lower spine. Her doctors said there was 'nothing to worry about in the x-rays' and that she had 'just badly twisted a large group of muscles which were now protesting'. They had strapped her up in a makeshift corset that made her sit upright like a manikin. Her dislocated shoulder had been 'popped' back into place shortly after she and Her Majesty had been rescued from the wrecked Royal Rolls-Royce.

Margaret Thatcher had visited the Queen at Woodstock yesterday evening and found her monarch much cheered by the company of her consort Prince Philip, the Duke of Edinburgh whom, after her Prime Minister's intersession, the RAF had flown south from his hospital bed in Scotland despite the vociferous objections of his doctors. Although the Duke of Edinburgh was still wheelchair-bound, he was itching for the fight and every word that passed his lips threatened to prompt a smile from his temporarily incapacitated wife.

The events of a week ago hung like a grim pall over Oxford.

The Prime Minister relived the nightmare at RAF Brize Norton every time she shut her eyes.

When the speculatively launched Mark XM41 Redeye Block I shoulder-launched surface-to-air missile had detonated on impact with the starboard outer Pratt and Whitney JT4A turbojet, of the US Air Force Douglas DC-8 carrying the Acting Chief of Staff of the US Army and Commander-in-Chief designate of all Allied Forces in Europe and his Staff; the Prime Ministerial bodyguard, and the men of the Royal 'protection squad' had acted as one to 'guard' their charges.

Margaret Thatcher's Royal Marines and the Queen's protectors, drawn from the Black Watch, had carried the two women to, and not to put too fine a point on it 'thrown' them into the only available remotely safe place on the exposed tarmac expanse of RAF Brize Norton; the nearby Royal armoured Rolls-Royce. Everything had happened so fast neither woman actually recollected how or when their numerous injuries had subsequently occurred. Two members of the Black Watch and two Royal Marines had fallen on the two women to shield them with their bodies, the stricken jetliner had crashed literally yards away, and as the disintegrating aircraft had cart-wheeled past a giant ball of burning aviation fuel had briefly enveloped the vehicle. It later transpired that the Rolls-Royce had been struck by and violently tipped onto its roof by the impact of a detached section of the undercarriage of the downed DC-8.

General Harold Keith 'Johnny' Johnson – a survivor of the Bataan Death March and a hero of the Korean War – and everybody else on board the US Air Force plane struck by the missile fired by two Irish Republican Army men had perished in the crash. As had seventeen men on the ground including thus far, eight Royal Marines of the 'AWP'; members of the so-called 'Angry Widow's Praetorians', the name the Royal Marines of Margaret Thatcher's personal bodyguard had proudly adopted amongst themselves. Three of her faithful AWPs had died lingering deaths from horrific burns in the last two days, and the new commander of the detachment had reported to her earlier that morning that another man was 'not long for this world'.

The shooting down of two aircraft; General Johnson's DC-8 at RAF Brize Norton, and less than an hour later Flight 616, an RAF Comet at Cheltenham had come as sickening body blows to Margaret Thatcher and her government. On board Flight 616 returning from Malta, had been the First Sea Lord, Sir David Luce, several senior staff officers, twenty-six seriously injured service personnel and civilians, their eight attendant nurses, and the Soviet code books and cipher equipment seized from the captured Turkish destroyer *Mareşal Fevzi Çakmak* after the Battle of Malta.

The IRA atrocities had been no less unnerving to the members of the United States Presidential delegation which had flown to England to discuss the delayed ratification of the new US-UK Mutual Defence Agreement – or more accurately, non-ratification - and to discuss the way forward in the Mediterranean.

What made the atrocities at Brize Norton and Cheltenham all the more soul destroying was that in the last week it had become apparent that contrary to the Prime Minister's hopes and expectations, Jack Kennedy had decided to come to England not to embrace the transatlantic alliance but to finesse its public downgrading for his own domestic political reasons.

Margaret Thatcher had been well aware that certain members of the Kennedy Administration had never supported the US-UK Mutual Defence Treaty, and that others close to the President were getting 'cold feet' about it. However, when Jack Kennedy had offered to come to England to 'iron out' recent 'local difficulties' she had taken this as a token of good faith on his part. Likewise, the visit of General Johnson to set up a 'skeleton headquarters staff' in England ahead of the formal announcement that, in due course, he would take over as Commander-in-Chief of All Allied Forces in the Mediterranean had seemed like a positive signal. Presciently, several of her own ministers, notably Tom Harding-Grayson her Foreign Secretary, Home Secretary Roy Jenkins and Barbara Castle, her fiery Labour Minister had said aloud what many of her confidants took for granted; that 'putting all the United Kingdom's eggs in any kind of American basket is a mistake'.

Although she had been disappointed that the Kennedy Administration was reluctant to discuss matters ahead of the visit other than in terms of generalities, a week ago she had genuinely hoped for the best and secretly prepared herself for the worst. In hindsight the 'worst' had turned out to be unimaginably bad.

In less than an hour last Monday everything had changed. The atrocities at Brize Norton and Cheltenham, both perpetrated by terrorists using modern state of the art equipment sourced from US military arsenals, the body blow of the news from the Middle East and the confusion in the immediate aftermath of the downing of the two jets had briefly paralysed the machinery of government.

Special Air Mission 26000, the President's aircraft, had landed away at RAF Coningsby; and the plane bringing members of the government of the Irish Republic to England had been instructed to turn around and had flown straight back to Ireland...

There was a quiet knock at the door.

"Come!"

Sir Henry Tomlinson, the greying, tired-eyed Head of the Home Civil Service and Secretary to the Cabinet of the Unity Administration of the United Kingdom – UAUK - entered the former Don's rooms. As always, he had a large hard back notebook under his arm.

"Cabinet has assembled, Prime Minister," he informed her. "And awaits your convenience."

"Thank you, Sir Henry."

The older man - he was in his sixties and she still only thirty-eight – viewed his Prime Minister with a quiet, almost fatherly pride. Notwithstanding that the recent disasters had taken a heavy physical toll on her, or that not even her immaculate coiffure or marvellously presented matching blue top and skirt over a pure cream blouse could mask her near exhaustion, she was undoubtedly *in control*, and magnificently unbowed.

The Cabinet Secretary held out a hand for his Prime Minister to steady herself. Margaret Thatcher might project an image of indestructibility; he knew that she was anything but. Less than a fortnight ago she had lost the man she loved – Admiral Sir Julian Christopher – and every day since it seemed some new disaster had befallen British arms or prestige, with each successive body blow further undermining her grip on the premiership and the nation's place in a World that was ever more horribly dangerous.

"What are the papers saying about the Cabinet reshuffle?" Margaret Thatcher inquired brusquely as she cautiously stood up, attempting to find her balance without provoking fresh waves of pain from her damaged lower back.

"Very little," Sir Henry Tomlinson said. "The 'Irish measures' seem to be attracting the most attention."

"Hum!" The Prime Minister sighed.

Since neither the Kennedy Administration nor the Government of the Irish Republic thought that smuggling advanced weapons across the North Atlantic to enable 'criminals' to shoot down aircraft in England was a *big thing*; nevertheless, the Unity Administration of the United Kingdom - the UAUK - had taken steps to ensure that in future both would understand exactly how *big a thing* it was!

One hundred and eighty-nine people – one hundred and forty-seven men, thirty-six women and six – three boys and three girls under the age of ten – children had been killed in last Monday's terrorist outrages. There had to be consequences or those complicit in those 'war crimes' would go on to commit further, heinous atrocities in the name of their godforsaken cause. Margaret Thatcher felt personally responsible for ensuring that there were *consequences*.

This was not the time for half measures.

One. As of midnight yesterday, the trans-shipment of goods of any description to ports or airports or by road from the United Kingdom and Northern Ireland to the Irish Republic was absolutely prohibited.

Two. The United Kingdom had asserted the absolute right to stop and search any vehicle, aircraft or vessel at sea on route to, or suspected to be on route to the Irish Republic.

Three. Diplomatic relations with the Irish Republic had been suspended indefinitely.

Four. In the absence of effective action by the Irish Republic the United Kingdom reserved the right to strike at – after the event or pre-emptively in self-defence - and destroy, without let, hindrance or notice 'terrorist' targets within the Irish Republic.

Two days ago, a third terrorist, a former British army non-commissioned officer, had been captured in Gloucestershire. The man had been living rough in the country. When cornered he had tried to kill himself but only succeeded in shooting off most of his right ear.

Margaret Thatcher had authorised the use of 'special interrogation techniques' on all three IRA men in custody. It was the first time she had signed off on *torture* but she had done it without a qualm.

"Via the Swedish legation the Irish Prime Minister is claiming that our quote 'Imperialist bully boy tactics amount to a blockade and that it will inevitably lead to a second great famine," Sir Henry Tomlinson declared, his tone blandly neutral.

"Well," Margaret Thatcher huffed irritably, "he should have thought about that before he allowed the IRA to embark on a proxy war in support of *his* party's avowedly 'United Ireland' platform!"

The Cabinet Secretary would have reminded his Prime Minister that although the Irish Taoiseach's Fianna Fáil party did in fact still publicly pay lip service to the goal of reuniting the six counties of Ulster with the twenty-six counties of the south, it no more wanted to actually attempt to govern the north than it wanted to discredit itself with its natural constituency by going to war with the IRA. However, right now the Prime Minister's emotions regarding the person of her Irish counterpart, former IRA man Sean Lemass were too raw, and the feelings abroad in the country were too febrile for the voice of reason to have any chance of prevailing. Perhaps, there would be time later when reason might have a chance to be heard?

Privately, Sir Henry Tomlinson was a little surprised, and enormously relieved that the extraordinary force of nature that was Margaret Thatcher, had – for all her faults and inexperience in government – firmly vetoed any 'loose talk' of immediate military action, or reprisals, against the Irish Republic.

In this troubled age a wise man was always thankful for small mercies.

Chapter 4

Monday 13th April 1964
Hall of the People, Sverdlovsk

Fifty-eight-year-old Marshal of the Soviet Union Hamazasp Khachaturi Babadzhanian was the last of the hastily called conference's participants to arrive; having flown up from the Advanced Headquarters of Army Group South at Ardabil in Azerbaijani Iran that morning at first light.

As his Mil Mi-6 helicopter had rattled over the miraculously intact city of Sverdlovsk from the airport, Babadzhanian had secretly wondered how long the Yankees and the British would leave this untouched place and others, like Chelyabinsk to the south unbombed. It now seemed likely that had the collective leadership – with whom he was meeting that afternoon – authorised a second city-killer strike on Baghdad after the destruction of Tehran that Kennedy, and or, his lackeys the British, would have attempted to complete the work they had left unfinished in the Cuban Missiles War.

The other thing he wondered about; and this was a thing that was probably giving the collective leadership more than a little pause for thought, was why the Americans had let *that* woman be the one to issue the ultimatum?

'The Soviet leadership is hereby given notice that any further use of nuclear weapons by it, its allies or its proxies will result in an all-out strike by the United Kingdom against the forces of the Soviet Union and any surviving concentrations of population or industry within the former territories of the Soviet Union, or in any territories deemed to now be under Soviet control.'

There was no mention of Yankee B-52s or missiles standing ready in their invulnerable silos in the American Midwest.

Just: *'RAF bombers stand ready at the end of their runways at four minutes notice to go to war. Other RAF bombers are airborne at this time ready to strike within minutes of the receipt of the order to attack!'*

Babadzhanian did not speak English. However, he had listened to *the* woman deliver her message a dozen times; trying to learn what lay beneath the words. Although he did not understand the words she was saying – other than in the translation, obviously – he completely understood the unbending steel in *that* woman's voice.

While both his armies - 3rd Caucasus Tank Army on the right and 2nd Siberian Mechanised Army on the left, and his Army Group mobile artillery – were equipped with a small number of tactical, essentially battlefield nuclear weapons, the Soviet Union, what was left of it, no longer possessed a viable strategic first strike strategic option. Apart from a couple of dozen turboprop Tu-95s and a handful of operational jet Myasishchev M-4 *Molot* long range bombers the Red Air Force had no means of attacking the continental United States of America. Although some kind of attack might be mounted against the

British, all the available intelligence suggested that the United Kingdom retained a functioning air defence system, so even this 'option' was to all intents, *theoretical* and therefore not to be trusted. Possessing nuclear weapons was no use unless you could use the damned things!

This was clearly not a problem for the British or for the Americans. In the last seventy-two hours RAF V-Bombers had moved into position at Malta, Cyprus and at Dhahran in Saudi Arabia.

Babadzhanian did not personally believe for a single moment that the Red Air Force's claims to have rebuilt 'an impregnable umbrella of radars, missiles and fighters' over the 'home cities of Sverdlovsk and Chelyabinsk' was worth a bucket of bear shit!

The Yankees and the British did not need to waste missiles on what was left of the Mother Country, they could simply fly across it and bomb it at will!

Besides, somebody somewhere had had to call time on the madness.

Of the great cities of the Soviet Union only Sverdlovsk, until 1924 *Yekaterinburg*, remained. Many towns and smaller cities elsewhere had survived the Cuban Missiles War, but Moscow, Leningrad, Kiev, Minsk and *all* the other 'great' cities were seas of rubble. That places like Odessa on the Black Sea coast, and areas of the southern Republics, Turkmenistan, Uzbekistan and Kazakhstan survived, or that towns and bases in the wilderness of the Siberian steppes, or that places like Tomsk or Barnaul had escaped the war, mattered little because at least two-thirds of the pre-war population of the Union of Soviet Socialist Republics had been consumed by the fires and practically everywhere there had been famine and disease, unspeakable hardships beyond sane comprehension. That, after all, was why the decision had been taken to fight on; to wrest back something of that which had been lost, to seize and to hold clean, unburned land with sufficient natural resources to be able, someday to alleviate the catastrophic situation of the Mother Country.

Sverdlovsk's population had been around eight hundred thousand before the war, since then it had doubled. The surviving cities had become beacons for the survivors, each one an oasis in a cold, foodless, shattered landscape. Even though killer epidemics swept through the overcrowded city, and the daily food ration was barely enough to keep the young, the old and the infirm alive, the factories of what had been the Soviet Union's fourth or fifth largest city had become the anvil upon which the first halting steps towards national reconstruction and rebirth had been hammered out the previous spring.

Sverdlovsk had first become a centre of heavy industry under the Five-Year plans of the 1930s. Later when Soviet industry was relocated east out of the reach of the advancing Germans in 1941 and 1942, the great Uralmash - an abbreviation of 'Urals Machine-Building Plant' – facility became the keystone of a massive expansion in national industrial capacity. During the Great Patriotic War Uralmash built blast furnaces, rolling mills, presses, cranes and drilling and drag-line equipment for the mining and metallurgical industries of the Urals and Siberia. Guns, armour plate, the hulls for tanks and self-propelled artillery had poured out of the factories of Sverdlovsk. After that war, Uralmash was redesigned and rebuilt, and production had largely switched to peaceful outputs but always with the caveat that in the event of war, the factories would again turn ploughshares back into swords. Thus Uralmash, having escaped the Cuban Missiles War, was now the great smoking hub of the new Soviet Union's war production. There had been arguments about further dispersal; in the end the concentration of all the Mother Country's surviving eggs in the single basket of the Sverdlovsk-Chelyabinsk 'undamaged zone' had been the only way to ensure that at least two full strength mechanised armies could be put into the field, and as importantly, in theory at least, mechanically sustained for a sixty-day campaign...

Babadzhanian shivered at the thought that, if he or his comrades of the collective leadership made a single mistake, Sverdlovsk might go the way of Moscow, Kiev and all the other great cities of the motherland.

Defence Minister Marshal of the Soviet Union sixty-four-year-old Vasily Ivanovich Chuikov, stepped up to Babadzhanian and slapped him jovially on the shoulder. It was the first time the two men had met since Babadzhanian's 'battlefield' promotion three days ago.

"Cheer up, Comrade Marshal," Chuikov observed, chuckling like a bear with an ulcer, his gnarled oddly cherubic features creasing this way and that as he smiled.

Babadzhanian straightened to attention before the other members of the collective leadership, nodding respectful acknowledgments before stepping forward to shake hands and exchange the ritual kisses.

The years were catching up with sixty-year-old Alexei Nikolayevich Kosygin. His face had a grey hue and his eyes were rheumy, when he breathed his chest rattled and as soon as he had greeted the newcomer, he sagged gratefully back into his seat at the over-large pine table aligned with one end of the rectangular hall.

Fifty-seven-year-old Leonid Ilyich Brezhnev, the General Secretary of the Central Committee of the Communist Party of the Soviet Union, was the de facto 'chairman' of the ruling triumvirate.

Unlike his old friend Alexei Kosygin, he was in good health, radiating bull-like strength and confidence. Throughout his career people had underestimated Brezhnev's feral intellect and his innate political nous, and like every man who had risen through the Party during the Stalin years he was as tough as an ox and a born survivor.

He and Kosygin were alike and superbly matched in that respect. Of the two Kosygin had been closer to Stalin, so close that he had daily feared for his life and never left home without updating his wife on what to say to the secret police – the NKVD in those days - if he failed to return, or if *they* knocked on the door in his absence. Brezhnev had been Nikita Khrushchev's man, leapfrogging Kosygin in the Party pecking order in the years before the Cuban Missiles disaster; but both men were wise enough to put past differences and old suspicions behind them.

"Comrade Alexei Nikolayevich and Comrade Leonid Ilyich," Chuikov guffawed, "are nervous that the advance has stalled around Tabriz, Comrade Marshal?"

Hamazasp Khachaturi Babadzhanian had been born in Armenia. Chuikov was one of the few men alive who sometimes employed the Russian form of his name, *Amazasp Khachaturovich Babadzhanyan*, which he detested. For all that he was a soldier of the Union of Soviet Socialist Republics he was no Russian, was intensely proud of his ancient Armenian ancestry and his roots in a culture that pre-dated the upstart 'Russian' interlopers of the last millennium. That today the Minister of Defence had not troubled to tease him was a good sign, confirming that no matter how panicked the civilians in the room were by the setbacks and delays in the Zagros Mountains, Chuikov was relaxed.

"Tabriz is too heavily garrisoned to be taken by an airborne assault," Babadzhanian stated. "Even if my airborne component had not been critically weakened by the Malta operation," he paused, tempted to point out that he had objected to that 'unnecessary diversion' at the time, "I decided that the surviving elements of 51st and 53rd Guards Airborne Regiments were better employed securing the lightly defended communications hub of Urmia. This blocking operation has been entirely successful and casualties thus far have been minimal. Leading elements of 3rd Caucasus Tank Army have now bottled up the weak Iranian force defending Qoshachay. A reconnaissance unit has patrolled twenty kilometres west of that town to the outskirts of Mahabad which is only lightly defended. Mechanised units of 3rd Caucasus Tank Army will probably be in Piranshahr near the Iraqi border by the end of the week."

The Commander of Army Group South spoke with calm, detached professional assurance.

"What about Tabriz?" Kosygin asked quietly.

"The garrison has little or no armour or artillery. Iranian air activity is non-existent. Frankly, local partisan groups are giving my boys more problems in that sector than the troops inside the city. We control all the roads into the city. We have partially disrupted the city's water supplies. 2nd Siberian Mechanised Army is now relieving 3rd Caucasus Tank Army, freeing it to resume the advance south. Once we have significant armour and sufficient logistical backup *in depot* at Mahabad, brigade-strength battle groups will be deployed west to the north of Dukan Lake and south to break through the Iraqi border defences opposite Erbil."

Brezhnev stirred like bear from hibernation, his eyes hard.

"What do you make of the reports of civil war in Iraq, Comrade Vasily Ivanovich?" He asked of Chuikov.

"I think the Iraqis are pissing their pants!" The Minister of Defence and the man who *was* the Red Army retorted with a grumbling chortle of satisfaction.

Babadzhanian shrugged.

"I think that was always going to happen," he declared. "Whereas, I always assumed that if we attempted to strike south through Iran, sooner or later the British would probably stiffen the Iranian Army's backbone."

"What's to stop the British or the Americans doing the same in Iraq?" The General Secretary of the Central Committee of the Communist Party of the Soviet Union persisted, unconvinced.

"That might still happen," Babadzhanian agreed, unflinching under Leonid Brezhnev's gaze. "Or if they think they are going to lose control of the oil fields of the Persian Gulf they might just 'bomb us back to the stone age'," he added dryly.

Chuikov grunted but said nothing. By the time one had one's back against the wall it was far too late to start worrying about what happened next.

Babadzhanian frowned.

"*Operation Nakazyvat*", Operation Chastise, "is not going according to plan, Comrades," he confessed. "That said it is going better than we had dreamed possible. In approximately one week from now my forces will launch the second and most crucial stage of the operation. If 'Action North' succeeds it may convince the Iraqis, the British and the Americans that our real objective is not Abadan Island, and a lodgement on the northern shores of the Persian Gulf threatening future operations again Kuwait and the Arabian Peninsula; but simply the seizure of Mosul, Erbil, Kirkuk and the oilfields of northern, Kurdish Iraq. In this scenario they will assume that our seizure of Sulaymaniyah is no more than a prudent 'straightening of our defensive line. If you recollect from my original notes on *Operation Nakazyvat*, I was at pains to emphasise that regardless of what forces the Iranians, the Iraqis, the British, the Yankees and their Arab lackeys managed to scrape together to block our path south, unless some or all of those forces can be drawn forward – that is, to the north – away from likely defensive positions in the marshes of the Southern Iraq or in prepared lines south of Khorramshahr and guarding Abadan Island, we might face the prospect of achieving all our stated strategic objectives but be too weak to hang onto them. I can fight one, perhaps two major battles of 'movement'; I do not have the resources or the logistics train to fight a battle of attrition all the way south and then to assault and over run pre-prepared major defence lines."

He let this sink in.

"If the enemy swallows the lie that all we want is the oil of Kurdish Iraq they will deploy their forces to block us south of the line Sulaymaniyah-Kirkuk. Once that re-deployment commences, I will destroy the enemy, drive south, invest Abadan Island and then," he sighed, "we shall see what history has in store for us."

Chapter 5

Monday 13th April 1964
RAF Brize Norton, Oxfordshire, England

Lady Marija Calleja-Christopher had been - now that she had had a little while to think about it – in a state of grieving shock for most of the last week. The fact that it was the first time in her life she had been away from Malta would have been quite sufficient, of itself, to have thoroughly disorientated her; but that was not the half of it.

The United States Air Force C-130 Hercules transport rumbled noisily to a halt on the hardstand some fifty yards away. Nothing happened for about a minute and then the note of the engines altered and fell, and the rear ramp began to descend slowly to the cold tarmac.

Marija briefly reflected on her own journey to England a week ago. It had been her first ever flight, for her in the comparative luxury of a jetliner rather than the draughty cargo bay of a propeller-driven military workhorse.

She waited for the first passenger to emerge from the cavernous hold of the newly arrived aircraft, trying very hard not to fidget and fret with anxiety in front of the others. Like Peter, her husband of a little over five weeks, she was very aware that she always on show now. Always before she could afford to be Marija Calleja, nurse, midwife and sometime unofficial leader of the Women of Malta protest movement, the dutiful daughter of her dockyard superintendent father and loving Sicilian mother; but now she was a 'lady', the wife of a Royal Navy Captain and the hero of the Battle of Malta, and no matter how much they would have preferred to have been anonymous newlyweds, in public whether together or separately, alone, they were *always* 'on parade'.

Even their grief was a public thing.

There was a further hiatus while the ground crew fussed around the cargo ramp of the US Air Force Hercules.

Marija's thoughts replayed her – her and Peter's – traumatic arrival in England a week ago today.

No sooner had their Comet jetliner rolled to a stop in the dark and the drizzle at Cheltenham than she and Peter had been whisked away by machine gun hefting stone-faced Royal Marines to a grand old house in the country near the airfield where they had been kept, under guard until the next morning. Neither she or her husband had slept that night; thinking about the burning wreckage on the ground near the end of the runway, the armoured cars and fire engines rushing by in the opposite direction as they and the other VIPs on their flight were ushered through the airfield buildings – the old racecourse grandstand, still with signs pointing, bizarrely to the *PARADE RING* and to the *WINNER'S ENCLOSURE* – to waiting cars. Had it not been for the comforting circle of her husband's protective arms that night she would have been utterly lost.

Iain Macleod, Her Majesty's Secretary of State for Information, with whom Marija had chatted to pleasantly for well over two hours during the flight back from Malta while Peter, bless him, had slept like a baby, had hastily bade the young couple 'adieu' at the airport and disappeared with his minders. Nobody had really known what was going on, just that there had been a crash; which was a thing that they could all see with their own eyes!

It was only the next day that the dreadful truth had emerged.

In fact, all through that awful next day one dreadful thing after another had been 'made known' to the shell-shocked couple.

Lady Patricia Harding-Grayson, a kind, softly-spoken elegantly maternal lady, had arrived in Cheltenham to 'brief' them at around eleven o'clock last Tuesday morning.

Before she commenced her 'briefing' she had handed Marija a 'Priority Cable' from 'The Office of the Military Governor of Malta'.

This is to confirm that Mr P. Calleja and Mrs M. Calleja of Tower Street, Sliema, are unhurt and their family home only lightly damaged. The aforementioned couple have been informed of your safe arrival and that of Mr J. Calleja, in England with your husband.

The telegram had been transmitted to Oxford over the name of Air Vice Marshal D.B. French, DSO, DFC, Officer Commanding, Malta.

However, the written confirmation of her parents' safety had been the last good news brought to them by Lady Patricia Harding-Grayson.

Marija had not immediately registered the fact that their visitor was none other than the wife of the British Foreign Secretary, or that her somewhat drawn, tired initial appearance was on account of her friend, the Prime Minister, for whose children she acted as an unofficial governess, having spent the night in Hospital in Oxford because she had been injured in the same unspeakable 'atrocity' in which Her Majesty, Queen Elizabeth had suffered what had initially been feared to be 'life threatening' injuries.

In any event there had been a lot of 'Lady Patricia' this, and 'Sir Peter' that, and superfluous 'Lady Marija-ing' before Peter had put his foot down and said: 'Look, I'm Peter, my wife is Marija.'

'Oh, thank goodness for that,' their grey-haired, willow-thin visitor had groaned with relief. 'I am *Pat*,' she had smiled momentarily. 'Especially, to my friends and now that I've met you both I think that's exactly what we'll all be when we get to know each other a little bit better.'

It had not taken very long for the Foreign Secretary's wife to become worryingly serious.

'Let's all sit down. I'm afraid I have some very bad news.'

The aircraft which had crashed at RAF Cheltenham was one of the aircraft returning from Malta ahead of Peter and Marija's flight. On board had been the First Sea Lord, Sir David Luce and a number of badly wounded service men and civilians, a flight crew of six, and several nurses. There had been no survivors.

A little earlier on Monday afternoon an American Air Force jet carrying senior officers to take up posts in England and the Mediterranean had crashed, like the De Havilland Comet at Cheltenham, while making its final landing approach to RAF Brize Norton. However, whereas the Cheltenham crash had happened short of the airfield, at Brize Norton, upon crashing the aircraft had disintegrated and ploughed into the middle of the awaiting reception committee. Mrs Thatcher, the Prime Minister, had sustained a dislocated shoulder, numerous minor abrasions and bruises and a twisted spine; Her Majesty the Queen had been severely concussed, broken her left ankle and upper left arm somewhere between being picked up by her bodyguards, her literally being thrown into the protection of her armoured Rolls-Royce, and that vehicle being violently overturned after being struck by a large piece of wreckage.

The Prime Minister, the Queen and some thirty other casualties from Brize Norton had been taken – many by helicopter – to the Churchill Hospital in Oxford. At that time although it was not known how many people had died in the crash, either on board the US Air Force DC-8 jetliner or on the ground, or at Cheltenham, the assumption was that the death toll would eventually approach around two hundred.

'You'll be pleased to learn that Her Majesty was sitting up and taking nourishment this morning,' Pat Harding-Grayson had reassured the younger couple.

'Two aircraft don't just crash?' Marija's husband had queried.

'No, the RAF and the Security Service, MI5, think that both aircraft were shot down by Irish Republican Army terrorists armed with modern American-made shoulder-launched anti-aircraft missiles.'

The older woman had hesitated before moving on to news that – even in comparison to news of the atrocities at Brize Norton and Cheltenham - was so bad that at the first telling it hardly sank in. Both Marija and her husband had stared at the Foreign Secretary's wife as if she was mad.

Pat Harding-Grayson, having anticipated the young couple's entirely understandable incredulity had patiently reiterated what she had just said; breaking the news that in some small part of her conscious mind Marija had *always* feared - ever since the rumours first circulated about her missing elder brother Samuel after the sabotage of HMS Torquay - might contain more than a germ of truth.

By then Sam had become distant, estranged from everybody in the family except perhaps, her father. Lately, she had got to know Sam's wife, her *sister* Rosa well, they had talked endlessly and the unhappiness of Rosa's cold married life to her brother had become evident, adding substance to Marija's suspicions. In retrospect they had all known that something was wrong; just not *what* was wrong with Sam. And now she knew; now they all knew what had been so unspeakably wrong these last few years with Sam.

And it was too...*incredible*.

She had refused to believe it at first.

'I'm sorry. There is no doubt about any of this.' Pat Harding-Grayson had warned the young couple. She had viewed Marija maternally, wanting to hug her and to make the evil go away. 'I wish there was an easy way to say this. But there isn't. I am sorry. I am so sorry.' She had quirked her lips apologetically and dropped the mind-numbing, shattering bombshell. 'Your elder brother, Samuel, was arrested at the Citadel in Mdina on the afternoon of the assault on Malta. At the time of his arrest, he was in the company of a Soviet spy – whom you knew as Arkady Pavlovich Rykov – he was wearing a Soviet paratrooper's fatigues and carrying a Red Army hand gun, which at that time he was holding to Admiral Sir Julian Christopher's head. My information is that Sir Julian had already sustained a fatal injury by that time. Your brother was apprehended by a woman you knew as Sarah Pullman; a woman who is in fact a long-time, trusted agent of the Secret Intelligence Service, MI6. Subsequently, when he was interviewed your brother confessed to having been in the employ of the Soviet intelligence services - the KGB - for many years. Furthermore, during this interview he admitted complicity in numerous terroristic attacks and assassinations in the Maltese Archipelago and to have been a trusted associate of the Soviet agent Rykov for many years. Since Malta is currently under a state of Martial Law the C-in-C, Air Vice Marshal French, has summary powers over the treatment and disposal of enemy spies and persons against whom there are prima facie grounds to suspect of involvement in gross acts of treachery, or in the commission of war crimes against the civilian population. Air Vice Marshal French, having reviewed Samuel's Security Service file and his freely given confession, found your brother guilty of participation in war crimes against the civil population and of treachery on grounds of his activities aiding and abetting an enemy spy.'

Tears had been welling in the Foreign Secretary's wife's eyes.

'Yesterday,' she went on, 'at dawn, Samuel was executed by firing squad in the exercise yard of Paola Royal Military Prison.'

Marija had cried all the way from Cheltenham to Oxford, she had been inconsolable. At some stage after their arrival in the city somebody had tried to call Peter away; he had told whoever it was to: 'Go to hell!' In a tone of voice, she had never heard him use, nor ever imagined him capable of.

It was this which had slowly, hurtfully broken her out of the first circle of her grief.

Did her Mama and Papa know yet?

Had anybody told her little brother Joe?

The hero of the Battle of Malta had been taken to the local hospital in Cheltenham for observation overnight. He had almost had to be poured out of the aircraft the previous evening, a little delirious.

Before the disasters of Monday afternoon, the arrangements for a big, victory-type parade through Oxford had been well advanced. Wednesday had been the day originally nominated for the event, at the conclusion of which there would be an investiture at Christ Church

College.

Peter was to be awarded the Victoria Cross.

Joe was to be awarded the George Cross.

But all that had been delayed, put on hold.

Marija had offered her services as a nurse at the Churchill Hospital; and initially, been turned down. Nobody in Oxford took her 'Maltese' nursing certification seriously. She had asked to speak to her 'new friend' Iain Macleod, explained the situation and the next day started work – as a 'volunteer nursing assistant' - on one of the children's wards at the hospital.

It had been a mercy to be busy, to be in some small way *herself* again for a few hours last Wednesday, Thursday and Friday mornings. Albeit as a glorified 'nanny' rather than as a 'proper' nurse.

She had been worried the hospital would object to the journalists and photographers that followed her around on Wednesday, her first day. Her over-sized uniform had been stiff and starchy and the cold and wet of the alleged spring day had made her bones feel old. However, once the interlopers had departed, she had instantly felt at home and all the other nurses had been very friendly, except for Matron and everybody understood that no Matron was ever supposed to be friendly in any hospital Marija had ever been in.

Her husband, meanwhile, had been 'the most wanted' man in Oxford.

Well, Peter, along with Alan Hannay – excepting Joe who was still under 'wraps' in hospital in Cheltenham - and all the other heroes of HMS Talavera's final desperate action had been 'wanted men'.

Marija had learned that the BBC was hurriedly making a documentary film about the battle. It seemed that at the very moment she and her sister Rosa had watched HMS Talavera with horrified, baited breath as Peter's ship raced out of the Grand Harbour amidst a forest of giant shell splashes, that a BBC film crew had captured the whole thing in glorious, dramatic Technicolor from the top of the ramparts of Valletta. She shivered to think of that moment; knowing then as now what it had portended. Peter's father had told him to '*cut your lines and get out to sea*', understanding that whatever he had said to *his* son that Peter would surely steam at full speed *towards* the sound of guns.

To her astonishment the newspaper people and the BBC had wanted to talk to her also.

On Saturday she and Peter had sat down in a room at Merton College and been 'interviewed' by a man called Barry Lankester. He was a nice man, very polite and a lot more nervous about the whole thing than either she or her husband. It had been Barry Lankester's film crew, set up to shoot a few scenic 'filler' and 'background' shots of the Grand Harbour from the lower Barraka Gardens, across the anchorage from Kalkara Creek and Royal Naval Hospital Bighi, from where Rosa and Marija had watched HMS Talavera's break for the open sea and her destiny, which had caught *everything* on camera.

After a while Marija had relaxed a little.

She had told her personal story; her long recovery from her childhood injuries suffered in the German bombing in 1942, how much she owed to Surgeon Captain Reginald Stephens and to Margo Seiffert, her friend and mentor who had been murdered by a Red Army parachutist during the assault on the Citadel at Mdina. She almost started sobbing uncontrollably more than once; Peter had squeezed her hand and taken his cue to explain how he and Marija had been pen friends half their lives and but for the October War might never have met, face to face.

'Yes, I know it all sounds a little like a modern fairy tale. But the war changed everything, of course,' he had observed, in that marvellously winning self-effacing way of his. 'If nothing else good came out of it that night when the balloon went up the whole dreadful thing made me realise what a prize clot, I had been all those years. After that, well, I just wanted to get to Malta. Even when I was standing on the bridge of the Talavera in a North Atlantic winter storm the morning after we got bombed off Cape Finisterre, and the ship was wallowing around like a drunken matelot on his way back to his berth after a run ashore, trying to sink under our feet, all I thought about was how I was going to get from there,' he had smiled and shaken his head ruefully, 'to Malta. It's a funny thing,' he had added, 'I never really thought I was a terribly brave fellow. I still don't think I am, by the way. It's just that when I'm in a tight spot I think of Marija and everything becomes, well, clear, simple.'

Marija could not wait to return to their lodgings at Corpus Christi College that evening. Her husband was still black and blue, sore and healing under his new uniform so she had been gentle with him. It was the first time they had made love since the morning of the Battle of Malta when her adorable, clever, honourable and unbelievably stupidly courageous spouse of less than six weeks had done his absolute level best to get himself killed!

Yesterday morning there had been a message from Iain Macleod's Private Office asking if she and Peter could attend a short meeting at Oriel College. In welcoming the couple into his lair, the normally charming, ebullient Minister had been unusually diffident.

'A decision has been made,' he had hesitated, 'by me, actually, on the advice of the Director General of the Security Services, to permanently embargo any information relating to the arrest and execution of your brother, Lady Marija,' he had explained.

They had been on 'Iain' and 'Marija' terms on the flight back to England.

'Might I inquire why, Mr Macleod?' Peter had interjected, betraying no hint of censure.

'Firstly, full disclosure in this matter will almost certainly give more comfort to our enemies than anybody connected to the dead man.' At this juncture he had looked to Marija with apologetic eyes. 'Secondly, you had to know, you both *had* to know because you will become, if you are not already, *public figures* who will, inevitably, be confronted with rumours and suchlike in the coming years. Frankly, knowing what really happened will help you avoid, let us say, offering inadvertent hostages to fortune. I should tell you that Samuel's widow, Rosa, has already been fully apprised of the situation and has undertaken to go along with the 'official line'. She seems to be a most sensible young woman. She stipulated the proviso that a certificate be issued legally assuming that Samuel had in fact perished when HMS Torquay was sabotaged earlier this year. I believe she considers herself to be affianced to Lieutenant-Commander Hannay and that the possession of this 'certificate' will facilitate their marriage at the earliest possible time.'

The Minster of Information had made no attempt to sweeten the pill.

'The fiction that Samuel was an innocent dupe of Red Dawn zealots murdered on board HMS Torquay will be the *official line* herewith. Your brother Joe has *not* been *briefed* in this matter, nor have your parents in Malta. They can *never* know the truth about Samuel.'

Marija had been angry and shocked, belatedly understanding why her brother Joe had been kept, virtually 'incommunicado' in hospital in Cheltenham. While he was in hospital and she was here in Oxford they could not share inconvenient *secrets*.

'So,' she had objected, 'I must now lie to my family about my brother?'

'Yes,' Iain Macleod had confirmed, without so much as a threat to dissemble. He had spread his hands wide, imploring the young couple to understand.

'Look, we live in a world in which all the old courtesies and decencies are buried under a layer of radioactive ash. Most of the people in this country are hungry a lot of time, there's hardly any electricity; very few private citizens have their own cars, most people work for the ration tickets that feed their families. There is no real economy, all things considered life is pretty miserable, and there isn't much that *we*, as the government can do about it at the moment. And that was before this *thing* in the Middle East blew up in our faces. If we lose the oil from Abadan, we'll be completely at the mercy of the bloody Americans again. If that happens, goodness only knows what will become of us. But and it is a huge but,' the Minister for Information declaimed, raising a hand as if in salutation, 'in the next few days Barry Lankester's film about the heroes of the Talavera and her brave Captain's fairy tale princess wife will be on every movie screen in the land.'

Marija had pulled a disapproving face.

'You are a princess, my dear,' the man had told her, rather sternly. 'And Peter is a genuine British hero straight out of the pages of *Boys' Own!*' Iain Macleod had had to pause for breath at this point. 'And if you think I am going to deny the British people the chance to bask in a little of *your* reflected glory you are sadly mistaken!'

Pat Harding-Grayson had been Marija's sometime companion most of the last week. Marija had met the 'Prime Ministerial twins' twice, once for tea in Margaret Thatcher's rooms in Corpus Christi. The Prime Minister had been somewhere else on business, which had been a pity. The twins were bright and friendly; particularly Carol who had asked her a series of polite questions about Malta; Mark had only wanted to know about the big battle.

Pat tended to materialise whenever there was a possibility Marija was going to encounter ordinary people, or worse, the gentlemen of the press. Pat was it seemed, Marija's chaperone.

Marija realised passengers were disembarking from the Hercules. She was a little taken aback when the first person she recognised walking down the ramp was Clara Pullman. Clara looked...*different.* The other woman smiled towards Marija, but waited in the shadow of the Hercules's tail plane.

Maria took her appearance as her cue to approach the aircraft, paying no heed to the other passengers emerging from the Hercules.

Clara waved, glanced back into the cargo bay.

Rosa appeared, walking stiffly but hardly limping at all.

She stepped onto the cold tarmac.

"Sister!" Marija screeched, completely oblivious of the half-dozen cameras clicking thirty feet to her right. In her excitement she almost but not quite forgot that she *could not* run. That was a mistake she had made back at the beginning of February and fallen flat on her face; ensuring that the first time the man she had loved half her life actually laid eyes on her, she looked like she had been beaten up!

Compromising she hurried, threatening to skip.

In moments Marija and Rosa fell into a joyous embrace.

A man in a wheelchair swathed in blankets, his face hidden by the rim of a hat drawn down over his brow, was pushed around the young Maltese women by a stoic middle-aged woman with straw-coloured hair shivering in the chill of the northern spring. The man glanced at the two young women as they trundled past. He said something to the woman propelling his chair forward, and she retorted with an impatient snort.

In their delight to be reunited neither Rosa nor Marija even noticed their passing.

They laughed, sobbed, clung to each other in relief and...*hysteria.*

For both of them the last week had been a giddy rollercoaster of extreme emotions and for reasons that only they could understand, there was nobody in the world either of them needed to be with more at that moment.

They had been very distant sisters-in-law until Samuel had disappeared, presumed dead in the wreck of HMS Torquay in January. Then Marija's friend and protector, Jim Siddall had been killed by a booby trap bomb investigating Sam's workshop and Rosa badly injured. Rosa had been shunned, all but disowned by her own family and Marija had befriended her; what else would she have done in the circumstances? Thereafter the two women had been inseparable until a week ago when Marija had flown to England. To be together again was sublime.

The women stood back.

Rosa bit her lip.

"I can never tell Alan," she whispered, knowing her sister would understand.

Marija nodded jerkily, blinking back tears.

Both the women were misty eyed, close to breaking down.

"Peter knows," she murmured, aware that other people were approaching. "But nobody else can ever know."

Rosa nodded, tears trickling down her cheeks.

The sisters hugged again, this time clinging to each other for dear life as if they were afraid they were about to be parted forever.

Chapter 6

Margaret Thatcher swept into that morning's appointed Cabinet Room to an accompaniment of scraping chairs and a stentorian chorus of 'Good morning, Prime Minister'. Last Thursday, in consultation with her deputy, James Callaghan the leader of the minority Labour and Co-operative Party element of the tottering Unity Administration of the United Kingdom, it had been decided to alter the structure of the government machine and to create a formal 'War Cabinet'. Today was the first meeting of *that* new sub-committee of the full Cabinet.

Several members of the UAUK had objected to their exclusion from the 'inner circle', one – Barbara Castle, the Secretary of State for Labour – had protested bitterly about 'the decision to go to war' having 'gone through on the nod' before Cabinet had had an opportunity to 'discuss it'. The feisty Member of Parliament for Blackburn had not, however, resigned over the issue. Margaret Thatcher had reminded all her colleagues that if they could not support her in this 'hour of crisis' that they ought to seriously consider their 'positions now rather than later'. While she had no inclination to attempt – like Winston Churchill – to fight this new war single-handed, she had no intention of allowing ministers who ought to be solely focused on their own department's domestic responsibilities to be 'distracted' by military and strategic considerations that were in no way their 'proper business'. In the current crisis the fact that she honestly did not think that she would still be Prime Minister in a few weeks' time was oddly *liberating*.

"Please," she enunciated primly, "everybody sit down."

Margaret Thatcher eased herself into the hard chair that one of her Royal Marine bodyguards, a walking wounded survivor from the Brize Norton *atrocity*, had brought down from her Private Office in the minutes before the War Cabinet convened. Like his charge, the man – Corporal David Sampson, on detached service to Oxford from his unit, 45 Commando - had moved stiffly as he shepherded the Prime Minister to her place at the long oval table positioned in the middle of the commandeered former ground floor common room. Sampson, like several of his 'oppos' who had suffered minor wounds at Brize Norton, having stubbornly refused to be put on the sick list was restricted to 'inside duties'.

At least one of Margaret Thatcher's AWPs escorted her everywhere, even inside the medieval walls of Corpus Christi College. Like their comrades of the Black Watch in the Royal Protection Company, the Royal Marines of the Prime Ministerial Bodyguard had taken the 'outrage' at Brize Norton a week ago, as an unforgivable slight upon the proud escutcheons of their units. Notwithstanding the circumstances and the death and wounding of so many of their brothers in arms, each and every man regarded the attack upon and the harming of their respective charges as being a profoundly personal insult.

The AWPs former commanding officer, Captain Hamish McLeish a Charterhouse educated, charming, red-headed former England rugby player, who had always treated Margaret Thatcher as if she was a senior member of the Royal family, had died of his injuries three nights ago. The Prime Minister, noting the look in the eyes of her AWPs, had taken his replacement, thirty-five-year-old Major Sir Steuart Pringle aside and reiterated that she 'did not want anybody getting shot just because they inadvertently look at me in the wrong way!'

'Oh, absolutely not, Ma'am," the Royal Marine had promised.

Margaret Thatcher had sighed with undiluted exasperation.

'*Ma'am* is how one addresses Her Majesty the Queen, Major Pringle,' she had complained, wondering if she ought to be addressing the man as *Sir Steuart*, given that he was, strictly speaking, 10th Baronet Pringle? 'I am *just* the Prime Minister. Therefore, *Prime Minister* or *Mrs Thatcher* will suffice in future.'

The Royal Marine had smiled toothily at her. 'Your wish is my command, *Ma'am*,' he had acknowledged, his face a mask of taciturnity. She had given up the unequal battle at that stage. Humbled that her faithful AWPs seemed to think nothing of dying for her; they could jolly well address her however they wished!

"Thank you, Corporal Sampson," she murmured, dismissing her limping minder. "I shall be occupied in here for some time. I shall be very unhappy if I discover later that you have not taken this opportunity to rest your injured ankle in the meantime."

"Yes, Ma'am!" The Marine replied respectfully as he briefly came to attention.

"Good. I'm glad we understand each other," she declared, uncertain if either of them actually remotely understood each other, deciding that *other* than in their suicidal devotion to her she hardly *understood* her brave AWPs at all.

The man turned and marched painfully out of the room, his booted feet clumping loudly on the bare boards. The big oak doors shut at his back and the cast of characters confronted with the nation's latest disaster waited for their beleaguered leader to kick off proceedings.

Margaret Thatcher was in no hurry; the best estimate was that the first Red Army tanks could not possibly reach the northern shores of the Persian Gulf in less than thirty days. Anything could happen in that time. She looked around the Cabinet table which today, seemed sparsely occupied.

To her left was her deputy, fifty-one-year-old James Callaghan, the big, lugubrious man who behind the scenes was fighting a dogged rear-guard action to hold the rump of the Labour and Co-operative Party together. The sitting member of Parliament for Cardiff South and Penarth, he was also Secretary of State for Wales. Ultimately, the fate of the UAUK was in his hands; for if his Party split away from what remained of the national government of 'Unity' there would probably have to be a General Election and nobody around the table knew what was likely to happen if the country went to the polls in the middle of a new war.

Beyond Callaghan sat the forty-eight year old MP for Abingdon, Airey Middleton Sheffield Neave, DSO, MC, the newly appointed Secretary of State for the Intelligence Services as the head of a new Ministry of National Security, a department created at Margaret Thatcher's diktat to 'rationalize, amalgamate and electrify' the 'complacent, incompetent, fragmented dog's breakfast' that comprised the United Kingdom 'intelligence community' in the wake of the 'disastrous failures of MI5, MI6 and the other intelligence organs which have comprehensively undermined *everything* we have achieved since the war!'

Airey Neave had escaped from Colditz, joined MI6 and been the man who read the indictments to the leading surviving Nazis at the Nuremburg War Crimes Tribunal. Following the October War, he had been Margaret Thatcher's number two at the Ministry of Supply, after Defence the most important department in the land, before stepping into her shoes on her elevation to the Premiership. He remained her closest, most implicitly trusted friend in government and he had been the obvious man to take on the poisoned chalice of the re-organised 'Intelligence Brief'.

Sir Henry Tomlinson, the Cabinet Secretary sat to the Prime Minister's right, and beyond him Sir Thomas Harding-Grayson, until December the Permanent Secretary in the post-October War Foreign Office. With the death of his predecessor, Sir Alec Douglas Home in the regicidal attack on Balmoral, he had been co-opted into the Cabinet by the then Prime Minister, Edward Heath. Recognised as one of, if not the finest mind in Whitehall before the war and in the way of these things side-lined because of it, like Airey Neave he was one of Margaret Thatcher's closest friends and confidantes.

Fifty-year-old Iain Norman Macleod, the Minister for Information – basically, the UAUK's principal propagandist and apologist – also held the posts of Leader of the House of Commons, and Chairman of the Conservative and Unionist Party. In normal times he would have been Margaret Thatcher's political bellwether and conscience; however, in the five turbulent months of her Prime Ministerial career to date he had been far too busy fighting fires and plugging the gaping holes below the waterline of the ship of state to worry about anything so ephemeral as the state of the Party in the country, or any of the normal minor politico-ideological or doctrinal schisms over which a man in his position would have endlessly obsessed prior to the cataclysm.

Across the table to the Prime Minister's right sat the Secretary of State for Defence, forty-five-year-old William Stephen Ian Whitelaw the MP for Penrith and the Border. He was a man well thought of in the Party, possibly a future leader even though he had only been elected to Parliament in 1955. Margaret Thatcher was beginning to suspect her bossiness and impatience with the old-world courtesies and niceties of the pre-war age somewhat irritated 'Willie' and that clique of landowning, public school and Oxbridge educated old-school Tories to which he was intimately affiliated. Educated at Winchester and later Trinity College, Cambridge, Whitelaw had distinguished himself serving with the Scots Guards in World War II and at the time of the October War had been Parliamentary Secretary to the Minister of Labour. But for illness he would have joined Edward Heath's post-war United Kingdom Interim Emergency Administration and, alongside Iain Macleod and others been in pole position to step into his shoes...

The Prime Minister caught herself in mid-thought.

There would be time enough to worry about conspiracies and the shifting ground beneath her feet another day. The Chiefs of Staff of the three armed services flanked Willie Whitelaw.

To his right sat General – soon to be promoted Field Marshall - Sir Richard Amyatt Hull, Admiral Sir David Luce's successor as Chief of the Defence Staff; the United Kingdom equivalent to the American Chairman of the Joint Chiefs of Staff Committee. The fifty-six-year-old veteran of the Italian campaign and the final battles in North West Europe of the Second World War had been the last Chief of the Imperial General Staff (CIGS), a post abolished in Edward Heath's time. The professional head of the British Army was a no-nonsense, quietly bluff man upon whom the most senior military post in the kingdom had naturally devolved.

At Willie Whitelaw's left elbow sat fifty-one-year-old Air Marshal Sir Christopher Hartley. Hartley had been promoted to his current post out of the blue when the former Chief of the Air Staff – Sir Charles Elworthy – was sent to Philadelphia in the thankless capacity of the UAUK's 'Military Legate to President Kennedy'. Unlike Elworthy, Hartley was a larger than life, 'can do' man but no diplomat. Educated at Eton College, Balliol and King's College Cambridge, he had taken part in zoological expeditions to Sarawak, Spitsbergen and Greenland before becoming a master at Eton in 1937, only joining the RAF Volunteer Reserve in 1938; and thereafter enjoying a distinguished career flying night fighters during the Second World War. Prior to the October War he had been Air Officer Commanding 12 Group, Fighter Command. Even in middle age he remained a tall, strongly built man never happier than when he was out in the country, shooting or walking.

Hartley had hugely impressed Margaret Thatcher on their first encounter as being exactly the sort of *let's get on with it and do it* sort of man she needed by her side in a crisis.

Although it was becoming clear that his predecessor, Sir Charles Elworthy's role in America was becoming increasingly invidious, there were no plans to recall him to his former post. Serendipitously, the UAUK's High Commissioner to New Zealand, the Hon. Sir Francis Cumming-Bruce, who had been in post since 1959 was pencilled in to return to Oxford to assume a role on Tom Harding-Grayson's personal staff; and the Foreign Secretary had suggested the High Commissioner's post in Wellington might be a convivial recompense 'for the iniquities Sir Charles has suffered at the hands of our transatlantic *allies* lately'. In any event bringing Elworthy – who had been born in Timaru, on New Zealand's South Island - back to Oxford now that the Air Staff had 'bedded in' under new leadership was unthinkable in the current crisis.

Beside the Chief of the Air Staff the new First Sea Lord, Admiral Sir Varyl Cargill Begg seemed slighter, less assured and very much on his guard. This was hardly surprising because in the space of a little over a week both the men above him in the professional pecking order of the Royal Navy had been killed – the one, Julian Christopher in action, the other, David Luce murdered by the IRA – hastening him into a position for which there had seemed to be no vacancy for some years to come.

Fifty-four-year-old Begg had been the gunnery officer of the battleship HMS Warspite at the Battle of Matapan in 1941, in which 'sharp action' the Mediterranean Fleet sank three Italian cruisers - two of them, the *Fiume* and the *Zara* in literally two minutes flat – in a particularly savage night time encounter. After the war he had commanded the 8th Destroyer Flotilla during the Korean conflict, been the Officer Commanding the Naval Contingent at the Coronation of Queen Elizabeth in 1953, captained the aircraft carrier HMS Triumph and prior to attaining flag rank in 1957, had been Naval Aide-de-Camp to the Queen. At the time of the October War, he had been slated to take over from Julian Christopher in the Far East sometime in the second half of 1963.

Margaret Thatcher quirked what she hoped was a welcoming smile to the new First Sea Lord whom she hardly knew, and the impassive, female occupant of the seat to his right.

"Before we start I would very much like to welcome our two new 'recruits' to this Cabinet."

Admiral Begg half rose to his feet and nodded, returning the Prime Minister's smile. The woman beside him simply inclined her face a little to the right, her lips pursed in deep thought.

"The First Sea Lord and the Minister for Supply, Transportation and Distribution are most welcome," Margaret Thatcher went on.

She had not expected fifty-two-year-old Alison Munro to dance a jig, or in fact, to do anything whatsoever to go out of her way to pander to any of the wearisome prejudices, and erroneous expectations of her latest set of powerful male colleagues. Many women in her place might understandably have been intimidated in this company. Not Alison Munro.

Alison Munro *nee* Donald had been educated at the Wynberg Girls' High School in Cape Town – where her family had emigrated in 1925 – before returning to England to attend St Paul's Girls' School and going on to St Hilda's College, Oxford, where she had graduated with a degree in philosophy, politics and economics.

Very little in Alison Munro's life had come easily to her. Both her parents had died in South Africa when she was a young girl. Orphaned at the age of thirteen she and her three siblings – one of whom, her brother Ian was an Obstetrician in Scotland credited with inventing the first ultrasound diagnostic machine – had, remarkably, and successfully fought not to be separated.

Margaret Thatcher had initially cavilled at her friend Airey Neave's unqualified recommendation of Alison Munro as his replacement at 'Supply', compelling her to read the whole of the woman's file.

She had married Alan Munro, an RAF officer and test pilot whom she had met at university in 1939; when her husband was killed testing a Miles Magister training aircraft, she had been two months' pregnant with her son, Alan. Nevertheless, she had joined the Ministry of Aircraft Production during the Second World War, first as a typist but later as the personal assistant of the legendary Sir Robert Watson-Watt, the inventor of radar. She had worked such long hours beside the great man that within the Ministry that at one time she was rumoured to be his mistress; precisely the sort of gossip that a woman of Alison Munro's mettle was never going to dignify with a comment, let alone a denial.

The Prime Minister had been 'hooked' by the other woman's story by then. In 1945 Alison Munro had passed the Direct Entry Principal Civil Servant interview (in a year when only fifty candidates were actually selected) and joined the Ministry of Civil Aviation, then in the process of considering what to do with the United Kingdom's 600 plus – many of them wartime built – airfields. In the 1950s she was the leading figure in the negotiation of European and ultimately, world-wide air traffic regulation and rights. Margaret Thatcher had been tickled more than somewhat by one story from this period when dealing with the Air Ministry of the then newly reinstated Italian government. Asked by a former Fascist Air Force general, a man called Abbriata: 'What rank did you hold in the war, Mrs Munro?' She had retorted: 'General, I held no rank but I was on the right side!' Apparently, even the Americans had been in awe – and possibly despair – as she fiercely negotiated the rights for BOAC (British Overseas Airline Corporation), BEA (British European Airways) and other home-based airlines to fly to practically every corner of the world. By the end of her stint at the Ministry of Civil Aviation, the cigar-smoking, combative and tireless force of nature that was Alison Munro had risen to be Permanent Under-Secretary for International Relations in Whitehall.

In the years before the October War the idiots who ran the Home Civil Service – many but not all of whom were vaporised on the night of the October War – had transferred Alison Munro to the Railways Department of the Ministry of Transport, where a little over a year ago she had come to the Prime Minister's attention as being one of, perhaps, the only person in the Ministry of Transport who actually seemed to be doing something constructive to ensure that the national railway system was restored to some kind of good working order.

"Right," Margaret Thatcher declared, "let's get started!"

Chapter 7

Comrade Major General Konstantin Yakovlevich Kurochnik commanding the 50th Guards Special Airborne Brigade – comprised of survivors from the 50th, 51st and 53rd Guards Airborne Regiments - was, for once in his rambunctious life, in something of a quandary.

He did not know where the garrison of the picturesque, peaceful city on the Shahar Chay River, had gone.

On the face of it this was hardly any kind of problem. He had, after all, seized a key communications hub – the only passable roads west of Lake Urmia from the north and the east, to the south and the west to the Turkish border passed through it - for the loss of half-a-dozen casualties of whom only two had been killed. Moreover, the whole town now seemed completely quiescent.

Perhaps, he had speculated it was because this was essentially an Azerbaijani place and so many of his troopers understood and spoke, at least in a pigeon fashion, the local language?

Several priests, imams so far as he could tell because he was not religious – having never seen the point of all that mumbo jumbo - had come to his headquarters in the City Governor's Palace; they had been worried about their 'holy houses' and their 'holy days', as if he cared. None of that was any of his business; he came from a land where the state religion was agnosticism but there was nothing in his orders that said anything about enforcing 'unbelief' on 'believers'. That was never a good idea, especially when a man only had eight hundred lightly equipped infantrymen – that was what airborne troops had to be because otherwise the aircraft that carried them would never get off the ground – to hold a city behind enemy lines along a single relief road from the east around the top of Lake Urmia, with a population of somewhere between sixty and seventy thousand, all of whom were potential hostiles.

Kurochnik had been warned to expect to be opposed by tanks and artillery; if he could not achieve a secure lodgement within the city, he had been ordered to harass and tie down the garrison and block the road south to Mahabad.

Somebody had told him *Rezaiyeh* – his maps called it 'Urmia' but apparently the Shah, rest his blighted soul, or his father, no *probably* his father, had renamed the place back in 1924 – was the 'Paris of Iran'. Kurochnik had never been to Paris, and never would now. However, *Rezaiyeh* or *Urmia*, or whatever it was called these days, was a not unattractive place for his veterans to rest up and feel the sun on their faces. From his position on the flat roof on top of the City Governor's residence he could see most of the built-up area, and the oasis green of the scrubby, forested area between the east of the city and the hazy blue grey of the waters of Lake Urmia. Beyond the lake a volcano-like mountain reared up. North and south-west of *Rezaiyeh* there were ribbons of barren tundra alternating with broad swathes of undergrowth, and trees filled the river valleys. After the arid mountains around Ardabil and Tabriz, this place was like that mythical land the Yankees and the British talked about...

What was it called?

Kurochnik lowered his binoculars, searched his memory.

"Shangri-La," he muttered to himself. "That's the place! Shangri-La..."

"Sorry, sir," one of his runners asked apologetically.

Kurochnik belched a guffaw of laughter.

"Nothing, kid," he grunted. His boys – he still thought of the 51st Guards Airborne Regiment as 'his boys' even though he now commanded a combined force comprising his two hundred and fifty 'boys' and the nearly six hundred strong remnants of the 50th and 53rd Guards Airborne – had had to leave most of their communications equipment behind in Tehran and the 'Urmia Action' had been mounted at such short notice there had been no chance to replace any of the lost kit. Life was like that sometimes; so, he kept a coterie of about half-a-dozen 'runners', fit young guys close to him wherever he went just so he *knew* that whatever happened, he would still be able to talk to 'his boys'.

The High Command was worried about the northern flank of the force it planned to start feeding into Northern Iraq from Mahabad via the border crossings at Piranshahr and opposite Sardasht to the south. Anything that stopped those columns moving through Mahabad would be bad news. Here on the Urmia Plain the going was not so bad but to the west the mountains effectively barred vehicular progress other than on treacherous winding roads which, in places, were effectively single-track highways that had not been repaired since being buried for several weeks by last winter's snows. It was all very well for planners to claim that aerial reconnaissance confirmed all the roads were still open; Kurochnik was far too old a soldier to take a thing like that for granted and he hoped that the Army Group Commander's staff had not taken anybody's word for it either.

If he was the Army Group Commander, he would have had Spetsnaz crawling on their hands and knees all over those roads through the Zagros Mountains for the last month. Just thinking about those narrow, switchback passes gave him a bad feeling.

Raising his glasses to his face he tried and failed to make out the squat control tower at the city's only air strip, 'a neglected, pot-holed disgrace', as it had been described to him by one briefing officer. Actually, the strip was not that neglected or pot-holed, although the runway was only partly concreted. The main problem was that the 'safe landing area' was only about two thousand metres long and that was bad news for the bigger transports in Army Group South's already dwindling air fleet.

The Urmia Action had exposed just how badly the aircraft lost on the Malta Operation were now missed. Once the airfield, situated six or seven kilometres north from the centre of *Rezaiyeh*, roughly halfway to the tiny hamlet of Chonqeraluy-e Pol, had been secured it had taken two further trips for the planes assigned to the 'Urmia Action' to transport the remaining six hundred troopers from Tabriz.

Kurochnik heard the distance scream of jet engines.

The fighters, four MiG-21s, were flying at some three thousand metres above the plain. *Altitude* was an ambiguous word in these localities since *Rezaiyeh* was some one thousand three hundred metres above sea level. The fighters roared south and returned a few minutes later, this time much lower and rocketed across the city less than two hundred feet above the rooftops before pointing their noses to the heavens and with their afterburners glowing red, blasting straight up into high clouds scudding across the mountains.

There was absolutely nothing quite like a show of strength!

It was a pity the concrete part of the runway of the only airstrip this side of Tabriz was too short to allow any kind of serious jet fighter or bomber to operate out of it!

More prosaically, Kurochnik regretted that while the Red Air Force possessed just about enough advanced supersonic aircraft for a 'show of strength', it did not seem to have any old fashioned, slow unspectacular propeller driven spotter planes to spare for doing boring, mundane little things like discovering what exactly lay beyond the trees, mountains and the valleys to the south and the west. There could have been a whole armoured division hidden out there and the first he would know about it was when the opening salvo of an artillery barrage fell on his perimeter!

What did he know?

He was a mere Colonel; correction, Major General, he had been informed of his promotion to Major General as he boarded the transport to lead the assault on the so-called Urmia Air Base.

It was nice to know he was a General at last; although not so good to still be commanding only a 'regimental' sized 'brigade'.

He sighed, turned on his heel and strode towards the steps down to the street. He had requested urgent airborne resupply; loads of ammunition for his mortars, as many 7.92-mm rounds as possible, and respectfully observed to his superiors that a few of the new, very scarce, shoulder-launched anti-tank missiles would be good, too. Headquarters had told him to make do with what he had. It seemed that stores previously earmarked for the 51st Guards Airborne Brigade had already been reallocated to other units 'more likely to face serious enemy resistance'.

It was as Kurochnik was walking into his first floor 'operations room' that he felt the shock of the distant explosion through the soles of his boots. The ground flinched another two times before the sound of the first big explosion rumbled into the room like the roiling commotion of great waves breaking on a distant shore.

In a moment he was running back to the steps to the roof.

"It's the air base, sir!"

Even as Kurochnik was attempting to focus his binoculars on the rising mushroom clouds of the huge explosions enveloping Urmia Air Base more detonations crashed out. These blasts were much louder, closer, in the south of the city.

Kurochnik's mind was churning with possibilities.

The bridges over the river had been rigged for demolition!

The Iranians sent their people to the west to be trained; not the conscript foot soldiers but all their officer class and most of their technical specialists. In the past the Iranian armed forces had had British and American personnel embedded in their ranks, *advising* and *supervising*, trying to stop the locals constantly breaking all the expensive kit they had acquired from the West in recent years.

But Urmia was not any kind of Iranian Army training base...

His boys had *not* stumbled over any obvious booby traps. Yes, they had discovered a few mines hurriedly laid in culverts and by the roadside north of the city; but otherwise, nothing...

The building around him seemed to convulse.

Kurochnik found himself on the ground coughing up the gritty dust of pulverized mud brick and stone. Strong hands hauled him to his feet.

"I'm fine!" He snarled. "Fine!"

His mind was racing faster and faster. This was only the beginning. In an hour it would be dark and then things would get very, very bloody.

The reason his boys had had such an easy time at the air base, the reason that, a couple of amateur snipers excepted, the 51st Guards Airborne Brigade had been able to walk into Urmia unopposed was that the whole city was a trap.

Like an idiot he had voluntarily put his hand into a meat grinder.

"RUNNERS!" He bawled like a black bear with a Snow Leopard biting his leg. "RUNNERS!"

Chapter 8

Monday 13th April 1964
Corpus Christi College, Oxford, England

Airey Neave leaned forward and rested his elbows on the Cabinet table as he surveyed the faces of his colleagues. The Prime Minister had invited him to explain his 'new brief' and to describe the 'new department' that he had been cobbling together over the weekend. Or rather, not so much 'cobbling together' as *spot welding* those overlapping parts of the disparate, feuding organisations he had inherited wherever they abutted uneasily against another one of his collection of unwieldy 'services'.

"The Prime Minister has instructed me to form a Ministry of National Security," he explained briskly for a thing like this was always best done quickly.

Edward Heath had toyed with the idea of bringing the entire 'Intelligence Community' under a single umbrella last year but one or other of the competing Director Generals had talked him out of it every time the matter rose anywhere near to the top of the agenda. However, the fiasco of the march to near war with the Americans in November and early December last year, the whole ghastly Red Dawn imbroglio, the knowledge that but for the suicidal heroics of the Royal Navy Malta would have fallen to a Soviet invasion, the shooting down of two jetliners by IRA terrorists over *England* which had very nearly resulted in the assassination of both the Prime Minister and *the Queen*, and finally, the news that the Red Army had over run northern Iran and was now threatening to sweep all the way south to the Persian Gulf, *without so much as a forewarning whimper from the code breakers in Cheltenham, or a vaguest suggestion of a problem from MI6 or MI5* had been the final straw!

Sir Roger Hollis, the MI5 man under whose watch the atrocities at Brize Norton and Cheltenham had occurred had been sacked, as had the Director of the Government Communications Headquarters at Cheltenham, along with his deputy and the head of security at that place.

Hollis and his *'collaborators'* - the Prime Minister's own word - had had several of GCHQ's most senior code breakers locked up in Gloucester Prison at the time Malta was under attack, two Soviet tank armies had been parked on the northern borders of Iran and three IRA assassins had been running amok in the land. They and Hollis 'had had to go' and Margaret Thatcher had not just 'sacked' them but had them placed under arrest at Government House outside Cheltenham in case they were of a mood to 'make trouble' among their 'old friends'.

It was now Airey Neave's job to persuade GCHQ, the Security Service (MI5) and the Secret Intelligence Service (MI6) to work 'nicely' together for the good of the country. This was easier said than done given that these institutions were self-evidently not naturally preoccupied with what everybody else regarded as the 'good of the country'; traditionally each had sheltered elements significantly more exercised by their own status and influence than any lightweight, ephemeral populist concept of a common understanding of patriotism.

"Bringing all the organs of the Intelligence Community under one umbrella is not a thing that can be done overnight," the former escapee from Oflag - an abbreviation of *Offizierslager; 'Officers Camp'* - IV-C, or as the man in the street would know it 'Colditz' Castle explained, allowing himself a rueful smile. "However, I believe we have made a damned good start.   After consultation with the Prime Minister, I have appointed Sir Dick White as the first Director General of the National Security Service, of which GCHQ, MI5 and MI6 have now become the primary subordinate branches.   Dick White has got his best people interrogating the Soviet military personnel taken prisoner on Malta, and, of course, the three IRA men in our custody. A raft of other initiatives are under the most urgent consideration, others have been implemented or are being implemented at this time. I regret that it would be inappropriate to discuss these in detail even in this august forum and I make no apology for this."

The Soviet-Turkish code books and cipher equipment captured when the Turkish destroyer *Mareşal Fevzi Çakmak* had surrendered to HMS Alliance in the aftermath of the Battle of Malta, feared lost when the Comet airliner carrying them back to England was shot down while coming in to land at RAF Cheltenham a week ago, had been discovered late on Saturday afternoon.   The code books were intact, the cipher equipment mangled beyond repair.   No matter, the cryptologists at Cheltenham had pulled out all the stops and been working non-stop on 'breaking' previously 'unbreakable' intercept material for the last forty hours.

This endeavour, being conducted under the codename '*Jericho*' was so secret that only nine people in Oxford even knew that there was a classified project called *Jericho*.

That morning a messenger from GCHQ had reported that the 'experts are already into routine housekeeping traffic' and that 'the coding books in our hands are *live* for at least the next fifty-three days', with the caveat, 'unless, of course, the Soviets change their encryption protocols before then.' Unfortunately, this latter possibility was 'very likely', since no code book was routinely employed until the end of its originally scheduled 'life span'.

Airey Neave did not care about that.   If the Soviets changed their codes, so be it, there was nothing he or anybody else could do about that.   The important thing was that GCHQ was reading the Soviet High Command's chit-chat *NOW*...

It went without saying that he was not about to broadcast this to all and sundry; in this room the '*Jericho* approved list' only included himself, the Prime Minister, James Callaghan, Willie Whitelaw and the three Chiefs of Staff.   At this time there were just fourteen names on the 'list' outside the environs of GCHQ.

Fortuitously, the provisions made to guard *Enigma* in the Second

World War provided an excellent historical model on which to base the Draconian security arrangements put in place around the cryptographic gold mine that HMS Alliance had delivered to their cause.

Several of the men and women who had broken that German *Enigma* code over twenty years ago were now at the coal face unravelling 'FOOL'S GOLD'.

Fool's Gold was the coverall security 'box' within which *Jericho* lived. Or rather, the largest of the many 'boxes' in which *Jericho* lived because most of the people at Cheltenham busily beavering away night and day to 'get into' *Jericho* had absolutely no idea what they were actually working on.

The best security systems *always* worked that way.

"I have already received representations on behalf of Sir Roger Hollis and others," he went on, not troubling to hide precisely how unimpressed he was by such representations. "None of which I am prepared to entertain. The message needs to get out to fellow Honourable Members of Parliament that we are in the middle of a war and that I don't give a fig what bloody school or club a fellow once went to or belonged to!"

"Here! Here!" Margaret Thatcher said irritably. She met the eye of the Chief of the Defence Staff, General Sir Richard Hull. "CDS," she smiled, tight-lipped, using the title never formally adopted by the Army Chief's predecessor, Sir David Luce. He had preferred simply to be acknowledged as 'First Sea Lord'. "CDS, would you brief colleagues on the latest news from the Mediterranean and the Middle East please?"

"Recovery and policing operations continue on Malta, Prime Minister." Sir Richard flicked a thoughtful glance towards the Foreign Secretary, who indicated for him to continue. "Air operations in the theatre have been disrupted by what appears to be a unilateral declaration of a 'no fly zone' over much of what was pre-war, French sovereign territory. The declaration was issued by a body calling itself the Provisional Peoples' Republic of the French. That said, there also appears to be a Provisional Government of South France, which is also making similar declarations. This latter body is responsible for a declaration warning that any 'ships of war' entering a two hundred miles 'exclusion zone' from the French Mediterranean coast will be liable to attack. Frankly, we don't know how seriously to take this but as colleagues will know we began routing all flights to and from Portugal and Malta so as to avoid *contentious* air space in the days before the Battle of Malta, thus adding over an hour to transit times. The French naval base at Toulon was pretty hard hit during the war so apart from a small squadron based in Corsica, which may or may not owe allegiance to one or both of the 'Provisional Governments' on the mainland we have only the most sketchy of *feels* for the naval, or for that matter, the aerial capabilities of those regimes."

Tom Harding-Grayson waved for him to go on.

"I'll pick up on this later, Sir Richard," he grimaced.

The soldier nodded.

"As I say, recovery and policing operations continue across the Maltese Archipelago. After aircraft from the USS Independence attacked two presumed enemy submarine contacts, one sixty nautical miles east and the other, seventy miles south of the Archipelago on Thursday last week the Central Mediterranean 'threat board' has been blank. Despite adverse political developments in Philadelphia, the US Sixth Fleet remains, effectively, at the operational disposal of the C-in-C Malta, Air Vice-Marshal French. That said, thus far none of the promised extra transport aircraft from the USA have materialised. Given that the US Air Force has not filed flight plans or requested clearances in this connection we are proceeding on the assumption that the onus to reinforce our garrisons in the Middle East will fall upon us. In any event, forces deployed during the Cyprus Operation have been warned for transfer to depots we hope to be permitted to set up in Southern Iraq, Jordan, Kuwait, Oman and Saudi Arabia. My Staff is in conversation with the Saudi Arabian authorities about exploring the possibility of utilising war and other stores positioned in that country by the US Armed Forces prior to their withdrawal last year. I apologise it this sounds a tad woolly but I know Cabinet does not want to get bogged down in detail at this stage. I have sent a personal representative to the theatre to assess the situation on the ground and to report back to me at the earliest time."

Margaret Thatcher raised an eyebrow.

"Major General Carver," the Chief of the Defence Staff reported. "A damned fine officer, Prime Minister."

"He was in command of the 3rd Division in Germany at the time of the recent war," Willie Whitelaw added. "He was out in Cyprus planning the move of his Division to that island when the, er, balloon went up."

The Prime Minister nodded for Sir Richard Hull to carry on.

"It happens," he announced, presaging a surprise morsel of news that was not uniformly grim, "that as a result of the minor rapprochement with the regime of the late Shah in the last few months – at least at a staff level – that we have men, and therefore potential intelligence 'eyes and ears' on the ground in Iran."

"Really," Margaret Thatcher said in surprise. "We do?"

"Yes, Prime Minister. Our fellows were specifically instructed to keep away from Tehran so as to avoid inflaming local factional sensibilities. Most of our people are in the south, in liaison and training roles with the Iranian Army. Their presence was what enabled us to co-ordinate the operations of the Abadan garrison with local Iranian armoured formations to repel the recent illegal incursion of the Iraqi 2nd Armoured Division."

"Yes," the Prime Minister breathed unhappily. She had only been informed *afterwards* that a large force of Iraqi tanks had manoeuvred so as to threaten Khorramshahr and the northern refineries of the Abadan Island complex. She had stiffly informed the CDS that in future she wanted to be informed *before* rather than *after* British forces engaged in offensive operations against the forces of a country that was, nominally, still an ally. "But you are saying that we have other forces in Iran?"

"Yes. A mixed detachment of SAS and SBS men under the command of Lieutenant-Colonel Frank Waters, VC; its mission was one of schooling Imperial Iranian Army counterparts in north-western Iran. They were using the city of *Rezaiyeh* as their base."

Margaret Thatcher looked to her Foreign Secretary for help.

"Old sweats from the days when our fathers campaigned in Mesopotamia," Tom Harding-Grayson smiled whimsically, "would have call *Rezaiyeh* by its pre-Pahlavi Dynasty name of *Urmia*. It is situated close to the conjunction of the borders of the south eastern corner of the Anatolian littoral of Turkey and the north-east of Kurdish Iran. That places it pretty much right in the middle of where in olden days the 'Great Game' was played out between ourselves, the French and the Russians." He looked to Sir Richard Hull. "Presumably, our boys were keeping an eye 'on things' while they were playing soldiers with the locals?"

The Chief of the Defence Staff laughed grimly.

"*Our boys*," he guffawed, "are *always* keeping an eye on things *wherever* they are, Tom!"

"Quite so," the other man concurred.

The Chief of the Defence Staff sighed.

"Colonel Waters has made contact with Abadan and reported the city of *Rezaiyeh* as being in the hands of Soviet airborne troops. His scouts also report columns of tanks and mechanised infantry on the road between Qoshachay, which is also known as Miandoab, to Mahabad, which would be entirely consistent with other intelligence to hand, that the Soviets plan to decamp onto the ground around the headwaters of the great rivers of Mesopotamia in north eastern Iraq via the passes through the Zagros Mountains in the vicinity of Piranshahr and Sardasht. Enemy combatants who have fallen into Colonel Waters's hands talk about 'driving on' to Erbil and Mosul. We don't know if the northern oilfields are the objective just of the first phase of the invasion, or just some ruse to draw the Iraqi Army and anybody stupid enough to follow suit, to the north of Baghdad."

"Why would it be bad to fight the invaders north of Baghdad, General?" Margaret Thatcher inquired.

Sir Richard Hull sucked his teeth for a moment.

"Fellows on my Staff served in that part of the World during the Second War and just afterwards, Prime Minister. If anything goes wrong there is nowhere to anchor a secure defensive line between Kirkuk in the north and Basra in the South."

The Foreign Secretary coughed.

"Iraq is not a cohesive entity in the sense that we in Europe would understand a nation state, Margaret," he observed. "There are the Kurds in the north, the Sunnis in the middle surrounding Shia Baghdad, and the Shias in the south. Each religious and ethnic group detests and mistrusts *all* the others and these divisions run through the Iraqi Army like the cracks in a broken pane of glass, ready to shatter without warning. If the Soviets wanted to hold the north it would be hard, but not impossible to winkle them out, assuming we weren't bothered about the blood and treasure we'd expend in outrageously copious quantities in the process. If the Soviets drive south, they *must* reach the Persian Gulf, or sooner or later they will be embroiled in, and probably destroyed by the internecine civil war they will have unwittingly brokered by destroying the illusion of Iraqi statehood."

"That's assuming the Iranians don't get their act together first," the Chief of the Defence Staff added. "The Soviets are sitting pretty at the moment because all the best Iranian armour is deployed in the south threatening Basra and surrounding Abadan."

Tom Harding-Grayson shook his head.

"On precisely the *wrong* side of the Shat-al-Arab," he bemoaned.

"And probably not under the command of somebody who actually knows how to use it!" Sir Richard Hull complained.

Margaret Thatcher wearied of this digression.

"Will the Red Army drive to the south like *your* man says, Airey?" She demanded, turning to her old friend.

"Ah, *my man*," her friend sighed.

Airey Neave honestly and truly did not know what to make of the man who claimed to be, and *seemed* to be the former deputy of the former Rumanian leader Gheorghe Gheorghiu-Dej, Nicolae *Ceausescu*. If the man was who he claimed to be he was a potential intelligence gold mine.

"He's adamant," her Minister for National Security assured her. "But then he admits he didn't know about the attack on Malta until the ship he was on board started bombarding Valletta!" He paused, glanced to the Foreign Secretary. "Tom's offered to have a chat with *Ceausescu* this afternoon, Margaret," he went on. "The fellow is due to be flying into Brize Norton about now. As you know, I've got my doubts about the fellow despite what Dick White's *lady friend* says. I'll feel a lot happier when Tom's given this *Ceausescu* and Miss Piotrowska his seal of approval."

Margaret Thatcher moved onto the next item on her agenda.

"What's actually going on in Philadelphia, Tom?"

"Contrary to what we were given to understand on Friday," he began, running a hand through his thinning hair, "Congress did not vote to immediately suspend all overseas military assistance and co-operation. That vote will actually happen later today. Regrettably, it looks like the motion will pass both Houses of Representatives. A lot of 'representatives' seem to think the whole thing in Iran is just a 'limey plot' to draw them into 'another foreign war'. Likewise, there is now no foreseeable prospect of the Senate ratifying the US-UK Mutual Defence Agreement. This is important because it was the legal basis of the Kennedy Administration's policy, vis-à-vis military, economic and diplomatic co-operation with us; and in less than a week's time the period of grace of ninety days after the signing and formal exchange of initialled copies of the treaty, expires. After that date no

American officer or official can operate under its terms without committing a criminally indictable offence within the jurisdiction of the United States Government."

President Kennedy had flown to England last week not to forestall this *disaster* but to dress it up as something it was not, and to publicly distance himself and his Administration from the latest colonial adventurism of perfidious Albion. Although the exercise had been frustrated by a new catastrophe, there had been indications that the Kennedy Administration had been back-sliding on the commitments made in January for several weeks.

Temporarily, the Battle of Malta and the timely intervention of the US Sixth Fleet had created an impenetrable smokescreen of mutually congratulatory rhetoric which had shrouded the real picture for a few more days. Notwithstanding, it was now clear that the Administration, in league with the House of Representatives was opportunistically using the UAUK's retaliatory and essentially defensive sanctions against the Irish Republic as a convenient excuse to ditch the US-UK Mutual Defense Treaty, and thus appease the deafening clamour of the America First movement. It now seemed likely this had been the Kennedy Administration's plan from the outset; if there had been no atrocities at Brize Norton or Cheltenham the President would have had to have manufactured another *provocation* to justify storming out of the 'Anglo-American Summit'. In the event the IRA had made it easy for him; he had hunkered down overnight and flown home the morning after he arrived in Britain. There had been no window for a meeting of minds; Margaret Thatcher had not been released from hospital until two hours after the President's aircraft had taken off bound for Philadelphia; and by the time SAM 26000 touched down the UAUK's planned 'Irish Sanctions' were already headline news on the East Coast.

Margaret Thatcher had always known that placing her trust in Jack Kennedy was a huge risk, literally a leap in the dark. Back in January the gamble had been worth the candle, if for no better reason than that anything was better than the outbreak of a shooting war with the United States. Nevertheless, having hoped for the best and prepared for the worst, it did not mean that she was anything but appalled by the steepening downward trend of recent Anglo-American relations. She did not so much feel as if she had been let down; as if she had been *betrayed.*

Margaret Thatcher understood that Jack Kennedy was confronting apparently insuperable problems at home. In retrospect the failed assassination attempt on the life of Dr Martin Luther King in February – an event which had gone practically unremarked outside the United States - had lit the fuse on renewed widespread and bloody civil unrest across the South. At the same time the President's reversal of the 'peace dividend' defence cuts having reinvigorated the American military, had enraged and alienated the powerful vested interest lobbies which had been counting on spending the proceeds of that 'dividend' to feather their own nests. And all the while a great

American city, Chicago, was cut in half by the battle lines of what was with the coming of spring likely to become a war zone.

All in all, Jack Kennedy's decision to run again for the Presidency had only served to unite his enemies. Worse, at the same time the Southern Civil Rights Movement was planning to 'March on Philadelphia' the first court hearings of the cases against the leading figures of December's failed coup d'état – the so-called Battle of Washington – were shortly scheduled to commence. It was hardly surprising that the Kennedy Administration was so fixated with crises at home that it was determined it seemed, to turn a positively Nelsonian blind eye to the terrifying developments in the Middle East.

"I will be speaking to Secretary of State Fulbright this evening," Tom Harding-Grayson announced. "Always assuming he actually takes my call this time!"

Margaret Thatcher blanched at this.

One school of thought still maintained that J. William Fulbright was the one remaining voice of reason in the Philadelphia White House. The Secretary of State's avowedly internationalist stance was, the Administration's apologists claimed, the last bulwark against a return to isolationism.

The Prime Minister had grown impatient with such sophistry. Things had reached the point where the country needed to know where it stood.

Was the United States at its back or not?

"No, Tom," she said, biting back her annoyance. "No, no, no."

All eyes fell on her in the sudden silence.

"Please inform the Philadelphia White House that I wish to speak to the President this evening. Please make sure that they understand that if the President is unable to take *my* call there *will be* consequences!"

Chapter 9

Monday 13th April 1964
Christ Church College, Oxford, England

"Ah, we meet again, Rachel," Tom Harding-Grayson observed ruefully as he stepped forward to take his visitor's hand. "As lovely as ever, I see?"

The woman greeted this remark with weary forbearance. Her hair, straw blond was cut short almost like a man's and the grey-blue dress she wore was an abysmally tailored sack that was far too thin for the chill of the late April day in England. Worse, she had foregone the use of makeup for several days and she felt horribly, inconsolably guilty and ached with loss. Not one scintilla of her guilt attached to the butchering of the Red Army parachutists – somewhere between twenty and thirty, she had not been counting - she had gunned down in her rampage through the Citadel at Mdina on the afternoon of the Battle of Malta, no, it was more subtle and insidious than that.

She kept asking herself if she could have done *anything* to warn *anybody* what was about to happen? If she had kept closer to Arkady Rykov, might he have let something slip? What had she missed?

"You look older, Tom," she said, looking around the Foreign Secretary's cluttered office. The state of the office reflected the mind of the man; endlessly curious, acquisitive, restless. His was a mind that worked in unique ways and saw things few of the people around him would ever see.

"I feel older," he confessed. "I should probably ask you what you've been up to the last ten years," he went on dryly, "but I won't."

The woman frowned.

"Just drink poison and I'll tell you everything you want to know."

Tom Harding-Grayson chuckled.

"The Shah of Iran came to a sticky end," he remarked for no particular reason. Except that they both understood it was anything but a casual observation.

Rachel Angelika Piotrowska's eyes narrowed a fraction.

Otherwise, her composure was perfect.

"He was a pig," she replied blandly, "like most men." She shrugged. "The bastards didn't have to kill those girls. That was cold."

"Very *Russian*, you mean?"

"No, Russians are human beings too. What we and the Americans did on the night of the war; that *was* pretty cold, too."

"More the Yanks than us, actually," the man objected dryly.

Rachel fixed him with a quizzical expression.

"The first we knew about it was when the Soviets started lobbing medium range ICBMs at us from the Baltic," he explained. His tone was that of a man explaining away the foibles of a dissolute younger brother, as if to say *'these things happen'*.

"You're joking?"

"No. We lost over forty V-Bombers on the ground. One day our people will find out what really happened on that night," he shrugged. "Hopefully, future historians will endorse the RAF's decision to fly east not west that night."

The woman stared at him.

"We didn't start it? The war, I mean?"

The Home Secretary shook his head.

"No. So far as I can tell JFK wasn't taking Harold MacMillan's calls the day of the war. For what it is worth, our hands are clean. We only attacked the Soviets *after* we came under attack ourselves."

The man waved for Rachel to take a seat in a well-worn upholstered chair near the guttering fire. She sat down and ruminated on the coals in the hearth, her thoughts roiling with the implications of what she had just been told. She waited for her host to make the next move.

"Presumably," Tom Harding-Grayson probed, "your spell in Tehran with the Shah would have been your last assignment before Dick White sent you off the grid looking for our friend Arkady Pavlovich Rykov?"

Rachel nodded, her lips sealed and her eyes drawn down again into the glowing remnants of the fire.

"That was before the war, of course," the man mused out aloud.

"You didn't *order* me to come here to discuss Arkady, Tom."

"I didn't *order* you to do anything. That's Dick White's job."

The woman snorted disdainfully.

"I ought to put a bullet in that man's brain."

"I don't think you'd be very popular with Airey Neave if you did a thing like that!"

Rachel fixed the Foreign Secretary with a hard, dangerous look.

"Airey, too," she added with a sigh. "I suppose they told you I didn't want to come back to England."

"No?" Tom Harding-Grayson's expression had become unyielding. He had heard the tales about what his former protégé had done in Mdina at the height of the Battle of Malta; and queried the wisdom of bringing her back into the fold. But then the twin imperatives of bringing the man who claimed to be Nicolae Ceausescu, the First Deputy Secretary of the Communist Party of the People's Republic of Romania to Oxford, and the necessity of neatly tidying up the loose ends contingent upon the execution of the traitor Samuel Calleja had concluded the debate. "Why ever not?"

Rachel ignored the question.

"You should talk to Ceausescu," she said abruptly.

"This fellow really is Nicolae Ceausescu?"

The woman nodded.

"How do you know? How could you know that?"

"I met him several times before the war. That would have been after you got yourself sent into internal exile, Tom," she remarked, nowhere near as cattily as she intended.

Rachel did not have her heart in clawing out Tom Harding-Grayson's eyes, figuratively or for real today. All her anger was gone; burned out by the knowledge of the grief that she was partly responsible for bringing to the lives of her good friends Marija Christopher and Rosa Calleja. Even though she had only known the younger women a relatively short time, they were her friends, Marija particularly had been there for her when she was at her lowest ebb and even now Marija did not blame her for any of the bad things that had happened. If Marija and Rosa were *sisters*, she had become their honorary step *sister*.

"Bucharest was a dreary, horrible place but perfect for talking to the Russians," she went on. "Switzerland, Berlin or Vienna were always far too public, and there were always too many people looking over your shoulder. The first time I met Ceausescu he thought I was a KGB whore. He almost wet himself with relief when he discovered I was actually only interested in 'opening up channels of communication' with the West. A direct line to the 'Free World' was always going to be his trump card when he finally wormed his way to the top. He'd keep Romania under his thumb and still enjoy the benefits of having *friends* in the West. The thing you must never forget with little shits like *Nicolae* is that it is all about them. I doubt if he's given his wife and kids – the ones he left behind in Bucharest for the KGB to pick up – a second thought since he escaped from Romania."

"And what about the other times you met him?"

"Courier in plain sight," she murmured, somewhat elliptically.

Her meaning was not lost on the man.

"This man is the real thing then?"

"Yes."

"What about the woman with him?"

Rachel smiled, she had to.

"Eleni. The little monster was the reason her nephew and her uncle died," again she sighed, 'but in some twisted way I think she genuinely loves the little shit. Still, I'm hardly one to talk, I suppose. Not after I let Arkady Pavlovich get so deep inside my head that I started to forget who I was..."

When the Foreign Secretary and Rachel Piotrowska entered the small ground floor annexe where Nicolae Ceausescu and his *nurse* Eleni had been *parked* awaiting Tom Harding-Grayson's convenience, the middle-aged Greek woman immediately began to complain about the treatment she and her 'friend' had received since they had got off the plane earlier that day.

Rachel held up her hands.

"I'm sorry. People are going hungry in this country," she explained in the woman's idiosyncratic, very Cypriot tongue. Then she looked at the one-legged prematurely aged man viewing her with cool, calculating eyes from where he sat in the creaky old wheelchair the people at RNH Bighi on Malta had found for him. Rachel switched to Russian and spoke slowly so that Eleni could understand a word, here and there, as she spoke. "You should not complain about your treatment, Comrade," she cautioned sarcastically. "The people in this country have every right to have you shot for your part in the *Krasnaya Zarya* abomination."

"*Red Dawn*," the man hissed, his English was grotesquely, clumsily accented with his mother Romanian vowels, "was," he hesitated, struggled for the right word, "*inflict*, yes, inflicted on *my* people!"

And there it was in a nutshell.

Nothing that had ever gone wrong in Nicolae Ceausescu's life was his fault; always he had been betrayed, let down, disappointed by others and that was never, ever going to change because that was the sort of man he was.

"If you say that often enough, they will put you up against a wall and shoot you," Rachel told him in Russian.

Tom Harding-Grayson had pulled up a chair for Rachel, which she accepted with strained good grace. The Foreign Secretary sat directly in front of the man in the wheelchair and looked him straight in the eyes.

"Ask him if he knows who I am and if he doesn't know, tell him please."

"You," Nicolae Ceausescu stuttered, pre-empting Rachel, "Foreign Minister..."

"Very good," Tom Harding-Grayson nodded. "Tell him you will ask the questions, Rachel. You will ask the questions in Russian and he will reply to you in the same language so that you can translate whatever he says to you word for word."

He waited while the woman conveyed this to their 'guest'.

Nicolae Ceausescu shrugged and nodded.

Eleni began to protest but he stilled her babbling by a single touch of her arm. She frowned and shut her mouth, glaring at Rachel.

"Tell me," the Foreign Secretary invited, "about your life and career, Nicolae Ceausescu?"

Rachel translated obediently.

"What do you want to know?" Was the answer in Moskva Russian that she repeated verbatim in English; and so, it began. It put her in mind of the first time Tom Harding-Grayson had 'debriefed her' all those years ago. So long ago that she had still been a scrawny student nurse at St Bart's Hospital. In those days 'Sir Dick' White had been the poster boy of MI5, just plain Richard Goldsmith White, and Tom Harding-Grayson had still been a full-time spook masquerading as a Principal Officer at the old Foreign and Colonial Office.

"Your life story, *Nicolae Ceausescu?* Only your life story? We can start with your date and place of birth, the names of both of your parents, their dates of birth and places of birth, and then you can tell me about your siblings?"

Now that he understood the game the one-legged man in the wheelchair relaxed a little; desperate to convey to his interrogators that he was unafraid, in control and that he sympathised with their dilemma.

He started to talk and went on talking until Tom Harding-Grayson held up a hand. Notwithstanding Rachel's personal verification of the man's identity – however unlikely and implausible it seemed that he was actually who he said he was and had survived the adventures that he claimed to have survived – he had had to be certain. Before the October War MI6 would have had a weighty file on Ceausescu; that had gone up in flames in the war but the Foreign Secretary knew enough about the *real* Nicolae Ceausescu to be able to make an informed judgement.

If this man was an imposter, he was a superbly good imposter.

Not many people in the West knew that Nicolae Ceausescu had owed his rise to the deputy premiership of the People's Republic of Romania almost entirely to a chance encounter with the man who became his mentor and protector, Gheorghe Gheorghiu-Dej. Ceausescu had been a member of the Romanian Communist Party since 1933 at the age of fifteen. That was the year of his first arrest by the Romanian authorities. He had been in and out of prison throughout his teens. During the Second World War the pro-Fascist regime of Ion Antonescu had cracked down hard on all known and suspected communist sympathisers and activists; and Ceausescu had seen the insides of several internment camps; Jilava in 1940, Caransebes two years later, and in 1943 first Văcăresti, and then Târgu Jiu in the Carpathian Mountains.

It was at Târgu Jiu that he first shared a cell with Gheorghe Gheorghiu-Dej, the man who within a year would become the leader of the 'prison faction' of the Romanian Communist Party, and the Party's General Secretary.

At Târgu Jiu the prisoners ran their own cell blocks; the result of an unofficial pact that guaranteed that nobody would attempt to escape. Gheorghiu-Dej used this 'freedom' to assert his control over the other inmates, running so-called 'self-criticism sessions' in which Party members were forced to confess to their failure to interpret the gospel of the Marxist-Leninist dialectic *as understood by Comrade Gheorghiu-Dej.* Nicolae Ceausescu's role in the 'self-criticism sessions' was as his master's bully boy, enthusiastically beating up 'comrades' who refused to engage with or were insufficiently enthusiastic in their 'self-criticism'.

After the war Ceausescu's rise had been meteoric. He had become a major general in the reformed Romanian Army; Gheorghe Dej's deputy minister of defence and his mentor's most faithful ally on the Central Committee of the Party by 1952. By 1954 he was a full member of the Romanian Politburo, and long before the October War Gheorghiu-Dej's 'enforcer' had become the absolute master of the Securitate, the feared and loathed *Departamentul Securitāsii Statului* – the Department of State Security – and consequently, the natural leader in waiting.

It had been a heady, breakneck rise for the third child of an impoverished drunken, wife-beating despotic father in Scornicesti in the obscure rural south of the country who had run away from home at the age of eleven to live with his elder sister Niculina in Bucharest...

Eventually Tom Harding-Grayson had held up a hand.

"Well, Nicolae Ceausescu," he conceded, a half-smile on his lips but cold purpose in his eyes, "now that we have established that you *may* be who you claim to be, let us talk about how exactly you came to know the particulars of *Operation Nakazyvat.*"

Chapter 10

Tuesday 14th April 1964
Oxford, England

The United States Ambassador to the Court of Woodstock had been unusually quiet, almost non-communicative most of that afternoon. He remained so now. This troubled Joanne Brenckmann as the couple walked unhurriedly down Beef Lane towards St Aldate's Church.

The security people had wanted to get out the armoured limousines for the half-mile or so journey from the new embassy, located almost in the shadow of Oxford Castle, to the Foreign Secretary and his wife's rooms at Christ Church College. Walter, her husband, had irritably and with rare discourtesy towards subordinates, brusquely vetoed this suggestion.

'I didn't come over here to hide in the goddammed Embassy!'

He had called the head of protocol back a few minutes later and apologised for his 'rudeness and inappropriate language'. The poor man had been so surprised he had not known if he was coming or going! Walter's predecessor had treated the Embassy staff like hired help; whereas her husband's quietly spoken, 'gentlemanly' demeanour and her own, somewhat 'down home' attitudes to housekeeping and the domestic management of the Embassy – a compound comprising several old buildings linked with passageways and what might once have been 'priest holes' – had promoted a relaxed, collegiate atmosphere more in keeping with their surroundings in historic Oxford.

Regrettably, the recent 'security nightmare' had largely curtailed the husband and wife's freedom to stroll in and around the old city. They had come to look forward to their early morning or late afternoon 'walks', during which they would dip into tiny shops, leisurely peruse the shelves of antiquarian bookshops and generally behave – quite unashamedly – like two 'hick' sightseers.

Today two Secret Servicemen strode ahead of the Ambassador and his wife, others guarded their backs and at points along the planned route rifle-armed British Military Policemen stood sentinel with suspicious eyes.

What troubled Joanne Brenckmann most was that her husband usually told her *everything*, well, not really top-secret military things – she did not want to hear about those things and she did not expect him to tell her them anyway – but *everything* else. Late last night he had taken a call from the State Department in Philadelphia. It had been a long call, well over an hour and afterwards Walter had not come to bed until the early hours of the morning. Even when she had snuggled close and wrapped her arms around him, he had still not slept.

"Something bad has happened?" She prompted. Her voice was

barely more than a whisper. "I mean, something *else* bad has happened, sweetheart?"

Her husband's stride faltered for a half-step.

When he was silent Joanne probed further; it was the last attempt she planned to make to find out what was eating him up inside. Whether it was about his time in the Navy, a legal matter, or the *latest* dumb thing the Administration had done back home she had far too much respect for her husband's discretion to push him too far beyond his self-imposed boundaries.

"I mean something that's not in the news yet?"

Walter Brenckmann grunted, shook his head.

"After what happened to the President's vote in the New Hampshire Primary," he explained wearily, "I was afraid the Administration would go down the 'America First' route; but I never thought it would happen so soon."

Jack Kennedy had won the New Hampshire Primary with thirty-one percent of the vote against a field of no-hopers. It was unprecedented! The President of the United States of America had only attracted the support of 'thirty-one percent' of *Democrat voters* in New Hampshire!

New Hampshire had not torpedoed the re-election campaign but it had given it a nasty jolt. Congress's now obvious intention to vote to reject the US-UK Mutual Defense Treaty agreed in January – to *reject* rather than to indefinitely *defer* ratification as was often the practice in election year – had brought things to a head. No 'America First' candidate could claim ideological purity if he stuck his neck out and went into bat for the *rejected* open-ended treaty with the 'old country'. Theoretically, the President had the option of ignoring Congress, of issuing a new Executive Order in the interests of 'national security'; and that was what Walter Brenckmann had tacitly assumed the Administration would opt to do. JFK had won a global nuclear war by placing American vital geopolitical strategic interest *first, second, third, etcetera*. If he wanted to stand on an 'America First' platform nobody had *his* credentials and Walter had assumed that *his* President had the moral courage to *stand* up for, and to account for his actions before the American people. One of the reasons he now felt so bad was that it was clear that he had been suckered in to believing that when *his* President spoke, *his* words actually meant something.

"I was sent here to lie to our friends and allies," he murmured wearily. 'That's what ambassadors do; I suppose. But I thought things would be different. More fool me."

Joanne squeezed her husband's hand.

Eighteen months ago, they had held each other while they waited for a second, killer bomb after the strike on Quincy. Back then in their Cambridge basement, not knowing if the world – their world, leastways – was about to end they had had the comfort of being together, inseparable in life and soon, in death. Nothing that had happened to them since that night had been so simple, or so *real*.

Joanne missed home, Boston, and her circle of girlfriends, but she had loved her short time in England. She had met so many new people, so many potential lifelong friends and the idea that *her country* might let down *any* of the people around her in Oxford and elsewhere in England was, or rather, had been *unthinkable* until that moment.

She stopped herself asking another question, knowing that her husband would explain in his own good time.

"The line in the sand the British want the President to draw is several thousand miles east of the one the Administration has in mind," he said eventually.

They followed the road as it curved around the flank of St Aldate's Church to their left and Pembroke College to their right. Ahead the thoroughfare of St Aldate's itself, still bustling with pedestrians and traffic cut north through the city. On the other side of the road were the walls of Christ Church College, where the Foreign Secretary and his wife had rooms.

"And the British don't know this yet?"

"I don't know, honey."

Walter Brenckmann had thought Christ Church College was a medieval castle of some kind the first time he had been ushered inside its cloistered walls, and walked out into the great grassy quadrangle within. Today he felt like a man offering himself – and his wife – as hostages to fortune; torn between his loyalty to his flag, the oaths he had taken as an officer and later upon assuming the role of ambassador, ties of reason and friendship and the indescribable ache of knowing that some lies were just plain inexcusable between *allies*.

Notwithstanding that the fare was always blander and less plentiful than when the Harding-Graysons were guests of the Embassy; the Brenckmann's were regular dinner guests in the Foreign Secretary's rooms at Christ Church College. Joanne had sent half-a-crate of various Californian wines ahead, just to oil the wheels of diplomacy, although as the door opened and Pat Harding-Grayson's smile welcomed the 'ambassadorial couple' she was beginning to wonder if the wine might not just be to drown their sorrows.

The Brenckmann's and the Harding-Graysons had hit it off from the outset. They were of an age, more or less, and each of the parties *liked* each other. Moreover, it helped, especially on evenings like this, that they understood how not to let secrets come between friendship.

"I was hoping to pay a courtesy call on Her Majesty," Walter Brenckmann remarked over drinks around the customary, guttering fire before dinner. "I gather that she is a little more herself, Tom?"

The British Foreign Secretary grimaced.

"Yes, Her Majesty is much more cheerful now that Prince Phillip has joined her at Woodstock. He's still fairly badly crocked, of course."

The American Ambassador could not help but wince.

One day the true story of the failed plot to murder Queen Elizabeth II and her family at Balmoral last year would emerge. When it did the fingerprints of traitors in the United Kingdom, terrorists in Ireland and God-alone knew how many rogue – or worse, not so rogue

– CIA operatives were going to be all over the attempted regicide. Both men knew this; and consequently, both men wanted the day of reckoning to be delayed as long as possible.

"I look forward to meeting His Highness," Walter Brenckmann avowed solemnly.

"We both do!" His wife added brightly. Already in the relatively short time they had been in Oxford, Joanne Brenckmann had struck out on her own, determined to have a role other than as 'the woman on the Ambassador's arm'. She had visited local schools, hospitals, spoken to Women's Institute meetings and had reached out to the growing community of 'Government and Civil Service' wives who had followed their husbands to Oxford from the former seat of administration in Cheltenham. On occasions when her husband's schedule had been changed at short notice, she had stood in for him at several charitable and other events. Whereas, few people in the street instantly recognised Walter, Joanne was constantly in the local papers, a familiar face in Oxford and beyond.

If Tom Harding-Grayson was aware that his guests were a little preoccupied he gave no hint of it.

"What's this I hear about your youngest boy earning himself unwanted notoriety out in California, old man?" He inquired jocularly of the US Ambassador.

"Oh, that," Walter Brenckmann chuckled. He winked at his wife. "Sam's his mother's son. Jo's been dealing with most of the flak!"

"We didn't find out the half of it until a few days ago!" Joanne Brenckmann explained. She and Walter were a well-honed party double act; having discovered long ago that all the tricky things in marriage were best handled *together*. This was one of those times when Walter would play it straight and Joanne would play it for laughs. She met the Foreign Secretary's wife's eye, and smiled resignedly. "Sam's a musician," she explained, as if that said it all. "He gets that from my side of the family. The older boys take after Walter. Walter junior is in the Navy and Dan is an attorney, they're both sensible boys. Well, most of the time. But Sam..."

"Sam's a musician," the long-suffering father sighed.

"Actually, he's a very talented one," the proud mother countered. "He has a contract with Columbia Records and his first 'single' is coming out in a week or two. He's been recording an 'album', a long-player apparently. Of course, we wouldn't know about any of this if it wasn't for the letters Judy, that's Sam's wife, sends us!" Joanne knew she was gabbling but did not care. "They met in Bellingham in Washington State on the day of the war and they had all sorts of adventures before they got back to California. Anyway, if it wasn't for Judy who seems a very practically-minded young woman, we'd be completely in the dark!!

Joanne was so distracted thinking about her prodigal son, his new wife and her first granddaughter – named for her dead daughter Tabatha – that her voice had grown a little distant and moisture had begun to fill her eyes. The well of loss rose suddenly, her bottom lip trembled before she caught herself.

Her husband stepped in.

"The story is a bit confused," he declared, touching his wife's arm. "Sam, or his manager, by all accounts an eccentric club owner called Doug Weston seem to have fallen foul of a dirty cop in Los Angeles. A club Sam was performing at, *The Troubadour*, got fire-bombed back in December and somehow or other, goodness knows how, Sam and Weston, the owner of the club got arrested. It all happened around the time of the unpleasantness in DC and they both got 'lost' in the California 'correctional' system for several weeks before things were cleared up. Jo and I are under orders not to breathe a word about it, any of it, to any living soul. Not that we've got a clue what *really* happened, anyway!"

Joanne Brenckmann had recovered her composure.

"It could only happen to Sam!"

Over soup – potato with trace elements of leek and onion – Tom Harding-Grayson and Walter Brenckmann started one conversation, while the wives set off on another.

"In a funny sort of way," the British Foreign Secretary remarked affably, "now that I've had a little time to think about it, the situation developing in Iran may be a blessing in disguise."

"Oh, how does that work, Tom?" The US Ambassador knew exactly how 'it' worked. His heart sank because in that moment he knew, without a shadow of a doubt, that his friend had understood *his* government better than he had long before he accepted the ambassadorial post in England.

The Foreign Secretary put down his soup spoon.

"That night of the shooting in the Oval Office," he prefaced, with not one scintilla of animosity in his tone, his expression or in his level gaze. "Iain Macleod and I found ourselves in a little room down in the White House bunker discussing what happened next. What of the peace we had just concluded? And more importantly, upon whose head the crown of leadership should now rest back in England? I was very much the junior partner in the negotiations between Iain and Jim Callaghan – then as now the Deputy Prime Minister. Margaret's name came out of the hat. There were various reasons for that but in retrospect, the two things that recommended the lady to my 'political' colleagues was that she was not of the generation responsible for sleepwalking into the October War; and that given her tender years and lack of experience at the top table of government, that she would be 'controllable'." He shook his head and chuckled. "The thing none of us realized was that of us all, only Margaret really understood what she was getting herself into and that one day, Jack Kennedy would, sooner or later, 'let us down again'."

"Tom, I, er..." But Walter Brenckmann's heart was not in the fight.

"An Ambassador, as one wise and very cynical man once said, is *an honest man sent abroad to lie for the Commonwealth*, my friend," the British Foreign Secretary comforted him. "I for one have no doubt that you have been an *honest* man in your dealings with the Unity Administration of the United Kingdom." He shrugged, picked up his soup spoon, paused. "As I say, it is good to know where we all stand on things."

Walter Brenckmann stared at his friend.

Tom Harding-Grayson smiled sympathetically.

"Margaret will never forgive Jack Kennedy," he declared wearily. "Margaret can be very pragmatic about some things, but others well, she can be infuriatingly *moral* about the *big* things. Even if President Kennedy gets re-elected in November, granted, that's not very likely, but even if he does, he'll be gone from the scene in fairly short order I imagine. Margaret could be Prime Minister for the next twenty years, and, as I say, she won't ever forgive the United States for *letting us* down a second time."

Walter Brenckmann groaned out aloud.

"I've been considering my position," he confessed.

Pat Harding-Grayson was frowning hard.

"Oh! For goodness' sake, Walter!" She cried in exasperation, and looked to Joanne Brenckmann for support. "Joanne, you're not going to let him be an officer and a gentleman over this nonsense, surely?"

Before the wife of the US Ambassador could reply, Pat Harding-Grayson turned on her husband.

"Really, Walter, if you insist on doing the *right thing* we'll be in a fine old situation! So far as Margaret's concerned you are 'the last honest American in Oxford'. If you go Fulbright will probably send us another ignorant, bigoted dolt like your predecessor and we'll be at each other's throats again in no time flat!"

Walter Brenckmann opened his mouth, planning to defend his Secretary of State. While he could not envisage any circumstances under which J. William Fulbright would ever endorse an ambassadorial candidate who was a 'dolt'; in the present climate whoever replaced him in Oxford was hardly likely to be another anglophile.

"I don't like being anybody's patsy," he admitted.

Tom Harding-Grayson sipped his soup.

"That's understandable," he agreed between sips. "Try looking at it another way." Sip, sip, sip. "Our countries are about to have a major falling out. Again. Something of an undignified *contretemps*, I daresay. Regrettable but inevitable, and so forth." Sip, sip. "The one redeeming aspect of the whole affair will be, assuming that you don't go all *honourable* on us, is that you will still be around to carry on apologising for the behaviour of your government," sip, sip, "and that you happen to be the one American in Christendom that Margaret will probably actually carry on listening to, Walter."

Joanne Brenckmann realised then – if she had not already - that she was still very new to the game of being a diplomat's wife. She had thought she was a fast learner and had been making quite a good fist of things up until then.

Did I really hear Tom say what he just said?

She looked to Pat Harding-Grayson, to the Foreign Secretary who was finishing his soup as if everything was normal, and finally to her husband who was deep in thought behind lawyerly inscrutable eyes.

Her country was going to betray all the people she had been shaking hands with, the futures of all the babies she had cooed over and rocked in her arms, and each and every one of the men, women and children she had met on the streets of Oxford. Her President was going to betray them and he had meant to do it all along.

And there was absolutely nothing she could do about it.

Chapter 11

Wednesday 15th April 1964
Mahabad, West Azerbaijan, Iran

Marshal of the Soviet Union Hamazasp Khachaturi Babadzhanian's helicopter put down in a storm of dust on the eastern bank of the Mahabad River.

The river was rising, soon the valley below the city would flood and the annual cycle of inundation would begin again. On another day Babadzhanian would have been curious and watched with more attention as his Mil Mi6 had raced low across the delta of the Simineh River where it fed into Lake Urmia on the trip from to Qoshachay, where the aircraft had put down to drop off several men, pick up others and to have its tanks topped off. Now that the winter had released its grip on the land the low ground was green with verdant new growth; and the broad valley of the Zarriné and the Simineh Rivers was turning into a Garden of Eden high in the mountains of Iran.

Mahabad was an ancient city nestling in a bowl-like valley in the mountains. Its population was mainly Kurdish rather than Azeri like the cities to the north and the west. Founded in the mists of time in the era of the Safavid dynasty its original name was *Savoujbolagh*, a Turkish word meaning 'cold spring'. Mahabad was one of those mystical places in Asia Minor that had history in its veins, and the blood of countless generations running in its gutters. It had been ruled by the Hasanwâyhids in the tenth century, sacked by descendants of Tamerlane, and after centuries of tribal conflict fallen under the Mukri Kurds – major players in the wars between the Safavid and Ottoman Empires - until the first half of the twentieth century.

Mahabad was a name coined only as recently as 1936, and between 1942 and the end of 1945 it had actually been occupied, like swathes of Northern Iraq and Persia, by the Red Army. That was why Army Group South had such good maps of the region and it had been possible to develop the movement plans of both 2nd Siberian Mechanised Army and 3rd Caucasus Tank Army, using the first-hand experience of surviving veterans who had actually served in the region during that period.

"What's the latest news from Kurochnik?" He demanded as he strode into the forward Headquarters of the 10th Guards Tank Division. Men had leapt to their feet and stood to attention like marble statues on his arrival.

"Comrade Major General Kurochnik reports harassing attacks on his perimeter for a second night, sir!" Babadzhanian was told. "Not so bad last night but he still lost another twenty men."

Using the bulk of his remaining airborne troops to leapfrog ahead and secure Urmia on the right flank of the two passes through the mountains into Iraq had been a risk; but a risk which had seemed entirely calculated at the time he had signed off on it. Babadzhanian hated this wooded mountain and valley country; there was no visibility, no easy way to root out enemies hiding or dug into the forests or lurking in the rocky gullies high above the narrow roads. Everywhere he went, the local civilians looked at him and his men with dull, inscrutable eyes. He mistrusted their passivity, their muteness; it was as if the people in the villages, towns and cities of Azerbaijan viewed the invaders as simply the latest interlopers to march through their lands and would soon be gone. In a way they were right, lines of communication units were 'occupying the ground' behind his tanks but that was all. That the Shah was dead mattered little to these people of the mountains. Up here in the wilderness of the north and west what went on in distant Tehran was of little consequence, one set of faraway overlords was the same as any other.

Babadzhanian's brief visit to Sverdlovsk had been a waste of time made bearable only by the decision to release two of the five infantry brigades held in the inappropriately named 'strategic reserve' at Chelyabinsk. The men of the brigades in question were mainly conscripts, their numbers no doubt swelled by men who recognised that life in the Red Army was marginally better than in a penal battalion; nonetheless, he could use the brigades to free up 'real soldiers' currently engaged on guarding his lines of communication. The harsh truth was that there were no 'real soldiers' available to replace casualties like the two hundred dead and wounded veteran airborne troopers in Urmia in the last forty-eight hours.

Up until a week ago there had been an Iranian regimental-size mechanised garrison at Urmia, equipped with at least half-a-dozen American supplied M-48 tanks, supported by mobile artillery and a company-sized transport unit. Thus far Kurochnik's paratroopers had *only* been up against fiendishly pre-positioned demolition charges and booby traps, and pinned down by small arms fire and sniping. So where were the tanks that had been in Urmia a week ago?

In the country to the west of Mahabad a couple of well positioned tanks – or at a push a man with a machine gun or a rocket launcher, in fact – could block one or both of the vital passes needed for the armour steadily rumbling down the road from Tabriz and Bonab.

Babadzhanian's two powerful tank armies; on paper they had a combined order of battle of some fifteen hundred tanks, two thirds of them modern T-62s, over two thousand other armoured, or all-terrain vehicles and a strength of approximately two hundred and forty-five thousand men, of whom about half were front line 'effectives', was currently strung out across hundreds of kilometres of mountain and upland valley roads. His unstoppable 'iron fist' was presently, in purely military terms, the biggest traffic jam in the World!

Whereas, 10th Guards Tank Division had raced ahead – wearing out its T-62s and exhausting its men – at breakneck speed investing or bypassing towns and villages, never resting in one place more than a few hours, ninety percent of the rest of Army Group South was, to

Babadzhanian's mounting exasperation crawling, nose to tail in its wake like a huge, bloated, lethargic caterpillar. The trouble was that because he only had transporters for one in four of his main battle tanks the roads all the way back to the Soviet border were littered, and sometimes blocked, by broken down T-58s and T-62s, not to mention countless miscellaneous cars, trucks and fuel bowsers. Even though he had known this would happen and he had planned for it – there were fifty salvage and recovery teams led by Red Army combat engineers patrolling the 'lines of advance' roads, repairing breakdowns and clearing the way for the endless convoys – Babadzhanian fretted constantly about the slow pace of advance of his main force.

Any kind of guerrilla insurgency, or worse, airstrikes by the Yankees or the British would be a disaster. As it was the sheer weight of his tanks and the volume of vehicle movements over ill-maintained and crumbling roads was fast degrading and destroying the very routes upon which *all* the ammunition, fuel, food and the thousands of things vital to sustain the drive south depended.

The situation would not be anywhere near as critical if the Red Air Force was doing its job. The useless pricks flew a few token fighter sorties over the line of march; dropped a bomb or two now and then and whined constantly about the 'lack of forward operating bases.'

The Iranians, or perhaps, the Iraqis had shot down a couple of Red Air Force reconnaissance aircraft over the Zagros Mountains three days ago and since then the 'flyboys' had virtually given up 'breaking trail' for his men on the ground!

The Red Air Force was supposedly subordinate to him in this operation, 'supposedly' being the operative clause. He had fired off angry signals to Sverdlovsk, hoping somebody would light a fire under the Red Air Force's collective arse, but he was not holding his breath waiting for a response.

Babadzhanian leaned over the unsteady plot table.

Viewed from the south Urmia dominated the ground to the north, sitting squarely between the lake on the right and the Zagros Mountains on the left. Presently, the spearhead of 2nd Siberian Mechanised Army was trundling down the road to Miandoab on the right, to the left 50th Airborne Brigade was holding Urmia, albeit taking casualties in the process. Problematically, if the garrison at Urmia had already decamped those casualties were in vain and Babadzhanian probably had armour – granted, a relatively small force – positioned either on his flank or threatening to block the road to Piranshahr.

He cursed under his breath.

He looked up, manufactured a saturnine smile for his men.

"I hate these fucking mountains!" He declared, knowing that he could afford to speak his mind in the company of fighting men such as those who surrounded him.

This prompted half-hearted smirks.

"Right," Babadzhanian decided. "There ought to be enemy tanks somewhere between here and Urmia. How quickly can you put together a battle group to move up the road to Urmia to seek and destroy them?"

The question was posed with a jovial intensity to the commander of the 10th Guards Tank Division, a man of his own age with a weather-beaten face and a shaven head that exhibited the white, gnarled scars of the day back in 1943 when a single German Tiger tank had knocked out three of the four T-34s of his troop in a clearing in the Taiga outside Kursk. His gunner had put a seventy-five-millimetre round through the side of the Nazi behemoth but not before the Tiger's eighty-eight-millimetre canon had put a solid shot into his tank's engine compartment.

Major General Vladimir Andreyevich Puchkov had been with Babadzhanian in Budapest in 1956 and was one of the handful of trusted veterans whom he had consulted in drawing up the original plan for *Operation Nakazyvat*. He knew the 'Piranshahr spearhead' was safe in Vladimir Puchkov's calloused hands.

"Urmia's over a hundred kilometres up the road," Puchkov thought out aloud. "I don't have the fuel to get half-way. Not up *that* road."

Babadzhanian smiled thinly.

The two men understood each other completely. They were moving through country in which the enemy was everywhere, but nowhere in sufficient strength to mass against the invader. Puchkov's 'drive' up the road towards distant Urmia would be noticed within hours and with a little bit of luck it would release the pressure currently being applied to Kurochnik's paratroopers in the city. *This* and the air strikes Babadzhanian was going to *demand* happen later this afternoon. He was perfectly happy to start shooting Red Air Force officers if that was what it took to get action!

"Just make it look like you mean business, Vladimir Andreyevich."

"Oh, I'll do that, sir! I'll have my boys on the road in two hours," the commander of the 10th Guards Tank Division promised, a grin forming on his lips and the light of battle glinting in his grey green eyes. For a tanker he was a big man, six feet tall and as broad as a bear. Around him the men of his headquarters staff were smiling.

Babadzhanian saw it and was heartened.

In the Red Army traditionally everything was subservient to discipline; but blind obedience alone was not enough in modern warfare fought on the move with increasingly complex and deadly weapons. By reputation Puchkov was a ruthlessly hard taskmaster. However, like Kurochnik, trapped up in Urmia he was a martinet with a heart of gold whom his men tended to follow with almost suicidal devotion. Like both of his two pugnaciously aggressive subordinates, Babadzhanian too understood that while men would sometimes obey an order to follow one into the jaws of death, only a *real* leader could persuade them to do it willingly.

Such leaders were scarce in the Red Army, as perhaps they were in any army. When one recognised the abilities of a man such as Kurochnik or Puchkov, Babadzhanian was duty bound to give them the opportunity to express their talents and occasionally, to guard their backs when things went wrong. He had no intention of leaving Konstantin Kurochnik 'out on a limb' at Urmia.

"Carry on," he said. Babadzhanian did not need to tell Puchkov his business. While he might otherwise have specified the strength of the force to be sent, timescales, specific objectives; that was wasting time when one was dealing with a man of Puchkov's proven professional abilities and experience. The Army Group Commander turned to the communications officer. "Do you have a secure scrambler link to the Air Force?"

Within a minute Babadzhanian was *telling* the numskull at the other end of the line at the forward Red Air Force Controller Station outside Tabriz *exactly* what needed to be done *before* nightfall along the roads into Urmia from both the north and the south.

How was Konstantin Yakovlevich Kurochnik supposed to do his job when the Air Force lacked the gumption to carpet bomb the ground beyond his perimeter? Sometimes, he really did not believe, even after all these years, that *he* still had to explain *these* things to the idiots running the Red Air Force.

Slamming down the handset in disgust he shook his head.

"Get me Comrade Major General Kurochnik on the line!"

Babadzhanian drank foul camp fire coffee from a metal mess tin as he waited.

"I've ordered the Air Force to burn you several hundred metres of clear ground to the north and the south of the city," he informed his hard-pressed airborne commander.

"That should stop the bastards creeping up on my boys tonight, sir!" The other man had chortled, seemingly without a care in the world. "We found a depot with brand new Yankee radios. The locals had never unpacked the bloody things! I reckon they had at least eight tanks based here, sir. Yankee M-48s judging by the spares inventory of the workshops on the outskirts of the town. They pulled out so fast they didn't have time to wipe out the maintenance schedules posted on the walls of the garages!"

"You had a tough night again last night?"

"This thing doesn't feel right, sir. My boys reckon there were hostiles infiltrating the central areas of the city around midnight. If it wasn't for the sniping, I'd get on with a systematic house to house search."

"Do you still think you have hostiles in the city?"

"I'd put money on it, sir. I reckon we've got two, maybe three shit hot snipers operating in the city. My boys can't even get close to them. They're acting like a team, covering each other's backs. The sort of thing our Spetsnaz boys are trained to do. From what I've seen of the *Iranian Army*," he went on, the words dripping with contempt, "I wouldn't have thought they were capable of playing these games with *my* boys."

Babadzhanian digested this. Unable to form a settled opinion he ended the conversation. Kurochnik did not need him to tell him his business any more than Puchkov.

Having come down to Mahabad to stand at the cutting edge of the great sword the collective leadership had placed in his hands, to symbolically lead from the front, Babadzhanian badly needed to step back and *think*.

Back in Tabriz *his* headquarters staff – like all staffs in the Red Army – looked to him to do its thinking for it. Down here the minutiae of divisional movement, deployment and logistics was Vladimir Andreyevich Puchkov's problem. Here in Mahabad Babadzhanian could stand to one side and ask himself if things were really going as well as they seemed to be going.

He was confident that Kurochnik would hold out, block the road south and therefore protect his vulnerable right flank should Iraqi or renegade Turkish Army units decide to get involved, which was unlikely. He had gambled that the Yankees and the British would initially be too shocked to react; and not recover in time to mount a sustained aerial attack on his forces while they were at their most vulnerable, stretched out in convoy along hundreds of kilometres of mountain roads.

Thus far, his gamble had paid off.

However, it would all be for nought if the enemy attacked his armoured spearheads in the two high passes to the west at Piranshahr and Sardasht.

Chapter 12

The Secretary of State anticipated that the forthcoming summit would be a bloody affair but he was confident he held all the cards that mattered. Not least among these was the unassailable *fact* that nobody in the Administration had *ever* given the British *any* kind of undertaking, or guarantee that American armed forces would participate in *any* military adventure 'east of Suez'. The British might have *implied* the existence of such implicit unwritten promises in the tone of the soon to be defunct US-UK Mutual Defence Treaty; but that however, was *their* problem.

The President had only agreed to the 'Philadelphia Summit' for domestic political consumption. How better to explicitly proclaim one's 'America First' credentials than by spurning a fresh British demand to get involved in yet another one of their interminable post-colonial wars?

The recent firestorm over the Unity Administration of the United Kingdom's *alleged* attempt to appoint a *British* Supreme Commander of All Allied Forces in the Mediterranean had satisfactorily poisoned the well, and now the rebirth of the *Soviet Menace* in the Middle East had serendipitously created a 'magic moment'; one of those once in a generation 'moments' when the public imagination and the national consciousness might be seized by a re-born charismatic leader. And that was exactly what John Fitzgerald Kennedy planned to do at the Philadelphia Summit.

America First!

It was no coincidence that the morning papers were carrying more 'leaks' purporting to prove 'beyond doubt' that the USS Scorpion had been sunk last year – not in error by US Navy Grumman S-2 Tracker anti-submarine aircraft flying off the USS Enterprise – but in a 'cowardly pre-planned attack' by an unnamed Royal Navy *'super silent advanced diesel electric submarine'* operating as HMS Dreadnought's 'backup'.

Fulbright blanched somewhat at the heavy-handedness of the rumour mill; he wondered at how newspaper editors and TV producers could look themselves in the eyes of a morning. *Newsweek* apart practically everybody else seemed only too happy to accept every unsubstantiated piece of nonsense that spewed out of the House of Representatives, or from anybody who had ever been associated with the Administration.

Ben Bradlee, Bureau Chief of the newly relocated Newsweek Office in Philadelphia had been trying to get Fulbright to give him an interview for weeks but the Secretary of State knew better than to humour Bradlee. Jack and Bobby Kennedy had tried to tempt him back into the fold in February but Bradlee had steadfastly refused to 'buy into' the 'party line'. Presently, most of the media was playing the Administration's tune with just enough minor, whispered discordant notes to make it look as if it was not entirely in the President's pocket; but the last thing anybody in the Philadelphia White House wanted was a former Kennedy family insider like Ben Bradlee getting his hooks into the facts of what was actually going on.

In the last forty-eight hours more inflammatory stories had emerged from 'sources within the Sixth Fleet' detailing how 'inept and incompetent' the British forces in the Mediterranean had been to quote, allow an 'obsolete big-gun Soviet invasion fleet to creep up on Malta undetected'.

Fulbright was painfully cognisant that these 'reports' neglected to mention that the powerful US Navy squadron assigned to provide long-range radar coverage for the Maltese Archipelago, and its primary shield against airborne and seaborne attack had gone missing during the critical hours.

It was telling that nobody in the Navy Department had lifted a finger to contradict the latest *Scorpion lies* or the new rash of misinformation coming out of the Mediterranean. As for the Administration; three brass monkeys could not have been any more publicly 'neutral' about the undermining of the *alliance* supposedly set in stone by the US-UK Defense Treaty signed in January.

Fulbright took little or no pleasure in his part in the campaign; but politics were politics and nobody got any prizes for coming second in a Presidential race. More to the point, while stabilising the situation in the Mediterranean was entirely defensible as being in the immediate vital national security interests of the United States, right now a major war in Iraq and Iran was not.

If America had actually needed Middle Eastern oil *right now* it would have been different but it did not, nor would it need Arab oil, or have to contemplate any of the compromises and accommodations that came with ensuring its smooth uninterrupted supply, in the foreseeable future. Given the lack of competition for what, pre-October War had been relatively scarce reserves of wellhead crude, American domestic requirements could presently be easily satisfied from internal US production, Central and South American, even Indonesian oilfields and according to recent geological surveys, eventually from Alaskan fields. In the absence of competition from other modern industrialised competitors, the abundance of Middle Eastern oil was in the short to medium-term – at least five to ten years according to which economist one spoke to - superfluous to American needs.

Fulbright was a pragmatist. Foreign policy was not about making friends it was about doing what was right for one's own country. America had enough problems of its own without another war. Besides, once the fighting was over somebody would have to pick up the pieces afterwards and potentially that was a much more lucrative deal...

"I had expected better of you, Bill," Lord Franks, the urbane, scholarly man who had cut an increasingly embattled figure in Philadelphia in recent weeks said sadly, as the two men shook hands.

Fulbright raised an eyebrow.

"How so, Oliver?"

The British Ambassador viewed the bigger man thoughtfully.

Fifty-nine-year-old Oliver Sherwell Franks's first spell as Ambassador had been between 1948 and 1952. He was a man used to being around powerful men and intimately acquainted with the ways, means and nefarious mores of Realpolitik. Yet even he had been somewhat taken aback by the hypocrisy and cynicism evident in the most recent pre-meditated craven foreign policy U-turn of the Kennedy Administration.

That he had seen the volte face over the US-UK Mutual Defence Treaty coming for some weeks made it no less unpalatable. The furore over the false, presumably State Department sponsored stories, about the late Sir David Luce's prospective elevation to the post of Supreme Commander All Allied Forces (Mediterranean) had been the final signpost on the road to the Administration's perfidy.

The signalled ritual denouement of the 'special relationship', this time most likely permanently was to be stage-managed around the forthcoming Philadelphia Summit. The networks and the press had already been primed to expect the President to stand up for 'American' vital strategic interests, to confront 'unreasonable demands from its European Allies', and not to 'fly in the face of the expressed will of Congress'.

Not for the first time Lord Franks had asked himself if the Kennedy Administration knew what it was doing? Right now, he was desperately seeking some indication that somebody in the White House understood, really understood, that the World was going to be a very different place the day after America betrayed its own soul?

"I am not one of those people who believe that those who fail to learn the lessons of history are condemned to repeat the mistakes of those who went before us," Lord Franks said resignedly. "However, it seems obvious to me that the United States has forgotten the consequences of its decision to shun the League of Nations and its isolationist stance in the 1930s. We in the old world eventually forgave you for coming late to two World Wars, mainly because everything turned out for the best in the end. Now it seems that after weeks and months of fine words; the Administration plans to leave *us* in the lurch. Very much in the manner of a suitor who has had his sordid pleasure with his putative partner under false pretences and subsequently jilted her at the altar."

Fulbright's face was suddenly a hard mask.

"And you have the nerve to ask me 'how so'?" The Englishman observed with such impeccable civility that it almost but not quite veiled his quietly seething contempt. "Presumably, it was *your* people who encouraged the Argentines to invade the Falkland Islands?"

The Secretary of State visibly flinched at this softly spoken accusation.

"That's nothing to do with us, Oliver."

"No. What else does the CIA have up its sleeve? Further rabble rousing in Ireland, perhaps? Or should we expect miscellaneous assassinations throughout the Commonwealth? Or perhaps, another attempt to murder the surviving members of the Royal Family?"

The directness of the attack had rocked the veteran Senator from Arkansas back on his heels. It was all the more shocking because Lord Franks seemed oblivious to the presence of several senior State Department staffers who had heard every word he just said.

"Clear the room please!" Fulbright barked.

Lord Franks waited until the doors closed at his back.

"The first duty of a politician is to get elected, Oliver," the Secretary of State said grimly. "Do you honestly think that if Jack Kennedy loses in November that the first thing his successor will do is buddy up to the old country?"

Oliver Franks shook his head.

Not in disagreement but in despair.

The question of whoever came out on top on 3rd November 1964 was so irrelevant to the scale of the crisis in the Middle East, it beggared belief that his American *friends* had eyes only for the demands of the immediate electoral cycle.

"If Jack Kennedy gets re-elected in November things will be different," Fulbright assured the British Ambassador. "The Administration will want to do the right thing by its friends..."

Lord Franks turned on his heel and walked away.

"Oliver, I..."

As the British Ambassador listened to the sound of his own feet ringing on the stone floor, he could not help but recall Winston Churchill's words, voiced in the darkest days of another war.

'We shall prove ourselves once again able to defend our island home, to ride out the storm of war, and to outlive the menace of tyranny, if necessary, for years, if necessary, alone...'

Chapter 13

The Secretary of State for Defence was the last man to arrive in the ancient room of a displaced College Fellow. Forty-five-year-old William Stephen Whitelaw, a veteran of the campaign in North-West Europe in 1944 and 1945 was going about his business with a fresh spring in his stride, and an odd lightness of heart. Part of his good humour was because he was feeling fitter and generally better within himself than he had at any time since the night of the October War; but perversely, now that the worst had happened and things looked uniformly grim, this was a time for *action.*

Moreover, the great outstanding question left unanswered from the cataclysm – had the USSR been destroyed or just severely mauled? - had now been comprehensively resolved and in the next couple of days he, and everybody else in England would discover exactly what all those fine American promises, hedged around by innumerable abstruse caveats and clauses, amounted to in reality. One way or another within a matter of days the government would know the precise depth of the dark, airless hole into which recent events had plunged it!

It was 1940 all over again...

The room appointed for the morning's conference with the Chiefs of Staff looked out over Mob Quad, a quadrangle of the college that had a middling to fair claim to be Oxford University's oldest seat of learning. Of course, the other two claimants to this status; Balliol and University Colleges, fiercely disputed Merton's claim and had done so for centuries.

Merton had been founded by Walter de Merton, Lord High Chancellor to both Henry III and Edward I, who had drawn up statutes for a self-governing college and organised endowments to support it in 1264. Balliol's charter dated to 1263 but thereafter the matter of which college possessed greater intrinsic antiquity was blurred by questions surrounding the physical existence of this or that institution. Merton College – or to give it its full name: The House of [the] College of Scholars of Merton in the University of Oxford - had not actually laid down foundations in its present site in the south east corner of the city until 1274, while the supporters of Balliol and University Colleges made rival pre-dating claims.

In any event, Merton's Hall, Chapel and front quadrangle were built in the quarter of a century after 1274, and Mob Quad, constructed between 1288 and 1378. The Merton College Library, situated in the Mob Quad was, allegedly, the oldest continuously used academic library in the World. But then Oxford Colleges routinely made so many claims about these things that it was often very hard to know which to take seriously.

In any event, as a Cambridge man Willie Whitelaw tended to take any claim by an Oxford man on behalf of his college with a very large pinch of salt.

"Dreadfully sorry to keep you all waiting, gentlemen," he declaimed, shouldering into the room with a sheaf of files under his left arm. "I was bearded by our new Supply Supremo. Mrs Munro doesn't take any prisoners so I had a Devil of a time making a break for freedom!"

Privately, the Secretary of State found it a little peculiar to be in a government run by a woman, and was still struggling to come to terms with a Cabinet that was not only led by a woman – albeit a remarkable, if prickly example of the gender – containing two others. He had had as little as possible to do with Barbara Castle, his counterpart at the Department of Labour, and conceded that a leftie like her was the ideal person to deal with the bloody trade unions; but Alison Munro's department, the greatly expanded Ministry of Supply, Transportation and Energy, was intimately connected in every way with what his bailiwick was all about; *making war.*

From the expression of sympathy on the faces of the three Chiefs of Staff, Willie Whitelaw divined that each man had already had his own baptism of fire at the hands of the second 'woman of steel' in the UAUK Cabinet.

"She is a most formidable lady, sir," General Sir Richard Hull, Chief of the Defence Staff remarked ruefully.

"Yes, indeed!" Willie Whitelaw dumped himself at one of the two vacant chairs around the old – everything in Merton was 'old' – common room table which had been brought into the annexe for this conference. "I was informed on the way down to this place that the Prime Minister's plane has landed at Philadelphia and her party has arrived safely at the Embassy."

General Hull cleared his throat.

"I briefed Charles Elworthy on the current military situation before I came across to Merton College, Minister," he explained, merely as a matter of form. Air Marshal Sir Charles Elworthy was the UAUK's 'military legate' to the Kennedy Administration, an increasingly thankless post that would soon be, if it was not already, redundant. "I also took the liberty of asking Major General Michael Carver to attend Merton College this morning with a view to making himself available to report directly to the Chiefs of Staff and, yourself."

"I understood the poor fellow was only due to fly into Brize Norton an hour ago?" The Secretary of State queried.

"Just so, Minister. He should be here in the next few minutes."

Willie Whitelaw gathered his wits.

The Prime Minister had decided that whatever came out of her 'summit' with President Kennedy, that the United Kingdom would 'draw a line in the sand' in the Middle East. Abadan Island and any government in the region willing to resist the Soviet invasion of Iran – and inevitably, soon Iraq – would be defended by British arms to the limit of the nation's resources.

Colleagues had already come to Whitelaw and observed that 'the PM seems to be a bit one-eyed about all this', but actually for all her faults, *the woman* was right about the one vital thing; if the country stood back and let the Red Army drive to the northern shores of the Persian Gulf it would be the end of *Great* Britain. He, like his Prime Minister, did not want to live in *that* Britain.

"Before we attack the meat of today's session," he decided, turning to the new First Sea Lord, Admiral Sir Varyl Begg. "Where are we with Operation Sturdee, First Sea Lord?"

Operation Sturdee – named for Admiral Sir Frederick Charles Doveton Sturdee, the victor of the Battle of the Falkland Islands in December 1914 – was the codename for the planned deployment of as many as eight modern conventional Oberon and Porpoise class submarines in response to the Argentine seizure of the Falklands Archipelago and other British territories in the South Atlantic.

"HMS Walrus and HMS Cachalot are two days out from Devonport bound for Simons Town, Minister. HMS Olympus and HMS Oberon are currently making ready at Gibraltar. They will sail for the Cape within the next forty-eight hours. Three other Oberons and Porpoises are being made ready for operations in the South Atlantic. The Ice Patrol Ship Protector has successfully rendezvoused approximately mid-way between South Africa and South Georgia with the South African destroyer Jan van Riebeeck and the frigate HMS Llandaff. All on board the Protector are reported safe and well. At least four Oberons and Porpoises will be on station around the Falkland Islands not later than 18th May, Minister."

The day before the Battle of Malta aircraft of the Argentine Republic had bombed Port Stanley and Argentine Marines masquerading as whalers and scrap metal dealers had landed on South Georgia, seizing the settlements of Grytviken, Port Leith and Stromness,

At the very time Malta was coming under bombardment from ships of the Red Navy, and nearly two thousand paratroopers and Spetsnaz of the Red Army were swinging beneath their parachutes over the most important British base in the Mediterranean, at least as many Argentinean soldiers were coming ashore at Port Stanley on East Falkland and raising the white and blue flag of the Argentine Republic over government house. There were unconfirmed reports that the small force of Royal Marines 'defending' the distant archipelago had fought practically to the last man and there were, apparently, gruesome stories emerging in the newspapers in Buenos Aires of 'British soldiers' and 'Imperialistic criminals' – civilian administrators - having been 'shot while resisting arrest'.

"Very good," Willie Whitelaw acknowledged. "I will advise the Prime Minister that an ultimatum should be broadcast as planned to the Argentine authorities and to all South Atlantic shipping, that as of 1st May all vessels encountered within a two hundred miles 'total exclusion zone' around the archipelago will be attacked and sunk without warning."

There was a business-like knock at the door.

"Major General Carver is here, Minister," Whitelaw's new private secretary, thirty-three-year-old Christopher Chataway, the former athlete and broadcaster, announced.

The Minister glanced to the Chief of the Defence Staff, who nodded. "Ask General Carver to join us please."

Willie Whitelaw had not been remotely surprised when he had discovered that the man the CDS had sent out to the Persian Gulf to 'report on the situation' was forty-eight-year-old Major General Richard Michael Power Carver. The Secretary of State's rose to his feet and extended his hand to the newcomer.

"How was your flight back, General?" He inquired solicitously as the newcomer was ushered into the room by Chataway.

Michael Carver viewed Whitelaw thoughtfully for a moment. Carver was a tall, handsome man with a superficially aquiline, praetorian dignity that gave strangers the impression that he was overly haughty, and inclined to purposefully distance himself from the milieu of those around him.

"Bumpy, sir," he said, the merest suggestion of wry humour in his hard grey eyes. He was carrying a somewhat careworn attaché case in his left hand and his uniform was creased, as bone weary as the man inside it. "Especially, the landing at Malta to refuel."

There was a noisy interruption as a tea trolley was pushed, rattling and creaking into the room by a co-opted Merton College porter whose sulky attitude made it abundantly apparent that the sooner his beloved and sorely missed 'Fellows' were reinstalled and the 'governmental riff raff removed' the better.

Earlier Willie Whitelaw had asked Sir Richard Hull if what he had heard about Carver was true. The Chief of the Defence Staff had guffawed at this.

'He's related to Wellington on his mother's side and some people maintain he looks a bit like the old Iron Duke. I don't see it myself in the paintings of the great man, and I'm sure Michael Carver would be mortified by the suggestion. He was at Winchester as a boy, detested it by all accounts. Afterwards, he went on to Sandhurst when he was eighteen; that would have been in 1933, hated that too at first. Legend has it that he almost went to New Zealand to train as a priest but fortunately somebody talked him out of it.'

Whitelaw liked the CDS personally and deeply respected his calm professionalism. He had hit it off with the bluff old soldier from the outset; his relations with Hull immeasurably reinforced by his meticulous disinclination to meddle directly in military affairs. Both men had been in Germany at the end of Hitler's War and broadly speaking, until the disaster of October 1962, they had earnestly hoped never to see the like again.

'In any event, in 1934 Carver passed out top of his class at Sandhurst,' the Chief of the Defence Staff had explained. 'He won the King's Gold Medal, the Anson Memorial Sword, the prizes for economics, military history and military law, and won a five-year Army

Scholarship. A year or so after he left Sandhurst he got into a set to with dear old Percy Hobart,' Percy Cleghorn Stanley Hobart was the man who had written 'the book' on British Army armoured warfare tactics in the years before the Second World War, 'apparently old *Hobo* Hobart once felt moved to have a chat with him about *insubordination.* Hobart was a one off, he really was. The story goes that he told young Carver that *the secret of success in the Army is to be sufficiently insubordinate!'*

Both men had chortled at that juncture.

'Carver almost resigned his commission around 1938. He's not a very clubbish sort of chap, not a man who really enjoys mess life and all that and I think he was bored stiff in the pre-war Army. Some clot had sent him out to Egypt as the transport officer of a camp near Heliopolis. Still, it turned out all right in the end. Hobo Hobart brought the 7th Armoured – you know, the brigade that ended up being *The Desert Rats* – out to the Middle East and suddenly Carver was back in the thick of things; as he was for most of the Second War, actually. Like all the other chaps who were there in Egypt from the start he traipsed up and down the North African coast for a couple of years until Monty arrived to sort things out, then he was in Italy, and Germany of course. By the end of the war, still just thirty he was a brevetted Brigadier in command of 4th Armoured Brigade. Like everybody else he reverted to his substantive rank, captain, when the Army shrank back to peace time proportions. A lot of good men went straight back to Civvy Street because of that; Carver stayed in the service even though it took him the best part of fifteen years to work his way back up to substantive brigadier. That was when he got command of the 4th Brigade in West Germany in 1960. In between he'd held key technical posts with the Ministry of Supply, been head of exercise planning at the Supreme Headquarters Allied Powers in Europe, and held senior staff posts in East Africa and so on. He was Director of War Plans between 1958 and 1960.' The Chief of the Defence Staff had finished his peroration with the opinion that: 'Practically everybody in the Army who knows him, even the people he's upset, think he's the cleverest man they've ever met.'

The table was rectangular, ten feet by about seven but of such antiquity that its dimensions had probably been fixed by eye rather than by rule. The CDS had been sitting at one end, Whitelaw at the other with Sir Varyl Begg and the Chief of the Air Staff each sitting alone on the long sides. A chair scraped and the newcomer sat down beside the First Sea Lord.

Carver opened his brief case and pulled out several folded maps.

Then he sat back and waited to be called to account.

"What do you have to tell us, General Carver?" Willie Whitelaw asked, raising his tea cup to his lips.

The drink tasted so foul he wondered if the disgruntled Merton College porter was actually a closet Red Dawn sympathiser intent on poisoning the men at the apex of the faltering British war machine.

Chapter 14

Captain Sir Peter Christopher, VC, had been surprised and – truth be told - less than ecstatic to receive the summons to meet the Prime Minister's flight at Brize Norton at less than twelve hours' notice yesterday morning. Marija had been typically stoical about their unexpected separation; whereas he had felt desperately guilty abandoning her in a strange and for the time of year unseasonably cold and rather miserable land.

'Rosa will be here to keep me cheerful,' Marija had comforted him in that serenely accepting, happy way with which she greeted practically every setback. 'You will only be away for three days. It is not as if you are going away on a long voyage, or anything. And besides, if you are going to be with the Prime Minister, I know you won't have an opportunity to be stupidly brave or to get yourself killed, husband!'

Privately, Peter guessed that Rosa – the widow of Marija's executed elder brother Samuel – would be hanging on Lieutenant-Commander Alan Hannay's arm every minute that HMS Talavera's former Supply Officer was off duty.

Every man who had survived Talavera and Yarmouth's unequal battle with the Soviet invasion fleet had been raised – substantively – one grade or rank. Consequently, Peter's 'personal steward', formerly acting or probationary Petty Officer Jack Griffin was now much to his horror, a full-blown Chief Petty Officer. In comparison Alan Hannay had received the news of his promotion with no little sangfroid.

Alan had subsequently been given the onerous task of co-ordinating with the other interested parties – the Royal Household, the Army, the Air Force, the Mayor of Oxford, the Prime Minister's Private Office, and the Chief Constable of Oxfordshire among others – the arrangements for the 'Battle of Malta Parade and Investiture'. This event was now scheduled to take place on the afternoon of Tuesday 21st April; the parade being 'through Oxford' and the investiture, mainly the awarding of medals for bravery and suchlike, at King's College. Some doubt remained over the practicability of the 21st April since it was not known if Her Majesty the Queen would be sufficiently recovered to take the salute on the steps of Oxford Town Hall, or to officiate at the investiture by that time.

Peter Christopher was not looking forward to the 'big party', as Alan Hannay kept referring to it. Nor were his emotions yet settled on the question of how he viewed inheriting his father's baronetcy, or the somewhat premature addition of the letters 'VC' to his name wherever he went, and to whomsoever he was introduced by a third party.

There was not much he could do about the 'Sir Peter; but he had not yet actually had the Victoria Cross, cast from the metal of a

Russian gun captured at Sevastopol in the Crimean War, pinned on his chest.

'Detail, old man,' Alan Hannay had informed him. 'The bally thing has been gazetted and that's that!'

Peter's had been one of four Victoria Crosses awarded in respect of the naval part of the Battle of Malta. Commander John Pope, in command of HMS Yarmouth had been promoted Captain and awarded his VC posthumously; and his widow was being brought to Oxford to receive his medal. Petty Officer Stanley George who had, in effect, taken command of the by then wrecked Yarmouth, organised other survivors to restart the emergency pumps, and from the auxiliary steering position near the stern of the burning frigate, somehow threaded a course through the reefs and run the ship aground in the shallows of St Paul's Bay, saving tens of lives, was Yarmouth's second VC. Talavera's second VC was to be pinned on the narrow chest of one of the smallest big men in the Royal Navy, Warrant Officer – formerly Chief Petty Officer – Nevil 'Spider' McCann, the destroyer's Master at Arms who had been everywhere at the height of the battle, directing the damage control teams that had kept the ship afloat long enough for her to launch the torpedoes that had 'won' the aforementioned battle.

Alan Hannay was one of several men awarded the Distinguished Service Order, most likely because somebody in the Admiralty had said 'we can't give everybody a bloody VC!' In the closing stages of the battle the dapper, amiable, impeccably courteous and modest son of a Suffragan Church of England Bishop had stood alone on the gun platform on top of the shot-riddled after deckhouse engaging a twenty-three-thousand-ton battleship at point blank range with twin twenty-millimetre calibre Oerlikon anti-aircraft cannons! After the battle Spider McCann had found him, covered in blood, literally standing ankle-deep among the body parts of the other gun crews.

Jack Griffin was another man who ought to have won a VC; but he was perfectly happy with his Distinguished Service Cross. Like every surviving Talavera he took the greatest pleasure of all in the George Cross the Queen was due to pin on Joseph Calleja's broad chest next Tuesday.

Practically every member of Talavera's torpedo crew had been killed or wounded early in the battle. If Joe Calleja had not known how to operate the quadruple 21-inch tubes; and more important, had had the gumption and the raw courage to operate them under murderously heavy fire, Talavera and Yarmouth's dead would have died for nothing...

Margaret Thatcher's blue eyes had fixed upon Peter Christopher. He had got the oddest sensation that she was reading his thoughts.

'I am advised that you are still somewhat incommoded by your wounds, Captain?' She had asked yesterday, anxiously hustling him towards a waiting chair at the pre-set coffee table in her private rooms at Corpus Christi College.

He had been touched, and a little embarrassed by her concern since she herself was obviously moving with stiff, careful deliberation as a result of the injuries she had sustained only nine days before at Brize Norton.

'I was,' the woman had started, before choking on the words she had meant to say. 'Terribly, terribly affected by the news of your father's death.'

Peter had been shocked to see the tears welling in the Prime Minister's blue eyes, and by how close she was to completely breaking down. She had forced a tight-lipped smile.

'He and I were very close,' Margaret Thatcher had said, recovering her poise with a monumental effort of will. 'When I was in Malta at the happy time of your wedding your father proposed marriage to me; and I accepted that offer.'

'I'm sorry, I had no idea...'

The woman had shaken her head. 'Contrary to Service rumours your father had no ambitions to succeed Sir David Luce as First Sea Lord. At the end of his tenure at Malta he planned to retire. At that time, we would have married.' She sniffed, looked away for a second or so. 'But it was not to be. Everything your father told me about you and everything I have subsequently learned about you, Captain Christopher, indicates to me that you are not a man who lives in the past, or dwells upon things that we cannot change.'

Peter had not known what to say and judged it best not to risk making a fool of himself saying something just for the sake of saying something.

'I apologise for tearing you away from your lovely wife,' Margaret Thatcher had continued, suddenly all business. 'I am travelling to Philadelphia tomorrow morning, just myself, the Foreign Secretary, Iain Macleod and a few people from our private offices. The mission is essentially political but I have for some time been worried that I have nobody on my personal staff capable of giving me up to date military advice based on recent, that is, post-October War experience in battle. I have spoken to the First Sea Lord and he assured me that he has no professional objections or reservations if I ask you to become, on a temporary basis, for this *mission* only at this stage, my Naval Aide-de-Camp.'

Peter recollected that he had behaved like an idiot.

'Oh, I, well... That's...'

To his astonishment the Prime Minister had smiled one of those smiles that instantly dazzled a man.

'Sir Varyl told me that you would want to go back to sea as soon as possible. He said that despite everything you had been through, you would be aching to get back into the fight.'

'Well, yes, actually...'

'The First Sea Lord also told me that he had no intention of giving you the opportunity to get yourself killed again *so soon.*'

Peter had confessed he had no idea what the duties of a Prime Ministerial Aide-de-Camp amounted to. The lady had smiled and he had been, well...*under her spell.* That was then and this was now.

Somebody on the BOAC Boeing 707 on the long flight across the North Atlantic had mentioned that the Philadelphia White House 'used to be a bank of some sort'. And that it was modelled on 'the Pantheon' in Rome. Peter had though that sounded a little crass and had therefore, been completely unprepared for the scale and the grandeur of the building into which he, spic-and-span in his best brand new expertly tailored dress uniform with the strange fourth – Post Captain's ring – on its cuffs, had followed the Prime Minister.

He had tried not to stare, mouth agape, at the reception committee awaiting the small British party.

The men standing in line all looked incredibly familiar and yet, completely different in the flesh and the one woman, small and elegant like a movie star. It was utterly bizarre.

The man at the head of the line looked just like the President of the United States of America, next to him stood a woman who looked exactly like Jackie, the President's wife, and there was an older more grizzled man who could have been Lyndon Johnson. It got stranger and stranger. Who was the big man in a US Air Force uniform covered in medals? Or the broad, dignified, commanding figure at the Vice-President's shoulder; or the man in steel-rimmed spectacles who looked like an accountant...

"Mister President," Margaret Thatcher announced proudly. "Allow me the honour of presenting you my Aide-de-Camp, Captain Sir Peter Christopher, VC, lately of Her Majesty's Ship Talavera."

Peter Christopher blinked dazedly into the green eyes of the most powerful man in the World.

He heard a stranger's voice say: "I'm honoured to meet you, sir."

"And I you, Sir Peter. Once Prime Minister Thatcher and I have hammered out our differences, you and I old Navy salts ought to exchange notes over a medicinal drink!"

"I look forward to that, sir."

And then the First Lady was smiling up at him. He had not realised she was so short – barely Marija's height - until that moment.

Lyndon Baines Johnson's grip was hard and dry.

Peter thought General Curtis LeMay was going to crush his right hand. When the older man released it, he was sorely tempted to check if anything was broken.

The Secretary of State, J. William Fulbright was the first person to assign Peter the consideration appropriate to him in this elevated company. He was after all the most junior captain in the Royal Navy. He simply nodded acquaintance and passed him on down the line.

Robert McNamara, the US Secretary of Defense smiled apologetically, and like Fulbright passed him swiftly down the line again.

General William Childs Westmoreland grabbed his hand and clung to it, slowing his progress and delaying his escape.

"Good to meet you, Captain," he grinned, a twinkle in his eyes. "Welcome to the major leagues."

Chapter 15

Major General Michael Carver rested his hands on the folded maps he had retrieved from his attaché case. His long, almost delicate fingers drummed briefly, involuntarily on the table top while he took several seconds to collect and order his thoughts. Even had it been in his nature to dive into his report without pausing for breath he was mindful that this was the most important, probably momentous, briefing he was ever likely to deliver, and this gave a man as cerebral as Michael Carver, very good reason to take his own sweet time.

"I had the opportunity to read and to consider the transcript of the preliminary debriefing of the 'special source' who came into our hands shortly after the Battle of Malta." He was curious to know the identity of the 'special source', and ideally, he wanted to talk to him, or her, face to face as soon as possible. However, that would have to wait. "My first reaction to *this* new intelligence is that it is entirely consistent with the general *schema* that, having spent the last few days on the ground in the Gulf, I would adopt if I were in the shoes of the Soviet High Command and I had determined to park *my* tanks on Abadan Island; and thus, threaten the entire Middle East with further *adventures* at a time of *my* choosing."

Carver looked around the table, his gaze thoughtfully inscrutable.

"My GSO5," he went on – he was currently Officer Commanding 2nd Division based in Winchester and had taken several members of his Divisional Staff with him to the Middle East, including his chief 'planner' – "is currently working up a document detailing the assumptions and the reasoning behind this *summary* briefing. With your permission I will address the matters at hand in the Gulf under three broad headings."

General Sir Richard Hull, Chief of the Defence Staff nodded.

"One," Carver began, "the enemy and his intentions. Two, the balance of forces in the region. Three, the military options open to us."

Nobody objected so he continued.

"One. The enemy and his intentions. If our 'special source' is correct two Red Army mechanised armies are currently strung out across the mountains of north western Iran. At this time this 'force', probably comprising as many as two thousand tanks and perhaps five to ten thousand other vehicles and as many as three hundred thousand men is extremely vulnerable to air attack. This is especially the case because thus far there have been few reports of significant Red Air Force operations. This may be because there are no airfields capable of handling fast jets available to the enemy in that part of Iran and that therefore, support operations must be mounted from relatively long ranges from bases inside Soviet territory to the north; or simply that the Red Air Force does not have many operational aircraft. It is self-evident that the objective of the Soviet offensive is to invade Northern Iraq via the passes at Piranshahr and Sardasht. I say 'self-evident' advisedly, because from jumping off points in the Iranian Province of Western Azerbaijan around Miandoab-Qoshachay and Mahabad, the Soviets might as easily advance in a south-south-easterly direction down the eastern flank of the Zagros Mountains to directly threaten Abadan."

The Secretary of State for Defence stirred.

"Surely that would be the most direct route to Abadan, the key strategic objective in the region, General Carver?"

"Yes, sir.   However, but that would be to see things from our perspective, rather than that of the enemy."   This the soldier said didactically but instantly quirked a fleeting smile.   "Abadan Island is only *one* of the enemy's objectives, sir. By driving south directly along the line of the foothills of the Zagros Mountains the Soviets would be putting all their eggs in one basket, so to speak, and would risk sacrificing their freedom of manoeuvre in the event of a sustained counter-attack by the relatively powerful, albeit somewhat fragmented, Iranian forces present in the south.   I believe it would be a huge mistake to form our plans on the assumption that the Soviets' *only* objective is Abadan."

"If not Abadan, then what?" Willie Whitelaw inquired.

Michael Carver had hoped not to be drawn into general, less specific and quantifiable areas, so soon. With a sigh he bit the bullet.

"I think it is reasonable to assume that the Soviets have thrown everything they've got into *Operation Chastise*." A Russian speaking member of his staff had complained that 'chastise' was only a vague translation of '*nakazyvat*' but Carver thought it was good enough, if only because it almost certainly spoke accurately to the mindset of the enemy. "The kitchen sink and everything," he grimaced, 'in the larder, too."

"And your point?" The politician prompted quietly.

"They wouldn't have done that if all they wanted to do was wipe out the Pahlavi Dynasty, Tehran and to conquer Iran as a way of exacting revenge on *just one* of their Imperialist foes, sir. I think what we have here is a gambler's last throw of the dice. A calculated, well-planned and up until the very last moment a brilliantly concealed last throw, but a last throw of the dice nonetheless. That is why although I consider it likely that the enemy's initial object is to conquer Iraqi territory north of the line Kirkuk-Sulaymaniyah, I suspect he will pause briefly in the north before striking south with everything he has got.

"Why pause in the north?" Willie Whitelaw asked, painfully aware that absolute clarity was essential.

"To regroup, to re-supply mainly by foraging and looting the resources of cities as far north as Erbil and Mosul, and to capture forward air bases for the Red Air Force. Moreover, by investing the north the enemy will almost certainly provoke the Kurdish elements of the Iraqi Army to join battle."

"Is there no possibility of containing the invaders in the north of Iraq?"

"In my opinion, no. None whatsoever. Shia Muslim elements of the Iraqi Army's high command have attempted to mount a coup in Baghdad, presumably taking advantage of the fact that the mainly Sunni-led armoured forces normally based around the capital – for reasons best known to local commanders – decided to launch an incursion into Iranian territory opposite Basra. While it is likely some of those forces in the south *may* move on Baghdad in the coming weeks, there is *no* possibility in my opinion that either the Sunni or the Shia-led formations will fight *together* against the Russians, or go out of their way to assist the Kurds in the north. The best we can do is to leave the Iraqis to their own devices. If we were so unwise as to attempt to intervene, the warring factions would just turn on us, sir."

Willie Whitelaw nodded.

"That is why the Soviets will drive south to the Shatt-al-Arab down the flood plains of the Tigris and the Euphrates?"

Michael Carver recognised that the politician had simply been quizzing him to confirm his own analysis of the situation.

"Yes, sir. The enemy's objective is not just to conquer Iraq and to seize Abadan Island and its refineries; it is to secure jumping off points for future adventures in the region and to gain access to warm water ports. The Soviets mean to transform the Persian Gulf into a Russian lake and to turn off the 'oil tap' to the West. At present, this latter is of critical importance to *us* because Abadan is our only 'oil tap', whereas, the other oil fields of the Gulf are currently of incidental significance to the United States. However, if and when the general world economy recovers from the recent war, as assuredly it will when the rebuilding begins in earnest, the availability, or non-availability of oil will become *the* critical *thing*. Whoever controls the oil will hold the rest of us to ransom. I say again, this is not just about Abadan and we would be making a bad mistake if we allowed ourselves to think otherwise."

There was a brief silence.

"The balance of forces?" Prompted Sir Richard Hull. The Chief of the Defence Staff's question was wholly rhetorical; today's 'briefing' was to ensure that his political masters understood precisely how naked the Emperor was, and did not get carried away with 'any damned fool ideas'.

"The garrison at Abadan has approximately three thousand effectives, of whom five hundred are from the 1st Australian Brigade. The majority of our people on the ground are lines of communications men. That said, two batteries of Bloodhound long-range surface-to-air missiles are now operational and we have established good radar and command and control systems around the Island. Armour; we have twenty-one Centurions and six Conqueror's. The latter aren't as nimble as the Centurions but they are very hard nuts to crack. No. 19 Squadron based at Abadan has a dozen operational Hawker Hunter fighters; and there are also a small number of transport aircraft on the Island. Plans are afoot to base several more Canberra medium bombers and reconnaissance aircraft at Abadan. War stores are being built up on an ad hoc basis. Elsewhere, we are in the process of evacuating our military contingent in Basra. Other than at Aden where we have the equivalent of four mechanised infantry battalions, our ground and air forces in the region are spread around in penny packets. The First Sea Lord will be able to speak to the Royal Navy presence in the area with immensely more authority than I, but essentially we are only talking about a couple of destroyers and various support vessels actually available for operations in the Persian Gulf at any one time."

Admiral Sir Varyl Begg nodded brusquely.

"In total," Carver continued. "We have something like sixty front line warplanes and approximately thirteen thousand service personnel in the region. I understand that the Australian government has offered to send significant reinforcements – warships and elements of a mechanised brigade - to the theatre. Obviously, we can fly out infantry and light equipment by air from the United Kingdom and Cyprus in fairly short order, albeit not in large numbers. Likewise, the RAF can reinforce existing units, always assuming airfields and such like are made available. One other thing; when the United States unilaterally pulled out of Saudi Arabia it is my understanding that they left three substantial 'war stores' depots in the Kingdom of Saudi Arabia. The war stores left behind included a large number of armoured vehicles, including M-48 tanks and all manner of munitions. Given that the Suez Canal is blocked and that heavy equipment will take at least two months to arrive in theatre from the United Kingdom – a little less from Australasian ports - the existence of those American depots should not be overlooked in any future plans."

"If we can't expect any help from the Iraqis," William Whitelaw posed, "who can we rely on, General Carver?"

"Several of the local Iranian commanders welcomed our *co-operation* in repelling the Iraqi armour that crossed the Arvand River at Basra." He shrugged. "I should imagine the Saudis are getting nervous at the moment as they look towards Philadelphia. I suspect both Syria and Jordan, for different reasons will attempt to observe states of 'armed neutrality' and hope the Red Army leaves them alone. The other military powers in the region are Israel and Egypt. Neither are geographically 'local' to the likely main areas of fighting, and Israel's active involvement in any way, shape or form would alienate all the Arab countries in the region and probably start new wars. As for Egypt, well, that's the one Arab country with a large, middlingly well organised, if not well led, army and air force. Equipped largely with 1950s Soviet weaponry, admittedly, but still militarily potent and more to the point it has a vested interest in flexing its muscles. However, as for the mechanics of in any way harnessing its military clout, that's not a question for me. The huge imponderable is what the Americans will do."

Willie Whitelaw nodded, lost in his thoughts.

"What indeed?" He mused softly. He looked up. "Item three. What are the options available to us, General Carver?"

The soldier resisted the temptation to unfurl his maps.

"Before I deal with that, sir," he apologised, "I think it would be helpful if I outlined, explicitly, what I think is likely to happen in the next few weeks."

"As you wish, General."

"Even were we to bomb the enemy in the mountains before he decamps from the Zagros Mountains, I don't think we can stop the Soviets occupying Northern Iraq. Once the Red Army is encamped in the north and has secured its supply lines, established forward air bases and advanced supply dumps, it will move south defeating any Iraqi Army formations it encounters. Most organised resistance will evaporate after the first battles; thereafter the Red Army's main enemy will be time and the hostile ground over which it is moving. By the time the invaders reach Basra they will have lost at least half their armour, almost exclusively to mechanical breakdowns and failures. At the stage when the Soviets will hope to be in a position to assault Abadan the invading armies will be stretched out over six or seven hundred miles all the way back into the mountains of Azerbaijan. The conquerors of Basra will be exhausted, short of fuel, ammunition, possibly hungry and much of the countryside and many of the cities in their direct line of advance will be in ruins. The Red Air Force will be in much the same state. Tanks and modern aircraft, and any kind of wheeled vehicle 'hates' the terrain and the climate of a place like Iraq. By the time the Red Army reaches Abadan it will have been fighting in daytime temperatures of well over a hundred degrees Fahrenheit for several weeks, at night the temperature can plummet to below zero, dust and grit and stones will have got into every conceivable piece of weaponry and machinery, tank tracks will be breaking and dropping off on *every* T-54, T-58 and T-62 every few miles, engines will overheat, seize up after an hour's running in the daytime heat, and there will have been no clean, potable water for the crews to drink for days or weeks. The average Russian soldier will be dirty, lousy, thirsty and sick, dysentery will be rife in the ranks and the farther south the army moves the less friendly the natives will become. At this time of year, the marshes for a hundred miles above Basra and all the way below it to the Persian Gulf are flooded, inundated by the snow melt coming down the Tigris and the Euphrates, no vehicle can go an inch off the road without bogging down and the Marsh Arabs have been resisting invaders for a thousand years. Tank commanders forced to stick their heads out of turrets to stop being roasted alive in the noon day heat will be picked off by snipers using rifles stolen from the corpses of dead British or Turkish soldiers killed in the Great War, stores will constantly be being pilfered. Whereas in northern Iran some Azeris would have viewed the invaders as liberators; in central and southern Iraq the Russians are just the latest unwelcome interlopers to be preyed upon, robbed and confounded."

Carver could tell his audience was growing impatient.

Reality was complicated and he was not about to apologise about it.

"Be this as it may," he said, wrapping up his introduction. "It is obvious to me that there is *no* way that we can stop whatever remains of the great Soviet invasion force which entered Iran approximately a fortnight ago reaching Basra, and," he hesitated, "taking Abadan by force majeure."

Chapter 16

Thursday 16th April 1964
The White House, Philadelphia, Pennsylvania

Peter Christopher sat in a chair behind the Prime Minister's right shoulder, one of countless advisors and middle-ranking military officers ringing the giant conference table. President Kennedy sat across the gleaming surface of the table, smiling fixedly at Margaret Thatcher.

The United Kingdom delegation; the Prime Minister, Sir Thomas Harding-Grayson, the Foreign Secretary, Iain Macleod, the UAUK's Minister of Information, and Lord Franks, the British Ambassador and three aides (Peter included) was hugely outnumbered by the President's entourage comprising key members of the Administration, the High Command of the US Armed Forces, and a host of immaculately suited and uniformed men, and several women.

"I am sorry, Jack," Margaret Thatcher declaimed, not bothering to cloak her growing exasperation. "Sending *one* aircraft carrier to the Indian Ocean at *some time* later this month or early in May does *not* in any *way* amount to meaningfully discharging your obligations under the US-UK Mutual Defence Agreement!"

Jack Kennedy deflected this barb with what he probably honestly believed was hard-nosed irresistible charm.

"*Margaret,*" he explained patiently, "you know how *personally* committed I am to *that* treaty. Unfortunately, the fact is that the House of Representatives has thrown it out. Besides, *that* Treaty does not, and was never intended to cover conflicts falling outside the old NATO sphere..."

"I recollect that a little over two months ago I was the one who talked *you* out of a retaliatory nuclear strike against the criminals suspected of sinking the USS Long Beach, crippling the USS Enterprise, attacking Cairo and blocking the Suez Canal at Ismailia. The Mediterranean and the Middle East were certainly inside the relevant *sphere of influence* at *that time!*"

Captain Sir Peter Christopher, VC, flinched. He honestly did not believe he had just heard a British Prime Minister talk to the President of the United States of America like he was a naughty school boy she had just discovered illicitly smoking a cigarette behind the bike shed!

He was even more astonished when it transpired that the Angry Widow had not so much said what she meant to say, but had only just begun to explain the error of *his* ways to her host.

"Margaret, I..."

"You have said your piece, Jack," Margaret Thatcher retorted, her tone increasingly hectoring. "It is abundantly clear that you do not understand what is at stake here."

Peter Christopher shut his eyes in horror because he knew what was coming next. He had conned Talavera straight down the barrels of the guns of a World War I battlecruiser and a big Soviet cruiser and he had only deliberately shut his eyes once. That had been when he had seen – yes, he had actually *seen* – a salvo of six hundred-and-sixty-pound rounds fired from the eleven-inch guns of the battlecruiser Yavuz hit the water several hundred yards directly ahead of Talavera; and ricochet off the iron grey Mediterranean seemingly directly at his head. One of those shells had passed only feet above the bridge, torn off the top of the gun director tower and scythed down the destroyer's towering lattice foremast as if it was a red-hot broadsword through butter. That had been the shell which had probably killed his best friend, Miles Weiss...

"*You* have seen fit to give me a lecture about how *my* government should behave towards the Irish Republic. *You* have assured me that in the event of the loss of Abadan Island and its refineries that the United States would in some way *guarantee* oil supplies to the United Kingdom. *You* have assured me that the Sixth Fleet is merely the precursor to a permanent American land, sea and air presence in the whole of the Mediterranean. *You* have assured me that steps would be undertaken to undo the damage done by predatory American conglomerates to British interests and companies in Africa, South America and the Far East in the immediate aftermath of the Cuban Missiles War. *You* have promised me that America intends to be, once again, at some point in the future as yet unspecified, the quote 'Policeman of the World'. *You* have also informed me that *you* view the question of the appointment of an American commander-in-chief of '*all allied forces in Europe*' as a high priority for your Administration. Last but by no means least *you* have indicated to me that there is no way that you can *sell* putting American GIs' boots on the ground in the Middle East to defend '*the last jewel in Britain's former Imperial crown*', namely Abadan."

President Kennedy thought, or rather, he hoped, that she had finished.

Peter Christopher *knew* that *his* chief had hardly begun.

The President opened his mouth to speak...

But got no farther.

"I think *we* need to understand each other a little better," Margaret Thatcher declared stridently. Beside her Iain Macleod looked like he wanted to bury his head in his hands, and Lord Franks's face was a rictus mask. Extraordinarily, the Foreign Secretary seemed to be on the verge of dozing off, giving every appearance of being completely indifferent to what was going on around him. Across the table several of the American participants were staring at the British Prime Minister with their mouths agape in disbelief.

"The United Kingdom's policy towards the Irish Republic is none of your damned business, Jack," the Prime Minister declared. "While Mr Lemass's government continues to tolerate the transhipment of American weapons to Ulster and to the mainland of the United Kingdom to facilitate indiscriminate murder and mayhem, his government and his people *will* be subject to appropriate *sanctions.*

For goodness' sake," she exclaimed angrily, "when Castro threatened you," she snarled, "you obliterated the whole of Cuba! Including," she added dismissively, "your own bases on that island!"

Iain Macleod groaned.

"Oh, no..."

Margaret Thatcher paused, scowling at the horrified expressions of her listeners across the other side of the table.

Peter Christopher thought that was the end of the conference.

Hopefully, he would get to see Marija one more time before the bombs started falling. It was not fair; he had not laid eyes on her face to face until ten or eleven weeks ago. They had only been married on 7th March. Notwithstanding his selfish personal feelings, it never occurred to him that *his* leader was in the wrong. She was *only* saying what any moderately informed man or woman in the street in Britain would say, were they to find themselves face to face with the American President who had deluged so much grief and misery on their heads eighteen months ago.

"Oil supplies," Margaret Thatcher said contemptuously. "Well, we all know how much our *ally's* promises amounted to throughout much of last year, *Jack.* I also know that tens of thousands, perhaps hundreds of thousands of *my* people died last year because of the failure of your Administration to make good on its promises, no, its obligations to help a NATO ally in need."

She drew breath and launched the next stinging rebuke.

"Yes, the Sixth Fleet is at Malta at this time. Had powerful elements of that fleet been at Malta instead of playing war games when they were supposed to be providing long-range radar cover for the archipelago, some three thousand Maltese civilians and many hundreds of brave British and Commonwealth servicemen would not have died when the Soviet invasion fleet appeared off the coast!" She huffed and puffed like a dragon getting her wind before spewing fresh fire and brimstone. "But for the courage and sacrifice of courageous young men like the officer seated behind me, Malta would now be a part of the Soviet Union. No thanks to the Sixth Fleet!"

Peter Christopher wanted to curl up and become invisible. His face burned impossibly hot, he grimaced feebly as every eye momentarily fell upon him seated faithfully at his mistress's right shoulder.

"Implicit in our discussions in Washington DC in January was an understanding that the jackals of Wall Street would be forced to recompense British and Commonwealth shareholders in those concerns illegally appropriated by American companies," Margaret Thatcher protested.

Oh! No!

She was actually wagging a finger at the President of the United States of America!

"However, there has been no movement on this issue, Jack. This is hardly surprising because the Administration has taken absolutely no action on it since January." She shook her head sadly. "As for rearming and becoming the 'Policeman of the World'? Well, that's a joke. Your proxies in Argentina have just invaded sovereign British territory. The Falkland Islands are not the *Malvinas* and the people on the islands are not bloody Argentines! They are British citizens! As for the Argentinean seizure of South Georgia, the South Sandwich Islands and laying claim to that part of Antarctica previously administered by *the Crown,* over which Buenos Aires has not, and never has had any title, frankly words fail me! That the United States should adopt a policy of 'no comment' on the matter is...despicable!"

Everybody really, really imagined she was finished at that point.

She was not. Not quite yet.

"Policeman of the World, indeed!" She added scathingly.

There was a horrible silence.

It was J. William Fulbright who eventually broke the unquiet quietness. He coughed and sat forward, resting his arms on the table. He sought out and held eye contact with Margaret Thatcher.

"Just for the record the Argentine government is not at this time any kind of 'client' of this Administration, Prime Minister. President Francesconi's government is completely beholden to the supposedly 'moderate' *Blue* faction of the Argentine military. The country is actually run by the Head of the Joints Chiefs of Staff, General Juan Carlos Onganía and by the Internal Affairs Minister, General Osiris Villegas. We have no control over *these* people and they do not listen to anything we have to say to them. For your information there has been an embargo on military sales to the regime since the last coup back in the fall." He spread his hands. "Speaking personally, I have a degree of sympathy with the, er, thrust of many of your *observations.* However, nobody has betrayed anybody here."

John Fitzgerald Kennedy had fallen silent.

He rested his chin on his left hand.

On that long ago inauguration day in January 1961 he had dreamed of what might be achieved in the next four years. He was a different man then, a young man still but not now. He had had the power to destroy the world but not to make all Americans equally free. He had had no power to stop madmen attempting to murder Martin Luther King on a public stage in Atlanta in February; no power to persuade an increasingly bucolic 'America First' Congress that there was a world beyond the boundaries of its debating chamber. Ultimately, he had had no power to extend the aid and succour that he yearned to offer to the infuriating, unique woman who had probably not yet finished berating him for his many and egregious transgressions. The reality was that even had he wanted to send US troops to the Middle East he had none to spare; the US Army was fully occupied holding the line in Chicago, rooting out insurgents in the Cascades and the length of the Rockies, attempting to keep the lid on the powder keg cities of Birmingham, Jackson, Atlanta and a score of other places. The news from Iran had been like the match that lit the proverbial blue touch paper, the whole of the South seemed to be on fire and worse, he was running for re-election.

The way things were shaping up if the 'America First' front runners got their act together he was going to be the first President ever to lose every single state of the Union in a General Election in November.

Whatever happened, he could *not* let *those* people win.

In the cruel calculus of these things if the price of keeping the barbarians from the gates of the city was drawing down the final curtain on the British Empire, then that was a price worth paying.

Pragmatically, if what it took to hold back the darkness was for John Fitzgerald Kennedy to become the cheerleader of the 'America First Movement', so be it.

"Margaret," he drawled, raising his face. "For all our failings I honestly believe that the future of freedom, democracy and reason in the World depends upon the survival of the United States of America. Ultimately, civilization rests in our hands. You may think this no more than hubris. You may think me bad, perhaps mad. It may just be that you and I won't ever see things the same way. None of that changes the reality of the situation."

Margaret Thatcher visibly bit her tongue.

The President's green eyes were resigned.

"The Sixth Fleet will render what assistance it may in the Eastern Mediterranean. Secretary of State Fulbright will facilitate what alliances and material aid can be secured from other parties in the Middle East. The USS Kitty Hawk will sail to the Indian Ocean, officially to assist in the evacuation of the dependents of US citizens and in other non-specific emergency relief work." He pursed his lips, let this sink in. "But that is all."

"I see," the Prime Minister acknowledged sulkily.

"Publicly, I will continue to take your government to task over its 'Irish policy'. What aid can be sent to the United Kingdom will continue to be sent, but if Congress blocks all routes, then that will be that. America has turned its back on internationalism. The mantra is now *America First* and I must follow that drum or this time next year, well, who knows?"

Oddly, now that the man had confessed his sins Margaret Thatcher's excoriating hostility cooled. The man had the dead of the October War on his conscience and now he was about to prostitute himself before the American people. In politics, she reflected, there were no right or good decisions; and sometimes the only realistic choices were between the lesser of two unthinkable evils.

"I came here to demand that we, *together*, draw a line in the sand," she said quietly, her tone that of a woman spurned, "I had in mind drawing that line in the deserts of Iraq or Iran. It never occurred to me, not for a single minute, that what *you* had in mind was drawing that line in the sand on the beach at Hyannis Port, *Jack.*"

Chapter 17

Lieutenant-Colonel Francis Harold St John Waters, VC, of the 22nd Special Air Service Regiment felt that he ought to be more surprised by the observational skills – or as witnessed by his experience of the last few days, the marked absence of the same – of the average Red Army soldier, whether he was an officer or a blank-faced private soldier. Honestly and truly, if he had been given the run around for two days and two nights in Urmia, not *once* setting eyes on one's enemy and had consequently had a large number of his chums blown to bits and picked off by snipers, he would certainly have been paying a lot more attention to his surroundings than these chaps!

Merging into the background in this country was a doddle!

The trick seemed to be to squat down on one's haunches by the roadside and look disinterested in everything for hours on end, occasionally holding out one's hand and muttering something that sounded vaguely Azeri – Farsi did not cut it around here if you were supposed to be begging – and nobody, absolutely nobody gave a fellow a second look providing you remembered not to look up while there was anybody near enough to see the colour of your eyes. The locals all seemed to have grey or tawny brownish eyes; his blue eyes would have been a dead giveaway that he was anything but *local*. If he ever got back to base; Stirling Lines in dear old Herefordshire as opposed to the embassy in Tehran which he was reliably informed no longer existed, he was going to have some fine old tales with which to regale the Mess.

'Frank' Waters was hot, sore, hungry and feeling his age. Although he was only forty-six; the trouble was most of the last twenty-five of those years had been *hard* years. He had almost bought it twice in the Western Desert, and again in Yugoslavia near the end of the Second War. He still had bomb fragments in his back from that cock up in Oman five years ago, and in the two decades between the excitement of playing hide and seek with the Afrika Korps and this latest little jaunt he had acquired a litany of minor injuries and breakages in training and other escapades. Vexingly, he still had intermittent mild Tinnitus in his left ear off from the time that bloody frog had caught him *in flagrante delicto* with in his marvellously pneumatic wife in Algiers; in the subsequent undignified melee the gun had gone off a tad too close to his head for comfort...

Anyway, what with one thing and another he was fairly close to half-way towards admitting that he was getting far too old for this sort of lark. Diving back into the fray had been immense fun but he had been around long enough to know when it was time to make oneself scarce.

Now, he had decided, was one of those times.

The Iranians he had been 'training' were outraged when he had told them that he and his men were 'off'. The locals were good sorts, just not very pragmatic. There was nothing wrong with dying for a good cause; but dying simply to make a point or in the name of one's family honour well, that was just plain stupid.

Waters had ordered his boys to saddle up and as they drove south the first line of Napalm strikes had illuminated the night at their backs. Fortunately, the two Land Rovers were five miles south by then.

A couple of *his* boys had been with him for years; the newer recruits had got squeamish over executing the prisoners. *The Rules of War!* What did the idiots think was going to happen if the Red Army got its hands on them? As for leaving 'prisoners' wandering about the countryside bursting to tell their 'comrades' all about British SAS men who were sneaking about in the night!

Frank Waters slowly stood up.

Life had been so much easier in those long-ago days charging about Cyrenaica with the Long-Range Desert Group. That was the ticket, none of this endless walking about in the sun pretending to be a bloody beggar!

Funny old thing, war...

"We're stringing the aerial now, boss," he was told as he picked his way into the trees where the Land Rovers were parked half-way between the Mahabad-Urmia Road and the mud brick ruins of what had every appearance of being a very ancient abandoned village.

"Keep up the good work, lads!"

Frank Waters's tone was relaxed, jovial. Out in the field he was an entirely different man to the 'barracks officer' that everybody tried their best to keep out of the way of. Back in the fifties in England and in his postings to the embassies in Bonn, Rome and Buenos Aires he had felt like he was in prison, a tiger caged, distracted now and then by predatory liaisons with other men's wives, bored beyond measure in his own ill-considered, ill-starred marriage. After the unmitigated 'fun' of the war years peacetime soldiering had been, well, a mighty let down and whenever he was at a loose end it was in his nature to go looking for trouble. The wasted years in foreign embassies, interspersed with stints training men straight off the Selection Course in Hereford and on the Brecon Beacons had brought out the worst in him. Of course, there was a silver lining to most clouds – as any old soldier will tell you – and eventually the people back home had got so fed up with him that they had banished him abroad.

His boys had gone in ahead of the invasion force at Suez in 1956; that had been a fiasco but a jolly good bash. He had chased Mau Mau killers through the Kenyan bush, hunted down communist insurgents in Borneo and Islamist fanatics in Oman and Yemen, served two tours on Cyprus where the women were irresistibly dark-eyed, and been on Malta at the time of the October War. The whole Cuban Missiles nonsense had seemed to him, even from a distance of thousands of miles, to be the most monstrous of cock ups by everybody concerned.

On the bright side it had opened up a wealth of opportunities for incorrigible cases like him!

Back in the makeshift 'camp' Frank Waters's mood was almost hearty.

Not even the thought of stale black bread and some kind of half-rancid sausage – all they had left of the food they had purloined clandestinely exploring Urmia after the Red Army had moved in – could dent his good cheer. When it got dark, they would move out, try and find a secluded place in the mountains to hide up; somewhere farther south from which they could sortie to snatch prisoners, and properly eyeball the traffic passing into and out of Mahabad. Command would need to know exactly what they were dealing with if this thing was half as bad as it looked.

Whoever was in local charge on the Soviet side seemed to know what he was doing. Whoever he was he could not know that the Iranian garrison of Urmia had mounted up in anything that had wheels or tracks and 'run away' to the north to hide in the hills; so, he was doing the sensible thing, sending a column up the road to Urmia to block any hostile force coming south; a few tanks, a couple of anti-tank guns and a company of infantrymen hefting RPG – rocket propelled grenade - launchers and heavy machine guns. And high in the sky there were suddenly the silver arrows of fast jets, circling, patrolling, waiting for *business*. Not that any of this was 'rocket science'. One look at a map and any soldier with two brain cells to rub together would know that the road from Qoshachay-Miandoab to Mahabad was the key 'choke point' in the advance of the Soviet armour. Anything, absolutely *anything* which seriously threatened the right flank of that long, exposed road across the high plain into the foothills of the Zagros Mountains was potentially a monumental disaster waiting to happen.

Frank Waters had recommended somebody in Middle East Command get his act together and bomb the road to buggery. Not for the first time in his eventful career his advice had thus far been ignored.

"Have we got through to the boys in Abadan yet?" He inquired, throwing off his hood. He liked to think he looked like a Bedouin; actually, he suspected he looked like a dirty peasant and smelled worse.

"Still working on it, boss."

A man offered Waters a mess tin with what looked like steaming mud in it. He took it gratefully, deliberately not asking what today's version of 'tea' was brewed from. It tasted like it might have been brewed from crushed tree bark and had the subtle bouquet of burned Camel dung. The old soldier hardly noticed, it was warm and wet and had been boiled long enough to kill most of the bugs.

Waiting for the radio link to be established he lowered himself to the ground and looked around the 'camp'. There were two men out on picket duty, and including him five loitering in the vicinity or sitting on the ground around him and the clumsy, boxy radio transmitter with its improvised whip and long wire aerial. He had lost two good men back in Urmia; his fault. He ought to have pulled out of the town sooner, at least an hour or so before he belatedly concluded the game was no longer worth the candle.

He put the thought to one side.

"We need to steal one of those old American charabancs we've seen the locals driving around in," he decided, no more than thinking out aloud.

After the 1945 war the Americans had pulled out with such indecent haste that they had left hundreds, possibly thousands of big Ford and Dodge four and six-wheeler Army trucks behind in Iran. Over the years the locals had resurrected a lot of them, obviously so because they were trundling up and down the roads even this far north. In fact, these trucks – all rusty and belching huge volumes of poisonous smoke – were pretty much ubiquitous, so much so that nobody, not even the Russians, gave them a second thought or look.

"After tonight we're going to have to ditch the Land Rovers. The chaps up in Urmia will have told HQ in Mahabad what they were up against by now. It won't take the enemy long to figure out that rascals like us are on the loose."

There were sage nods of agreement around Frank Waters.

That was when he knew what he was going to do next and a saturnine, predatory smile began to quirk at the corners of his mouth. He chuckled, tickled pink with the idea.

In his best Moskva Russian, he said: "My sobirayemsya delat' vid, byt' Russkimi, tovarishchi."

We are going to pretend to be Russians, comrades...

The idea did not instantly go down a storm with the three non-Russian speaking troopers nearest to him, mainly because they did not understand a word of what their leader had just said.

The man at the radio smiled broadly.

"We're going to dress up like Russians," he explained.

"My budem imet', chtoby ukrast' nekotoryye formy i gruzovik pervym. No my mozhem sdelat eto," Frank Waters went on, liking the idea more with every passing second.

"*We are going to have to steal some uniforms and a lorry first,*" the other Russian speaker translated. "*But we can do that.*"

Chapter 18

Thursday 16th April 1964
Merton College, Oxford, England

The Secretary of State for Defence very nearly swallowed his tea cup. It was all he could do not to spontaneously spew his mouthful of tea – a vile, disgusting brew served to the meeting by a surly, disenchanted Merton porter who viewed the presence of the Chiefs of Staff and their political master in *his* college as an outrageous affront to everything that was right and just in the world – in the face of the man who had moments before made an unforgivably, despicably defeatist statement.

"What do you mean?" He blustered angrily. "There's nothing we can do to stop the Soviets reaching the Persian Gulf and seizing Abadan Island?"

Major General Michael Carver viewed William Whitelaw, the forty-five-year-old Member of Parliament for Penrith and the Border with clear, unperturbed eyes. He sighed, exchanged a brief quizzical look with his direct superior, the Chief of the Defence Staff, General Sir Richard Hull who's minutely raised eyebrow and nod gave him leave to reply.

"Forgive me, Minister," Carver responded. "I thought that I had been at pains to make my meaning crystal clear?"

Willie Whitelaw stared at him, his tea cup poised in mid-air and his mind racing with bad possibilities and dire premonitions.

"The tactical calculus is straightforward," the handsome, patrician general continued. "The enemy has two thousand tanks, over a quarter of a million men and we have less than thirty tanks and discounting the other forces we have scattered around the region, we have approximately three to four thousand fighting troops on the ground. We can inconvenience the enemy with air strikes, and we can make trouble for the Red Army by stirring up and supporting local insurgencies along the enemy's line of advance – although personally I don't think the locals will need any encouragement from us to harry the invaders – and we can block the Persian Gulf at the Straits of Hormuz with our existing naval assets. What we cannot do, and what it would be a criminal waste of men and materiel to attempt to do is hold on to Abadan Island."

General Sir Richard Hull coughed.

"Given forewarning of General Carver's conclusions and the detailed reasoning behind those conclusions," he said regretfully, "the Chiefs of Staff concur with the view he has just expressed."

The Secretary of State clunked his cup and saucer on the table.

"I can't tell the Prime Minister that!"

Michael Carver sipped his tea, wrinkling his nose. He had tasted worse in the Middle East recently, but not much worse. Notwithstanding the World had gone to Hell in a hand basket the last couple of years; the politicians remained the same!

The First Sea Lord, Sir Varyl Begg spoke.

"I'm the new boy in this, er, *class*," he prefaced self-effacingly. "However, the logic of the situation in the Gulf is compelling, Minister. Self-evident, in fact because even if we had unlimited treasure to pour into the defence of Abadan – which we do not - and more importantly, its refinery complexes, those self-same invaluable *assets* would inevitably be destroyed in the course of their *defence*. The political ramifications of the actual situation on the ground in the Middle East are one thing, sir. The military realities are another completely; unless of course, *Arc Light* is back on the table?"

Willie Whitelaw vehemently shook his head.

Arc Light was the code word for a 'first' nuclear strike.

"We have several V-Bombers positioned at QRA in the region," Air Marshall Sir Christopher Hartley, the Chief of the Air Staff observed. "We have now established small stockpiles of tactical and strategic free fall bombs at Malta, Akrotiri on Cyprus, Dhahran in Saudi Arabia and at Aden..."

The Defence Minister turned on his three senior professional military advisors, ignoring Michael Carver, the bringer of disastrously bad news.

"Is that what you gentlemen are recommending?" He demanded, his customary urbanity disintegrating. With an effort he recovered his composure. Coolly he asked: "That we resolve this matter by starting another nuclear war?"

Michael Carver's voice cut across the sudden, cringing silence.

"No, Minister," he declared irritably. "It may well come to that but *that* is not the main substance of my recommendations to the CDS, this meeting or to the government."

Willie Whitelaw said nothing for several seconds. He was too busy blinking with bewilderment to form coherent words. Presently, he ran a distracted hand across his brow.

"What exactly are you recommending, General Carver?"

The most junior officer in the room was not about to hurried. Not for the first time he involuntarily patted the still folded maps before him on the table top as he carefully deployed his thoughts.

"My recommendations are predicated by two general assumptions, Minister. One; that we can expect little or no assistance from our American allies on the ground in the Middle Eastern Theatre of Operations. Two; that it will not be possible to transport sufficient quantities of heavy equipment, armour, artillery and the thousand and one things required to sustain a large, Corps or multi-division mechanised force in the field, from the United Kingdom to the Persian Gulf in time for it to be deployed in good order to interdict the Red Army's operations in Iraq. The former assumption must be hedged around by political caveats; however, even if – and it is a big 'if' – the Americans believed that their interests in Arabia are seriously threatened by the Soviet invasion of Iran and Iraq I would be remiss factoring in a significant contribution from them that I do not honestly believe will be forthcoming. The latter assumption is simply a statement of fact; we do not have the time – or for that matter the fully stocked depots in the United Kingdom – to enable us to massively reinforce our existing garrisons in the theatre."

Willie Whitelaw desperately wanted to jump in; but something held his tongue. Something that was ineluctably unspoken in the didactic certainty of Michael Carver's uncommonly sure-footed delivery.

"That is not to say that we will not eventually be obliged to pack up our camps, depart with our tails between our legs and leave the region to the tender mercies of the Soviet invader," Carver went on. "In the time available to us, say perhaps a month, two if we are very lucky, we can strengthen our air presence with a view to achieving local air superiority over the Persian Gulf, fly in infantry reinforcements and begin to collaborate with friends, and possibly former adversaries in the region in whose best interests it would be to form mutual defence *arrangements*. Specifically, this would involve building on existing professional relations between members of the British officer cadre in the region and the commanders of the surviving units of the Iranian Army positioned around Abadan. It means negotiating with the Saudi Arabian authorities to gain access to the US 'War Stores Depots' located at Al Jeddah, Riyadh and Dammam-Dhahran, and fully opening the former US Air Base at the last of those places to our aircraft. Thirdly, we must make our peace with Egypt. I repeat, at *any* cost we must make our peace with Egypt. Because if we don't make peace with *that* country then we shall never, *never*, expel the Red Army from the northern shores of the Persian Gulf. It goes without saying," he added ominously, "if we don't expel the Red Army from the Gulf, say before the autumn of this year, in a few years from now the whole Middle East will be a fabulously oil-rich Soviet Republic dedicated to the downfall of the Western World."

The Secretary of State for Defence mulled this wordlessly, knowing now that there was more, much more to come and that what he had intuitively misidentified as 'defeatism' was nothing less than brutal pragmatism.

"Within the framework of those assumptions and caveats," Michael Carver continued, "I have recommended the following to the Chiefs of Staff."

He paused for one last reflection.

"One; that we reinforce our existing garrisons in the theatre outside Iraq and Iran as best we may in terms of men and materiel. Two; that we withdraw the Basra garrison to Abadan. This has already begun. Three; that we make no attempt to interdict the Soviet invasion until such time as the leading elements of the spearhead of the Red Army approach, or ideally, have passed Abadan on the western side of the Shatt al-Arab to invest the Faw Peninsula. Four; at that time limited offensive *demonstrations* should be mounted to give the impression that it is our intention to make a stand at Abadan to cover the withdrawal of our forces at that place. Five; that all the facilities at Abadan be destroyed prior to our departure. In the meantime, the RAF must establish air superiority over the Persian Gulf, Southern Iraq, Kuwait and the Western Desert of Iraq. Six; that we must begin to build up whatever mobile forces resources permit, in Kuwait if necessary but ideally for deployment in northern Saudi Arabia. Seven; that at such time as the Red Army – by then with most of its surviving equipment in a poor state of repair and its manpower exhausted – digs into position along the northern shores of the Persian Gulf, offensive operations should be launched from the west and the east to cut the Soviet lines of communication mid-way between Baghdad and Basra."

Willie Whitelaw stared at the other man.

"Cannae," he murmured.

Michael Carver nodded.

Among his numerous accomplishments he was a military historian who had – before the October War – anticipated a retirement spent writing of old battles and campaigns, including those in which he had participated in the Western Desert, with a view to debunking no small number of popular myths about Erwin Rommel's career prior to Bernard Montgomery's arrival in the desert in 1942.

Every fighting general dreamed of master-minding his personal *Cannae*, of engineering and fighting a war-winning battle. Every subaltern at practically every staff college learned about *Cannae* but only once in a generation, or maybe two or three or four generations, did a general officer actually glimpse a fleeting opportunity to 'Cannae' his enemy.

The technology and the mobility of warfare might have changed since that August day of the Battle of Cannae in 216 BC in Apulia in southern Italy but the principles of war remained the same. On that day over two millennia ago the Army of the Roman Republic under the command of the consuls Lucius Aemilius Paullus and Gaius Terentius Varro, had been enveloped and destroyed by the much smaller Carthaginian army of Hannibal. The Romans had become so pre-occupied battering at the apparently weak Carthaginian centre that the powerful wings of Hannibal's army had swept around it, and much like a giant meat grinder, chewed the massed legions to pieces. Classical sources spoke of only fourteen thousand of the eighty-six thousand legionnaires of the Roman Republican horde escaping the slaughter.

"Yes, sir," Carver agreed. "But first we must allow the ground over which our enemy is advancing and the privations of that country take its toll on him, and," he looked hard at Willie Whitelaw, "by hook or by crook *you* must find me an armoured corps with which to *Cannae* these blighters!"

Chapter 19

Tuesday 21st April 1964
USS Kitty Hawk (CV-63), 187 miles West of Tarakan, Celebes Sea

Lieutenant-Commander Walter Brenckmann followed the other officers filing into the great carrier's long, low Wardroom. He had only just come off watch where he was three-quarters the way through qualifying to stand as Officer of the Deck (OOD) unsupervised. Standing watch on the bridge of the US Navy's biggest ship – the Kitty Hawk was over a thousand feet long, displaced over eighty thousand tons fully loaded, had a four-acre flight deck, carried over eighty aircraft and helicopters and had a crew of well over five-and-a-half thousand men – was roughly akin to being in command of a floating air base capable of steaming at thirty-three knots, or in land lubber's money, better than thirty-seven miles-an-hour. Walter Brenckmann did not think he was going to get used to that any time soon.

He had joined the super carrier while she was still in dock at Kobe undergoing a routine overhaul. Completed only in 1961 the Kitty Hawk had been in need of a 'two-year service' and now she was as good as new, working up to full combat efficiency with her re-constituted air wing and some six hundred new officers and men rotated into her company during the refit period.

Twenty-eight-year-old Walter Brenckmann only occasionally – he was far too busy most of the time - thought about the surreal days of last December when briefly, he had been at the eye of the US Navy's scandal of the century.

The chain of command of the Polaris boats of Submarine Squadron 15 based at Alameda in San Francisco Bay had been compromised; rogue firing instructions and targeting coordinates had been issued to at least one boat, the USS Sam Houston (SSBN-608). Even though he was wholly blameless in the affair; other than having been instrumental in bringing the 'problem' to the attention of his superiors, he had wrongly as it turned out, suspected his naval career was over. Instead, he had been promised a place on next year's Nuclear Boat Command Course and in the meantime, he had been posted to the Kitty Hawk, the flagship of Carrier Division Seven, as Assistant Anti-Submarine Officer and been given the opportunity to qualify for OOD duties.

After departing Japanese waters three weeks ago; Carrier Division Seven had visited Manila in the Philippines, before conducting a 'shake down' exercise in the Celebes Sea. There was talk of a 'good will' cruise down to Perth in Western Australia; Walter did not think that was very likely since relations between the Australian and New Zealand governments and the Kennedy Administration were still 'strained', according to the last letter he had received from his mother. She was in England now with Pa, and from what he gathered relations with the 'old country' were also somewhat 'strained' at present although Ma said she and 'the Ambassador' had already made a host of new friends 'in Oxford'.

Half-a-dozen letters had caught up with Walter in Manila.

Gretchen Betancourt, whom he had once gently rebuffed, had sounded as if she was genuinely much more her old self. She had been very badly injured during the fighting in Washington DC in December; hurt in the explosion in which Under Secretary George Ball had died and later shot twice by insurgents. Not that she was the sort of girl to allow a little thing like that to keep her down for long. The eldest daughter of New England Democratic Party elder statesman Claude Betancourt – who had been the late Joseph Kennedy's go to corporate litigator – Gretchen was a woman in a hurry. Notwithstanding she was hardly back on her feet and in no way fully recovered from her injuries she was, it seemed, now engaged to be married to Walter's younger brother Dan, and about to start 'defending' the leaders of last year's coup d'état!

As for Dan, according to Gretchen, he had got himself a 'nice little sinecure on the Warren Commission'. Dan had appended a short note to his fiancée's long, chatty letter: *Try not to run the ship aground – we've only got the KH and the Independence until they fix the Enterprise and get the other big boats back to sea! Take care, big brother.*

The Brenckmann family was settling down; a second letter from Ma had conveyed the news that his kid brother, Sam and his girlfriend Judy had 'tied the knot' having produced a daughter, Tabatha Christa a fortnight or so before Christmas.

Gretchen's letter had alluded to but largely brushed over the ongoing 'situations' in Chicago and the 'mountains in the West'. However, she had not mixed her words about the 'disgrace' the 'Administration has allowed to go virtually unchecked in the South'. These were subjects that Walter knew little about and had passed over in his reply to the woman whom he had only met half-a-dozen times in his whole life but for whom, and with whom, he had formed a strange, possibly unbreakable affinity in the fateful December days before she went back to Washington DC, and very nearly died for her temerity. He was glad she was marrying Dan. Dan loved Gretchen in ways Walter knew he could not. Besides, Dan was in Gretchen's thrall, and more than that Dan was the sort of 'good man' who would always be there for her when she needed him most.

Having served most of his career in the Navy in submarines where one never told anybody anything about proverbial 'diddly squat', it was a joy to be on board the Kitty Hawk, and for the while at least, to be a part of the 'visible' Navy. This had enabled him to write back *admitting* that he was on the ship that he was *actually* on board, *actually* naming places he had been and even sharing one or two pieces of harmless service gossip about his *actual* duties.

"ADMIRAL ON DECK!"

Every man snapped to attention as Rear Admiral William Bringle strode down the avenue of officers accompanied by the Kitty Hawk's commanding officer, Captain Horace Epes.

Fifty-year-old Bringle had been the carrier's first captain, commissioning the Kitty Hawk three years ago to the day at the Philadelphia Navy Yard. The US Navy like to do things in style, and everybody in the compartment realised that on the commissioning anniversary there was a real possibility that the Commander of Carrier Division Seven might be about to make a big announcement of some kind.

"Stand easy, gentlemen."

There were over a hundred and seventy officers, forty percent of them naval aviators from the Kitty Hawk's Air Group, crushing into the Wardroom with latecomers arriving all the time, since the summons had been sudden and without any prior warning.

Bringle, the Tennessee born Commander of Carrier Division Seven had graduated from Annapolis in the class of 1937. His first ship had been the Saratoga; thereafter he had trained as a naval aviator at Pensacola. At the time of Pearl Harbour, he had been CO of Cruiser Scouting Squadron Two operating off the cruisers Omaha (CL-4) and Savannah (CL-42). Later in the Second World War he had been involved in the invasion of Southern France in 1944, and the latter stages of the Pacific War, flying off the escort carriers Wake Island (CVE-65) and Marcus Island (CVE-77). He was the holder of the Navy Cross, the Distinguished Flying Cross and the French Croix de Guerre, had been CAG – Commander Air Group – on the fleet carriers Tarawa (CV-40) and Philippine Sea (CV-47) before a spell as Executive Officer of the Hornet (CV-12) in 1953. Successively Head of the Operational Intelligence Branch of the Chief of Naval Operations Staff and then Personal Aide to the Secretary of the Navy; he had been a shoe-in to command the Kitty Hawk in 1961, and his promotion to Rear Admiral in 1962 just before the October War, inevitable.

Walter Brenckmann had learned to recognise the *type*, the sort of driven, utterly competent, reliable leaders of men who naturally gravitated to the top of the service. Brindle was one of *those guys*. When he entered a room, everybody knew he had arrived; and when he was about to say something you knew, you just knew, that you needed to be listening with every sinew of your being.

The Commander of Carrier Division Seven took the microphone.

"I'll keep this short and sweet, gentlemen," he declared. "You will have heard the Commander-in-Chief's address to the nation last weekend in which he outlined the Administration's 'America First' foreign and military stance under which the strategic interests of the homeland, and specifically the defence of and the economic wellbeing of the Union will heretofore be the primary 'guiding light' of the remaining months of President Kennedy's term in office. In the last twenty-four hours the Navy Department has issued the following orders to all ships and sea and shore establishments."

Walter Brenckmann wondered if he was about to hear that the 'peace dividend' U-turn was about to be reversed, again. That the Navy was to halt its re-mobilization and that the big carriers and cruisers were *not* after all to be retrieved from mothballs and sent back to sea. It would be the ultimate betrayal of the service but not entirely any kind of surprise given recent history.

"This is to inform all serving personnel in the US Navy that the ships listed for return to service under ordnance January/Re-activation/010364 will return to service as per the plans drawn up by the Department."

Okay, there was going to be no immediate U-turn.

"Operations. General. All ships at sea and shore establishments will assume the lowest state of alert DEFCON FIVE until further notice or unless specifically warned to assume a higher state of readiness."

The Administration had had a big bust up with the British over what was going on in the Middle East but nobody was reaching for their guns right now. Walter Brenckmann breathed a silent sigh of relief.

"Ongoing operations. Subject: Naval Operations against forces of the former Soviet Union and or, affiliated or co-belligerent forces. In the Mediterranean Sea current rules of engagement remain unchanged; that is, US Sixth Fleet will continue its peace keeping mission in support of the British Royal Navy and may at discretion of CINCMED take such pre-emptive aggressive action as is necessary to protect Sixth Fleet ships and vessels in company with same."

Walter Brenckmann interpreted this somewhat tautological clause as giving CINCMED a license to shoot first and ask questions later; which seemed to completely fly in the face of everything the President had said in his broadcast about 'no more foreign adventures and AMERICA FIRST, SECOND, THIRD AND FOR ALWAYS!"

"The United States of America is not, repeat not at war with the Soviet Union. No officer in the US Armed Forces is authorised to initiate or to seek engagement with Soviet forces unless, or until it is, or is likely said US forces will be the target of direct Soviet aggression. While the customary rules of the sea and the right of all captains to defend their commands at need is unaffected by this constraint, the US Navy is not authorised to assume an aggressive posture against Soviet forces."

By now the Assistant Anti-Submarine Warfare officer of the flagship of Carrier Division Seven was glancing around to find out if he was the only man in the compartment who was starting to get a little confused. From the looks he got back he concluded that he was far from alone.

"Carrier Division Seven," Rear Admiral Bringle said jarringly. There was an edge in his voice because he was far from unaware of the changing, cooling mood in the compartment. *"Carrier Division Seven is directed to operate for a period of not less than thirty and not more than ninety days in the Indian Ocean. During that period Kitty Hawk and other ships will pay good will calls on Madras, Colombo in Ceylon, and Bombay. Depending on events in the Persian Gulf we may be required to protect US shipping and property, and to stand ready to provide humanitarian assistance in that region, and in an emergency to evacuate US citizens in theatre."*

The pitch of Rear Admiral Bringle's authoritative baritone fell as he finished reading from his prepared script.

"Carrier Division Seven is *not* operating under the rules of engagement that apply in the Mediterranean. The ships under my command will treat any United Kingdom forces encountered with strict *neutrality*."

A man behind Walter Brenckmann cursed under his breath.

"I don't fucking believe this crap!"

Others picked up and echoed the same sentiments.

The fleet commander's uncompromising bark instantly quashed the chorus of discontent before it could spread around the compartment.

"Gentlemen! The Commander-in-Chief has spoken. It is not for anybody on board any ship of Carrier Division Seven to question the President's orders. We have been given our mission and woe betide any man under my command who does not discharge his duty. Officers under my command are responsible for carrying out *my* orders. Every man in this compartment swore to honour the flag and to obey the orders of the Commander-in-Chief. It is not for us to ask the reason why; we live to serve."

Normally, there would have been a mutter of agreement.

Today there was just the barely perceptible motion of the great ship under one's feet, the soft swishing of the air conditioning fans, the distant rumbling of the huge Westinghouse turbines deep in the bowels of the Kitty Hawk and the muted scream of jet engines spooling up on the flight deck.

And a quietness of the soul that Walter Brenckmann had last experienced on the day after the night of the October War; when as the Torpedo Officer and Assistant Missile Officer of the USS Theodore Roosevelt (SSBN-600) he had been alone in the claustrophobic cabin he shared with the quartermaster officer in the hours after he had participated in the flushing of the boat's birds.

To this day he did not know where those birds had landed.

Nor did he ever want to know.

However, right now he was feeling a little bit sick in his stomach in much the same way he had been on that awful morning eighteen months ago in the hours after the USS Theodore Roosevelt had flushed her last bird.

Chapter 20

Tuesday 21st April 1964
Blenheim Palace, Woodstock, England

Her Majesty Queen Elizabeth the Second, by the Grace of God, of Great Britain, Ireland and the British Dominions beyond the Seas Queen, and Defender of the Faith had greeted the hero of the Battle of Malta and his wife with a rueful apology once the normal bowing and scraping had been got out of the way.

The Queen was seated in a high-backed chair supported by strategically placed cushions with her newly pinned and plastered left arm in a neatly fashioned blue linen sling, and her equally 'plastered' left ankle concealed beneath the long grey dress that covered her small frame from her neck to her feet.

"Do forgive me for not getting up to welcome you, Sir Peter and Lady Marija," she smiled. Prince Charles and Princess Anne had greeted the visitors to Blenheim Palace in lieu of their parents, Charles horribly shyly, Anne with eager curiosity. Their father, Prince Philip the Duke of Edinburgh had been waiting with their mother in the Library of the great house. The Queen's consort was haggard and prematurely aged and seated in a wheelchair beside the monarch; his eyes gleaming with bright interest and twinkling with fun now that he had finally been reunited with his family.

Peter Christopher had eventually found his voice.

"We are much relieved to find you so well after your ordeal, Ma'am," he forced out.

Both the Queen and her husband were viewing Marija with no little interest

"Your husband's father," Prince Philip explained to her, "was my Uncle Louis's protégé and later, his very good friend. I'm sure the old boy and Sir Julian – wherever they are now, bless them – are looking down on you and Peter here, patting each other on the back in pleasure to see you both together!"

The Queen had offered Peter her small hand and he had fearfully, terrified lest in his nervousness he should inadvertently crush it, taken it in his hand. Now he shook the Duke of Edinburgh's hand also. Marija, hopelessly tongue-tied and unaccountably, probably for the first time in her life a little awestruck, timidly offered her own hand to be shaken.

"I, we," she stuttered, "are honoured to be..."

"No, no, no," the Queen said lowly. "We've been so looking forward to meeting you both! The Prime Minister has told me all about Sir Peter's exploits," she explained, focusing on the nutmeg-haired, almond-eyed slim young Maltese woman who was patently overwhelmed by the occasion, desperately trying to put her at her ease. "And the exploits of your remarkable brave brother, of course, Lady Marija. I am right in thinking that you witnessed Sir Peter's ship leaving the Grand Harbour, while you were making your way to the Royal Naval Hospital at Bighi to offer your services?"

Marija was slowly getting used to the idea that Queen Elizabeth II was actually a human being rather than an unapproachable deity, and moreover, a mere woman like herself.

"My sister," she started to say, checked, corrected herself, "my sister-in-law Rosa and I, we knew we had to help."

Chairs had been drawn up for the royal teenagers and Peter and Marija disconcertingly close to the royal couple; soon fine china clinked musically and tea was being poured. Gradually, Marija's feet began to feel more securely *grounded* and her senses slowly settled to a new, anxious equilibrium.

The forthcoming 'Battle of Malta Parade' through Oxford to King's College ahead of the formal investiture initially rescheduled for that afternoon had been put back a further day to tomorrow. The Prime Minister's party had only returned from Philadelphia yesterday afternoon, and the Queen's physicians having previously demanded 'another day's grace' for the monarch at the weekend, Wednesday had been finally set in stone as the date for the 'party', as Alan Hannay now called the event.

The RAF C-130 Hercules transport which had brought Rosa and the woman Marija had formerly known as Clara Pullman back from Malta, had also brought home the greater part of the expensively fashionable trousseau of the late wife of a former Commander-in-Chief of the Mediterranean Fleet, Vice Admiral Sir Hugh Staveley-Pope. Lady Pamela Staveley-Pope who had been vacationing with friends in Villefranche-sure-Mer at the time of the October War had been two decades her husband's junior, and possessed of a figure not dissimilar to Marija's. Somebody had mentioned the existence of the trousseau, hung and boxed in the Verdala Palace, the official residence of the Governor of Malta, to Lady Patricia Harding-Grayson, Marija's self-appointed 'Oxford chaperone' and miraculously, the RAF had delivered the fantastic wardrobe to the college rooms of the flabbergasted young wife of the 'Hero of the Battle of Malta'.

Today Marija was wearing – at Pat Harding-Grayson's suggestion because she had had no idea what to wear to an 'audience' with *the Queen* – a silky calf-length beige frock that had probably cost more to buy than a nurse in either England or Malta earned in a year before the war!

"Joe Calleja was the real hero of the battle," her husband blurted.

"My brother has been in hospital in Cheltenham," Marija added hesitantly. "He was more badly wounded than we knew at the time but he is due to travel to Oxford this afternoon. I hope he is well enough for me to hug. Without thinking I hugged him the day after the battle and I think I nearly killed him..."

"Your parents must be very proud?" The Queen put to her.

"Yes. I have not seen them since before the battle. Everything was very confused after the fighting was over and then we came to England. I have written to them but they may not have got my letter yet."

Peter Christopher cleared his throat.

"We hope to travel back to Malta in the near future, Ma'am," he said, resigned to the fact this might not be possible for some time. His father's body was to be flown back to the United Kingdom later in the week; and a full State Funeral was being planned. "Marija lost a very dear friend, and members of Talavera's crew are buried on Malta. We never got a chance to say our farewells..."

That was when Marija had broken down and Peter had gone to her to wrap her in his arms. A footman and a lady in waiting had stepped forward; the Queen had waved them away.

Marija had sobbed.

Prince Charles and Princess Anne had stared at their feet; the Duke of Edinburgh had reached over and taken his wife's one unencumbered hand in his own. The Queen had waited patiently, serenely.

"Forgive me, Your Majesty," Marija sniffled, recovering a little of her poise. "Ma'am, I mean..."

"There is absolutely nothing to forgive, my dear," the Queen looked up and motioned for her children to make their exits. Soon the adults were alone.

Prince Philip had fixed Peter Christopher in his sights as the younger man resumed his seat.

"How was your first visit to the lost colonies?" He inquired, archly tongue-in-cheek much as if the two men were swapping tall stories in the wardroom of a destroyer.

"Short but not terribly sweet, sir."

In those brief spells when he had not been involved in the rancorous politicking of the – by any standards, disastrous Philadelphia Summit – the American media had been alternatively pushy, curious, and basically, in his thrall. While the political consequences of the comprehensively *broken* 'North Atlantic Alliance' had rumbled around him he had gone on the Ed Sullivan Show (broadcast for 'one night only' from downtown Philadelphia), later been frantically interviewed by at least half-a-dozen radio reporters, endured a torrid press conference at the British Embassy, and got spots in front of his eyes from being constantly photographed wherever he went.

"Actually," he explained, able now to view the experience with a slightly clearer perspective, "I think the people at the Ministry of Information made a mistake not letting Marija come with me. The American newspaper and TV people were constantly asking me when I'd be back with Marija."

The Queen sensed he was about to say more.

She waited.

"That was the oddest thing, Ma'am," Peter went on, "the newspaper and the TV people were interested in the Battle of Malta, and Marija, but they seemed either unaware of or completely indifferent to the Soviets invading Iran. Nobody over there really felt as if what was going on in the Middle East was anything to do with them. There was all this 'America First' song and dance; yet they assumed, took it completely for granted in fact, that *we* were still their best friends. As I say, it would have all been rather bizarre if it wasn't so worrying."

The Queen moved on, she was much better at small talk than either of her guests, and very aware that this audience was every bit as stressful for them as being under attack in Malta a little over two weeks ago.

"I'm informed that at least a hundred of your brave Talaveras and men from HMS Yarmouth will be marching tomorrow, Sir Peter?"

"Seventy-one Talaveras and forty-one Yarmouths, Ma'am. Because of the delay in holding the parade several of the walking wounded have sufficiently recovered to attend the investiture, and I believe that as many as fifty or so family members have been able to get to Oxford."

At this the Queen smiled.

"I confess that I have been very wicked," she confessed serenely.

"Very, my dear," Prince Philip agreed.

Peter and Marija exchanged baffled looks.

"I have been keeping secrets. Just before you arrived at Woodstock, I was notified that an RAF Comet carrying several prominent Maltese citizens had landed safely at Brize Norton," the Queen announced, effecting severity. "I am reliably informed that among their number there happens to be a certain Mr Peter Calleja and a certain Mrs Marija Calleja."

Marija rose unsteadily to her feet and was about to attempt to dance an ungainly jig when she recollected, belatedly where she was and who was watching.

And then she started to cry again.

Chapter 21

Brigadier Mirza Hasan Mostofi al-Mamaleki's family had been in the service of the Pahlavi dynasty since the early 1920s. A tall, handsome man in his early forties with a lovingly tended moustache in the old luxuriant style, wearing battlefield fatigues cut by his family's long dead Savile Row tailor which drew the eye to his lean, muscular frame he presented a haughty, unbending presence as he straightened to his full height when his guest was ushered into the half-wrecked office building.

The newcomer was like al-Mamaleki a tall man unencumbered by excess flesh, but unlike the Iranian he was of slighter build and of a thoughtful, scholarly mein and his creased uniform betrayed evidence that since the two men had last met, he had travelled far and wide.

The two officers saluted crisply.

Major General Michael Carver's stern physiognomy creased into a half-smile that spoke of many old soldiers' woes; and al-Mamaleki's expression briefly mirrored his friend's. They had first encountered each together many years ago at Sandhurst. Carver had been delivering a series of lectures – as a XXX Corps veteran of the Western Desert - offering an incisive, well-reasoned critique of the shortcomings, strengths, weaknesses and eventual victories of the British, and in those days, *Empire,* Generals who had overseen the Desert War. Afterwards they had corresponded occasionally, bumped into each other – literally, in Pall Mall, where al-Mamaleki was taking the airs while his wife supervised the suiting and booting of their twin sons ahead of their first term at St Paul's School – at oddly frequent intervals.

They shook hands.

"Isn't this a thing, Hasan?" The Englishman grimaced.

"Cannae?" The Iranian inquired softly, pleased and not a little relieved to see with his own eyes that his friend had returned to the desert, for they had both realised that the message and the advice he had taken back to Oxford from Abadan was the sort of thing that might have easily got him cashiered.

"By the leave of the Chiefs of Staff and the Secretary of State for Defence," Michael Carver confided lowly even though the two men had dismissed their respective staffs, "I was invited to put *our* plan before the Prime Minister. To cut a long story short – notwithstanding that I was brutally frank about the chances of actually pulling it off - *she* has given *Operation Lightfoot* her full support. The RAF and the Royal Navy have been directed to send every available aircraft and ship to the Gulf. Middle East Command has absolute priority for reinforcements and materiel, and a 'diplomatic offensive' is at this time being mounted to establish whether certain 'third parties' in the region might be prepared to participate in what as you and I appreciate only too well, is probably their only realistic hope of salvation."

The two men stepped back to study each other.

"What of the American weapons stores in Saudi Arabia?"

Al-Mamaleki's English had been learned in Hampshire while he was a pupil at Winchester College, preparatory to his time at Sandhurst. He spoke with a languid drawl only slightly impaired by an adult life spent mostly in or around the bases, depots, headquarters and palaces surrounding Tehran. Before he had assumed command of the 3rd Brigade, he had been a court insider, one of a small clique of 'personal' military advisors to the Shah. Another man would have regarded a field command as a demotion; not al-Mamaleki, the man considered by *outsiders* – that is, men outside the moribund, complacent hierarchy of the Iranian Army – to be the nation's finest 'tanker'. A known favourite of the Shah, his superiors had banished Mirza Hasan Mostofi al-Mamaleki to the distant south where he could 'play his tank games to his heart's content without bothering anybody else'. He was one of those officers whose self-evident gifts and effortless competency tended to perturb his elders and betters, whose very existence threatened the status quo and vexingly questioned established strategic preconceptions and long protected tactical shibboleths. He was a maverick, and worse he was a very charismatic maverick; his men loved him and nobody in the surviving Southern Command of the Iranian armed forces had thus far dared to gainsay anything he was doing in the critical 'Abadan Sector'. However, even al-Mamaleki was treading on thin ice operating so openly *alongside* the old 'Imperial Oppressors'.

No man knew this as keenly as Michael Carver.

"Entreaties will be made to the Kingdom of Saudi Arabia; more than that I do not know," he explained. "What I do know is that the assumption in England is that the Americans will stand on the side-lines." His expression became apologetic. "Forgive me, Hasan, I have not inquired after your wife and daughter. Are they safe in Isfahan?"

Al-Mamaleki nodded.

"Yes, the garrison has restored order in the city and re-opened the roads to the south and the east. The Russians have as yet made no attempt to probe south of Tehran. As we anticipated they continue to use the line of the Alborz Mountains to cover their southern flank. I have received reports that the Air Force is attempting to harry the enemy's supply lines," he shrugged, "but the Soviets have MiG-21s and our handful of *Yankee* Super Sabres are greatly outmatched. And in any event, we only have a handful of aircraft available at any one time, and to attack the Russian columns they must operate at the extreme limits of their endurance."

What remained of the Iranian High Command had begun demanding V-Bomber strikes – using conventional iron bombs – against the Soviet forces streaming through the mountains and investing Tabriz; but without fighter cover and at least the semblance of local air superiority nothing would persuade the RAF to risk its few remaining strategic assets just to 'block a few roads in the hills'.

Whatever Michael Carver privately thought of his RAF colleagues the last thing he wanted to do was to dissipate *any* of the 'assets' he possessed ahead of the coming crisis. Besides, like any sensible hangman he wanted his enemy to put his head in the noose before he kicked away the ground beneath his feet.

"For the time being we do what we can," he sympathised. "What of your 3rd Brigade?"

Al-Mamaleki grinned roguishly.

His pre-war 'brigade' of some eighty tanks and six thousand men had swelled into a widely dispersed force of approximately two hundred British-supplied Centurions and US Army cast-off M-48s, supported by some thirteen thousand men. The tanks and men under his command now equated to a large armoured 'division' supported by elements of two mechanised infantry brigades. It had been the 3rd Brigade that had – granted with timely British support - hurled back the Iraqi thrust into the holy soil of Persia a few miles north of where they now stood; and increasingly, it was a magnet for every man in the Iranian Army who actually wanted to fight. Whereas, other units in the south were suffering a death by a thousand cuts, afflicted by desertion and plummeting morale; Al-Mamaleki's command had become a rallying point.

"Give me the signal and I'll drive all the way to Baghdad, my friend."

The Englishman smiled and shook his head. They both knew that it was exactly this sort of reckless bravura that Marshal of the Soviet Union Hamazasp Khachaturi Babadzhanian was counting on to hammer home his current overwhelming tactical and strategic advantage.

"But then we'd be at war with Iraq as well," he observed. "Perhaps, if we could fight one war at a time, Hasan?"

Al-Mamaleki vented a laugh straight from the pit of his belly.

"True. The Russians will roll over *them* anyway!"

"Quite so." Michael Carver agreed, quietly hoping that the Iraqis would fight hard enough to blunt the Soviet spearheads rather than just surrendering en masse, gifting the invaders fleets of tanks and other vehicles to replace its own wastage. "I don't think the Red Army will linger long in the north once it breaks out of the mountains. If I was in command of the Iraqi Army, Heaven forefend, I would draw the invaders into a battle of attrition for control of Sulaymaniyah. Sulaymaniyah is the key to the north; the place to bleed the Soviets dry."

"It will never happen!" The Iranian Brigadier grunted. "The Sunnis will leave the Kurds to their fate and the Shias of the south will watch and wait, and see what happens. That is the Iraqi way. Of course, if I drove towards Baghdad somebody in Iran would put a knife in my back for going to help the Sunnis." This he said philosophically, half in mordant jest. "For all its troubles Iran is a real country, the old Persian bonds bind us together even though we don't all talk a common language and we've been ruled over by usurpers and pretenders for most of the last forty years. The blood of Cyrus the great, Darius and Xerxes runs through my veins, and the history of a mighty empire is in my soul in the way the ghosts of Babylon *ought to* but never will run in the veins of *those* people across the Zagros Mountains!"

One of al-Mamaleki's great uncles had been Prime Minister of Iran over fifty years ago, his elder brother, one of the Shah's ministers had gone missing in the capital at the start of the invasion; assassinated or simply consumed in the nuclear strike which had obliterated seven-tenths of Tehran. He was of the ruling class and everything he did, and every attitude he held reflected as much.

Michael Carver understood that if the day came when his friend's tanks stood astride the Basra to Baghdad road then nothing short of a new bloodbath was going to remove them. If *their* grand strategy came to fruition, they would be re-drawing the map of the Middle East for a generation or more. Whether their political masters understood this was a moot point; in any event, it was hard to think of any likely consequence being remotely as bad as leaving Red Army tanks in command of the northern shores of the Persian Gulf threatening the whole of Arabia.

They could talk about 'Cannae', double envelopment and a crushing victory for ever and a day but nothing could actually obscure the reality of their situation. They were outnumbered ten to one and al-Mamaleki's 'brigade' supported by the Commonwealth garrison of Abadan was presently the only significant 'allied' force between Suez and Hong Kong. The huge war stores depots in Saudi Arabia were in the wrong place and it did not matter how many infantrymen could be flown into the Middle East from the British Isles, the Mediterranean and Australasia, without another armoured force at least as large as al-Mamaleki's command to hand there could be no modern-day Cannae anywhere, let alone somewhere on the flood plains of the Tigris and the Euphrates between Basra and Baghdad.

"I think you're wrong, Hasan," Michael Carver offered cautiously. "Some of the Iraqi Army units will fight. Maybe not in the north but around Baghdad, possibly, and certainly before Najaf and Nasiriyah; moreover, above Basra in the marshlands the Soviet's lines of advance will hit any number of pinch points. Even local insurgencies will take their toll."

"Ah, ever the strategist, Michael!"

The older man smiled.

"For my sins. But," he sighed, "you and I both know that the ground is the ground. Mesopotamia was the death of a British army not so many decades ago; it may well be again for another invader. The mere mention of places like Kut and Amarah and Basra still make old soldiers blanch. What has been will be again. If I had honestly believed I wouldn't have been laughed out of court, I might have had the courage to suggest to my masters that," he shrugged, "a solid case could be made for letting the Russians have Iraq and letting them stew in their own juices. Give it five or ten years and they'll choke on Iraq; just like everybody else has from time immemorial!"

His Iranian friend gave him a quizzical look.

"If that happened the whole region would be on fire in the end."

"Perhaps," Michael Carver conceded. It was academic, anyway. There was nothing he could do to stop the Red Army swallowing the poisoned fruit of Iraq whole, except, for the time being, initiating the process of erosion. "But everything *will* be different, even if we win, Hasan."

The other man guffawed and patted his shoulder.

"*Different* is a lot better than *defeat*, my friend."

Chapter 22

The Right Honourable Airey Middleton Sheffield Neave, the Member of Parliament for Abingdon and the recently appointed Secretary of State for National Security in the Unity Administration of the United Kingdom, invariably paused for thought when he came across his former protégé, Margaret Thatcher in her full war paint; especially, on those days when it was readily apparent that the lady had got out of bed that morning with a bee in her bonnet. He knew his friend the Prime Minister must still be in discomfort – sometimes excruciating pain in fact – from the back injury she had suffered at Brize Norton but nobody who did not know her well would have noticed anything amiss. She was quite simply, magnificent. Today she was positively glowing and the light of battle glistened in her steely blue eyes.

"Why Airey, this is a pleasant surprise!"

It was said with a brisk, business-like curtness that a stranger would have interpreted as dismissive. However, Airey Neave knew the Angry Widow too well to make that mistake.

They were alone in the Cabinet Room where Margaret Thatcher was rifling through a red dispatch box, eager not to waste a single moment before her day became totally subsumed by the twice delayed celebration for the deliverance of the Battle of Malta.

Airey Neave approached and was invited to pull up a chair.

"I thought you'd like to know that the boys back in Cheltenham are beginning to 'read' *Jericho*," he announced very, very quietly. "They're still working on selected older intercepts, obviously," he went on, smugly, "but we're also *reading* stuff that's less than thirty-six hours old now."

Margaret Thatcher had looked up in the middle of a document.

She nodded, returned briefly to the page in her hands.

Presently, she smoothed the sheet on the table before her and gave her friend her full and undivided attention. GCHQ – the Government Communications Headquarters – at Cheltenham would have been 'into' *Jericho* even sooner but for two unfortunate happenstances. Firstly, MI5 had locked up four key directors of that organisation – including the legendary Chief Cryptanalyst Hugh Alexander – because they had had the temerity to attempt to communicate to her that GCHQ was, due to mismanagement, lack of prioritisation and resources, in a dangerously parlous state. And secondly, because the aircraft carrying the priceless cache of cipher books and manuals seized by HMS Alliance's boarding party from the captured Turkish destroyer *Mareşal Fevzi Çakmak*, had been shot down by an Irish Republican Army terrorist using an XM41 Redeye Block I shoulder launched surface-to-air missile as it attempted to land at RAF Cheltenham on Monday 6th April.

Until the weekend before that atrocity and the heinous outrage at Brize Norton, when the aircraft bringing the Allied Supreme Commander Mediterranean (Designate), General Keith 'Johnny' Johnson and his Staff to Europe, had also been shot down by a Redeye missile smuggled to the IRA from a supposedly 'secure US Army facility in Virginia', and very nearly killed herself and *the Queen*, Margaret Thatcher had in hindsight been almost completely in the dark about the United Kingdom's proud history of code breaking. She had known nothing about the 'secret' lineage of GCHQ, nor remotely comprehended the magnitude of the unspeakably bad things that happened to a country in the modern world, if it lowered or neglected its cryptographic guard for a single second.

Jericho was the *only* thing that gave her hope for the future.

It had been the existence of *Jericho* – not her incandescent rage that the IRA had been permitted to perpetrate two such *atrocities* on English soil and very nearly kill the Queen – which had moved her to sack the Director General of MI5, Sir Roger Hollis, and to create Airey Neave's Ministry of National Security.

The calculus was very simple; Hollis had put several of the kingdom's finest code breakers in prison so as to sidestep embarrassing questions about the shortcomings of the security services; therefore, he had had to go.

Jericho had almost been lost because of the failings of MI5; and even after the precious cargo of cryptographic gold dust had been recovered, because of MI5's incompetence since the October War there had been a wholly unnecessary delay in 'getting into it'.

Sir Roger Hollis was lucky he was only under house arrest.

It had been Airey Neave and Tom Harding-Grayson who had accompanied the Home Secretary, Roy Jenkins, to her rooms at King's College on the night before the abominations at Brize Norton and Cheltenham to *acquaint* her with the 'affair of the Cheltenham four' - who had been unjustly incarcerated at Her Majesty's Prison Gloucester by MI5 - and the true story of Great Britain's glorious past age of cryptographic pre-eminence. Even now two-and-a-half weeks later every time she thought about that evening her mind turned somersaults of astonishment and bewilderment at the secret history that incredibly, nobody had thought to tell her about until *that* moment.

Nobody, that was, apart from four GCHQ departmental heads whose warning letter had been intercepted by MI5! Airey Neave had handed her the letter with the words 'you will have a lot of questions you need to ask after you have read this, Margaret'.

That had proved to be something of an understatement much along the lines of *'the cataclysm of the October War was a little bit unfortunate'*.

'Why on earth have I never heard about Bill Welchman and Alan Turing?' She had demanded. Thereafter, the story had emerged at a rush. To her surprise Airey Neave – whom she had always known had never really detached himself from his wartime, 1939-45, Special

Operations Executive and MI6 'friends' – had deferred to the Foreign Secretary, whom *she* had *never* realised had had any kind of past history with the intelligence services.

Tom Harding-Grayson had started talking about the people who had broken the German codes and practically won the war!

'Sit down, Margaret,' he had suggested. 'This will all come as a bit of a shock to you and yes, we ought to have had this little chat before now but well, so much has been going on and the sort of secrets we're about to discuss are *not* really the sort of thing any of us *ever* thought we'd *ever* divulge to *anybody*.'

Airey Neave had chuckled at this point.

'Not without somebody holding a gun at our heads,' he remarked.

Completely flummoxed and somewhat vexed she had scowled at the two men.

'Well, if it would help, I'll called in my AWPs so that they can hold guns to both your heads?"

Neither of her visitors had been entirely convinced that she was joking; and neither man doubted that had she asked her Royal Marine bodyguards – who took immense pride in styling themselves the *Angry Widow's Praetorians* - to put guns to their heads that they would have hesitated for a single second.

Tom Harding-Grayson had tried to paint a picture.

'There were four *wicked uncles*,' he had explained. 'Bill Welchman and Alan Turing, and Hugh Alexander and Stuart Milner-Barry; together they formed what one might call the *brains trust* that broke *Enigma*.'

'Enigma?' She had asked impatiently, not in any kind of mood to be subjected to a pointless history lesson about a war long won.

'*Enigma*,' the Foreign Secretary had echoed. 'The Germans used an electro-mechanical cipher machine called *Enigma* which was so fiendishly proficient at encoding their communications that they, the Germans, never once during the war considered the possibility that anybody could *break* it. You see, a message enciphered using an Enigma machine could be converted into a plain text in which every character of every message could be encoded in billions of different ways. To cut a long story short the four *Wicked Uncles* first broke the *Wehrmacht Enigma*, then they broke the even more fiendishly complicated *Kriegsmarine U-boat Enigma*, and then they helped the Americans to break the *Japanese* equivalent to *Enigma*, the supposedly unbreakable *JN-25 code*. In so doing, the *Wicked Uncles* practically invented two entirely new *sciences*; the science of *Traffic Analysis* and the science of *Electrical Computing*. Alan Turing was also interested in a thing call *AI*, that's *Artificial Intelligence* to simpletons like you. But that's a whole story in itself.'

First Airey Neave had spoken of 'Bill Welchman'. William Gordon 'Bill' Welchman had been thirty-three in 1939. He was a Marlborough schooled Trinity College mathematician who had been Dean of Sidney Sussex College, Cambridge. Alan Mathison Turing was twenty-seven at the start of Hitler's war, an old boy of Sherbourne College who had at the tender age of twenty-two been elected a fellow of King's College Cambridge for his proof of something called the 'Central Limit Theorem'. Thirty-two-year-old Stuart Milner-Barry had become a city stockbroker after winning Firsts in Classics and Moral Sciences at Trinity College, Cambridge. As long ago as 1923 he had won the first British Boys' Chess Championship and from 1932 onwards, he had represented England at chess. The fourth *Wicked Uncle* was Irish-born Conel Hugh O'Donel Alexander, aged thirty in 1939, who like his friend Stuart Milner-Barry was a former Trinity College man and an international class chess player. Before the war he had taught mathematics at Winchester College.

Earlier that year that idiot Hollis and his blundering underlings had arrested Hugh Alexander – one of the men who won the Second World War – for having had the courage to attempt to inform *her* that all was not well at GCHQ!

'Bill Welchman ran Hut Six,' Tom Harding-Grayson had explained. 'Hut Six was in the business of attacking the German Army's Enigma and *Traffic Analysis*.'

The Prime Minister had looked blank.

'Traffic Analysis is what you do with the plain language part of every transmission,' Airey Neave had offered, trying and failing to be helpful.

Tom Harding-Grayson had given him a look which asked: 'Who is telling this story? You or me?'

Having settled this issue, the Foreign Secretary had ploughed on regardless.

'The only plain language parts of any given Enigma message – or of practically *any* intercept – are the *FROM* and the *TO* components, although to a casual observer these also will also seem like apparently meaningless codes. However, once Bill Welchman and his people had worked out, for example that WA58Z was the Third Panzer Grenadier Regiment of the Second Panzer Division, and a simple signal triangulation exercise established that it was mostly broadcasting from the vicinity of say, Amiens, Bill's people *owned* WA58Z forever. For example, by the time of the Dunkirk fiasco at the end of May 1940 Hut Six had deduced the complete – and I do mean *complete* – German order of battle in the West. So, before we had actually *broken* a single Enigma message, Bill Welchman was able to pick up the phone and tell the powers that be *not* to worry about carrying on fighting the Battle of France because we had *already lost it*. Fortunately, that was just in the nick of time for the Navy to start pulling what was left of the British Expeditionary Force off the beaches of Dunkirk. Consequently, Winston Churchill did not get thrown out of Downing Street in early June 1940 and, eventually, *we* won the war.'

The Foreign Secretary had not worried overly if he was teaching his Prime Minister to 'suck eggs'. It was critically important that she understood exactly what HMS Alliance had captured on the *Mareşal Fevzi Çakmak*.

'*Traffic Analysis* tells one where and what one's enemy is

'physically' doing; where his forces are deployed, his state of readiness and consequently where one's own defences are the most vulnerable. It also tells one where the best place to attack him has been in the past, and might be again in the future. Traffic Analysis is so vital that frankly, without it and the 'complete picture' it gives you of the enemy's strength and dispositions it is immaterial whether one can, or cannot *read* his coded radio transmissions. Bill Welchman, a certifiable genius by any measure, was the first man to understand this and to put his 'big idea' into practice. Military intelligence, all intelligence in fact, is about *context*. *Facts* tell you nothing in the absence of *context*; incidentally, that's a common journalistic, academic and political misunderstanding!'

Margaret Thatcher had been positively rapt by this stage.

'Alan Turing?' She had asked.

'If Bill Welchman was a certifiable genius, I hardly know where to begin with Alan. Alan Turing ran Hut Eight. Hut Eight's job was to crack the U-boat Enigma. SHARK. Turing was a truly remarkable fellow. After the war he was on the short list for the British Team at the London Olympics for the marathon, he was still one of the top five or six long-distance runners in the country even though he would have been in his mid-thirties by then. Turing was the man who designed the first electro-magnetic machine, 'a computer', to speed up the code-breaking process. He was *the* master logician who had sat down and worked out, in his own head, how such a machine would work, built it, eventually got it to work and basically won the Battle of the Atlantic. Granted, albeit with a little bit of help from the Royal Navy. We had had some early success reading SHARK in 1941 and 1942 but then the bloody Germans started using an extra 'rotor' on the naval version of the Enigma machine and breaking SHARK became exponentially more problematic. It was Bill Welchman, who by 1943 was in charge of mechanisation at Bletchley Park, as well as being the poor chump who was responsible for liaising with the Americans, who actually designed a modification to Turing's code-breaking machine – his *bombe* – that speeded things up so efficiently that we could start reading SHARK again. Bill Welchman and Alan Turing became the 'big men' at Bletchley later in the war; with Milner-Barry and Hugh Alexander respectively taking over the running of Hut Six and Eight from about 1943 onwards.'

Margaret Thatcher had been burning with questions.

'What happened to *The Wicked Uncles*? Apart from Hugh Alexander, I mean?'

Airey Neave had picked up the story at this point.

'Poor Turing was driven to suicide in 1954. The local police in Manchester persecuted him because he was a known homosexual and nobody in authority who knew anything of his exemplary wartime service raised a finger to help him. The whole affair was a disgrace. Bad show all round.'

'Oh, and what about Welchman and Milner-Barry?'

'Bletchley Park was comprehensively dismantled after the war. A pale, penny-pinching shadow of the wartime Government Code and Cipher School was set up at Eastcote in Middlesex in 1946 but GCHQ, again in a parsimonious sort of way, wasn't established in Cheltenham until the early 1950s. Stuart Milner-Barry joined the Treasury in 1946, I think. He was an Under-Secretary by the time of the October War. He went missing the night of the war. Bill Welchman got so fed up with the penny-pinching of the Atlee Government that he moved to the United States in 1948. The last I heard he had become an American citizen and he was a top man in the National Security Agency in Virginia.'

And now after a gap of over eighteen long, lost years, GCHQ and one of the legendary *Wicked Uncles* – Hugh Alexander - who had won the Second World War, was back in business reading *Jericho*.

Airey Neave was smiling like a Cheshire cat.

The Prime Minister could not but help ask herself how much pain and grief might have been averted if governments of the day had built on, instead of throwing away everything that Bletchley Park had achieved in the seventeen lost years between the end of Hitler's war and the disaster of the October War?

"I hope you're not trying to keep me in suspense, Airey?" Margaret Thatcher half-asked, half-cautioned her friend as she focused on the here and the now.

"I wouldn't dream of it, Margaret." The Secretary of State for National Security was having trouble stifling a chuckle. "One of the first intercepts we fully decrypted was from the forward HQ of the Red Army's 10th Guards Tank Division describing a series of attacks on its columns along the road from Mahabad to Piranshahr by *guerrillas*. It seems the division's movement schedule has been put back between four and five days and a whole mechanised corps is backing up along the road all the way back to Qushachay and Malekan!"

"Guerrillas?"

"Yes. If I didn't know better, I'd start thinking the Red Army is getting acquainted with my old chum Lieutenant-Colonel Francis Harold St John Waters, VC, rather better than they'd like."

Margaret Thatcher looked at her former mentor with more than a tincture of incredulity in her eyes.

"Surely one man can't possibly be responsible for holding up a whole tank division for five days, Airey?"

"Ah, well, that's the thing," the man guffawed cheerfully, "if what's going on in those mountain passes between Mahabad and Piranshahr is really Frank Waters's work, there's no way he's going to be satisfied holding up just *one* division for *just* five days, Margaret!"

Chapter 23

Wednesday 22nd April 1964
Sarukani, Lahijan-e Sharqi District, Iran

It was the sort of country where the only place you could hide was in plain sight. Nevertheless, it was beautiful country, especially at this time of year when the winter wind no longer blew and the heat of the mid-day sun was yet to sear the flesh of exposed faces and limbs red brown. Like an old soldier anywhere and from any age, Lieutenant-Colonel Francis Harold St John Waters, VC, was always thankful for small mercies.

Behind the groaning, pitching and rolling old Ford six-wheeler they had 'requisitioned' in Mahabad four days ago the sooty black mushroom of smoke rising from the burning carcass of the T-62 slowly drifted downwind on the breeze falling off the sheer-sided mountains on the northern rim of the valley. In the seconds after the huge detonation – a little less than half-a-mile away - all the other vehicles in the column had halted, Red Army officers had jumped out and stared back. The numerous local villagers caught up in the monumental traffic jam had started hitting their horns; oddly, the Russians still seemed to be under orders not to do anything to alienate the civilian population, a thing that came hard to most Soviet soldiers.

Frank Waters could see how much the Russian rank and file wanted to start shooting the grubby old men and women who peered into their trucks as if they were inspecting cattle sent to market. The invaders wanted to start taking hostages, making 'examples' but somebody at the top had had the common sense to not compound his present difficulties by inciting a general guerrilla insurgency along the whole length of his chaotic lines of communication. In this sort of country every household had a long rifle of indeterminate vintage in a cupboard; in this sort of country somebody was always feuding with somebody else and if people got shot well, that was just the way things were. In country like this, two or three men with rifles could block the Mahabad to Piranshahr road at any point between here and the border with Iraq.

Frank Waters and his small gang of SAS cut-throats and brigands had come across the T-62 by the side of the narrow road along the side of the valley. To the right of the road was the rubble of burned-out hovels and a path leading to the foothills of near vertical mountain slopes, to the left a pattern of fields, flat on the flood plain of the valley running into the hazy south east.

The tank had shed a track and been bulldozed off the road; its three-man crew had been easy to *deal with* in the dark as they slept around the embers of the small fire they had cooked their rations on the previous evening.

A man never called out if you cut his throat the *right way*. Hauling the beggars up into the turret had been harder than Frank

Waters had expected; an indication that he and his boys were not exactly in tip top physical shape anymore. Never mind, the turret had probably been blown a hundred feet in the air when the improvised demolition charges went off in amongst the 115-millimetre rounds stored below the dead gunner's knees...

It was a pity the T-62 had been short of fuel.

Another fifty or sixty gallons of fuel would have made a nice *fireball* and taken out more than just the half-a-dozen nearest vehicles when the demolition charges lit off. Still, one could not have everything.

Frank Waters's stolen Spetsnaz fatigues were filthy, his unshaven face was so grimy he would have looked like a native of these parts had he wrapped a blanket around himself. It was the dirtiness and the fact of his fortnight-long unkemptness that made it so easy to blend in with the Red Army. The invaders were already filthy, tired, angry and because of the incompetence of their quartermasters, hungry. The roads down which provisions, fuel and ammunition were supposed to flow were blocked with stalled columns, and nobody had either predicted the inevitable bottlenecks, or possessed the native gumption to do anything about it.

Of course, his own modest *interventions* and *mischief-making* had somewhat exacerbated the Red Army's difficulties but honestly, whoever imagined he could drive hundreds of tanks and supporting vehicles down roads like these without one, destroying the roads, and two, creating the world's worst traffic jam ought to be shot!

"Shit!" Muttered the driver sidelong under his breath. "Those boys up ahead have got KGB patches on their collars, boss!"

Frank Water's did not hesitate.

"Everybody out! Piss break!"

This said he kicked open the passenger door to the cab of the ancient Ford and dropped stiffly to the ground. He made a big play of stretching and yawning, pulling his forage cap on and off and scratching his head as his men and the driver gathered along the hill side of the truck, ostensibly to relieve themselves, as he watched the approaching Red Army policemen. Unlike the fighting soldiers upon whom they preyed like a parasitic infestation, these fellows were spotlessly clean, immaculately turned out and pinkly well fed. Big men hefting freshly oiled Kalashnikovs.

Frank Waters contemplated reaching for his Makarov pistol.

No, bad idea!

He stepped up to the nearest KGB man.

"Chto yebat' proiskhodit, tovarishch?" He bawled angrily.

What the fuck is going on, Comrade?

"Identiy dokumenty, tovarishch kapitan," the man demanded doggedly.

Identity papers, Comrade Captain.

Lieutenant-Colonel Francis Harold St John Waters, VC, of Her Majesty's 22nd Special Air Service Regiment treated this demand with the disdain he normally reserved exclusively for cavalry officers.

"Go fuck yourself!" He yelled in the man's face. "And salute a superior fucking officer, you miserable little shit!"

The other man, an NCO with a flat oriental face who obviously could not tell the difference between a Moskva or a Kazakh accent – Water's knew he sometimes flipped between different accents when he shouted at somebody in Russian – flinched and thought about raising the muzzle of his Kalashnikov.

"Where's your commanding officer? And why the fuck aren't you shitheads doing something about this fucking snarl up?"

As an aside the scarecrow SAS man waved for his men to get back into the truck.

Now that they had had a look around and knew what they were up against they needed their guns.

Frank Waters eyed the sky; it was still two hours to full darkness. This was going to get very, very bloody he thought to himself as the NCO's commanding officer, a weasel-faced Senior Lieutenant strutted between the lorries and armoured personnel carriers trapped on the winding dust road to the west.

The veteran SAS man took one look at the man and knew he was not about to talk his way out of this particular fix.

He heard his men dropping down to the ground behind him; and the clicks of firing pins. His four surviving troopers all had loaded Kalashnikovs. Thus far he had seen eight or nine KGB men – although there would be more nearby -plus the officer heading towards him.

These roving KGB 'police squads' were usually fifteen to twenty strong.

Fifteen or twenty of these bully boys against five SAS men; okay, that was a fair enough fight.

The real problem was going to be the other thousand or so Red Army soldiers stuck on this stretch of road within a few hundred yards of where he stood. Well, after they stopped cheering and spitting on the corpses of the dead KGB men on the ground, anyway.

Frank Waters gazed one more time across the valley to the grey-black mountains beyond. The green of the valley floor contrasted against the darkness of the rising ground, the patchwork quilt of fields and irrigation ditches had probably not changed for hundreds of years. Alexander the Great might have ridden through this pass once, likewise the legions of Darius and Xerxes, the Safavids, the Ottomans and latterly, the sad Pahlavis had each tried to imprint their marks upon this land. When the soldiers had passed through things always went back to the way they had been before, as if nothing had ever happened. No matter how frenetically great men kicked up the dust of history, it settled again sooner or later, burying their footsteps.

"All right! All right!" He complained testily. "I'll give you my fucking identity documents!"

He sighed as he reached back into the cab of the truck and his hand closed around the butt of the Makarov pistol.

There was a roaring in his ears.

Bloody tinnitus!

Except it was not tinnitus.

What's that infernal screeching sound?

One moment Frank Waters was standing up on his hind legs idly wondering why he had not been shot yet and the next he was scrabbling under the Ford six-wheeler; and around him was absolute bedlam.

Absolute, fiery bedlam...

The insane, ear-rending scream was inside his head and all around him.

The first jet flew so low over the stationary column that its engine kicked up a giant rooster's plume of dirt and dust. Anybody who had not hit the ground and tried to get off the road or under cover was already dead and dying by then. Thirty yards behind the Ford truck a Napalm canister bloomed and its deadly modern version of Greek fire billowed and boiled down the road.

The second jet dropped another Napalm bomb as it rocketed down the valley from north to south.

There were further explosions, time seeming to elongate, the flashes of fire and the hammering of guns was suddenly deafening.

And in the aftermath; there was absolute silence.

Utter, ear-splitting silence in that horrible moment before the groans and the screams of the dying and the terribly maimed, filled every corner of Frank Waters's shocked conscious mind.

Chapter 24

Wednesday 22nd April 1964
Blenheim Palace, Woodstock, England

Captain Sir Peter Christopher, VC sipped the sickly-sweet fizzy wine – it seemed there was no Champagne left nowadays – as the 'gala reception' for the heroes of the Battle of Malta went on around him. He was feeling tired and a little light headed but strangely optimistic about...*everything* really. This was 'odd' given that the country was going to the dogs in a hand basket, the Americans seemed to have wiped their hands of their international commitments and practically everybody assumed that the Middle Eastern oil tap was about to be turned off forever; and all things considered there was not actually, on the face of it very much to be 'optimistic' about.

Like a prize idiot he had assumed Marija's queasy tummy and lack of appetite was probably to do with the change in the climate and the blandness of the food here in Oxford. She was a child of the sunshine and accustomed to the vegetable and fish rich diet of her native Maltese Archipelago. They had been so busy since they arrived in England – he had been away on the trip to Philadelphia – and what with all the events they had attended, the attention from the newspapers, the radio and the television people, he had thought it entirely to be expected that Marija would need a little time to acclimatise.

He was a prize idiot...

'Husband,' Marija had explained with shy patience when he had asked her, for the umpteenth time that morning, *how she was feeling* after she had rushed to the bathroom to be sick, 'I am not nervous. I am looking forward to the parade and the awarding of the medals to *all my brave Talaveras*. My sickness is to be expected. It is nothing for you to worry about. This I know because I am a midwife, yes?'

He had blinked at his wife like *a prize idiot*.

'Oh,' the penny had still not completely dropped.

Entirely on account of the fact that he was a prize idiot of the first order...

So Marija had had to explain further.

'It is very early but I am pregnant, husband.'

His wife's almond brown eyes had lowered momentarily and then she had sniffed, tears forming.

'There's no doubt?' He had blurted, like *a prize idiot*.

'No,' she had confirmed patiently. 'I am a midwife, remember?'

Instantly, he had worried about his wife spending most of the coming long day on her feet, and started looking around for several yards of cotton wool with which to wrap his beautiful princess for the next however many months it took to produce their *daughter*.

Marija was quietly, implacably insistent that their baby would be a *girl*.

Peter Christopher liked to think he was the most rational, scientific of men but if his wife said their child was a girl, who was he to argue? Marija said she had known she was carrying their daughter from the day of the Battle of Malta; before that she had only 'suspected' it. She had told him this news with seraphic certainty and even *a prize idiot* like him knew better than to press her. It seemed that Rosa, her sister-in-law, soon to be married to Alan Hannay – Peter's father's former Flag Lieutenant and briefly, Talavera's Purser and Supply Officer – had already been let in on 'the secret'.

Rosa was a little shorter than Marija, a shapely, dark-haired woman in her mid-twenties with smiling eyes that belied the dark secrets that she, Marija and Peter were sworn to keep to themselves for the rest of their natural lives.

For Rosa, the execution of her traitorous husband had been a merciful release from a desperately unhappy marriage, and summarily resolved the long weeks of doubt and suspicion following Samuel Calleja's disappearance at the time of the sabotaging of HMS Torquay in the Grand Harbour. She had been ostracised by her own parents, been the object of a vicious whispering campaign only halted when Marija had publicly stood by her. In retrospect Peter had discovered that his father had put down a smokescreen of misinformation to protect Rosa, Marija and him, and the reputation of the Royal Navy, and to 'disappear' the traitor Samuel Calleja from history. His execution – as an *unknown enemy soldier guilty of war crimes against the Maltese people* - by firing squad at Paola Prison on the morning Peter and Marija had flown to England had completed the process of expunging his memory. In due course human remains would be discovered in the wreck of HMS Torquay, whose broken bow and stern sections still lay beneath the waters of the Grand Harbour; and those remains would subsequently be solemnly identified by reference to dental records as those of Marija's older sibling, and the case would be closed, forever...

Peter Christopher realised he was wool-gathering.

Admiral Sir Varyl Begg, the man who had stepped into the late Sir David Luce's shoes as First Sea Lord was standing directly in front of the 'Hero of the Battle of Malta'.

The younger man suspected that he was about to be taken into the confidence of the man who was, if not 'God' then God's chosen representative in the Admiralty. In a crowded room filled with a hundred conversations there was an unlikely privacy; an opportunity to communicate important matters without fuss, bother or any of the normal constraints of rank and position. In other words, this was an ideal moment to have a short, to the point, man to man *talk*.

"Sir Peter's father and I never really hit it off," the First Sea Lord confessed to Marija, who was literally, hanging off her husband's arm while viewing him with a beatifically sunny smile as she inclined her head to listen very, very closely to every word he was about to say. "But he was undoubtedly the Navy's finest 'fighting admiral'." Sir Varyl Begg grimaced. "He will be sadly missed. Notwithstanding, that is, Sir Peter is a man cast from exactly the same mold!"

"Very good of you to say so, sir," Peter muttered, reflecting for the thousandth time that day how much easier it had been conning Talavera into the mouths of huge Russian naval rifles, than it was being compelled to present a sitting target for an endless barrage of compliments.

"How do you two feel about a two-year tour of duty in the lost colonies?" The First Sea Lord inquired wryly.

The question momentarily bewildered the tall young naval officer and his nutmeg-haired wife; both of whom peered quizzically at the older man for several seconds.

"I have come to the conclusion that your husband has fought quite enough battles for the time being, Lady Marija," the First Sea Lord explained sternly. "Things in the Persian Gulf may or may turn out as badly as we fear they might. Whatever happens *out there* or in the South Atlantic, or wherever else in the World fresh disasters and tribulations occur in the future, diplomacy and the business of the Navy will continue. Life continues and it so happens that the political and the naval consensus is that Sir Peter needs to be kept as far away as possible from the sound of guns." He smiled ruefully. "If only because whenever he hears the sound of distant artillery, he has proven an unrivalled propensity for steaming towards it at maximum speed!"

Marija nodded. "This is true," she agreed seriously. "It is a thing I have chastised him about many times, Sir Varyl."

The young woman's intent scrutiny briefly incommoded the professional head of the Royal Navy. Marija's gentle scrutiny had that effect on most men.

"Yes, well, absolutely," the First Sea Lord muttered, recovering his composure and recollecting what he had meant to say next. "It happens that Sir Peter is, among officers of his rank, supremely qualified to act as the Admiralty's 'technical' Liaison Officer to the Office of the Chief of Naval Operations of the United States Navy. The post was one envisaged by the US-UK Mutual Defense Treaty which we, on this side of the Atlantic, are keen not to see consigned to the dustbin of history quite yet."

Marija was genuinely baffled and since she did not subscribe to the view that she ought to be seen but not heard when in public with her illustrious husband, asked a question before Peter could get a word in edgewise.

"But the Americans have betrayed *us*?"

"Yes," Sir Varyl Begg admitted. "But we can't afford to get carried away with newspaper headlines and suchlike. We and the Americans have more things in common than not. For example, we don't want to be at each other's throats, ever again. At the urging of the government, I am sending Sir Peter and a small supporting 'team' to our embassy in Philadelphia to work with Lord Franks, our ambassador, to ensure that whatever else goes wrong that we never again *stop* talking to our American *friends*."

"Oh," Marija sighed, suddenly afraid she was going to be separated from her husband of less than two months, *again*.

Peter Christopher had digested what he had been told and was immediately able to put Marija's mind at rest.

"For extended overseas diplomatic postings it is normal for officers to be accompanied for the full duration of that service by their spouses and families, my love," he said softly, bending his lips down to her ear. He straightened and met the First Sea Lord's gaze. "Might I inquire as to the makeup of my 'team', sir?"

"Who do you have in mind, Sir Peter?"

"Alan Hannay as my number two; acting in the capacity of my personal and social secretary, sir. I'll need a security *presence*, as opposed to a *detail*, I have in mind Chief Petty Officer Griffin to head it."

"Griffin? The fellow who was on the torpedo tubes with Lady Marija's brother?" The query was partly rhetorical because the First Sea Lord knew who Jack Griffin was, and his chequered history.

Marija sensed his disquiet. "Jack won't let *us* down in America," she said in a tone which brooked no dissent. And so, it was settled.

"We'll send you all over to New York in style on the Queen Mary," Sir Varyl Begg declared, sealing the deal. "That will give the Ministry of Information people plenty of time to plot their 'charm offensive' with the Americans."

Peter wanted to say he had hoped to have another seagoing command, that the fight was unfinished and that his place was not thousands of miles away from the action. He made no such protest; knowing it was pointless. The Navy and as importantly, the Ministry of Information wanted him mending old fences, building new bridges across the Atlantic and generally reminding all and sundry that the United Kingdom remained a going concern. Diplomatically and probably militarily, a time of famine and distrust was besetting the two old allies; and he and Marija were being sent to the United States in an attempt to limit the damage.

"The Prime Minister, the Foreign Secretary and the Secretary of State for Information will brief you fully before your departure. The Queen Mary will be sailing from Southampton on the 30th of this month."

Alan Hannay had seen the First Sea Lord button-holing his friends and once the coast was clear he, with Rosa Calleja inseparably attached to his left arm, approached Peter and Marija.

"We are all going to America," Marija announced.

"Oh. I thought that was enemy territory?" Alan Hannay grimaced.

Peter Christopher had been lost in his thoughts.

It had been a peculiar day all round.

First there was Marija's marvellous news. Then the inspection of the assembled surviving Talavera's and Yarmouths; and the parade bathed in kind, unexpected sunshine along streets thronged with waving and cheering people, the march past and salute – with Her

Majesty, literally propped up, flanked by her consort, Prince Philip, and most of the UAUK's senior members – and the investiture a little later in the great quadrangle of King's College.

His father's sword, flown back to England from Malta, felt odd at his side; likewise, the full-dress uniform adorned with a whole row of campaign and other medals he had not known he had been awarded until a day or two ago.

Two splendidly ornamented ladies in waiting had hovered – one to each shoulder – to catch the Queen if she faltered during the investiture.

The Victoria Cross hung heavily on his breast as afterwards he stood to the front of the parade beside Talavera's other 'VC', former Master at Arms, Nevil *Spider* McCann, the man who had kept the destroyer afloat long enough to fire her torpedoes. The Queen had presented Commander John Pope's VC to his widow, Mary, a tearfully proud brunette accompanied by her sons, aged twelve and ten. Her Majesty had spoken to the Pope boys like a fondly protective aunt, and placed a comforting arm on Mary Pope's arm. Chief Petty Officer Stanley George who had taken command of the wrecked Yarmouth as she reeled away from the battle, had been the fourth man to receive his VC.

Joseph Calleja, cutting a somewhat paler and reduced figure from his stockier, fleshier pre-Battle of Malta self, had been the first man presented to the Queen. The Maltese dockyard electrician who had been sacked by the Royal Naval Dockyards of Malta - several days before he jumped on board HMS Talavera when all his fellows were leaping ashore - on account of his trade union activism and openly avowed Marxist politics, had stepped shyly up to the diminutive figure of his monarch to receive his George Cross.

He had leaned close to hear what the Queen was saying to him.

He had responded in a hoarse whisper that had failed to carry to the ranks behind him; she had talked again. Their conversation had only ended after about a minute.

Joe Calleja had smiled, bowed his head and stepped back.

There had been tears in his eyes as he had walked stiffly, limping still, to join Marija, who was standing a little to one side surrounded by government ministers and several large, heavily armed Royal Marines.

Brother and sister had hugged as if they had not seen each other for ten years...

Peter Christopher looked to his wife and she returned his gaze. They were suddenly like islands in the stream, the room was moving around them, and they were uncaring, oblivious of anything but each other.

He quirked a smile and she reflected it back for they were attuned precisely to each other's thoughts.

"Well, Lady Marija," Peter Christopher remarked fondly, "it seems that fate has decreed that our *daughter* will be born in America..."

Chapter 25

Forty-six-year-old Gamal Abdel Nasser, since 1956 the President of the Egyptian Republic halted in the long, vaulted cloister and raised his right hand in greeting at the approach of his old friend and fellow 'Free Officer' from the revolutionary days of 1952.

Muhammad Anwar El Sadat, the man who was in all but name Nasser's deputy, was a dapper, lean man in exactly the way his friend and leader was not. Where Nasser was a broad, increasingly heavy-set man who cut a commanding figure by sheer dint of his physical presence and spoke with a compelling gravitas or impassioned eloquence as the occasion required, Sadat cut a slighter figure. The same age and military generation as his friend, Sadat was a cerebral, calculating man who had only really come to the fore since the Cuban Missiles War. Previously, he had been one of several confidantes of the President, now there were those in Cairo who whispered that he was the 'power behind the throne'.

This was untrue, no man in the regime was more devoted to or loyal to Nasser than Anwar Sadat; but the rumours and the gossip irritated both men. Like many men who had come to power in a coup d'état they were intensely preoccupied with notions of 'legitimacy' and forever looking over their shoulders to see where the next threat was coming from.

Unseasonal south eastern winds had churned up sand storms in Sinai and buffeted Cairo in recent days and Sadat – who had been visiting the ongoing recovery and salvage work at Ismailia where the Suez Canal was still blocked by four sunken merchantmen and an Egyptian Navy frigate – had radioed the Heliopolis Palace earlier that morning warning that he might be delayed.

The two men had spoken often of the 'unseasonal' weather which had afflicted Egypt since the October War. Last winter the Nile floods had come early like a biblical nightmare, flooding parts of Cairo, inundating huge swathes of the Delta, killing thousands, and ever since there had been drought, absolute and dust dry, with the great Nile falling to unprecedented low spring levels. The weather was not so much 'unseasonal' as simply, dreadfully, 'wrong' as if the war had in some malevolent fashion unhinged normal Saharan and sub-Saharan climatic patterns. Flood one month and weeks of sand storms two months later; each so extreme as to make a God-fearing man wonder if the events of October 1962 had been so terrible as to anger Allah, *alayhi as-salām*.

Peace be upon Him...

Nasser had put back the meeting with the visiting US Secretary of State, J. William Fulbright two hours in the hope that his friend would fight his way through the sand storms by then. Important as the

Secretary of State was, that evening Nasser was scheduled to address a council of restive senior Army and Air Force officers and in the present atmosphere of 'uncertainty', each and every one of his political imperatives revolved around the preservation of his own support and the unity of Egypt. Moreover, since these were considerations that American foreign policy and post-Cuban Missiles War military deployments had singularly failed to take into account; whatever message J. William Fulbright was bringing to Cairo in the latest round of his so-called publicity seeking 'shuttle diplomacy', was very low on Gamal Abdel Nasser's personal priority list.

Nevertheless, the diplomatic niceties had to be observed.

"We'd never have kept the Americans waiting in the old days," Anwar Sadat observed dryly as the two friends fell into step.

Their feet and those of their coterie of ever-present bodyguards – both men were at the top of the hit lists of disenchanted factions in the military and any number of religious extremist splinter factions – rang on the gleaming marble floors of the corridor.

Until as recently as 1958 the Presidential Palace located in the heart of Cairo had been the Heliopolis Palace *Hotel*. Built by the Heliopolis Oases Company between 1908 and 1910 in what was then open desert east of the Nile as the centrepiece of a new suburb of the capital, it had been Africa's most luxurious hotel when it opened its doors on 1st December 1910. Designed by the Belgian architect Ernest Jaspar in what purported to be the local Heliopolis *style* – a lavish and overblown melding of the European Neoclassical with Persian, Moorish Revival and Islamic influences – it had been constructed by the two largest civil engineering concerns in Egypt, both foreign, *Leon Rolin and Company*, and *Padova, Dentamaro and Ferro*. Internally, the hotel's power and other utilities mimicked the technological marvels becoming common in Germany, France, the United Kingdom and North America, all installed lavishly with little or no expense spared. For example, *Siemens and Schuepert* of Berlin had been contracted to install the hotel's cabling and modern electrical wizardry. Notwithstanding, the hotel had always been something of a white elephant, out of place and time. The Heliopolis Palace Hotel's original French management were long gone, and within five years of its gala opening the building had become Cairo's major military hospital, a fate it suffered again in the Second World War. Between the two World Wars and afterwards, its decline hastened by the waning of British imperial power the hotel had become a half-forgotten vanity project slowly falling into disrepair, increasingly neglected until the 1950s when the Egyptian Government had begun casting around for an appropriate setting for a new Presidential Palace, a Palace fit for the leader not just of a nation that traced its lineage back to the Pharaonic epoch; but that was self-evidently *the* most powerful, leading Arab polity of the modern era.

For its current role – if never a viable business proposition in its former incarnation - the old hotel was perfect. It sat in a Cairo suburb surrounded by great buildings constructed in the grandiose *Heliopolis*

Style, it looked and felt palatial inside and out, it had over four hundred rooms, a great Moorish reception hall, numerous magnificently appointed large public rooms presented like something transplanted straight from Versailles, and an enormous Central Hall which might have been created specifically to host grand state occasions. The apex of the dome of the Central Hall – which had formerly been the grand dining room – stood one hundred and eighty feet high, and the lavishly decorated ceiling was supported by twenty-two Italianate marble columns. To each side of the Central Hall there were other public rooms, one planned as a banqueting hall and the other as a large billiard room. Although much of the original furniture had been lost during the World Wars, stolen or sold off to keep creditors at bay; here and there mahogany chairs and tables – supplied by *Maples of London* – survived.

The President of the Egyptian Republic – Nasser had been Head of the United Arab Republic, which had merged Egypt and Syria between 1958 and 1961 before infighting in the Syrian regime had torpedoed the alliance – liked to remind his guests that the Heliopolis Palace was so large that a narrow-gauge railway had been installed in the basement running the entire length of the building!

Nasser understood that the great Palace impressed the British hardly at all; Americans only when they paused long enough to actually notice their surroundings, and most Arab visitors – although they admired some of the Moorish Revivalist and Islamic characteristics of the imperialistic hubris of the former French and British overlords - privately asked each other what all the fuss was about?

The point about the Heliopolis Presidential Palace was that it impressed the people that Nasser actually wanted to impress; the Egyptian people.

J. William Fulbright was Nasser's latest US Secretary of State. First, he had had to deal with John Foster Dulles. President Eisenhower's man in the State Department had been preoccupied with propping up the Shah of Iran and in meddling in Asian and Southern American affairs. Notwithstanding that Dulles had been against the Anglo-French invasion of Suez in 1956, within months he had violently taken against Nasser and by 1958 American arms shipments had ceased. Dean Rusk, President Kennedy's first Secretary of State had broadly held to this 'anti-Egyptian, anti-Nasser' line; effectively driving Egypt farther into the Soviet Union's sphere of influence, meaning that most of Nasser's Army and part of his Air Force was now equipped with relatively modern but now increasingly hard to maintain Russian equipment.

The first time Nasser had met Fulbright, the new man had seemed to be a much more pragmatic man than either of his predecessors, and much less concerned with 'old history'; but now, like his predecessors he was clearly flexing his muscles.

Before flying to Cairo, Fulbright had spent two days in Tripoli, the one stable major city in Libya still nominally under control of the old

Italian colonial regime. This administration was partially estranged from the Fascist Tuscan league government of the Italian homeland; a situation the Americans badly wanted to remedy as a bulwark against *Egyptian* territorial ambitions in Cyrenaica. The rest of Egypt's western neighbour was slowly fragmenting into warring tribes and enclaves and, for the time being, nobody was doing anything to extract or exploit the oil reserves which eventually, would be Libya's economic salvation.

It was Nasser's working assumption that Fulbright's main interest was in sufficiently pacifying the warring factions in Libya to facilitate the influx of US-based oil companies. On a previous visit he had acted virtually as the agent of American companies interested in clearing the Suez Canal at Ismailia and developing the recently discovered oil fields in the Sinai. These previous meetings had left the President of Egypt undecided whether Fulbright was a statesman or simply the overseas representative of corporate America.

Nasser remained uncertain whether Fulbright had the remotest understanding of *anything* in the Middle East. In fact, he was confident Fulbright was blissfully unaware that members of Nasser's High Command viewed the events taking place in Iraq and Iran as a 'once in a generation' opportunity to 'annexe' the 'failed Libyan state' and bring it under 'the protection' of an Egyptian dominated 'commonwealth'.

Libya was falling apart, rapidly becoming a threat to itself, its neighbours and to the free movement of seaborne traffic along the North African coast. An Egyptian military intervention in Libya might even be seen, if handled correctly, as a statesmanlike act of kindness rather than aggression throughout much of the Arab world.

Nasser prided himself on being a realist. He yearned for pan-Arabist unity but recognised that 'unity' could never be bought by war, especially not when the entire region was already like a powder keg ready to blow up. Everywhere was chaos, new threats encircled Egypt at the very time his regime had embarked on a program of massive social and economic reforms. Too many of his people still lived in poverty, worrying daily where their next meal was coming from. Egyptian industry, such as it was, was incapable of sustaining the country without external meddling. While he dreamed of a cultural revival to throw off the shackles of the colonial past, his people needed him to concentrate on projects like the High Aswan Dam, not foreign adventures. His people needed food, jobs, schools for their children and hospitals for all, not just the rich and the lucky. Moreover, while Nasser's personal popularity with the masses remained his real powerbase, there were always plots and coups rumbling just beneath the surface.

Problems never arrived singly; there were Red Army tanks in northern Iraq and Iran, on his western border lay a lawless Libya, the Suez Canal was blocked and therefore the income from it indefinitely suspended, his attempts to support republican rebels in North Yemen had alienated the pro-western elements of the Saudi Royal Family, and now the American Secretary of State had demanded an audience at forty-eight hours' notice...

In this the twelfth year since the Free Officers had toppled the corrupt regime of King Farouk, Gamal Abdel Nasser was acutely aware that nothing was ever quite so straightforward as it seemed. Just when he had imagined the World was an impossibly complicated place in which few, if any of the really important things were resolvable in his or any other man's lifetime, Fulbright's visit threatened to throw another wild card into the great game.

Had, he wondered, the Americans got wind of the meeting he and Sadat had had with the British Foreign Secretary, Sir Thomas Harding-Grayson and Field Marshall Hull, the Chief of the United Kingdom Defence Staff at Sharm el-Sheikh *three* days ago?

After that short, terse conference beneath a hurriedly erected tent on a desert air strip – one of those ultra-secretive meetings where all aides and flunkies were banished well out of the hearing of the participants – Nasser and Sadat had looked at each other in stunned silence, as if daring the other to confirm what they had just been discussing only minutes before. Both men understood that for all their bluster and obsession with protocol and 'form' that the British could – if push came to shove – be the most ruthlessly pragmatic people on earth. Even so, what their guests had broached in the cold of that Arabian night had rocked the two men to the very core of their beings.

Seven-and-a-half years ago a British Prime Minister had likened Nasser to Hitler and Mussolini, and plotted with the French and the Israelis to invade his country and to remove him from power. The resultant Suez Crisis had very nearly fractured the Anglo-American 'special relationship', fatally undermined what was left of the British Empire, driven Anthony Eden from office, and changed the political centre of gravity of the whole Middle East for a generation. And yet in that tent in the desert in the middle of the night in Sinai, a British Foreign Secretary and the most senior officer in the British Army had baldly invited the Egyptian Republic to reshape the map of the Middle East...

Gamal Abdel Nasser and Muhammad Anwar El Sadat strode confidently into the reception hall where J. William Fulbright and his overlarge coterie of suited and stern-faced staffers awaited their pleasure.

Three days ago, both Sir Thomas Harding-Grayson and Field Marshall Sir Richard Hull, had made the effort to acquaint themselves with sufficient of Nasser's mother tongue to greet him in his own language, and to contritely apologise for suggesting that the rest of their exchange be conducted in English.

But no American Secretary of State ever made *that* sort of concession to a *mere* Arab. So, at both Nasser's and Sadat's shoulder stood interpreters.

The American Ambassador, sixty-one-year-old John Stothoff Badeau, an Arabist who understood Egypt and the Middle East better than practically any other living American with whom Nasser enjoyed frank, friendly and mutually respectful personal relations, had read the runes and was doing his best to hide his dismay. The Kennedy Administration had sent him to Cairo in 1961 to 'mend fences' but almost immediately cut the ground from beneath their ambassador's feet by taking Israel's side in the United Nations and by describing Nasser's regime as 'Castro-like', and Nasser himself as a 'socialist', and a 'Soviet stooge'.

Badeau knew for a fact that Gamal Abdul Nasser was none of those things as he stepped forward and introduced his chief to Nasser in *Egyptian*, signalling that he planned to be his Secretary of State's translator.

Nasser looked J. William Fulbright in the eye.

The American met his stare, unblinking.

That was when Nasser knew that although Fulbright must have heard about the meeting with the British in the Sinai; he had not yet drawn any of the obvious conclusions. If he had, he would have brought senior military officers with him rather than the pale-skinned, sweating State Department second-raters standing at his back.

For all that the US Sixth Fleet, with its big grey warships swinging around their anchors in the Grand Harbour at Malta like some occupying armada pretended that it had made the Mediterranean an American sea, it was only the British who actually had the will and the courage to fight.

Before Fulbright had opened his mouth to speak Nasser, and at his side, Anwar Sadat, were already redrawing their thoughts about the proposition put to them at Sharm-el-Sheik.

If the United States really was disengaging from its former – mostly unspoken – commitments East of Suez then the rules of the game had just changed.

Suddenly, sitting on the fence awaiting developments was no longer an option.

Chapter 26

Thursday 14th May 1964
Advanced HQ, 3rd Caucasus Tank Army, Sulaymaniyah, Iraq

Major Generals Vladimir Andreyevich Puchkov and Konstantin Yakovlevich Kurochnik snapped to attention as Marshal of the Soviet Union Hamazasp Khachaturi Babadzhanian walked into what had been – up until seven days ago - the dining room of the residence of the Military Governor of Sulaymaniyah.

It went without saying that the aforementioned officer had decamped, as had most of his men, heavily encumbered with their wives, children and looted chattels as soon as they had discovered that a column of Red Army tanks was coming down the road towards Sulaymaniyah from Dokan in the north. The Red Air Force had wanted to bomb the road south; Babadzhanian had vetoed the idea. Roads clogged with refugees and the remnants of a fleeing army would block any attempt by the enemy to mount a counter attack on Sulaymaniyah; and the Red Air Force needed to save every rocket and bomb because it was abundantly clear that Army Group South's supply and communications lines were an unmitigated shambles.

Partly, this was because his two armies were attempting to traverse some of the worse tank country on earth – the Alborz and Zagros Mountains - in the face of guerrilla interdiction and occasional locally devastating, air attacks but mainly it was because the Army Group's hastily thrown together quartermaster corps was simply not up to the job. Babadzhanian had already sacked the commander of that organisation, a supposedly reliable officer with good pre-war Party connections, but God himself was not going to turn around the disastrous 'supply situation' overnight. Right now, his army and his air force were going to have to fight with what it had to hand and basically, he was not going to waste any bullets or bombs, let alone critically scarce aviation fuel 'shooting up' an already fleeing enemy.

"I visited the western bridge over the Tanjaro River. Well, what's left of it," Babadzhanian announced conversationally to the two men he regarded as the best fighting generals in Army Group South. Vladimir Andreyevich Puchkov, the commanding officer of the 10th Guards Tank Division had driven his armour through impossible country at breakneck speed and at times got so far ahead of the following units that he had completely lost touch with the rest of 2nd Siberian Mechanised Army for days on end. Konstantin Yakovlevich Kurochnik had parachuted into Tehran at the outset of *Operation Nakazyvat,* had led the 50th Guards Airborne Brigade at Urmia, and now commanded the 3rd Siberian Mechanised Division.

In the next twenty-four hours Babadzhanian planned to unleash his two hardest charging generals on separate, but vital new adventures. His armies were strung out across northern Iraq all the way back to Azerbaijan; any other man might have called a halt, waited for the logistical nightmare to resolve itself and for his armoured formations to regain some semblance of coherence on the plains around Sulaymaniyah.

Any other man at any other time...

The politicians back in Chelyabinsk were panicking. If they had not been so terrified of Defence Minister Marshal of the Soviet Union Vasily Ivanovich Chuikov, the other two members of the collective leadership, Alexei Nikolayevich Kosygin and Leonid Ilyich Brezhnev would have had Babadzhanian's head by now. Unfortunately, not even Chuikov, the most decorated soldier in the history of the mother country had been able to stop the idiots inflicting that maniacal shit Andropov and his brainless fucking KGB troops on Army Group South!

Babadzhanian got angry just thinking about those bastards crawling around *his* armies looking for traitors, deserters and so-called fifth columnists. Any remaining sympathy he felt for Comrade Yuri Vladimirovich Andropov, Deputy First Secretary of the *Komitet Gosudarstvennoy Bezopasnosti* – who had by all accounts had a rough time of it in Bucharest before the Red Army had put down those *Krasnaya Zarya* fanatics - had evaporated within twenty-four hours of his arrival in Iraq. The bloody man seemed intent on taking out his anger not on the enemy but on *Babadzhanian's* soldiers, who had quite enough on their plates getting through the mountains, conquering half of one country and the whole of another, without having to look over their shoulders all the time worrying about the fucking KGB!

The Army Group Commander took a series of deep breaths to help collect his thoughts. Babadzhanian needed no encouragement from above to press on. If he once permitted the invasion to descend into a war of attrition along fixed defensive lines all would be lost.

In twenty-four hours, Puchkov's 10th Guards Tank Division would strike towards Jalawla, some one hundred and fifty kilometres to the south; while simultaneously Kurochnik's Siberians would race to Kirkuk, over a hundred kilometres to the west to cut off the cities of Erbil and Mosul from the rest of the country.

Last night the RAF had dropped two very big bombs on the bridge carrying the Sulaymaniyah to Kirkuk road over the River Tanjaro west of the city. The river was still in flood but one of the bombs had landed close enough to the eastern foundation of the structure to so badly undermine it that most of the bridge had collapsed. The second big bomb had left a crater in the road nearly thirty metres in diameter and five deep. During the same raid one, perhaps, two other aircraft had dropped as many as forty, one-thousand-pound bombs on the city itself.

The raids marked a step change in the intensity of the war.

Up until now the Red Air Force had been engaged in a cat and mouse skirmish with the dwindling handful of Iranian fighter bombers – none any kind of match for Mig-21s – and isolated incursions and strafing attacks by Iraqi aircraft, neither of which were in any way coordinated, and rarely followed up by second strikes. But last night the British Royal Air Force had taken down a key bridge and turned the centre of Sulaymaniyah into a blasted Hellhole. Any serious thought of using the city as a staging post for the next stage of the invasion had suddenly been rendered null and void; it seemed the enemy – the *real* enemy – understood what was in *his* mind and had no intention of permitting *Operation Nakazyvat* to play out according to *his* plan.

Already Babadzhanian had adapted, altered his immediate objectives.

Forget about subduing the north of Iraq; that would have to wait for another day. He would take Kirkuk, and Erbil and Mosul if he could, quickly without a serious fight, otherwise the latter two cities would be isolated, the roads to the south blocked and the bulk of his forces would head directly towards Baghdad. If necessary, he would feed his tank divisions into the fight piecemeal.

Forty-eight hours ago, the plan had still been to command the north, now the priority was the race to Baghdad.

He looked to Puchkov, the weather-beaten, scarred veteran of the Battle of Kursk who had been with him in Budapest in 1956. That had been a filthy business, not that he had ever lost any sleep over the counter revolutionaries his men had killed in seizing back control of the city. The rebels had hung Hungarian secret policemen from lamp posts in front of the Soviet Embassy; what the fuck did they think was going to happen after that?

"I wouldn't be surprised if the British take out the southern bridge over the Tanjaro tonight," he remarked, apparently idly.

Puchkov chuckled.

"I'd best send my combat engineers down that way to put it back up again in the morning, sir."

"Yes, you do that." Babadzhanian sniffed. To cap his woes, he had come down with a dose of dysentery the last few days and he was running a fever. That was the trouble campaigning in a country run by fucking savages! "Keeping open the roads west and south is the absolute number one priority at this time," he added, knowing that the two senior commanders did not need to be told this or to receive his personal imprimatur to do what needed to be done. "Once we've got more air strips operating Comrade First Deputy Director Andropov has promised us half-a-dozen penal battalions to repair the roads. Until they arrive round up any able-bodied civilians you can find and put them to work."

He made eye contact with Puchkov and then Kurochnik.

"Effective mobile strength?"

"Fifty percent," Puchkov retorted, as if this was hardly any kind of problem.

"Forty percent, perhaps," Kurochnik reported. He had only been in command of 3rd Siberian Mechanised Division thirty-six hours but did not for a moment contemplate falling back on this as any kind of excuse for any suggestion of vagueness in his report. "That's forty percent that can move at a couple of hours' notice, sir."

Babadzhanian looked to the former paratrooper.

"I want you to seize Kirkuk not later than 20th May."

Kurochnik nodded.

Babadzhanian turned to Puchkov.

"Think your boys can be in Jalawla by then?"

"Yes," the shaven-headed commander of the 10th Guards Tank Division confirmed grimly.

Babadzhanian had no intention of telling either man how to do his business. Time was short and any moment now he was going to have to run – or at least move hurriedly – in the direction of the nearest latrine.

He turned to another subject.

"I was informed we had taken a senior British prisoner?"

"They've got him outside, sir."

"Bring him in."

The bearded, scarecrow figure almost fell on the ground before the Army Group Commander as his burly minders pushed him into the room. The man was filthy and his uniform – which might once have resembled the battledress of a Spetsnaz trooper – was tattered and blood-stained. It was not immediately apparent if the blood belonged to the swaying, blinking forty- to fifty-year-old man who stank of urine, faeces, gasoline and every other imaginable stench endemic in the mud and soil of the lands around Sulaymaniyah.

The prisoner made an attempt to straighten to his full height.

The effort hurt him; no matter, he was of that generation who respected the uniform and the rank of an enemy even if he despised the man inside it and everything he stood for.

"Who are you?" Babadzhanian demanded.

"Waters," the other man croaked, paused, cleared his throat and coughed a chest-rattling cough. "Lieutenant-Colonel," he went, translating the rank into its nearest Soviet equivalent in Russian. "Francis Harold St John Waters."

Babadzhanian scowled.

The Prisoner went on in Russian: "Yesli vy dumayete, chto ya sobirayus' rasskazat' vam svoyu krovavuyu nomer i polka vas yest' yeshche odna krovavaya veshch' idet, tovarishch!"

If you think I am going to tell you my bloody number and regiment you've got another bloody thing coming, comrade!

The Commander of Army Group South was more impressed by the jovial manner in which the prisoner had said it than offended by the other man's sentiments.

"Is that so?" He inquired coolly.

"Da, vot chto eto takoye. Vy mozhete popast nas yemki menya seychas, tovarishch."

Yes, that's about the size of it. You can get on with shooting me now, comrade.

"You are a long way from home, Comrade Colonel?"

The conversation went on in Russian.

"So are you, old son!"

"Waters? Why do I know that name?"

"I tried to kill Rommel once," the prisoner suggested, clearly trying to be helpful as if the two men were having a man-to-man chat to pass the time of day rather than discussing pressing military matters. "Well, twice actually but that was a long time ago. You have the advantage of me, sir. To whom do I have the pleasure of speaking?"

"Babadzhanian. Marshal of the Soviet Union."

Frank Waters tried very hard to come to attention.

In his enfeebled, somewhat battered, hungry state it took him some seconds to realise that the Russians in the room were ignoring him and talking too fast for him to catch more than a few words.

Strangely, they did not seem to be discussing how to execute him. That was a relief, although the way he felt right now it was not that much of a relief. Presently, Marshal of the Soviet Union Hamazasp Khachaturi Babadzhanian fixed him anew in his sights.

"I have instructed my officers to clean you up, feed you and insofar as it is within our powers to attend to your injuries. You will not be shot quite yet. Unless, of course, you attempt to escape."

"Obviously," Lieutenant-Colonel Francis Harold St John Waters grinned, "I can't make any promises about that. Sorry. Nothing personal. The chaps back home wouldn't understand it if I suddenly turned over a new leaf."

Babadzhanian almost but not quite smiled.

The other generals in the room were a little baffled by the prisoner's idiomatic Moskva Russian; nevertheless, they caught his meaning.

They exchanged old soldier's looks; and shrugged one to the other.

It was a well-known fact that the English were mad.

Chapter 27

Friday 15th May 1964
Military Port, Limassol, Cyprus

Squadron Leader Guy French had watched the big grey guided missile destroyer slowly navigate the partially blocked main channel into the bay, her side manned and her flags dipping in respect as she passed close to the wreck of HMS Blake and manoeuvred to come alongside the dock.

Out in the harbour barges and small service boats still clustered around the stricken Blake, lying on her side in less than forty feet of water. The Blake had been sent to Cyprus to remove the forty or so nuclear warheads at RAF Akrotiri ahead of the feared Red Dawn invasion of the island. She had been preparing to sail for Malta at the time of the attack and over half her crew had died in the initial explosion or later from burns or radiation sickness.

During the ongoing salvage operation, the cruiser's side had been peeled open with oxyacetylene cutting torches, and in the last couple of weeks clearance divers had commenced the task of removing the nuclear weapons from submerged compartments.

Every time Guy French let his eyes wander around the ruined port he tried, and failed to imagine, what it must have been like when that ancient ferry carrying a cargo of refugees from Turkey had been vaporised by the detonation of the Hiroshima-size tactical nuclear weapon in her hold. He honestly did not know what kind of mind would put a weapon like that on a civilian ship, sail it into a port and set it off. Sometimes, the thought of it was so awful that it temporarily eased his own doubts about his part in the October War.

On the night of the war, and sometimes since he had told himself he had been – in the cold jargon of these things – 'suppressing medium range mobile ballistic missile batteries', which might otherwise have laid waste the entire United Kingdom; but whatever he told himself the reality was that his aircraft had dropped two city-killer size thermo-nuclear bombs close to places where he knew a lot of people – tens of thousands, perhaps hundreds of thousands of people - *had* lived...

Guy French's CO had told him that HMS Hampshire was the newest ship in the fleet and there had been no time to run the normal trials. Her crew had come on board, her tanks had been topped off, her 4.5-inch main battery magazines half-filled, provisions for a six-week cruise loaded and then she had sailed for Portsmouth to take on her 'special' cargo ahead of a high-speed run to Cyprus.

The County Class destroyer – a few fresh rust stains on her hull plates apart – was plainly brand new. The big pendent number 'D02' on her flank was blackly clean cut.

They said the big bombs stacked on the ugly cradles welded to the destroyer's helicopter landing pad, were World War II vintage Grand

Slams and Tallboys; ten ton and six-on general purpose high explosive weapons designed to penetrate several feet of reinforced concrete, or to burrow deep into the ground before exploding and undermining otherwise indestructible targets. Dropped by aircraft of No. 617 – 'The Dambusters' – and No. 9 Squadrons in the last year of Hitler's war bombs like these had sunk the Tirpitz, destroyed supposedly impregnable German U-boat pens, smashed the giant V-2 launch site at Wizernes, disabled the long-range guns with which the Nazis planned to level London at the Fortress of Mimoyecques, and methodically knocked down the great railway bridges and viaducts of western Germany ahead of the advancing Allied armies.

Many of the bombs produced during that war had since been used in trials but it transpired that somebody, somewhere, had decided to hold back a cache of the mighty weapons. Just in case. After the 1945 war the United States had built its own version of the bombs, several of which had been liberated from former US Air Force bases in the last year. The US versions of the Grand Slam and the Tallboy were prosaically called T-14 and T-10. Altogether there were seven ten-ton and nineteen six-ton bombs on board the Hampshire. If Guy French had been on board, he suspected he would have winced every time the ship hit a big wave.

The bombs were so big that only the Handley Page Victor V-Bomber had a bomb bay large enough to accommodate them internally. A Victor could carry either a single Grand Slam or two Tallboys and the powers that be had determined that while the seven Avro Vulcans sent to the Middle East would operate from Saudi Arabian airfields or from Abadan, the six Victors sent to the Eastern Mediterranean would be based in Cyprus; three at what had been Nicosia Airport, and three at Akrotiri. Two Vulcans and a single Victor would also be based at RAF Luqa on Malta, but the deployment of the additional Victor, and a force of six additional aircraft, all Vickers Valiants had been delayed pending the completion of an extension to the existing main runway at Luqa. On completion of this deployment half the surviving operational V-Bomber Force would be based close enough to support British and Commonwealth forces in and around the Persian Gulf.

Two of the Cyprus-based Victors had been sent to Iraq again last night, one with a Tallboy on board and the other with thirty-one thousand-pound general purpose bombs; both aircraft had returned safely at around dawn.

HMS Hampshire's arrival, two days ahead of schedule was timely because the single Grand Slam and all four Tallboys 'shuttled' to Cyprus by Valiants based at Coningsby in England had been expended in the last two nights. The chaps in the Mess at Akrotiri had been of the opinion that it was high time the RAF delivered a 'Welcome to Iraq' greeting card to the invaders.

Honour satisfied; everybody could get on with the war now.

Before the Navy had stepped in with its generous offer to cart a ¬hole bunker full of big bombs to Cyprus there had been much talk about 'wearing out' and or 'risking' the remaining Victor Fleet – fourteen to seventeen operational aircraft at any one time – moving big bombs to the Eastern Mediterranean. In the event, four Grand Slams and six Tallboys had been left behind in England and the Navy had offered to have the Hampshire undertake a second 'high speed run' to finish the job as soon as she got back to Portsmouth. But that was only after she had taken on board all the warheads recovered from HMS Blake, and returned home via Malta and Gibraltar dropping off several 'tactical nukes' at each base.

With the news of HMS Hampshire's mission everybody in the Akrotiri Mess now agreed that despite their initial reservations, the Navy was actually useful for something!

Guy French had spent most of the last year flying RAF turboprop transport aircraft and De Havilland Comets. Although he had been a 'Vulcan man' for his whole operational career there simply were not enough Vulcans to go around anymore; certainly not enough serviceable kites to keep a fellow like him in regular employment. Perversely, more pilots and miscellaneous fully trained aircrew had survived the war than either Vulcans or Valiants. He had literally jumped at the opportunity to volunteer to come to Cyprus to 'train up' on Victors – for which pilots were actually only slightly more numerous than operational aircraft – in the second, right-hand co-pilot's seat.

Although being based at cold, wintry Brize Norton was not quite as miserable as it sounded – because of the proximity of Oxford - the chance to come out to sunny Cyprus and the promise of flying a V-Bomber again was almost too good to be true. Even better, everybody knew that of the three V-Bombers the Handley Page Victor was the most advanced and sophisticated of the three. Basically, it put old cart horses like the Vickers Valiant, or the American B-47 or B-52 in the shade.

The Victor was still the biggest aircraft in the world to have broken the sound barrier in level flight – allegedly, some bright spark had put the nose down for a few seconds with the throttles more or less open and hey presto, his kite had registered 1.1 on the Mach meter – and in comparison, with every other big bomber in the sky its design remained cutting edge over a dozen years after its maiden flight. Notwithstanding, he still missed his beloved Vulcan. Nobody believed him when he said flying a Vulcan was like flying a giant Spitfire...

Somebody at his shoulder was admiring the huge bombs on the destroyer's deck.

"Blimey, I've never realised how big those bastards were up close!"

Guy French involuntarily reached to his upper lip and ran his forefinger through his moustache. Handlebars were getting a bit passé these days but he was proud of his 'bars' even though it did not go down so well with the girls as the clean-shaven look.

Girls...

He had been engaged before the October War.

He had survived; God alone knew how.

Greta had not; nor had the tiny village outside York where she and her parents lived survived that awful night.

Even sixty or seventy feet away as the big destroyer edged towards the quayside the bombs on the helicopter pad looked *very* big. Guy had not realised that they were actually *that* big. Now if a fellow dropped one of those chaps on a half-way worthwhile target in Iraq or Russia or anywhere else, well, *that* really would be a thing.

Killing tens of thousands of people you had never known and never would know was murder – whichever way you cut it, it was murder, no point quibbling about words at this remove – but dropping a Grand Slam or a Tallboy 'on the nose', now that would be a thing indeed.

If a man could do a thing like that before he died, he might die, if not happy, then at least a little more at peace with himself.

Guy French stared at the big bombs as crewmen pulled away the last tarpaulins which had kept them dry on the long voyage from Southampton. He stared, and kept on staring because he knew that tonight, for the first time in eighteen months there was an even chance he might sleep awhile without descending into the dreadful miasma of his nightmares.

'Grand Slam," he murmured aloud.

Grand Slam!

Chapter 28

Thirty-six-year-old Sultan bin Abdulaziz bin Abdul Rahman bin Faisal bin Turki bin Abdullah bin Muhammad bin Saud had been appointed Minister of Defence and Aviation only the previous October. The 12th son of King Abdulaziz had held several senior posts in the Kingdom while still a very young man and been instrumental in assisting his father in establishing a system of national governance based on Sharia Law. That he had always been a highly trusted member of his father's house was attested by the fact he had been appointed to oversee Aramco's – the Arabian American Oil Company's – construction of a rail link between Dammam on the Persian Gulf to Riyadh as a very young man in the late 1940s. Contemporaries knew him as a 'volatile and emotional' firebrand with no real military experience, other than a short spell in command of the Royal Guard, who had been elevated to his present role because of his birth and his loyalty to the current regime. However, within the Kingdom these were not things to be taken lightly and neither of Prince Abdulaziz Al Saud's guests that afternoon regarded the hard-eyed man in flowing Bedouin robes standing before them with anything other than wary respect and mild trepidation.

Until the events of recent weeks, the Minister for Defence and Aviation had been regarded as a pragmatist with both feet solidly planted in the American camp. Even when the United States had reduced its military presence in Arabia to half-a-dozen companies of clerks and guards for their three strategic war stores depots; he had never conceived of a day when the Kingdom's very existence would be called into doubt and the Americans would do...*nothing.*

Nothing was exactly what the United States seemed to be doing as Red Army tanks rolled into Iran and Iraq. At first, he had not believed the intelligence reports, mistrusted what *his* people had been telling him every bit as much as what he was hearing from the British Ambassador. Like Crown Prince Faisal, he too had bristled with indignation, humiliated to have to accept the presence of Royal Air Force V-Bombers on *his* soil because no matter how many times the US State Department offered 'guarantees' in respect of the 'territorial integrity of the Arabian Peninsula', as the war in Iraq rumbled ever closer to the borders, the airspace, and the waters of the Persian Gulf through which practically *all* the Kingdom's oil was exported to the outside world, *words* increasingly counted for nothing.

He and every other member of the government now felt like they had been duped by the Americans. His honour had been besmirched. He had trusted the Americans and they had, by failing to immediately send troops, aircraft and ships to 'guarantee the territorial integrity' of his country, insulted and betrayed the entire ruling family.

Prince Abdulaziz Al Saud tried very hard to veil his anger as he studied the faces of his hosts.

It was one of those quirks of circumstance that while not a fluent Saudi speaker, the British Ambassador, fifty-year-old Sir Colin Tradescant Crowe found himself almost by accident, admirably qualified to be his country's safe pair of hands in the worst of all possible times in the Kingdom of Saudi Arabia.

The son of a diplomat father he had been born in Yokohama, and educated at Stowe School and Oriel College, Oxford where he had acquired a first-class degree in history before taking up a posting in the Diplomatic Service in Peking between 1936 and 1938. Thereafter, he had served in Shanghai, Washington DC and Tel Aviv before returning to China during the Korean War. In Peking in the early 1950s British diplomats were fair game for so-called Chinese 'volunteers'; and Crowe's brother-in-law had been arrested and executed on trumped up charges of conspiring to murder Mao Zedong in 1951.

Crowe was one of those indefatigable never say die stalwarts of the old diplomatic corps; thus, it was hardly surprising when he was appointed as the prospective *Chargé D'affaires* in Cairo in 1957, a post he was only able to take up two years later in 1959 when diplomatic relations were resumed after the debacle of the Suez Crisis of 1956. It was largely down to Crowe that full diplomatic relations were finally restored between London and Cairo in 1961. His reward had been to be sent to New York as the United Kingdom's deputy Permanent Representative to the United Nations, a position rendered redundant by the Cuban Missiles War and the host nation's unilateral decision to withdraw from that crippled institution in February 1963. Needless to say, he had not been overly surprised to be handed again the poison chalice of repairing diplomatic ties with Saudi Arabia – broken since 1956 – the previous year. A modest, calm, very patient man with a gentle sense of humour he could be scathingly dismissive of 'old school' colleagues and 'time servers' who still behaved as if Britain ruled the waves and that there was actually such a thing as 'the Empire'. Here in the Kingdom his tact and charm, and for want of a better word – his transparent 'decency' – had mended many fences and enabled him to form new working relationships. Crucially, within the upper echelons of the Saudi Royal Family, Crowe was seen as a man with whom the Kingdom might do business.

However, the man standing at the British Ambassador's shoulder was – his reputation apart – an unknown quantity to Prince Abdulaziz Al Saud.

It was said that Sir Thomas Harding-Grayson, since December of last year the British Foreign Secretary and one of *that* woman Thatcher's 'inner circle', had once been ostracised by his superiors for his anti-American stance and the man's wife was, of all things, a famous novelist!

Of only average height, balding and in appearance older than his fifty-nine years, the dapper, suited Englishman stepped forward and nodded his head in a cursory bow.

"Thank you for altering your schedule at such short notice to do us the honour of meeting with us at this place, Your Highness," Tom Harding-Grayson said in halting Arabic.

"You speak our tongue, Sir Thomas?"

"Not so well as I did in my younger days I fear, Your Highness. It is many, many years since I was so 'graced' as to be last in this part of the World."

Prince Abdulaziz Al Saud gestured for his interpreter to step forward. There could be no scope for misunderstandings today.

"I am here today at the request of Crown Prince Faisal," he declared. "He met Secretary of State Fulbright yesterday. It was not a satisfactory meeting. Our American 'friends' wish to 'sell' us arms and to assure the Kingdom of their undying 'support', and have sought assurances that the war supplies depots at Jeddah and elsewhere will be 'respected'. This last matter I personally found to be most curious."

He waited for his interpreter to translate.

And looked the British Foreign Secretary in the eye.

The other man met his hawkish stare without blinking.

Sir Colin Crowe coughed politely.

"Might I suggest we retire to comfortable chairs, Your Highness?" He suggested.

He led the others to chairs around a low table. Viciously strong, bitter coffee was served in small cups and then the exchange resumed as if there had been no interruption.

"With respect," Tom Harding-Grayson observed, "the status of the war supplies depots is a thing which *ought* to preoccupy the United States, Your Highness."

"How so, Sir Thomas?"

The Englishman did not so much as bat an eyelid.

"Because my generals and air marshals want the contents of those depots so that they can better assist your armed forces in the defence of *your* borders, sir."

There was a deathly silence.

It went on for ten, fifteen, twenty or more seconds.

"My forces," the Minister of Defence and Aviation said dangerously, "are perfectly capable of defending the holy soil of the Kingdom."

The British Ambassador raised his coffee cup to his lips, thought better of it and replaced cup and saucer carefully on the table.

"At this time," he observed, "we do not think it is the Soviets' intention to immediately invade the Kingdom, Your Highness. However, we do think that the enemy's ultimate strategic objective is to command the waters of the Persian Gulf, to occupy most of Iraq and Iran, and to eventually *expand* his sphere of influence in the region to encompass the whole of the Arabian Peninsula. It is also our assessment that it is the Soviets' intention to seize or destroy all the oilfields of the region."

"That's madness!" Prince Abdulaziz Al Saud exploded.

Tom Harding-Grayson shook his head.

"With respect, sir. He who controls two-thirds of the World's known oil reserves has his hands around the throat of the whole World."

Prince Abdulaziz Al Saud did not need a Westerner to tell him what was patently obvious to the humblest beggar in Riyadh. This was after all why the prevailing mood within the Saudi government was one best categorised as one of 'barely contained panic'.

Had it not been for the Crown Prince's veto the Saudi Army would already have broken into the 'American Depots'. The Defence Minister had also spoken against such a precipitate and irreversible move but not out of any consideration for the likely reaction of the United States. His concerns were wholly prosaic; he did not have a sufficiently large cadre of trained men to use the majority of the weaponry stored at Jeddah or Dhahran and in the camp outside Riyadh. Untrained conscripts from the backstreets of the Kingdom's cities, or the sons of desert wanderers could not suddenly learn to drive and fight an M-48 tank, or handle a howitzer, let alone fly a modern jet aircraft, or for that matter, any kind of aircraft. Moreover, large stocks of general munitions – thousands of tons of shells and bombs - posed insuperable problems to his forces; if he let his people break into those depots, they would probably inadvertently blow up the damned places!

"The Kennedy Administration believes that the Soviets may content themselves with seizing the oilfields of Iraqi Kurdistan. The Central Intelligence Agency says that the Russians are too weak to invade the whole of Iraq. The Soviets have already decapitated the regime in Iran," Prince Abdulaziz Al Saud involuntarily winced as he said this, mindful of the grainy movie of the execution of the Shah of Iran, copies of which had mysteriously been delivered to several key ministries in Riyadh in the last week, "perhaps, all they plan to do is threaten your *Imperial* fief at Abadan?"

This savagely pointed barb bounced of Tom Harding-Grayson.

The British Foreign Secretary put aside the hypocrisy of being taunted about 'Imperialism' by a man who was currently in his present elevated post only because he happened to be one of the thirty or forty offspring of a former monarch of the Kingdom.

"No, Your Highness. That is not the objective of the Soviet High Command."

It was stated in a tone as unequivocal as the words.

Prince Abdulaziz Al Saud's eyes narrowed.

"How can you be sure, Sir Thomas?"

The Englishman smiled thinly.

"The Red Army will drive south to the Persian Gulf, Your Highness," he said. "It will assault Abadan. There is nothing you or I can do about that. True, we could start another nuclear war but I think we've all come to the conclusion that's not a terribly good idea. The RAF is flying in reinforcements every day but without heavy equipment and munitions we're up a creek without a proverbial paddle.   Every available tank and armoured vehicle in the United Kingdom has been, or is being, loaded onto fast merchantmen and sent to the Gulf via the Cape of Good Hope.   There's even talk of rushing HMS Ark Royal out of dry dock and using her for a fast run around the Cape loaded to the gunnels with all manner of war supplies.   But hardly any of that will arrive in time to be any use. Unless, of course, the Kingdom and its neighbours join us in the fight to save *your* oilfields and *your* systems of government and belief, from the Godless interlopers who mean to crush you *all* beneath the heel of a new Marxist-Leninist monster."

Chapter 29

Sunday 17th May 1964
Steps of the Cathedral Basilica of Saints Peter and Paul, Philadelphia

Notwithstanding that the American government, the newspapers, and the radio and television networks were horribly negative, even derisive about everything that the 'old country' touched, the two young Maltese women had adored practically everything else about America. Neither they nor their husbands had encountered so much as a scintilla of personal hostility since they had disembarked from the Queen Mary; to the contrary, they had been greeted – feted indeed – as if they were movie stars. Thus, it was with only mild trepidation but without surprise that the two *sisters* emerged from the sepulchral splendour of the Cathedral onto the steps down to North 18th Street to be greeted by an even larger than usual crowd. There were the normal photographers, a cordon of Philadelphia Police Department men, and their own bodyguards – led by Chief Petty Officer Jack Griffin, proudly wearing his scars from the Battle of Malta – and perhaps several hundred or more Philadelphians simply wanting to catch a glimpse of the visiting celebrities.

These 'events' had already developed their own rhythms and unwritten protocols. Marija and Rosa would pose shyly for the newspaper photographers, and smile nicely. The husbands would shift on their feet in the background like two self-effacing Englishmen abroad who honestly and truly did not know what all the fuss was about; and before they made their escape the couples would briefly hold hands separately, concluding events by standing together as a quartet for one final photo call and a self-conscious wave to the bystanders.

Often, as today, they would be cheered as they drove away in the big Embassy cars in which they were obliged to travel in the city.

The Ambassador had been very insistent about how they were to travel around the city.

'The average American citizen is by nature welcoming, friendly and wishes you nothing but happiness,' Lord Franks had explained. 'But as experience in Washington showed in December there are also some very strange and some very dangerous people about. In the city you must be careful at all times.'

Not that there was any chance of *not* being careful when Jack Griffin was in charge of one's security detail. Not only did their faithful guard dog growl and scowl at anybody who remotely gave his charges – particularly his 'ladies' – a cross look, at all times he was at pains to broadcast the impression that if anybody got out of line, he would not hesitate to crack their skull.

This morning the women jumped into the first car; knowing their husbands would want to talk about 'Navy' matters, specifically about their forthcoming trip to Norfolk, Virginia, home to the US Atlantic

Fleet. Jack Griffin had held the door for the women, scowling watchfully at the nearby crowd before dropping into the front passenger seat beside the driver. He was never far away when 'the girls' were outside the protection of the Embassy compound.

"What a lovely service," Rosa Hannay declared breathlessly. She was beginning to get over the sensation that she was completely in her *sister's* shadow. Until she had married Lieutenant-Commander Alan Hannay, DSO, two days before embarking on the Queen Mary at Southampton the women had been 'sisters-in-law', now they were just *sisters* and basically, each other's best friends. They were both newly married, transported thousands of miles from the misery which might have otherwise plagued them had they still been in their native Malta, and each was positively drunk on a diet of exciting new places, sights and sounds. And unashamedly a little overwhelmed by America, with which they were fast falling into love.

It was the second Sunday that they had attended Mass at the Cathedral Basilica of Saints Peter and Paul. The Cathedral was magnificent and it was hard to believe it was, in the scale of things, so *young*.

The Embassy staff had been eagerly awaiting the arrival of the two Navy couples. The advent of two newlywed catholic girls married to 'heroes' who had if not embraced, then taken on board their wives' Catholicism, had been seized upon by their Ministry of Information 'minders' with delight.

There had been an early and very public introduction to the Catholic Arch Bishop of Philadelphia, John Krol, who had proudly taken them on a tour of his great 'church'. Designed by Napoleon LeBrun who had also designed the Academy of Music in the city and later the Masonic Temple and a host of other ecclesiastical buildings in New York, the Cathedral had been built between 1010 and 1864. The Cathedral was and remained the largest Catholic church in Philadelphia – and incidentally, the city's largest brownstone structure - capable of seating two thousand worshippers. Built in a Romano Corinthian style it was modelled on the Lombard Church of San Carlo al Corso in Rome. According to Arch Bishop Krol its Palladian façade and aqua oxidized-copper dome drew on influences from the Italian Renaissance.

Marija had not had the heart to tell the good Arch Bishop that his church did not hold a patch on the Cathedral of St Paul's in the Citadel at Mdina, where she and *her* Peter had been married only seventy-one days ago. That would have been rude and un-Christian and besides, Lord Franks had been quite explicit about how he expected the two young couples to 'play the game'.

Lord Franks and his wife, Lady Barbara, a kindly and very distinguished woman, had entertained the newcomers to an English tea the day after their arrival in Philadelphia. Significantly, the otherwise ever-present men from the Ministry of Information had been summarily excluded from the *tea*.

'Things may be a little bit sticky for us here in America,' the

Ambassador had admitted. 'Back home there is no doubt a lot of loose talk about how the Americans have let us down, and so forth. That is *not* how most decent, hard-working, family-loving, God-fearing Americans view the situation. By the way, most Americans are transparently decent, hard-working, family-loving, God-fearing *and* instinctively *welcoming* in my experience and this is my second stint over here as Ambassador.'

The Christophers and the Hannays had listened respectfully.

'The Kennedy Administration has *not* betrayed *us*," Lord Franks had emphasised. "The United States is a democracy and the President cannot lead his people where they *will not* go. This is election year and if President Kennedy sends American GIs to the Middle East, he will be swept away in a landslide in November. You will find that the rhetoric and distemper of the American TV, radio and printed press is directed not at *Britain*, or at *British people* but at the *British Government*, and at what many Americans still perceive to be British *Imperial pretensions*. You will – generally speaking – be welcomed with open arms wherever you go providing,' Lord Franks had counselled, 'that you do not allow yourself to get drawn into politics. Under no circumstances are you to offer any opinion, positive or otherwise on the American body politic, its Byzantine machinations or upon the character or sayings of *any* of its players. Other than when you are in *this* building you should say nothing whatsoever about politics to anybody.'

Marija's husband had whispered to her afterwards that if they were not in the Embassy, they ought, actually, to assume that their conversation was being 'bugged'. She thought he was being a little bit paranoid and had indicated as much.

'We are a long way from home here, my love," he had sighed.

In the back of the Embassy car the two young women were tempted to pinch themselves. Life was suddenly even more marvellous. Marija had accepted that sooner or later she would have to leave Malta; she had never dreamed it would be in these circumstances or that she would be accompanied by her best friend.

"I wish we were going down to Norfolk with 'the boys'," Rosa decided, catching her breath and watching the streets rush past the window.

"We'd only get in the way," Marija giggled.

Rosa giggled, also. Their husbands had spent most of yesterday clambering over big grey warships in the Philadelphia Naval Yard; tomorrow there was talk of a helicopter ride out to a re-commissioned guided missile destroyer conducting trials just off the coast.

The men from the Ministry of Information had scheduled meetings with Congressmen and various other luminaries at City Hall, the American version of Parliament, tomorrow for the two women. Rosa thought it sounded dreadfully boring; secretly Marija was actually quite excited about the prospect.

But then everything was *exciting* about America!

Marija accepted that she and Peter had been sent across the

Atlantic to be 'ambassadors'; she understood why she was being treated like minor royalty and that everybody she met was on their best behaviour. But even so she was beginning to form a real feeling for the country around her, the sprawling mass of its cities, of a population descended from a hundred different races, tribes, places and religions all thrown together into a single bewildering, fascinating melting pot.

She had been born into and raised in a society which was, albeit on a vastly smaller scale, just such a melting pot. Her father was half-English, half Maltese distantly descended probably from Jews expelled from Spain around the time of Christopher Columbus, her mother was Sicilian, her maternal grandparents were possibly from southern Italy, she almost certainly had the blood of Phoenicians, Greeks and Carthaginians in her veins and yet she was *Maltese*. She was Maltese in the same way that all the people around her in Philadelphia, regardless of their ancestry and family traditions were *American*. Of course, nothing was that simple. She might be *Maltese* but she had married an *Englishman*; her children would be Maltese-English or English-Maltese, it mattered not which, like her own father. If the wheel turned once, it soon turned again for that was the way of the World. Another complication: if they were to be in America for two years not only would her first child be born in America, but possibly her daughter's younger brother or sister too before she and Peter returned home. Wherever home was to be?

"You haven't been listening to a word I've said!" Rosa complained with laughing eyes.

Marija shrugged apologetically and brushed the palm of her right hand across her abdomen. Rosa had that dark, Norman look about her sometimes. Of the two women she was the more naturally curvaceous, flashing-eyed. Rosa had always had boys in tow in her teens. Hers was an old Maltese family with a lineage mapped back ten generations; such short genealogies were superficial in the history of ancient Malta. In the last thousand years Norman knights, Christian crusaders, Ottoman Turks, Barbary pirates and the human flotsam of a score of wars had swept around, through, and sometimes washed up on Malta's unforgiving rocky shores. Marija was nutmeg-haired and almond-eyed, Rosa was dark haired and her complexion fairer, both were equally the children of their tiny archipelago situated at the crossroads of the Mediterranean, fought over, broken and rebuilt countless times through history; once pagan then Christian, Moorish and Christian again. Although they came from a place that would probably fit inside the geographical footprint of greater Philadelphia the two women were oddly at home in America...

CLANG! The women looked to each other. The driver gunned the Embassy car's engine hard; Marija and Rosa were forced back into their seats. Suddenly they grasped each other's hand. CLANG!

Splinters of glass sprayed into the car.

Behind their heads the rear window blew out.

Chapter 30

Tuesday 19th May 1964
USS Kitty Hawk (CV-63), Arabian Sea, 47 miles ENE of Al Hadd, Oman

Lieutenant-Commander Walter Brenckmann junior had been standing duty as Officer of the Deck shortly after dawn forty-eight hours ago when the Australian destroyer had approached Carrier Division Seven at flank speed with her bridge signal lamps blinking angrily.
YOU ARE IN RESTRICTED WATERS. PLEASE OBSERVE RADIO SILENCE.
Until then he had suspected – but not known for a fact – that Carrier Division Seven was steaming into hostile waters.
Walter had passed the word for the commanding officer of the Kitty Hawk, Captain Horace Epes to come to the bridge. Shortly afterwards, Captain Epes had requested the man in command of Carrier Division Seven, Rear Admiral William Bringle's presence on the bridge.
Captain Epes had been mightily displeased by the approaching destroyer's presumption. *Nobody* told a US Navy ship how to conduct its operations in international waters.
Rear Admiral Bringle had visibly stiffened with outrage.
Her Majesty's Australian Ship Anzac, a vessel completed shortly after the Second World War on the pattern of the Royal Navy's later Battle class ships had careened through the heart of Carrier Division Seven at better than twenty-five knots before slowing and turning in a wide circle to assume station on the Kitty Hawk's starboard flank at a range of less than two hundred yards; at which stage an abbreviated acrimonious exchange via a crackling, distorted FM radio link had commenced between the commanding officer of the Anzac, and Admiral Bringle.
'Please state your intentions, Kitty Hawk?'
'My intention is to go about my lawful business in international waters, Captain.'
Anzac's commanding officer had identified himself as Commander Steven Turnbull and he clearly did not have much time, or any innate sympathy, with the senior officers of foreign navies.
'I am instructed to inform you that the United States Navy has no lawful business in these waters, sir. Your government surrendered any *lawful* business your Navy might have had in these waters when it reneged on its obligations to its friends in these parts. Stand ready to receive the Commander-in-Chief of All British and Commonwealth Naval Forces in the Indian Ocean. His helicopter will approach your flagship from approximately due south within the next thirty minutes. On his arrival I strongly recommend you think up a better story than the one you've just given me to justify your presence in these waters, Admiral. I will hold position to starboard until further notice. Please notify me by signal lamp if you intend to alter course. That will be all.'

The link went dead.

Admiral Bringle had stared at the receiver in his clenched fist.

'Continue to recover aircraft,' he had grated, clunking the handset onto the bridge plot.

Kitty Hawk's Executive officer had hurried onto the bridge at that juncture.

'I have the deck, Mr Brenckmann!'

'You have the deck, sir!'

As promised the helicopter bearing the Commander-in-Chief of All British and Commonwealth Naval Forces in the Indian Ocean approached out of the south. After a terse radio conversation with Captain Epes, the Westland Wessex had swooped down to land abreast the carrier's big island bridge. Moments later a generously fleshed man of indeterminate middle years had emerged from the Wessex.

Walter Brenckmann, having been hastily dragooned into joining the reception committee for the flagship's unexpected visitor, had found himself at Captain Epes shoulder.

'Horace Epes, Kitty Hawk.'

The newcomer had viewed the carrier's captain thoughtfully for a moment; and then his cherubic, lived-in face had split with a broad grin.

'Nick Davey, Rear-Admiral, these days. I'm delighted to make your acquaintance, sir. I probably need to make my apologies to your Admiral for Steven Turnbull's rustic misunderstanding of the correct protocols. But what can you expect? That's our Antipodean friends for you!'

He had saluted and stuck out his hand which Kitty Hawk's commanding officer had, after an awkward hesitation, shaken. The commanding officer of Carrier Division Seven, the captain of the Kitty Hawk and the British Admiral had locked themselves in Admiral Bringle's day cabin for approximately fifteen minutes; thereafter Rear Admiral Bringle and Captain Epes had emerged with faces dark as thunder and Rear Admiral 'Nick' Davey, exuding charm and roguish insouciance had been whisked away by the Royal Australian Navy Westland Wessex which had originally conveyed him onto the deck of the carrier only minutes earlier.

The Kitty Hawk had been buzzing with rumours and outlandish gossip in the last two days, and now anybody who was not on watch or who could find an excuse to get up on deck or crowd around a vantage point on the ship's port side was watching the approaching squadron.

It was a somewhat rag tag sight but none the less impressive for all that.

At a distance the silhouettes of the three aircraft carriers exuded menace as their stark lines emerged out of the morning haze, while around them their escorts slowly quartered the azure blue waters.

The Kitty Hawk had suspended air operations over an hour before the flagship of the 'Australian, British and New Zealand Task Force' came over the southern horizon.

The modern all-gun cruiser HMS Tiger was streaming a huge battle flag from its tripod main mast, as was every vessel in 'Nick' Davey's motley fleet. Behind the Tiger, the only operational aircraft carrier, the twenty-two-thousand-ton HMS Centaur, had parked all her fighters and helicopters on her deck. Behind Centaur the HMAS Sydney and HMS Triumph, two decommissioned British wartime light carriers converted respectively to the roles of a fast transport and a heavy repair ship, shouldered through the four- or five-feet swells.

Through binoculars Walter Brenckmann blinked in astonishment to see that the flight decks of both *former* aircraft carriers were crowded with tanks, mobile howitzers and other vehicles amidships and forward and aft of the 'vehicle parks' with helicopters and aircraft. Most of the deck cargo was protected by dark tarpaulins but any fool could tell what was under them.

Her Majesty's New Zealand Ship Royalist, an aging Dido class British light cruiser completed in 1943, steamed ahead of the second echelon of the 'ABNZ' fleet. Several small Ton class minesweepers kept company with a big grey fleet oiler and another Royal Fleet Auxiliary vessel that looked like an ammunition ship. There were three bigger escorts, two of which Walter Brenckmann identified as the Voyager, an Australian fleet destroyer, and HMS Palliser, a British anti-submarine frigate.

In purely naval fighting terms, the approaching squadron was no match for the Kitty Hawk, or frankly, any two of her main escorts; but as a visible statement of intent the ABNZ flotilla made a fine sight. The two old-fashioned gunship cruisers bristled with naval rifles – always a more impressive sight than the clean, modernistic pylons of missile launchers – and the carriers, well the carriers just looked 'mean'.

"Those are Centurion tanks on the decks of the carriers," a man by Walter Brenckmann's shoulder said in astonishment. "Where the fuck did they get all those tanks and choppers?"

"Australia," he suggested. The Australian military had been buying small job lots of British tanks ever since the Korean conflict. There had to be at least thirty of the monsters on the decks of the Sydney and the Triumph, perhaps half the armoured inventory of the CMF – the Citizens Military Force of Australia – on those two old carriers. How many more had been stowed below? The Australians would have had to have emptied out their entire armoured 'locker' to send so many tanks abroad.

Who said the British Empire was dead?

Chapter 31

Tuesday 19th May 1964
The Embassy of the United States of America, Oxford

Lady Patricia Harding-Grayson and Joanne Brenckmann exchanged pecking kisses of greeting before settling in comfortable chairs in the Ambassador's private rooms. There was a quiet air of siege in the collection of ancient buildings next to Oxford Castle which had been allocated to the American Embassy; outside there were Coldstream Guardsmen in battledress and full combat webbing cradling loaded L1A1 rifles beside uniformed US Marines still equipped with pre-World War II ceremonial carbines. Policemen armed with Webley revolvers and long night sticks manned the cordons roping off the surrounding streets.

The word was that the British Guardsmen had orders to shoot anybody who attempted to break into the Embassy and that those orders came directly from the Prime Minister's mouth. Irrespective of how *disappointed* she was with their 'half-hearted transatlantic allies', Margaret Thatcher was determined that the rule of law be upheld and that the niceties of ensuring the safety of diplomatic envoys, their staff and their families should be scrupulously observed.

'Just because the Americans seem, self-evidently, to be incapable of protecting *our* people in Philadelphia that is no excuse for laxness on our part!' She had declared angrily in the House of Commons only the previous evening.

Yesterday, soon after the news from Philadelphia had arrived there had been a near riot in two streets adjacent to the Embassy as protesters attempted to break through to the compound; presumably to exact their own rough justice for the outrage perpetrated against the 'heroes of the Battle of Malta'.

"What on earth have you done with Walter today?" Pat Harding-Grayson inquired brightly. The Foreign Secretary's wife knew exactly what her new friend had *done* with her hard-pressed husband; the thing was to break the ice and to attempt to cheer up Joanne Brenckmann.

The Ambassador's wife rolled her eyes.

"He insisted on going down to Portsmouth as planned," she complained resignedly. In a moment she smiled. "Actually, I knew he was really looking forward to meeting up again with Captain Penberthy - he's the new Deputy Superintendent of the Naval Dockyard – and I *insisted* that he go."

"Captain Penberthy?"

"He and Walter got to know each other last year. David Penberthy was captain of HMS Talavera, Peter Christopher's commanding officer, and Walter, as the US Navy's unwanted liaison officer with your Channel Fleet spent most of his time carrying out *goodwill* visits to ships in harbour. David Penberthy and his officers were always very welcoming and, frankly, very *sympathetic* and understanding of Walter's position. David Penberthy was badly injured in the Battle of Lampedusa. He lost a foot..."

"Of course," Pat Harding-Grayson recollected. "That was when Peter Christopher took command and saved the day."

Joanne Brenckmann smiled uneasily.

"It is just dreadful that somebody could attack *their* cars like that!" She said shaking her head, ashamed for her countrymen. "Sometimes, I despair, Pat. I really do!"

The Foreign Secretary's wife had no intention of letting her friend brood on this.

"Well, fortunately, there was hardly any harm done. Lady Marija and Mrs Hannay escaped with only very minor injuries. From what Lord Franks has said the whole American body politic has united in its condemnation of the attack." She decided to change the subject. "So, Walter is spying on the Royal Navy at Portsmouth today?"

Joanne Brenckmann laughed.

"He's always wanted to stand on the deck of HMS Victory and climb up her halyards."

"Shouldn't Walter be more interested in how soon the Ark Royal will be ready for sea again?" Pat Harding-Grayson countered mischievously.

"Possibly," the US Ambassador's wife agreed as coffees were brought in.

"I'd forgotten what *proper* coffee was, you know?" Her guest confessed.

Joanne Brenckmann raised her cup to her lips, viewing her visitor thoughtfully over the rim. She and Pat Harding-Grayson were ever firmer friends but, and it was a big but, she was the wife of the US Ambassador and Pat was the – very worldly, very astute wife - of the British Foreign Secretary *and* the confidante of Margaret Thatcher. The Ambassador's wife could have no illusion that anything she said privately, or that anything either of them said to each other, was in any meaningful way *private*.

"What's Tom up to. Nobody's seen him in Oxford for several days?"

"My dear," the Foreign Secretary's wife laughed, "for all I know he could be tucked up in bed somewhere with his mistress!"

Joanne tried not to giggle like a schoolgirl.

Sir Thomas Harding-Grayson was far too busy to keep a mistress; even if he was *that* sort of man, which he was not.

"I'm sorry, I shouldn't ask."

Pat Harding-Grayson had been a little surprised by how adroitly her friend had 'played the game' virtually from the day she had arrived in England. For all that she gave the impression of never having been anything other than a Boston housewife and mother, a little *down home* and disinterested in politics and world affairs, Pat had always found Joanne Brenckmann to be a very shrewd kindred spirit.

"That's quite all right, Joanne. Actually, Tom is in the Middle

East. He flew out with the Chief of the Defence Staff to *assess the situation.* The man on the spot, General Carver is probably the best man we've got but the Prime Minister is determined to make sure that the *political* side of things does not get lost in the business of *war fighting.*"

Joanne Brenckmann absorbed this revelation.

Anglo-American relations were estranged but unlike in November and December last year, this time around, *nobody* was about to risk anything getting lost in translation via *normal* channels. The Kennedy Administration might not know anything about exactly how the British and their Commonwealth allies proposed to *fight* the rejuvenated Red Army in Iraq or Iran; but it knew that when Margaret Thatcher talked about 'drawing a line in the sand' she was in deadly earnest.

Joanne Brenckmann also knew that tomorrow there was to be yet another Parliamentary vote of confidence – the second in a month and the fourth in the short tenure of the UAUK - in the House of Commons in the Great Hall of Christ Church College. In a day's time there might be a new government, a new leader and that the United Kingdom's resolve to continue the fight could evaporate overnight. What then?

"And what is the *political* side of things?" Joanne Brenckmann asked innocently.

"What happens after the war in the Persian Gulf," Pat explained pleasantly. The two women could have been discussing table settings or a cake recipe.

The Ambassador's wife realised that in talking about 'the Persian Gulf' as opposed to Iraq or Iran her friend was making a big and potentially key distinction.

"The Gulf?"

Pat Harding-Grayson nodded.

"The Russians don't want to rule Iraq, they don't even really want Abadan. What they want is to control the Persian Gulf and to have access to the oceans of the World. They have oil enough for their own needs already; the oilfields of the Caucasus, and soon, if they haven't seized them already, the oilfields of Iraqi Kurdistan. We're the ones who *need* Abadan and you, the Americans, are the ones who *will* in a few years badly *need* the oilfields of north-eastern Arabia and Kuwait. Without that oil American industry will grind to a halt inside a decade and then there will have to be another, unimaginably bloody war over the control of the very same oilfields the Administration won't lift a finger to defend unless or until JFK is re-elected in November."

Joanne Brenckmann stared at her friend.

"I don't..."

She knew that she represented one of many back channels by which the UAUK kept in touch with the Administration in Philadelphia. There were too many things it was hard, if not impossible for the British to say directly to her husband, the Ambassador. There were so many nonsensical protocols designed to frustrate direct talking; and too many things which had to be deniable at a later date.

"*When* Margaret wins tomorrow's vote of confidence she wants President Kennedy to invite her to Philadelphia."

"Okay," Joanne whispered, thinking she understood.

"Everybody's had a chance to think things through now," Pat went on, keen to break this as gently as possibly to her friend. "However, although the Prime Minister still feels desperately let down by the President, she's come to the conclusion that if *we* are going to be the ones left holding the, er, *baby*, then it is only right and proper that there should be an appropriate *quid pro quo*."

Chapter 32

Wednesday 20th May 1964
Great Hall, Christ Church College, Oxford

When Margaret Thatcher rose to speak it was to a long and sustained chorus of jeers from across the other side of the hall and a stony silence from the majority of the *notional* friends at her back. She waited for stillness, for the bear pit to quieten about her. While she waited, she looked around at her surroundings struck by the sensation that she had never really seen this place as it was, or for what it had become before now.

Although the reinstitution of Parliament in Oxford had been her decision; the details of that edict and its physical implementation had been handled by others. The immediate post-October War capital of the United Kingdom had been established at Cheltenham almost by accident, the city having survived the war untouched, GCHQ being located within it and it having previously been identified as a possible 'governmental centre' in at least one existing war plan. However, Cheltenham had never been a viable long-term capital, not when Oxford, Birmingham, Manchester and historic cities like Winchester or Bristol had survived equally undamaged. But in November 1962 nobody had thought farther ahead than day to day survival; the decision to move to Oxford had come about because symbolically, *she* had decided that 'just surviving' was *not* good enough.

The British people deserved better than that.

The layout of the old chamber of the House of Commons in the now wrecked shell of the Palace of Westminster had owed its configuration to that of an earlier chamber, St Stephen's Chapel, destroyed by fire in 1834. The construction of St Stephen's Chapel within the old Palace of Westminster had been completed around the year 1297 during the reign of Edward I. It was only after Westminster ceased to be a royal palace that Henry VIII's son Edward VI had passed the Abolition of Chantries Act in 1547, making the chapel available for the Commons. Thus, St Stephen's Chapel had become the debating chamber of the House of Commons for nearly three centuries until its destruction by fire in 1834.

The mother of Parliaments was nothing if not faithful – some said 'the prisoner' - of its traditions and what it saw as its ancient prerogatives. In the rebuilt Victorian Palace of Westminster, the layout of the chamber of the Commons had been faithfully copied from that of St Stephen's Chapel; the Speaker's chair was placed upon the altar steps as if still in a church, where a lectern had once stood the Table of the House was positioned, and as they had from time immemorial the Members of the House sat facing each other in medieval fashion in opposing choir stalls. True to that tradition in recent weeks carpenters and joiners had been industriously re-creating those uncomfortable, tiered pews, intent on partially recreating the old bear pit in the image of its former glory.

Furniture requisitioned, borrowed and 'found' around the College had been returned and today the chamber smelled of freshly sawn wood, varnish and resin. The Prime Minister had been informed that the Chamber theoretically 'comfortably sat' some three hundred and eighty Members, preserving a standing area for 'gentlemen of the press'.

Oddly, although the Great Hall of Christ Church College was probably not that much bigger than the previous home of the Commons it seemed, to the Prime Minister, significantly less claustrophobic.

Margaret Thatcher had been Prime Minister for approximately six tumultuous and mostly disastrous months. Her attempts to rebuild the 'special relationship' with the United States had been doomed from the start, little or no progress had been made in beginning the great work of national reconstruction, she had split her own party, fragmented the political system of the country and presided over one military disaster after another. Back in the darkest days of the Second World War Churchill might have survived the Norwegian fiasco, the Fall of France, the supposed 'miracle' of Dunkirk, and later the fall of Singapore and a catalogue of disasters in the Western Desert at the hands of Rommel; but he had had years of experience in the highest government posts and *his* disasters had happened over a period of many years.

Her disasters had all happened inside six months and each new setback had come hard on the heels of the last. Yes, the Royal Navy had held on in the Mediterranean. Yes, Cyprus had been re-taken but the trouble was that these were isolated bright spots in a universally gloomy canvas painted by one humiliation after another. But for the suicidal bravery of the crews of two outgunned British warships Malta might have fallen; the outrages at Brize Norton and Cheltenham which had signalled the latest breakdown of Anglo-US relations closely following the Kennedy Administration's mendacious decision to respect the letter, rather than the spirit of the US-UK Mutual Defense Treaty that she had signed in January, had been the last straw.

The British people craved peace.

Her people wanted to rebuild, to properly grieve for and to come to terms with what had been lost.

Instead, all she had given her people was war and more war.

War without end...

Margaret Thatcher cleared her throat.

Although not a single hair was out of place on her head, every time she looked in the mirror, she saw the premature age lines in her face, the weariness in her blue eyes, and she seriously wondered how long she could go on...*alone*. The death of Julian Christopher still cut her to her soul. Had he been at her side these last few terrible weeks she could have faced anything. No matter how she bluffed and brazened her way through the intolerable obstacles placed daily in her path, she knew that her strength was, slowly, surely failing.

"There are those who say that after all we have been through," she declaimed, empowered and energised by the one thing which had never let her down, her anger. "There are those who say we should retreat back into our island home. There are those who are tired, tired of the battle to live day by day; tired of going to bed each night hungry, and sick to their hearts that their children are growing up in the World that *we* have made for them."

The Prime Minister had expected heckling, to be shouted down.

However, unhappy muttering aside her most vociferous public detractors on the other side of the chamber seemed unnaturally subdued. It was as if they too recognised at last that the country was at the crossroads.

"Today I have no intention of mounting a defence of my leadership of our country," Margaret Thatcher said. "Today, I propose to share with the House my view of the situation that we find ourselves in. I plan to speak plainly. This is not a time for eloquent extemporizations about what, in the best of all Worlds, we would do next or even, dare I say it, of what we might or ought to have done in times past. Today, we must address the reality of our situation."

She could feel the restiveness behind her on the government benches; and idly wondered who would be the first to plunge a knife between her shoulder blades.

"President Kennedy has invited me to America to discuss a new resolution of our long-term relationship. When an old friend offers such an invitation it must be accepted. If I remain Prime Minister after this day I will fly to America on Friday."

Margaret Thatcher let this sink in.

"Immediately prior to leaving my private office for this House I was informed that a Royal Navy submarine had attacked and sunk the Argentine aircraft carrier the *Indepencia*. The *Indepencia* was fifteen miles outside the declared air and maritime *Total Exclusion Zone* mandated by the UAUK," she paused as the mutter of voices in the hall threatened to sweep her away. "However, in the last twenty-four hours Argentine warships and aircraft flying from the *Indepencia*, have harassed and threatened British registered vessels sailing in international waters inside *and* outside the total exclusion zone. Another of our submarines has since attacked and sunk an Argentine destroyer that was attempting to illegally escort the 'arrested' British registered Motor Vessel *Stanley Caird* towards Argentine territorial waters after firing on and apprehending that vessel in international waters."

To the Prime Minister's surprise, the threatened uproar subsided to a whimper of bad-tempered growling. She had anticipated and prepared for many things; she had not seriously contemplated the possibility that Honourable Members on both sides of the House would be genuinely *shocked*.

"The blockade of the Falklands Archipelago will continue to be vigorously enforced. If the Argentine persists with the employment of aggressive measures against British shipping and interests in international waters or *anywhere* in the Southern Ocean inside or outside the specified exclusion zones, we will meet force with force. Honourable Members should know that the captain of every Royal Navy submarine deployed to the South Atlantic was handed a sealed envelope bearing orders signed by Flag Officer Submarines and countersigned by me. *Our* captains are authorised to take whatever offensive measures they deem appropriate including the sinking without warning of merchant vessels conveying supplies to the Argentine forces currently occupying the Falklands Archipelago in breach of international law."

Margaret Thatcher had found her second wind.

The pitch of her voice became hectoring, defiantly angry.

"RAF bombers have mounted attacks against Red Army troop concentrations and communications targets in Northern Iraq for the third successive night. During these attacks several large 'Tallboy' type six-ton bombs were dropped on bridges around Sulaymaniyah and elsewhere. No aircraft were lost or damaged in *any* of these missions."

The Prime Minister's gaze swept around the chamber.

"Neither I nor any member of my government will be supplying daily updates on the war in Iraq, or on the measures that we are taking to protect our interests in the Persian Gulf. However, I will tell you that if the High Command of the Soviet Union thinks, for a single minute that *we* and our *allies* will sit back and allow the Red Army to invade and *rape* Iraq and Iran without exacting a terrible cost on it in terms of men, materiel and morale, it is tragically mistaken. It is the policy of *my* government to resist tyranny; and while I live, *we* will never surrender. I say to the men in the new Kremlin – wherever that vile new incarnation of the evil empire may now be located in southern Russia – that no matter what ground your tanks seize *we* will never rest until you are expelled from it. You may defeat us in one battle, you may defeat us in many battles but we will never, ever give in. *You* are responsible for the abomination of Red Dawn, for the despicable use of nuclear weapons against civilian populations in Turkey, Greece, Cyprus and Egypt!"

She had grown breathless with rage; forced herself to take several deep breaths.

"*You* are criminals responsible for the obliteration of Tehran," she spat. "After that atrocity I warned *you* that a further use of nuclear weapons would result in an all-out strike against your remaining centres of population. I have not yet received an unequivocal acknowledgement of this warning. I demand that the Soviet High Command provide such an unequivocal acknowledgement not later than midnight on 27th May," she paused, "or be prepared to face the consequences."

Chapter 33

Thursday 21st May 1964
Heliopolis Presidential Palace, Cairo, Egypt

Muhammad Anwar El Sadat was a cautious, calculating man; it was no accident that he had risen to be the President of Egypt's right-hand man and at some stage, possibly, his friend Abdel Gamal Nasser's successor. But all that was a long way in the future – if it happened at all – for he and Nasser were relatively young men in their mid-forties, and Nasser was one of those rare, once in a lifetime, men who was touched with greatness. While Sadat was less enthralled by dreams of a pan-Arabic, or some kind of 'united' Arab Republic enfolding the 'Arab World' like a 'string of pearls' than his friend, if it was any man's destiny to reunite the 'Arab World' that man was almost certainly Nasser and *his* time was *now*.

Or if *his* time was not now then it was very *soon*.

Becoming embroiled in the Yemen civil war last year – contained mostly in the north of that country, thank Allah – was in retrospect a false start in the process of reunification. But of course, nobody had actually known what *sign* they were waiting for in the first place. The bombing of Ismailia and the Soviet Invasion of Iran and Iraq had changed all that. Egypt had been a Russian client in the years before the October War, and consequently its Army and Air Force was largely equipped with Red Army and Red Air Force surplus weaponry. The failed attack on Cairo – the missile launched, according to the United States and the British from within the borders of the old Soviet Union had detonated beyond the Pyramids of Giza – and the devastating strike on Ismailia, had given the government the excuse to round up former Soviet observers and advisors in the country, and hopefully, freed the Egyptian military from their grasp.

Nasser had no more wanted the Russians in his country than he had the British but timing was everything; and now fate had gifted Egypt a fleeting opportunity to achieve in weeks and months the task that Nasser and Sadat had hardly dreamed of even beginning in their own lifetimes. The prize was so immense it justified almost any risks and that was the problem, because if they were thinking in such terms then surely, so were their *real* enemies among whom they included both the Americans *and* the British.

Gamal Abdel Nasser was standing framed in the window of his opulent Presidential Office when Sadat was shown into his presence. Nasser had been staring out across the inner courtyard of the old hotel, lost in his thoughts. The *idea* of laying the foundation of an unbreakable United Arab Republic which might one day stretch from the Atlas Mountains of Morocco to the Zagros Mountains of Western Iran, and from the Anatolian plains to the Mountains of the Moon, the fabled source of the great Nile was fatally seductive. It was a thing more to do with myths and legends; a challenge best taken up by a modern-day Alexander and Nasser understood as much. However, with the Americans gone, the British otherwise engaged, the Iraqi Army routed by the invaders and the whole Middle East in turmoil; when would there ever be a better time to assert Egypt's ancient supremacy?

"So," the President of Egypt asked rhetorically, his tone thoughtful and strangely distracted, "it is true that a large British fleet has docked at Dammam?"

"Yes. There is talk of an *ANZAC* Brigade being formed for service in Kuwait," Sadat explained. "Australians, New Zealanders with modern tanks and artillery to fight beside the infantry formations the British have already flown out to the Kingdom."

"The British are making a lot of the bombing raids being carried out from Cyprus. What do our people in Iraq report?"

Our people in Iraq referred in the main to members of the *Muslim Brotherhood* too distant from Cairo to have been purged and harassed by Nasser's security service and a dwindling handful of Iraqi Army officers sympathetic to Nasser's dream of a pan-Arab republic, rather than any kind of coherent intelligence network.

The two men sat down, the President behind his desk and Sadat, weary from his travels in the chair before it. Notwithstanding their friendship there was never a scintilla of doubt as to who was the real master. There was a hiatus while strong bitter coffee was poured by acolytes and both men collected their thoughts.

Muhammad Anwar El Sadat had come a long way from his humble Upper Egyptian roots. Born one of thirteen children of a poor family at Mit Abu al-Kum in December 1918 to a Nubian father and a half-Sudanese mother, he had faced insults and racial jibes from the first day he was exposed to the milieu of Lower Egypt and the alleged sophistication of contemporaries and enemies from Cairo, Alexandria and the Delta. Throughout his adult life his opponents and detractors had never regarded him as being 'Egyptian enough', and latterly they sniggered behind their hands and accused him of being 'Nasser's black poodle'. As a boy his heroes had been Mustafa Kemal Ataturk, the leader of the 'Young Turks', Mahatma Gandhi, and as a young man he had been fascinated and excited by the early success of the Nazi 'Blitzkrieg'. It was shortly after graduating from the Royal Military Academy in Cairo in 1938 that Sadat, a conflicted proto-revolutionary had been posted to the Sudan – then a part of Egypt under the 'protection' of the British – where he had met Nasser and with other officers founded the *Free Officers*, committed to expunging the two great evils then afflicting their country; the British presence and the endemic corruption of the ruling royal regime.

During World War II the British had jailed Sadat for making approaches to the Italians and the Germans for help. He was by nature a profoundly political animal; during and after that war, acting on behalf of the *Free Officers* he was involved with and penetrated the *Muslim Brotherhood*, the fascist movement *Young Egypt*, and the pro-palace *Iron Guard of Egypt*. When in 1952 the *Free Officers* had overthrown King Farouk it was Sadat who had made the announcement over Egyptian radio. That had been a momentous moment in his life; and shortly 'Nasser's black poodle', the second most powerful man in Egypt and his 'master' had to make a decision upon which, literally, the fate of their nation hung.

"The British bombing is being undertaken by a small number of aircraft," Sadat reported. "We believe they have persuaded the Syrians, and possibly the Lebanese to allow the RAF to overfly their territory enabling the bombers involved to carry the heaviest possible bomb loads. The Soviets probably meant to use Sulaymaniyah as a concentration point and logistics hub, a 'pause point' before renewing their invasion. However, the bombing seems to have forced them to proceed in a somewhat 'piecemeal' fashion. If our Iraqi friends only stopped fighting among themselves," he observed resignedly, "the British bombing might actually have given them a chance to at least slow down, if not halt the Russians before they get to Baghdad. But," he shrugged, "we know that won't happen."

"Have the Iraqis started moving forces to reinforce the Baghdad garrison yet?"

Sadat shook his head. "No, the forces in the south have drawn back around Basra. For all we know they might be about to mount another idiotic incursion into Iran."

Nasser turned the possibilities in his head.

"You spoke to the Iraqi Ambassador?"

"The man was more concerned with seeking asylum for his family and business associates in Baghdad, than he was about seeking our help on the battlefield," his friend responded, quietly contemptuous. "He seems to be under the impression that the British or the Americans will come charging to Iraq's rescue at any minute. He kept on saying 'surely they will defend *their* oil' to me!"

Nasser nodded.

By the grace of Allah, he led a 'historic' country, not a collection of ethnically, religiously and culturally incompatible 'provinces' cobbled together by British and French diplomats over forty years ago at a now ruined French palace outside Paris. Egypt had existed throughout recorded history; it was *the* great power of the Middle East, situated astride both Africa and Arabia. From its history it derived intrinsic and legitimate nationhood and unity; Iraq had none of that for all the fact that its ancient Mesopotamian settlements had been the cradles of civilization. There was no such thing as 'Iraq' other than in the minds of map makers and long dead European politicians. Iraq was merely one of the more egregious of the blunders written into the Treaty of Versailles.

Iraq was not worth fighting for. But Basra?

Well, that was different, likewise Kuwait which the Russians would surely gobble up sooner or later if they gained a secure foothold in the Persian Gulf. If the Soviets ever established themselves in Southern Iraq and Iran what then of Egyptian claims to be a regional power?

There was also the matter of Egypt's own oilfields. Commercially viable fields had been discovered in the first decade of the twentieth century in the Gulf of Suez, other, as yet unexploited but potentially much larger reserves of oil lay under the Sinai Peninsula around Abu Rudeis and Ra's Sudr. New reserves were regularly discovered in both the Western and the Eastern deserts; had the World not gone mad in October 1962 Nasser's Egypt might have already been well down the road to becoming a major global oil producer by now. The riches that might have earned would have made it possible to fund his regime's raft of radical social reforms; made it unnecessary to go cap in hand to the old superpowers to finance great projects like the High Dam at Aswan.

Those oilfields, 'under the auspices of a new pan-Arab Republic, and those of Kuwait and Southern Iraq, perhaps, allied with those of Abadan and the adjacent Iranian oilfields might yet underwrite a new and lasting Arab economic, cultural and military renaissance'.

These were the exact words that had come from the mouth of a *British* Foreign Secretary! It was hardly surprising that Nasser and Sadat had looked at each other in askance, momentarily too stunned to respond.

'Of course,' Sir Thomas Harding-Grayson had continued, as if he was discussing some small and insignificant caveat in a ten-thousand-word long treatise on building sand castles, 'one cannot ever be entirely certain how things will play out. War is a notoriously messy business.'

Egypt was to have a 'free hand' in Libya; to be at liberty to restore order to that 'sadly perturbed land' and thus 'secure the southern flank' of the Central and Eastern Mediterranean theatre of operations. Moreover, the British had no objection 'in principle' to Cairo extending its 'influence' further west into, for example, Tunisia, or south into Sudan, etcetera. However, if Iraq succumbed to invasion, not just Arabia was threatened and 'British interests' were denied a hitherto relatively secure supply of oil, Egypt's own position in the region was inevitably undermined 'perhaps, for all time'.

Sir Thomas Harding-Grayson had proposed a pact; albeit the sort of diplomatic pact that nobody in their right mind would dare to write down in black and white, let alone append his signature to.

The British wanted three things. Firstly, at least one, preferably two Egyptian armoured divisions, with supporting infantry and logistics support to be transported around the Arabian Peninsula by sea to be ready for full scale offensive operations not later than 30th June. No, at this stage Sir Thomas was not at liberty to discuss the significance of that date or any other 'military matter.

Secondly, the above-mentioned forces would be placed at the disposal of and under the orders of the *Allied Commander-in-Chief, Middle East* for a period of not less than thirty days after the 'commencement of offensive operations.

Thirdly, *after* the cessation of hostilities in Iraq – there had been no mention of Iran in the contract – the United Kingdom and the Arab

Republic of Egypt would seek to establish good relations based on shared economic and geopolitical interests including a mutual defence pact covering the Eastern Mediterranean and 'those territories' surrounding the Persian Gulf.

Both Nasser and Sadat were military men who understood exactly what was on the table.

'Let us be clear; after we fight the Soviets in Basra Province?' Nasser had inquired of the British Foreign Secretary. 'You understand that it may not be possible for my tanks to *retire* immediately to their initial start lines?'

'Yes. That is not a problem.'

That was when Nasser and Sadat had known the gamble was worth the candle.

'It is all very simple,' the Englishman had explained. 'You have a free hand in the Western Desert all the way to the Tunisian border. Simultaneously, your Army has a chance to earn a glorious victory in the east. Thereafter, with your oilfields secure for a generation you will be able to afford to purchase the fruits of regenerated British industry with which to modernize your economy.'

Nasser had ordered the 1st and 3rd Armoured Divisions of the Egyptian Army to twenty-four hours readiness to move several days ago. At the same time, he had ordered units under the command of several of his most trusted men to 'guard' key installations and facilities within the capital. In a revolutionary state all large troop movements caused ripples of alarm and sparked in dissidents, sudden hopes of a new coup d'état.

"What is your advice?" Nasser asked his friend.

Sadat hesitated. When it became obvious that the regime was, to all intents, siding with the British against the Soviets the remaining *stay behind* elements of the phalanx of Russian experts and advisors who had avoided the round ups after the Ismailia strike, would almost certainly attempt to foment an uprising. The streets of Cairo would run with blood well before this thing began to play out, and if the adventure ended in failure both he and Nasser would probably pay for it with their heads.

"There are those who will never forgive us," he observed sadly. "But the British are right." The words stuck in his throat. "If we do nothing in a few years we will either have to bow to the Russians again, or perhaps, the Americans. Before the October War we believed that this was our destiny; that and the endless conflict with the Israelis."

"Ah," Nasser sighed, "the Israelis."

"I think the British are right that the Israelis will sit this thing out. In any event Palestine is a matter that we cannot resolve at this time."

"I agree." Nasser forced a grim smile. "Summon the Chief of Staff of the Army and the commanders of the 1st and 3rd Armoured Divisions to the Presidential Palace. I will personally give them their orders."

Chapter 34

Thursday 21st May 1964
British Embassy, Philadelphia, Pennsylvania

J. William Fulbright was having a hard time containing his anger and it was patently obvious to every member of the Embassy welcoming committee that morning. This was hardly surprising since he felt like he was not so much walking barefoot over hot coals, as tiptoeing into an invisible wall of *disdain* as he was ushered into the Ambassador's spacious private office. The fact that Lord Franks, the United Kingdom's Ambassador to the United States of America was at pains to pretend that nothing whatsoever was amiss, did not help; nor did the charming pleasantries of Lady Franks, or the immaculately neutral tones of the Chargé d'affaires, or the grim, fixed expression on the face of the tall, angry-eyed young naval officer who completed a reception line whose civility was of that particularly English, icily polite variety.

The Secretary of State waited for the Ambassador to separate himself from his retinue but when Lady Franks made her excuses and left to supervise the provision of tea and coffee, the Chargé d'affaires, fifty-five-year-old Sir Patrick Henry Dean, and Captain Sir Peter Christopher, VC, remained.

Fulbright had known Dean from before the October War, when Dean had been the last Representative of the United Kingdom to the United Nations. As for Peter Christopher, his only previous meetings had been those of the nodding acquaintance type which had given him no real insight into the younger man's temper or character. This was unfortunate because right now Peter Christopher looked like he wanted to hit him with a baseball bat.

"I know that the President has written to you," Fulbright said to Lord Franks while he looked to the young naval officer, "but I would like to take this opportunity to personally apologise to you, Sir Peter, and to send my best wishes and hopes for her swift recovery from her injuries to Mrs Hannay."

The 'personal security detachment' provided by the Philadelphia Police Department had permitted an imposter dressed in one of their uniforms - riding a *Harley Davidson* – to drive unchallenged up to the first of the two Embassy cars transporting the two couples back to the compound after attending Mass at the Cathedral Basilica of Saints Peter and Paul. The assassin had been able to fire several shots into the passenger compartment of the vehicle – carrying Marija and Rosa Hannay – with a Navy Colt forty-five and would have dropped a hand grenade through the shattered offside window of the car had not Jack Griffin, while the vehicle was travelling at over thirty miles-an-hour thrown open his front passenger side door and hurled himself under the wheels of the assassin's Harley.

The grenade had skittered away and exploded on the pavement

some distance from either Embassy car, killing an elderly man and seriously wounding his wife as the cars sped away, leaving Jack Griffin, bloodied but incandescent with rage beating seven bells out of the attacker. Whereupon, the hapless first Philadelphia PD men on the scene had attempted to arrest Griffin for apparently attacking one of their own, and had it not been for his ankle having been broken when he came off his motorcycle, the assassin would probably have escaped in the melee.

The end result of the whole outrageous farrago was that while Rosa Hannay had received superficial injuries from flying glass, and mercifully, Marija had not suffered so much as a scratch, Jack Griffin was still in hospital nursing injuries entirely consistent with those one might reasonably expect to sustain in falling out of a moving car, unseating a motor cyclist by the reckless, nevertheless effective expedient of rolling under his wheels, and from the subsequent brutal pummelling he had received at the hands of the Philadelphia PD.

"Thank you, sir," Peter Christopher responded stiffly. "Mrs Hannay's injuries are on the mend, sir. As you know, my wife was unhurt. Although," the younger man sniffed, biting back what he had been about to say before settling on a mildly accusative: "the same cannot be said for Chief Petty Officer Griffin."

It was the quiet, seething courtesy in what Peter Christopher said next that stung J. William Fulbright, in the moment and whenever he thought about it later.

"But for *Jack's* bravery and courageous self-sacrifice my wife and Rosa Hannay could very easily have been killed due to the negligence of the police and the *other* local and federal law enforcement officers into whose hands we had been so unwise as to entrust our safety."

Peter and Marija had already been visited at the Embassy by the Chief of the Philadelphia Police Department, Commissioner Howard Leary, one of the shortest policemen Peter had ever met. The man was barely an inch or so taller than Marija. Marija had been Marija, utterly charming; her husband had been moody and churlish, communicating in terse monosyllables for which his wife had gently chastised him after Leary had departed.

"That was deplorable," the Secretary of State agreed with no little gravitas.

"Quite, sir," Peter concurred. In truth his mood had not been improved by a meeting earlier that morning with Rachel Piotrowska – the woman he had previously known as Clara Pullman – whom, it seemed, was now an openly acknowledged officer of the newly formed National Security Service, of which GCHQ, MI5 and MI6 had become subordinate branches under the directorship of Sir Dick White. Clara, or rather, *Rachel*, had been a little vague about the purpose of her visit to Philadelphia which was par for the course with spooks.

Presently, she was 'talking' to Rosa, 'just to tie up a few loose ends', presumably concerning the 'Malta end' of the big lie that he and the two wives had been asked to live with in the wake of Samuel Calleja's execution. To 'facilitate' this little *tête-à-tête* Peter had been 'asked' to send Alan Hannay on 'an appropriate errand' for a few hours. Much as this was intensely galling he had sent his friend – if they had not been close, good friends before they came to America they were most assuredly that now - over to the Navy Department building in Camden to organise a 'proper visit' by Marija and himself early next week; a publicity exercise with photo shoots and such like, to persuade the American public that the hero of the Battle of Malta did not hold any grudges against the US Navy on account of its tardy late arrival at the actual battle.

Notwithstanding the recent provocation he did *not* hold any such 'grudges', and certainly not against the 'American public' or 'people'. His war had started in early December last year in the gun line bombarding Santander in Northern Spain, turned grim the next day when Talavera was bombed off Cape Finisterre, and red hot in the fire fight inshore at the Battle of Lampedusa. The desperate struggle to save the USS Enterprise south of Malta in February already seemed an awfully long time ago; and the events of the Battle of Malta after which he had been pulled out of the cold drowning sea by *American sailors* who had dived into the flotsam of Talavera's sinking to tie a lifeline around him, well, all that was very nearly just a bad dream. The last six months had rushed past in a blur and in the middle of it he had found, met and married the love of his life. Occasionally, he wondered if he had already lived his life and that everything that happened in the future, would be in some way diminished by what he had lived through and against the odds, survived these last few months. However, those were thoughts only for the darkness. Whenever he was with Marija he had no doubts that the best of his life was still to come and that as sure as night followed day, sooner or later he would find himself again standing on the bridge of another big grey warship. Although, hopefully never again leading *his* people so directly into the jaws of death...

Rachel Piotrowska would be talking to Rosa and Marija, who had insisted on being present during the 'interview', about Rosa's dead first husband. She would want to know, to double and triple check each and every one of Rosa's memories. Who had Samuel met? Who had he spoken to or of, his movements, habits, what he said in his sleep, on and on, for ever. It must be intolerable for Rosa not to be able to confide a single word of this, any of it to Alan. The worst of it was yet to come; one day the wreck of HMS Torquay would be raised from the bottom of the Grand Harbour where she had lain since January – her back broken by a Red Dawn saboteur's demolition charges - and on that day human remains *would* be discovered. Later *those* remains would be identified as those of Samuel Calleja (1932-1964) and buried, with due ceremony and presumably no little public fanfare. Samuel Calleja, the story would go, had been an innocent dupe of evil men and in years to come nobody would connect the execution of an unnamed Soviet parachutist for war crimes on 6th April 1964 at Paola Prison, with Marija's brother, and Rosa's husband. Or that at least was the great plan concocted by the Ministry of

Information because the country needed heroes and heroines, princes and princesses and whatever the actors in the great drama thought about it, they owed it to *their* people to accept and to play the roles which fate had randomly assigned to them.

Peter hated having to lie to Alan Hannay.

It felt like betrayal even though it was his duty.

Just as it had been his duty to drive Talavera into the big guns of those Soviet warships off Malta less than two months ago; and it was his duty to go along with the lie.

"Marija and Rosa survived, sir," Peter Christopher told the Secretary of State. "That is all I care about. That, sir," he added, "is the end of the matter. Marija and Rosa would be mortified if this unfortunate incident was allowed to in any way further sour the relations between our two countries."

The British Ambassador decided to take charge of the meeting.

"I have asked Sir Patrick and Sir Peter to be present," he explained with brusque courtesy as he waved the other men towards a circle of chairs near the high, old-fashioned windows that allowed sunshine to fill the room with warmth each afternoon. "Sir Patrick will minute whatever we have to say to each other, Secretary of State."

"This meeting is better 'off the record', Ambassador," Fulbright objected.

"Circumstances make that impossible, I fear."

The four men sat down, the Chargé d'affaires picked up a large lined hard back notebook and a propelling pencil. Sitting next to him with the US Secretary of State fulminating to his right Peter Christopher had no idea what he was still doing in the room.

"You wanted to speak to me," Lord Franks prompted. "You have the floor, Mr Secretary."

Fulbright had requested the United Kingdom's Ambassador attend him 'at his earliest convenience' at the State Department Building in downtown Philadelphia; Oliver Franks had politely declined that invitation. Acting against his own better judgement on orders from Oxford – orders that came from the very top – he had informed the Secretary of State that: 'I am to convey to you that since it is obviously unsafe for representatives of the Unity Administration of the United Kingdom to travel the streets of Philadelphia at present, that I must, respectfully suggest that *you* call on the Embassy."

"Your Prime Minister virtually threatened to nuke the Soviets if things went badly in Iraq," Fulbright stated unhappily.

"Yes," Lord Franks agreed. "That is what Mrs Thatcher said."

"That's madness!"

"What? Threatening nuclear war?" The Ambassador posed the questions rhetorically, wearily. "Or waging it without warning anybody first, Mr Secretary?"

Peter Christopher winced.

Then to his astonishment J. William Fulbright, the man who had inherited the poisoned chalice of America's disastrous post-October War foreign policy after the Battle of Washington in December last year, smiled. He actually *smiled.*

"That's below the belt, Oliver."

"I apologise," Lord Franks returned graciously. "I'm not sure President Kennedy took the Prime Minister seriously when she spoke about drawing lines in the sand. When she flies over in a few days' time she plans to re-iterate exactly what she means..."

"This is the wrong time for Mrs Thatcher to come over..."

"Fine," the Ambassador retorted. "The Prime Minister will make a personal visit. Perhaps, she'll bring over the twins. For a short holiday, as it were. Obviously, while she is over here it would be rude if she didn't make herself available to talk to the networks..."

"Dammit, Oliver! A head of state can't come to another country and start playing politics behind a President's back. You wouldn't countenance the idea of the President meeting the Irish Government delegation in Oxford last month..."

"That was because their surrogates keep trying to murder the Queen, Bill," Lord Franks reminded his guest. His tone was briefly that of a man who really did not believe that he was actually having to tell the US Secretary of State *any* of this. "In any event Mrs Thatcher *will* come to America. Unless you shoot down her aircraft, that is."

Fulbright sighed.

"Your Prime Minister told the Russians that there would be 'consequences' if they failed to prove – God knows how they are going to do that – that they aren't about to go nuclear again in Iran or Iraq?"

Lord Franks did not respond to this because he did not think he had been asked a serious question. It seemed to him that the Secretary of State had simply restated Margaret Thatcher's statement to the House of Commons of the previous day. He remained silent.

"What consequences?" Fulbright pressed.

"Oh, consequences," the Ambassador murmured. "Well, I think at the last count we had thirty or forty operational V-Bombers left. In the event of the use of nuclear weapons against our forces or our allies in the Middle East I should imagine we would drop every bomb we could lay our hands on," he went on resignedly, "on the, er, rump of what is left of the Soviet Union."

Chapter 35

Sunday 24th May 1964
Corpus Christi College, Oxford

The Prime Minister and her Secretaries of State for Defence and Supply and Transportation had walked over from Christ Church Cathedral where they had attended the morning service. Field Marshall Sir Richard Hull, the Chief of the Defence Staff had been driven straight to the meeting on the first floor of Corpus Christie College from Brize Norton, having flown back from Abadan in the small hours.

Upon the arrival of the Prime Minister the earlier attendees fell silent and rose to their feet. Margaret Thatcher acknowledged her Minister for National Security, the Director General of Security and the woman at his side with a terse nod.

"Let's get down to business," she demanded, settling at the head of the table which dominated the modestly proportioned former lecture room. To her front some twenty feet away a curtain had been drawn across the blackboard.

Four days ago, she had come within a dozen votes of being ousted from the premiership; had that happened the Unity Administration of the United Kingdom might have fallen, and an election of some kind would have had to have been called. Not for the first time in the last few weeks she suspected she understood something of what must have gone through Winston Churchill's mind in the darkest days of the Second World War; after Dunkirk, the fall of Singapore or Tobruk, or the news of yet another Atlantic convoy decimated by U-boats. However, like her she had recently learned that he too had been *reading* the innermost conversations of the enemy High Command, he too had *known* of his enemy's weaknesses, that he was not alone in confronting seemingly impossible dilemmas and that all was *not* yet lost. Like her he had known that to speak of such things publicly, specifically in his own defence was impossible, and that some things were so secret that they could never, ever be confessed.

Margaret Thatcher had been Prime Minister several months before *her* people had trusted her with Churchill's greatest secrets; and only then had she learned the unwritten, real history of Winston Churchill's eventually triumphant crusade against the Nazis. Thus, on Wednesday afternoon she had been forced to sit and take her *medicine*, compelled to be the object of the House of Commons' anger and mistrust, contempt and in some cases, undiluted scorn, totally unable to state in her own defence the one thing that would have instantly silenced nine-tenths of her detractors.

Jericho was still in play.

While the Red Navy had changed its codes at the end of April the Red Army, Air Force and the Political Bureau of the Soviet Ministry of Defence, which was now known to operate out of a bunker complex several miles east of Chelyabinsk, were still using the 'J416 Variant 03' code which had come into use as long ago as 16th January. This and the fact that an increasingly large number – literally scores – of formations in Iraq and Iran were routinely transmitting, and expecting to receive in return only *plain text* communications, meant that on some days the code breakers at the Government Communications Headquarters (GCHQ) at Cheltenham were sometimes reading messages before, or at around the same time as senior Soviet commanders in the field.

The only real problem with *Jericho* was that there was so much of it. The code breakers were being overwhelmed by its sheer volume, unable to prioritise what was gold dust and what was housekeeping as literally thousands of encrypted intercepts piled up waiting to be 'looked at'.

GCHQ at Cheltenham had been drowned in paperwork; neglected and run down after the October War, it had been in no condition to suddenly up its game. Tantalisingly, even though it was criminally short-staffed and incapable of managing the ever-accumulating deluge of intercepts – thus far GCHQ had decoded significantly less than one percent of the traffic intercepted by listening stations in the Middle East and the Mediterranean – the code breakers were nevertheless, serving up a daily stream of critical intelligence jewels.

Notwithstanding its difficulties, on the basis of traffic analysis alone Cheltenham had already built up a comprehensive table of organisation for, established the dispositions of, and calculated the approximate fighting strength of Marshal of the Soviet Union Hamazasp Khachaturi Babadzhanian's Army Group South. Each day as Red Army spearheads penetrated deeper into Iraq the picture was updated, often down to the level of how many serviceable T-62 main battle tanks a given unit had and whether it had sufficient fuel in hand to continue motoring the next day.

From this comprehensive 'Order of Battle' it was known, for example, that the leading echelons of the 2nd Siberian Mechanised Army and the 3rd Caucasus Tank Army had abandoned – temporarily or otherwise - over half their tanks and sixty percent of their supporting vehicles in the mountains of Iran or parked, broken down alongside the roads west, east and south of Sulaymaniyah. Moreover, it was readily apparent that the Red Army's logistics system had broken down to such an extent that the entire Soviet invasion had briefly stalled with the 10th Guards Tank Division sitting, completely isolated and cut off from the rest of the invasion force, in the ruins of Jalawla a hundred miles north-north-east of Baghdad, and 3rd Siberian Mechanised Division investing the city of Kirkuk.

Given that there were known to be Iraqi forces present in brigade, possibly divisional strength on the right flank of the chaotic Soviet line of advance around Erbil, Army Group South's position ought to have been if not untenable, then *precarious*. That the Red Army could get away with, as the Chief of the Defence Staff guffawed 'such a dog's breakfast of an advance' in spite of its 'comical logistical situation' was solely down to the 'disgraceful' inability of the Iraqi Army to 'get its act together'.

Margaret Thatcher looked around the table at today's membership of the War Cabinet. The regular members of the War Cabinet present were: Secretary of State for Defence, William 'Willie' Whitelaw, Field Marshall Sir Richard Hull, speaking for the Chiefs of Staff of the three armed services, and Airey Neave, the man her enemies now called *her* 'Security Supremo', or more unkindly *Beria* to her *Iron Lady*. Customarily, Iain Macleod, Minister of Information, Leader of the House of Commons and the Chairman of what was left of the Conservative and Unionist Party would have been present but he was currently hospitalised. He had been struck down by a mystery fever, collapsing in his office the previous evening. The Foreign Secretary, who tended to report to the War Cabinet on an 'at need' basis, had flown to Saudi Arabia yesterday. Today the Prime Minister had specifically requested the attendance of Alison Munro, a vital contributor to the War Cabinet's deliberations in her key position at Supply and Transportation, from within which department she was, more or less, single-handed, masterminding the ongoing 'build-up' in the Middle East.

Airey Neave was flanked by the Director General of the Security Services, Sir Richard 'Dick' White and his protégé Rachel Piotrowska, who had just got back from Philadelphia. The woman was due to fly out to America again with the Prime Minister on Tuesday to take up the post of Head of Station of MI6 in the United States. Margaret Thatcher had raised an eyebrow when Airey Neave had briefed her on this appointment but otherwise let the posting go unremarked.

Margaret Thatcher's gaze hesitated on Rachel Piotrowska's face.

The other woman was the same age as her; more *obviously* attractive despite being careless, a little languid in her manner and irritatingly elegant in whatever she wore. Tom Harding-Grayson had only given the Prime Minister the edited highlights of the other woman's extraordinary life and career; Rachel had survived the Lodz ghetto as a child, Ravensbrück concentration camp as a teenager, and worked for British Intelligence practically all her adult life. Then there had been that bizarre, incredible Kalashnikov-wielding rampage through the Citadel of Mdina in which she had single-handedly taken on practically the whole Red Army! The Prime Minister could not forget, nor would she ever forgive – even though she knew her resentment was irrational and unworthy – the fact that it had been in Rachel Piotrowska's arms that the man she had loved, Julian Christopher had died.

The Prime Minister's stare shifted onto Airey Neave's ruddy face.

"Presumably, since Miss Piotrowska is being *redeployed* to Philadelphia, we may infer that Comrade Ceausescu's *debriefing* has been satisfactorily concluded, Airey?"

Her friend nodded.

"Yes. Most satisfactorily, Prime Minister. There are always loose ends which will need to be tied up at a later date but Ceausescu has filled in a lot of what we had only previously surmised in very general terms, and provided a wealth of other high-level intelligence. Previous damage assessment analyses of the USSR have been thoroughly reviewed and amended as a result. Ceausescu was less helpful as to the true extent and capabilities of the 'rump' surviving Soviet Union, but again," the Secretary of State for National Security shrugged, "he has provided us with any number of revealing insights. Our working assumption that perhaps two-thirds of the USSR was effectively destroyed or badly damaged was broadly correct; where we were completely wrong was in assuming that there would be very few 'joined up' or large contiguous areas of territory completely untouched, other than by fallout. In retrospect, we and the Americans hugely underestimated the extent to which Soviet industry beyond the Ural Mountains remains intact."

The Prime Minister considered this for a moment. Before the October War, Soviet industry had become so centralised that a dozen, or perhaps a score of nuclear strikes taking out the cities which produced most of the tanks, ballistic missiles, jet aircraft, railway locomotives and so forth would have crippled the Russians' ability to wage offensive war every bit as effectively as laying waste the vast areas that had actually been destroyed. Sometimes, she wondered if the people who had been in charge before the war had had any idea what they were doing?

All that destruction, all those lives wasted...

"What do we do with Ceausescu now?" She asked, unable to wash the anger from her voice.

"We'll squirrel him away," Airey Neave reported. "We'll dust him off from time to time; if nothing else he'll be damnably useful as a *spotter.*"

"A spotter?"

Rachel Piotrowska cleared her throat.

Although she was at pains not to show it, she was weary, a little jet-lagged from her recent transatlantic interlude – thirty-six hours in transit, eighteen one way and twenty the other, so that she could spend a day with the 'Maltese wives' in Philadelphia making sure that everybody was on the same page vis-a-vis the Samuel Calleja 'legend' – and rather resented being drawn into such an overtly 'political' arena. This was not to say she did not fully understand Airey Neave's motives in wanting her to be at hand in case the Prime Minister asked him too many awkward questions. Because of this she felt herself not so much empowered, as required to contribute, at need, when required.

"Nicolae was heavily involved with the Romanian Securitate," she explained, matter of factly, "in fact he virtually owned the Secret Police in Bucharest. He is a walking 'reference book' that we can turn to whenever we want to identify a suspected Soviet or Eastern Bloc agent ͡er senior Eastern Block Communist official, Prime Minister."

Thatcher was struck by the lilting, very Polish accent the ͡ffected. It was as if she was searching for the ͡before her life became a lie. According to

Airey Neave she had been a courtesan and an assassin, and once briefly been the favourite mistress of the dead Shah of Iran. The Prime Minister took herself to task, realising she was losing focus again.

"There was a woman with him, I believe?"

"Yes, Eleni. A Greek-Cypriot woman," Rachel confirmed. "She is very attached to him. I feel sorry for her. She and Nicolae are presently being held in Scotland with several other 'defectors' and 'persons of interest' whose survival we wish to keep secret for as long as possible."

"Thank you," Margaret Thatcher said. "That will be all, Miss Piotrowska."

The men in the room half-stood as Rachel departed.

Everybody settled anew and the curtain was withdrawn from the blackboard revealing a composite map of the Persian Gulf and the surrounding countries assembled from several different sheets.

The Chief of the Defence Staff rose to his feet.

Sir Richard Hull's demeanour was that of an old soldier, calm and measured, and uncomfortably aware that everything he was about to say was hedged around with so many qualifications that if he tried to explain one-tenth of them they would still be here tomorrow afternoon before he got half-way through.

"Frankly, if we go looking for the holes in this scheme of ours," he smiled wryly, "we will worry ourselves to death and die asking ourselves why we didn't at least try to do something in the first place!"

"Quite so, Sir Richard," Margaret Thatcher observed tartly.

"However, I will," the Chief of the Defence Staff reminded her, "reiterate the point that regardless of whether the Egyptians fulfil their part of the bargain, we shall be in a fine old fix if the Saudis don't open up the war stores depots on their territory. If they *wait and see* much longer then they are going to end up facing the Red Army across *their* indefensible northern land borders on their own."

"I'm sure the Foreign Secretary will be communicating that to Crown Prince Faisal in Riyadh, Sir Richard." Margaret Thatcher could hardly credit that the Saudi Arabian government was still *haggling* over the terms of its only possible salvation. The way the Saudis were behaving it was as if they honestly believed that the Red Army would stop at the Kuwaiti border! Ever since the USS Kitty Hawk had arrived in the Arabian Sea the Crown Prince had been trying to play off the two old trans-Atlantic allies against each other!

"Provisional plans," Willie Whitelaw, the Defence Minister sighed, "are being made to land Egyptian forces directly on Kuwaiti territory. The port facilities at Dammam are better, obviously, but if the Saudis are going to make difficulties, well," he opened his hands, "we shall just have to get on with it."

The Saudi government - a conglomeration of feuding members of the Arabian 'nobility' who had more in common with medieval satraps in a Byzantine court than any kind of modern twentieth century administration – was schizophrenic about the presence of foreign troops on its soil. Nevertheless, for some reason the presence of the

USS Kitty Hawk and her escorts in the Arabian Sea had convinced a substantial faction within the ruling elite that the United States – against all the evidence - had not actually abandoned the Kingdom. At one level this naively wishful thinking ignored the fact that the US did not actually need Saudi oil; and on another level, flew in the face of the equally persuasive consideration that if it lost Abadan, the United Kingdom *did* need that oil. Who did the Saudis think was more likely to fight to stop the oil tap being turned off?

Tom Harding-Grayson had advised that the Saudis be allowed to play out their internal contradictions. The first priority was the use of air bases, port facilities and transit areas in and around the Dammam-Dhahran area; and the question of the American war stores depots should not be permitted to muddy the waters.

In any event other than the thousands of free fall bombs – of every imaginable non-nuclear type and size – stored in the war stores depots, little else in those great 'weapon dumps' in the desert was actually immediately usable by the British or the ANZAC, Australian and New Zealand forces currently being built up in the region. The US military used different calibre naval shells, tank rounds and small arms bullets, and the one hundred and fifty tanks – mainly M-48 Pattons – 'parked' in Jeddah and outside Riyadh had been partially disabled by the US Army prior to its pull out the previous autumn. Likewise, many of the artillery pieces and armoured personnel carriers required 'reactivation' before they could be deployed. It seemed that American planners had assumed a sixty to ninety day 'de-mothballing' window ahead of any future emergency, and de-commissioned much of their heavy equipment accordingly.

Tom Harding-Grayson was probably right in asserting that the Saudis had still not worked out that the reason the Americans had left mostly old, obsolete, disabled equipment and thousands of tons of World War II-type ordnance - bombs and shells – in Arabia was that they never intended coming back. Or rather, if they ever came back, it would be with modern, state of the art weaponry.

"Well," Margaret Thatcher sighed, "I'm sure that Tom will eventually persuade the Saudis that this is their fight, too. In the meantime, we should focus on the positives. In this connection I spoke again to both the Australian and New Zealand High Commissioners yesterday evening. No words of praise are sufficient to express my personal gratitude for the sacrifices they are making to help us."

Everybody around the table was astonished that their Australasian Commonwealth friends had dug so deep so quickly. Within days of the first tentative inquiry the Australian Navy had started strengthening HMAS Sydney's flight and hangar decks to carry forty-one-ton Centurion tanks, begun mobilizing reserve units and marching small airborne and special forces formations onto transport aircraft bound for the Middle East. New Zealand had raised two rifle battalions, and hurriedly found enough men to crew and fight the old cruiser Royalist – for many years relegated to the role of a training ship – and dispatched them to the Indian Ocean. When the Australian government was asked if it was prepared to release HMS Centaur, the aircraft carrier that Julian Christopher had left at Sydney to ensure that the Australian Navy always had at least one aircraft carrier available for operations, the Australian government had taken less than twenty-four hours to confer and agree to the Admiralty's plea.

At the last count there were thirty-nine Australian Centurion tanks and nearly six thousand ANZAC fighting men ashore at Dammam in the Persian Gulf. In addition to the Australian Navy destroyers Anzac, Tobruk and Voyager, some twenty Westland Wessex helicopters were to be operated from the deck of HMAS Sydney as soon as she had finished unloading her cargo of Centurions.

Those Centurions – including twenty-three up-gunned Mark IIs - were priceless. Although eight thousand troops had so far been flown into Kuwait, Abadan and Dhahran from the United Kingdom and Cyprus as yet, no heavy equipment had reached the Persian Gulf from England or the Mediterranean. Moreover, apart from the cruiser HMS Tiger and a few smaller ships which had made best speed around the Cape taking nearly a month to reach the Arabian Sea, no significant naval reinforcements other than the Centaur and the ANZAC contingent had yet reached the theatre.

Last night the Australian High Commissioner had proudly reported that a second consignment of eleven Centurion tanks – previously mothballed Mark Is of Korean War vintage – were loading on board a 'fast transport' at Sydney bound for the Gulf sometime in the next few days.

Sir Richard Hull was no less impressed with the ANZAC contribution than his Prime Minister but he could not allow himself to be carried away with the 'good news'. Even when the full ANZAC contingent was ashore Michael Carver would only have one – albeit a very capable - armoured 'brigade', supported by a single British mechanised infantry 'brigade' guarding Kuwait and the approaches to north eastern Saudi Arabia. In other words, he would have an approximately 'division-sized' formation in position to halt an 'Army' that outnumbered his units by somewhere between three-to-one and six-to-one in tanks, artillery and men. Potentially, the situation of the Abadan Garrison was much, much worse. Carver presently had thirty or so tanks and about four thousand men under his direct control; if the local Iranian commanders let him down the Red Army would wash over his handful of Centurions like a tsunami.

"The *other* problem with the Saudis," the Chief of the Defence Staff went on, "is that unless they permit either or both of our, and the *promised* Egyptian forces expected to start arriving in theatre before the end of June to move to jumping off points west of the Kuwaiti border we will not be able to properly exploit the opportunities presented by that ground."

Margaret Thatcher gave him a vexed look.

"May I be honest with you, Prime Minister?" The soldier inquired, smiling sternly.

"Of course, Field Marshall."

"Without the Egyptians, or the Saudis any other course of action other than static in-depth defence in Kuwait will be impractical. In that event sooner or later the Soviets will out flank our line and we shall be in a fine old mess. At Abadan everything depends on the Iranians."

Willie Whitelaw stirred uneasily, his jowly features rolling with angst.

Operation Lightfoot, Michael Carver's ambitious plan to 'Cannae' the Red Army north of Basra remained a pipe dream. It was much more likely that the only viable strategy was going to be to dig in along the northern border of the Emirate of Kuwait, withdraw from Abadan and attempt to deter the Russians from interdicting seaborne trade – the passage of tankers – in the Persian Gulf with air and sea power. It was a strategy of last resort and in many ways of despair that only delayed the evil day when the Soviets extended their malign influence over the entire Arabian Peninsula.

"We have exchanged one unreliable ally for a whole gang of new *unreliable* allies?" The Defence Secretary gloomily offered to the room at large.

The Chief of the Defence Staff politely dismissed this.

"Possibly, Minister. The situation on the ground is what it is."

The Secretary of State for Defence grunted. Normally a jovial, phlegmatic man his temper had become strained in recent weeks. He had been weakened by illness last year and looked prematurely aged, nearer sixty than fifty, even though he was still not yet forty-six.

"Forgive me," he conceded graciously, "you know your business better than I, Sir Richard."

Sir Richard Hull grimaced.

"Assuming the co-operation of significant Iranian forces and the presence, if not the whole-hearted participation of Egyptian and or Saudi armoured forces, at the very least I believe we have a fifty-fifty chance of giving the Soviets a dreadful fright. As to destroying the Soviet presence south of Baghdad," he shrugged, "and winning any kind of total victory, the odds against that are much longer."

Then a thought occurred to him out of the blue and the ghost of a smile quirked at his pale lips.

"That said, although our chances of winning a new Cannae in the deserts and marshes above Basra may be very remote," he confessed, whimsy still twinkling mischievously in his grey eyes. "If somebody had said to me before the Battle of Malta that but for the actions of a pair of small Royal Navy warships whose captains had been previously given leave to remove themselves from the battlefield, in charging headlong at a vastly superior enemy force, Malta would have been lost," he guffawed softly, "frankly, I would not have believed a word of it, Prime Minister."

Sir Richard Hull spread his arms wide.

"Who am I to throw cold water on Operation Lightfoot?"

Chapter 36

Sunday 24th May 1964
'Kursk' Bunker, Chelyabinsk

Two things had surprised Lieutenant-Colonel Francis Harold St John Waters, VC, since his capture in the Zagros Mountains by KGB troopers. Firstly, apart from at the beginning shortly after his capture, nobody had tried any real rough stuff; and secondly, that after his surprise encounter with Marshal of the Soviet Union Hamazasp Khachaturi Babadzhanian, he had received rudimentary medical treatment and been given enough food and clean water to keep body and soul together while he contemplated his next move.

Notwithstanding, it was still his working assumption that he could be taken out and shot at any time. There was a war going on and when all was said and done, he had been caught behind enemy lines, not only wearing a stolen uniform but with the dog tags of a dead Spetsnaz captain around his neck. Understandably, his captors had been very, very interested in how he had come by those!

'The poor chap was already dead,' he had explained apologetically. 'Sorry, nothing to do with me.' Which was the truth, the whole truth and nothing but the truth, insofar as it went.

He had not personally killed the man.

The irksome thing was that he had no idea whatsoever what had happened to *his boys*. After the air attack on the traffic jam east of Piranshahr he had regained consciousness on the roadside being prodded by the muzzles of a couple of Kalashnikovs. The sky had been obscured with oily black and grey smoke and the atmosphere had positively reeked of seared human flesh.

The Russians had asked him about his 'comrades' between desultory beatings – not nice but once you curled up into a foetal ball and got into the rhythm of rolling with as many of the blows as possible, it was a bit like being at the bottom of a scrum in particularly hard-fought rugby match – but Waters had got the distinct impression *his boys* had either made themselves scarce in the commotion or they were dead. Which was a bit of a shame; the Regiment hated it when a commanding officer walked back into Stirling Lines in Herefordshire on his own. The 22nd Special Air Service Regiment was very finicky about things like that. It was decidedly bad form losing *all* one's chaps and having the gall to survive to tell the tale because that was *not* the stuff of the *right kind* of Regimental legends. That sort of thing that was regarded as very bad form in the Mess, of an order of blaggardly behaviour on a par with seducing a fellow officer's wife, or worse, one or more of his teenage daughters. If the worst came to it, it was generally accepted – pretty much without exception – that it was de rigor for a fellow to die with *his chaps*, no ifs and no buts, and woe betide any man who transgressed that most sacred of unwritten Regimental laws.

Basically, the way Frank Waters looked at it, the Russians would be doing him a middlingly big favour if one morning they took him outside and shot him. He had had a bloody good innings and all things considered his long-suffering wife Shirley, and eight-year-old son, Harry, whom he had not laid eyes on since late 1959 would probably not miss him. He knew they had survived the October War; they had been in the Welsh Marches the night the balloon went up and his brother Eric, a sickeningly honourable good egg of a man had taken them in soon afterwards. Eric had been in the Navy in the Second War, later he had gone into the Civil Service. Now young Harry and his mother lived with Eric somewhere in the hills outside Sheffield...

Yes, it would be much better for everybody if he got shot, ideally attempting to escape because he had no intention of eking out a miserable declining existence in some fetid ice-cold Soviet gulag.

With this in the back of his mind finding himself unceremoniously bundled onto a draughty old Soviet turboprop transport aircraft two days ago had come as something of an unwelcome shock. Likewise, the fact that ever since boarding that aircraft he had been chained by the left wrist to one or other of four tough-looking green-uniformed KGB military policemen.

The KGB men had been ordered not to talk to him and vexingly, they were self-evidently, very, very good at 'guarding' problematic prisoners. These boys appeared not to notice the stench when he moved his bowels, contemptuously ignored his attempts to make small talk in various Moskva idioms and generally treated him like an idiot child. Equally infuriatingly, none of his KGB minders carried a personal weapon of any description so there was absolutely no chance of relieving any one of them of the same! To cap it all three of the four KGB policemen were twice his size and the fourth, a smaller species of Russian bear, was easily half as big as him again; even had he not been in a somewhat emaciated, weakened state these gorillas would have laughed themselves silly if he been so unwise as to try any funny stuff.

That morning he had been presented with an unbelievably badly-tailored brown suit, baggy skivvies and a shirt that was so itchy it might as well have been made of *hair*, a pair extensively darned woollen socks and scuffed, much worn black shoes and ordered to: 'Get dressed!'

He was unchained while he dressed.

The trousers were so roomy he had to hold them up with one hand, and the shoes painfully pinched his feet. Once he was re-attired, he was re-chained to the biggest of his guards.

"No funny business!" He was told in English.

"Perish the thought, old son," he had grinned.

His guards looked at him as if he was something malignant, they had just scraped off their boots.

The walls of the bunker complex were bare, sweating concrete and the soles of Frank Waters's shoes and those of his booted escorts clumped leadenly on the damp stone floors of the corridors down which they marched.

Suddenly the prisoner found himself in a brightly lit windowless room which had rugs on the floor, a big desk, and maps and pictures on the walls. These latter were old-style propaganda posters but undeniably they lent the subterranean office a certain brightness of character. Curiously, there was a big upright reel to reel tape recorder loaded with two silvery eight-inch spools on the right-hand side of the table.

The man behind the desk did not get up.

He nodded to the guards who forced Frank Waters to sit in a hard chair, manacled his wrists behind his back, snapped to attention, wheeled around and departed.

The captive studied his latest inquisitor.

Unlike him this man was wearing clothes that actually fitted him, and which, presumably, had not been recovered from a corpse at some indeterminate time in the last few months. Moreover, the man behind the desk had been able to shave that morning, wash and brush up; Frank Waters had not done any of those things for weeks and looked and smelled rank.

"Mne soobshchili, chto vy khorosho govorite po russki razgovornuyu?"

The middle aged, grim-faced man who had made no move to rise from behind his desk asked quietly.

I am informed that you speak good conversational Russian?

"Moy russkiy yazyk luchshe, chem razgovornym, comrade!

Frank Waters retorted, a little offended.

My Russian is better than conversational, comrade!

The other man registered this with a raised eyebrow. He was obviously not in any kind of a hurry.

"My name is Yuri Vladimirovich Andropov," he announced in Russian. "I am First Deputy Director of the Committee for State Security of the Union of Soviet Socialist Republics."

Frank Waters was impressed; if his interlocutor was to be believed, he was talking to the number two man in the KGB. Andropov, he realised, was sitting in a wheelchair and his face had about it that lopsided look that suggested it had been smashed and only partially put back together again. There was something vaguely reassuring about knowing the man in whose hands his life undoubtedly rested had had an even worse war than he had.

"How do you do, Comrade Andropov," he retorted, barring his teeth in a wolfish smile.

To the Englishman's astonishment the Russian's lips twisted into what might have been a rictus grin. The moment passed.

"You were captured in the uniform of a Red Army officer, Colonel Waters. You are suspected of gross crimes against the Soviet Union. You are a war criminal. I could have you executed at any time."

Frank Waters shrugged.

"Absolutely," he agreed. "I wish you'd bloody well get on with it, old son!"

Andropov viewed him silently with dull, inscrutable eyes.

"The food is bloody awful," Frank Waters went on. "And making me wear this bloody clown's suit is the last straw!" He frowned. "Where is *this* by the way?" He inquired cheerfully concluding on what he hoped was a civil note. As an officer and a gentleman, it behoved him to remember at all times that one was a guest in somebody else's country. "Somewhere east of the Urals, presumably?"

"Yes, Chelyabinsk."

"Ah, Chelyabinsk," Frank Waters sighed. "The city that bridges the Urals to the west with Siberia in the east." He felt a little stronger for knowing where he was; a man's place in the landscape mattered. "Is it true that like Rome, Constantinople and Moscow this city is built on seven hills, Comrade First Deputy Director?"

Andropov gave him a disdainful look.

"I don't know."

"Does the Leningrad Bridge still stand across the River Miass?" Frank Waters asked. "The famous bridge of the Urals to Siberia?"

"Yes. The Yankees never bombed the city."

Frank Waters tried to remember his geography.

"What about Sverdlovsk? That would be about two hundred kilometres north of here?"

"No, they didn't bomb Sverdlovsk either."

Frank Waters grimaced: "My, my, that was careless of them?"

How on earth had Strategic Air Command ignored both Chelyabinsk and Sverdlovsk?

Chelyabinsk was 'the Gate to Siberia', a crucial hub on the trans-Siberia Railway; the city that during Hitler's War and afterwards was generally referred to in Western military colleges as 'Tankograd' or 'Tank City' because at one time it had been the home of the biggest tank factory – the S.M. Kirov Factory No. 185 – in the World.

Sverdlovsk, in Tsarist times Yekaterinburg, had been the fourth largest city in the USSR before the war. Again, since the 1940s when Soviet industry was transferred east of the Urals to keep it out of the greedy clutches of the advancing Wehrmacht, it too had been a major industrial centre as well as a key regional communications hub.

The Russians had been so worried about their secrets in and around this part of the country that they had installed cutting edge surface-to-air missile defences before the October War. Missile defences so advanced that they knocked down an American U-2 spy plane flying at seventy thousand feet!

Frank Waters started to ask himself what else the masterminds in charge of SAC and the RAF V-Bomber Force had *missed* on the night of the war? Given that there were fully equipped Red Army tank divisions on the move south through the mountains of Iran he did not like any of the answers he thought of; because each and every one of them suggested the flyboys had missed an awful lot of their targets.

The First Deputy Director of the Committee of State Security was watching his prisoner with hooded, darkly suspicious eyes. Frank

Waters suspected the KGB man had been intimidating people all his life because he was very, very good at it.

He was even beginning to get a little twitchy himself.

Andropov came to a decision.

His right hand disappeared under his desk, presumably to ring a bell.

Within seconds two of Frank Waters's minders stomped into the room. There was a jangling of keys and his hands were freed by one uniformed KGB trooper, the other stood by the big clumsy reel to reel tape recorder on Andropov's desk.

The SAS man winced as the circulation returned to his hands in an agonising rush of pins and needles.

Andropov growled at the man next to the tape recorder and the spools began to rotate.

A woman's clear, rather pedantic oddly mesmeric voice filled the underground bunker room with hissing, hectoring urgency through the background mush of static and long-range signal attenuation.

'The Soviet leadership is hereby given notice that any further use of nuclear weapons by it, its allies or its proxies will result in an all-out strike by the United Kingdom against the forces of the Soviet Union and any surviving concentrations of population or industry within the former territories of the Soviet Union, or in any territories deemed to now be under Soviet control.'

Frank Waters recognised the voice of his Prime Minister. Once heard it was the sort of voice a fellow tended to recollect forever. Like most of his contemporaries in the Regiment and throughout the armed forces he had assumed 'the Angry Widow' would be a stop gap, here today gone tomorrow phenomenon, nobody had expected her to still be – literally – calling the shots six months later. But then nobody had ever expected the Prime Minister to be such a damned attractive blond bombshell either.

It was a funny old World...

'RAF bombers stand ready at the end of their runways at four minutes notice to go to war. Other RAF bombers are airborne at this time ready to strike within minutes of the receipt of the order to attack!'

"Here! Here!" Frank Waters guffawed softly before he thought better of it. He was in no fit state to survive a new beating and it was important to be able to stand up of one's own volition when the enemy shot one.

'I will tell you that if the High Command of the Soviet Union thinks, for a single minute that we and our allies will sit back and allow the Red Army to invade and rape Iraq and Iran without exacting a terrible cost on it in terms of men, materiel and morale, it is tragically mistaken. It is the policy of my government to resist tyranny; and while I live, we will never surrender. I say to the men in the new Kremlin – wherever that foul new incarnation may now be located in southern Russia – that no matter what ground your tanks seize we will never rest until you are expelled from it. You may defeat us in one battle, you may defeat us in many battles but we will never, ever give in. You are responsible for the

abomination of Red Dawn, for the despicable use of nuclear weapons against civilian populations in Turkey, Greece, Cyprus and Egypt. You are criminals responsible for the obliteration of Tehran! After that atrocity I warned you that a further use of nuclear weapons would result in an all-out strike against your remaining centres of population. I have not yet received an unequivocal acknowledgement of this warning. I demand that the Soviet High Command provide such an unequivocal acknowledgement not later than midnight on 27th May, or face the consequences.'

Andropov waved to his man at the tape recorder.

The reels stopped turning.

The silence was instantly oppressive.

"Is that woman insane?" Andropov asked sourly.

Frank Waters had no idea why the second-in-command of the KGB was asking him *that* question. He had never met the woman in question and one simply did not discuss a *lady* in company; it just was not done. Was nothing sacred with these people?

The barbarians were at the gate!

"No, sir," he said curtly.

"She talks about consequences? What consequences?"

Frank Waters chuckled. He could not help himself chuckling. Suddenly, he realised what he was doing in this bunker in Chelyabinsk and it more than somewhat tickled his sense of humour.

"Comrade Yuri Vladimirovich," he explained, his words hastened by the knowledge that both the big KGB policemen were itching for an opportunity to kick him around the room. "For my sins I have had a fair bit of experience of how a *lady* tends to react when she belatedly discovers that she has been taken for a ride."

Andropov's broken face creased into a contorted frown of incomprehension.

It was time to speak plainly.

"I have never met the lady," Frank Waters went on, struggling not to smirk, "but I rather suspect that the 'consequences' she has in mind are of the most violent imaginable kind."

Chapter 37

Joanne Brenckmann did not think she had ever met a prospective Head of Station of British Intelligence before. Although, the more she thought about it she realised she could have met dozens of 'spooks' without ever knowing it. What made today's encounter all the more surreal was that the woman in front of her seemed so 'normal', so 'pleasant' and on the face of it, 'open'.

Unlike his wife the Ambassador was not in the least surprised that Rachel Piotrowska had decided to pay a 'courtesy call' on him prior to leaving for Philadelphia.

"My wife does not know what to make of your visit, Miss Piotrowska," he smiled as his guest settled in an armchair in his private rooms. This was to be a 'private consultation' in the fine old tradition of such meetings.

Walter Brenckmann studied the woman over the rim of his coffee cup.

With her straw blond hair cut short like a man's and wearing a tailored jacket over a man's white shirt – top button undone - and grey slacks the shapely spy had made herself seem androgynous to casual observers. She wore no jewellery, scarcely any makeup.

"No?" Rachel smiled; her grey eyes gently amused. "Well," she prefaced, looking to Joanne Brenckmann. "The United Kingdom's relations with the United States are going through a rocky patch, there's no denying that. But," she shrugged apologetically, "if we're not the best of allies at the moment we certainly aren't any kind of enemies. More like two old friends who have had a bit of a falling out, that's all."

Her lilting accent was now that of a long time Polish exile; the Englishness of recent years was just a memory for she was no longer that person. Clara Pullman had died in Malta, Clara and each and every one of her former courtesan alter egos.

"I am not," she went on, "going to Philadelphia to spy on America or Americans." She was tempted to add 'unlike that idiot the CIA have posted to Oxford who has already been caught twice trying to bribe civil servants at the Ministry of Defence'. A scheme was in hand to get him sent home; he was a menace. Dick White had in mind an entrapment exercise, a good old-fashioned scoop for the press in which the CIA man or one of his senior associates was found in bed with 'inappropriate' male or female company.

"Oh," Joanne Brenckmann murmured, totally confused by Rachel's apparent candour.

"I am going to Philadelphia to make sure that nothing is lost in translation between the Administration, its intelligence agencies and the UAUK. Granted, I will have certain responsibilities vis-à-vis the

National Security Department desk at the Embassy in Philadelphia, and of course, I will be liaising with the various military attaches assigned to the Embassy. But I will *not* be recruiting 'spies' in America, and I will *not* be engaging in any activity inimical to the constitutional rights of American citizens."

"You'll be spending a lot of time on the cocktail party circuit then?" The Ambassador's wife observed sympathetically.

"Unfortunately, yes," Rachel agreed.

Joanne Brenckmann was starting to wonder what sort of country she and her husband would return to when their stint in England ended. They had only been away three months and yet things at home already seemed to have changed irrevocably for the worse.

It looked as if Jack Kennedy was going to sweep aside his opponents in the race to be re-nominated as the Democratic 'runner' for President; the Administration's volte face, suddenly embracing *America First* as its battle cry shouting 'let the British stand on their own two feet' and declaring that America would have no part in defending 'any part of the old British Empire' had turned the tide and brought sections of the Democrat main stream back on board the Kennedy bandwagon.

Richard Nixon, at one time the likely Republican candidate for the Presidency had been swept away – crushed between Jack Kennedy's Damascene conversion to the 'America First' crusade and the rising tide of support for Nelson Rockefeller's *independent* version of the isolationist bandwagon in the north and Governor George Wallace's equally *independent* racist, segregationist very nearly secessionist brand of hellfire white supremacism in the south. John Cabot Lodge, that most honourable doyen of the Great Old Party of Lincoln and Eisenhower presently cut a sad figure; notwithstanding he had once looked like a shoe-in for the Republican nomination he was already a no-hoper, running at below ten percent in national polls. People were already speculating that a Rockefeller-Wallace 'America First' or 'Independent Republican' or even 'Independent Democrat' ticket – however unlikely or outlandish it sounded – might 'walk into the White House' on 4th November. If that happened Joanne knew that she and Walter would be on the next plane home and it would only be a matter of time, in the present political climate, before they were both hauled up before some newly convened Kangaroo court or reformed House Un-American Activities inquisition to defend their 'outrageous and unpatriotic' pro-British proclivities.

However, that prospect was the least of her and her husband's worries.

The spring cease fire in Illinois brokered by Major General Colin Powell Dempsey, the sixty-one-year-old Washingtonian National Guard reservist who had single-handedly master-minded the suppression of the insurgency in the North West last year, had broken down within days of his sacking, at the behest of Mayor Richard Joseph Daley by the State Governor Otto Kerner. South Chicago, previously largely intact and 'viable' as the surviving half of the bomb-damaged Windy City, was now threatening to turn into a battlefield and what was left of the Kennedy family's Midwest political powerbase was disappearing down the plug hole of history.

Meanwhile, spurred on by the sudden sacking of General Dempsey, their military guru, the Confederation of West Coast States – Washington, Oregon and California – had activated their previously suspended 'Military Assistance Pact' under which Federal intervention in their affairs was strictly circumvented. The three states, including California, the most populous in the Union, had – within the last week - threatened to withhold Federal taxes until such time as its 'legitimate grievances' were heard and acknowledged in Philadelphia.

Across the South there were daily reports of riots and disturbances. Birmingham Alabama and several towns and cities across Mississippi, Georgia and Louisiana were under martial law. Tensions inflamed to breaking point by February's atrocity in Atlanta when Doctor Martin Luther King had been badly wounded, and six other members of his entourage killed or injured by a sniper's bullets, had been ignited by George Wallace's incendiary rabble rousing, Nelson Rockefeller's apparent indifference, and the Administration's failure to do anything at all about the invidious post-Civil War Jim Crow laws entrenching racial segregation across the former Confederate States.

At Doctor King's rally in Bedford-Pine Park in Atlanta in February over two hundred people had died, killed in the crush after the shooting had panicked the huge crowd of between seventy and eighty thousand people. The Bedford-Pine 'Incident' was now the rallying cry of a new and militant Southern Civil Rights movement which its leader, Martin Luther King, only recently sufficiently recovered from his wounds to appear again in public, was struggling to drag back towards its avowedly non-violent roots.

In a little over a week's time King was scheduled to walk at the head of his people on the first day of the *March on Philadelphia*. The Afro-American Southern Civil Rights movement was coming to the nation's temporary capital. Day by day the march would gather new members on its slow progress north, arriving in Philadelphia on 4th July, *Independence Day.* There was a general expectation that the *March* would end in dreadful violence long before then, that Martin Luther King would never live long enough to stand on the steps of City Hall, and share again with the American people his dream of a better, fairer more righteous future for *all* Americans in a land in which the colour of a man or woman's skin, his religion, creed or ethnicity no longer governed how he or she was viewed by his fellow citizens.

If Martin Luther King died who would be left to speak for non-violence?

What price peaceful civil disobedience in a society in which the voice of reason had been silenced?

What had happened to America?

People back home were reporting that 'everything that could go wrong was going wrong'. It was election year so nobody in Congress, let alone the Presidential contenders cared about anything except getting elected. Wall Street was in turmoil, the Stock Exchange was heading south at a rate of knots and everybody was waiting with baited breath for the first big bank to go bust. Chicago was not the only Great Lakes city in ferment, upper New York State around Niagara and where the city of Buffalo had once stood was bandit country, likewise the badlands south of Boston, where the ruins of Quincy had been taken over by the dispossessed, the homeless and the hopeless who had armed themselves by ransacking the ruined navy base and the wrecked warships in the docks.

The Administration's policy towards the nation's millions of refugees had become one of armed containment while it fought fires elsewhere as and when they flared, without any semblance of any plan or any over-arching 'big idea'. The wreckage of Washington DC and its surrounding heavily militarised 'martial law zone' might have been a ghastly metaphor for the state of the whole Union.

In Philadelphia, a relatively tranquil island of political sectarian gerrymandering kept 'peaceful' by a massive Army, Navy and newly recruited paramilitary 'Special Police Division', the House of Representatives blithely carried on as if nothing was amiss. While members of Congress and the Senate bickered angrily over the terms of reference of Chief Justice Earl Warren's Commission into the Causes and the Conduct of the Cuban Missiles War; the Department of Justice was preoccupied – to the exclusion of virtually everything else – with preparations for the forthcoming trials of the leaders of the attempted coup d'état which had sparked the Battle of Washington last December.

"We were appalled to hear about the attack on the Christophers and the Hannays in Philadelphia," Joanne Brenckmann said. "We all believed that Philadelphia was fairly safe, but to be attacked like that in broad daylight!"

"I met both Lady Marija and Rosa Hannay when I was on Malta," Rachel confessed. She had given up obfuscating about those parts of her personal history that were less than secret. "And again recently, the last time I was in America. They are both very resilient young women. I'm sure they have put the 'incident' behind them already."

"I understand that you have visited the United States many times?" Walter Brenckmann prompted, feeling he ought to help out his wife. He had been a little lost in his thoughts. His eldest son was on board the USS Kitty Hawk, part of Carrier Division Seven's ill-thought through presence in the Arabian Sea. His second son, Daniel, was an assistant counsel to Earl Warren, at the very epicentre of the ongoing political firestorm. His youngest boy, Sam, was out in California with his new wife and baby daughter; if things went wrong troops could soon be marching into that state to restore the Federal writ; while here in England he and Joanne found themselves having to repeatedly defend the indefensible.

"Yes," Rachel smiled wryly, mischief flickering in her placid eyes. "I have been to America several times."

In what seemed now like another lifetime she had met and been involved with, intimately in several cases, members of the current Administration and miscellaneous Congressmen and Senators. Dick White had sent her to Washington after the Suez Crisis for nearly a year; and sent her back again when JFK had beaten Nixon to the White House. Being in America in those days had been fun; without any of the normal dangers of her profession.

Returning to old ground in a new role, as oneself, unprotected by an assumed persona was another matter. This time she would be surrounded by potential enemies, by powerful men who had reputations and positions to uphold, men who would not welcome being reminded that their secrets were not their own. But then that was exactly why the new Director General of National Security wanted her in Philadelphia; to remind men who ought to have known better that the past never, ever really goes away.

"Oh?" The Ambassador queried.

"I was not always a spy," Rachel lied. "There are a lot of old acquaintances I intend to *look up* in the next few months."

Chapter 38

Monday 25th May 1964
Headquarters of Aramco, Dhahran, Saudi Arabia

The days when Thomas Barger, the President of the Arabian-American Oil Company (Aramco) might have felt uneasy facilitating a meeting between a British General and two senior Saudi ministers, were long gone. Notwithstanding he had spent half his life living and working in Saudi Arabia, Barger was as patriotic as the next man but business was business and his first loyalty was to the shareholders of his company, *not* to a United States government that was seemingly Hell-bent on wrecking US-Saudi relations for a generation and in the process, destroying practically *everything* he had achieved in his whole working life. Back 'home' there would be people, a lot of people, who were going to accuse him of having 'gone native'; but if it was left unchallenged the Kennedy Administration's one-eyed *America First* insanity guaranteed that the region containing something like sixty to seventy percent of the World's known 'recoverable' oil reserves, was about to be plunged into decades of chaos.

The very idea of the Red Army lurking on the northern borders of Kuwait and Saudi Arabia, and dominating the northern shore of the Persian Gulf sent an icy shiver down Thomas Barger's spine. Even if the Soviets did not immediately invade the oil rich north east of the Arabian Peninsula – the biggest oilfields were within only a few hours' drive from the Iraqi border and little more than an hour's flying time for a Red Air Force bomber based at Basra or Abadan – the Saudi regime, and almost certainly those of the sheikdoms and emirates along the southern shores of the Persian Gulf, not to mention Oman which commanded the approaches to the Gulf, would most likely fall.

And then what?

What, if anything, would remain after the bloodletting was over?

Whereas, nobody in Philadelphia seemed to have thought about any of this; it was clear that the British had thought about it a lot. The trouble was that they needed men, bullets and the co-operation of the sons of the people they had betrayed at Versailles all those years ago, and in Arabia forty or fifty years was just a blink of the eye when it came to remembering old slights and the honour of settling blood feuds.

Today's 'conference' was only possible because Thomas Barger – whom his Saudi 'stakeholders' and contacts regarded as part-Arab in exactly the way people back home suspected he was part-native – trusted him. Or rather, they trusted him to do whatever was best for Aramco, which was serendipitous because they recognised that what was good for Aramco was good for the Kingdom. Saudi Arabia was nothing, an arid impoverished wasteland without its oil.

The Kennedy Administration's talk of 'guaranteeing the territorial integrity of Arabia' was meaningless. The United States had access to oilfields in South America and Indonesia, there was oil in Canada and Alaska as yet untapped and with the post-October War collapse in the price of crude oil, American industry and consumers alike were content to enjoy their 'cheap gas' for as long as the party lasted. America did not *need* Saudi oil at the moment and that *fact* trumped every other consideration.

The Kingdom had been facing bankruptcy before the Soviet invasion of Iran and Iraq; now it was looking into the abyss and the ruling Royal Family was beginning to ask itself when, not if, it would be swept away in a bloody palace revolt. In such a climate it was hardly surprising that Crown Prince Faisal had sent two of his younger, most ambitious ministers to parley in secret with the emissary of the former Imperial overlords.

Newly promoted Lieutenant-General Sir Michael Carver had risen to his feet, straightened and bowed his head first to thirty-six-year-old Prince Abdulaziz, the Minister of Defence and Aviation, and then to Ahmed Zaki Yamani, the thirty-three-year-old Minister of Petroleum and Mineral Resources.

The British officer was immaculately, elegantly attired in a lightweight grey civilian suit. Not that his non-military garb concealed for a single moment the soldier within. Thomas Barger had recognised in Carver exactly what he guessed his Saudi friends and business partners would instantly see; in the man's patient, thoughtful presence there was none of the ignorant haughtiness of so many of his fellow countrymen, simply a respect for his surroundings and a lack of suspicion. Perhaps, here was a man that might, in some lights, be a tangible link back to the glory days of the Arab Revolt and the campaigns of Lawrence...

In Carver's aloofness there was a quiet dignity that was highly respected in this land. His bearing might have been that of a scholar or priest, his measured movements suggestive of a man always deep in his thoughts, an aesthete, the most cerebral of warriors, a man who would not flinch to do what had to be done.

"No Egyptian soldier will step onto the soil of the Kingdom," Prince Abdulaziz asserted as he shook the Englishman's hand. "Nasser is bent on a revolutionary course and has purged those sympathetic to the Kingdom's cause in his own land."

Thomas Berger translated fluently.

Michael Carver was a tall man at pains not to look down his aquiline, patrician nose at the Saudi Minister for Defence and Aviation. He nodded. Ideally, he would have placed the Egyptian armour 'promised' to him opposite the Syrian Desert of Southern Iraq but that had never been more than a staff college exercise, a hypothetical scenario. Only a small proportion of the Egyptian 1st and 3rd Armoured Divisions could be transported by sea from Suez around the Arabian Peninsula by sea in the next thirty days; by the end of June, he *might* have a couple of disorganised, rag tag Egyptian tank regiments ready to move although they were unlikely to be in any sense anywhere near what a British Army tanker would consider 'combat ready'.

Sir Thomas Harding-Grayson had been very specific about the nature of the game they were playing. Nasser and Sadat were not fools; they understood that their tanks were pieces on the regional chess board, no more or less. One fought wars not with the armies, air forces and navies one wished one had but with the ones one had to hand *now*. Nasser's tanks were a statement of intent, once *in theatre* they ensured that Egypt would be *engaged* in the long-term battle for the control of the Middle East, not a peripheral onlooker preoccupied with its local ambitions in Libya or its renewed ancient feud with Israel.

Most important of all; whatever happened the 'deal' ensured that Nasser was surgically removed from the Soviet orbit, forced to declare for the Western-led coalition against the invaders. This was a decision which would ring down the coming years regardless of what happened in the coming war.

Nor had it been lost on Michael Carver that the agreement Sir Thomas had initialled with Nasser had inextricably tied the United Kingdom to supporting - with nuclear weapons if it came to it - the region's one potential unifying power.

Michael Carver glanced to Ahmed Zaki Yamani before returning his full attention to the Saudi Defence Minister.

"I am here because I am convinced that it is in the best interests of both our countries that, at the appropriate moment," he waited while Thomas Barger translated before continuing. "That *we* fight our mutual enemy on Iraqi soil. I further believe that forces of the Royal Saudi Army and Air Force, bolstered by tanks, vehicles and munitions currently held in American 'War Stores Depots' within the Kingdom, supported by British armoured units and the RAF are capable of implementing such a strategy."

Prince bin Abdulaziz's eyes narrowed.

He was disconcerted by how directly the Englishman had confronted him with the reality of their situation.

At his shoulder Yamani coughed politely.

"Our forces are equipped with M-48, so-called 'Patton' tanks, General Carver," he said in English. Thomas Barger effortlessly stepped in and translated, in low confidential terms in flowing Arabic for Yamani's colleague, the Minister for Defence and Aviation. "These machines are no match for the modern Red Army tanks. Likewise, we have few modern jet fighter aircraft."

Carver thought about this.

He looked to the senior minister, Prince Abdulaziz.

"Well handled the M-48's ninety-millimetre gun is capable of doing great harm to the Soviet T-62. I am confident that your tanks, *well-handled*," he emphasised, "fighting alongside *my* Centurions are perfectly capable of greatly inconveniencing our foes."

Michael Carver was not a man who liked to deal in unequivocal predictions. However, on this occasion he saw no profit in hedging around his thinking with superfluous caveats and clauses. He had the forces to hand to allow him to blunt and possibly stall the Soviets at the Kuwaiti border and if absolutely unavoidable, with which to embroil the Red Army in an attritional bloodbath on Abadan Island; but those forces alone even with the ANZAC reinforcements presently coming ashore at Dammam were too weak to attempt to repel the enemy. To go onto the offensive, he needed 'mass', *more of everything* and even then, there were no certainties to be had. Somehow the Egyptians or the Saudis, hopefully the Syrians, and Iranian Army units fast evaporating through desertions and lack of leadership had to be drawn together into some kind of united fighting force to resist the invaders.

There was no point worrying about all the things that could go wrong. It was the worst kept secret in the Middle East that the Israelis had been planning *their* next war against their neighbours ever since the Suez Fiasco; likewise, that Nasser wanted a finger in every political pie and had been actively seeking to undermine practically every other regime in the region. Saudi isolationism, the Shah's ego-centric rule in Iran, the constant threat of civil war in Iraq, and to a lesser degree, in Syria and the escalating tensions created by the huge reserves of oil recently discovered in the Emirates along the southern shore of the Persian Gulf made for an explosively volatile mix. Ongoing low-level civil wars in Yemen and Oman, and finally, the withdrawal last year of the permanent presence of American troops, aircraft and warships from bases in Saudi Arabia had turned the Middle East into a powder keg in which the continuing British footholds at Abadan, Aden, Kuwait and a dozen other under-strength garrisons had merely complicated, rather than simplified the ungodly, horribly messy strategic picture.

Until that was, the Red Army had intervened.

Now there was a short window of opportunity; a heaven-sent common enemy against whom it was in everybody's interest to unite.

"Frankly, Your Highness," Michael Carver said, addressing the Defence Minister in the tone of a weary cleric confronting some esoteric or arcane doctrinal matter. "While it might not be wholly in your interests to fight the Soviets with us; it is certainly *not* in your interests to fight the Soviets alone, or to shrink back from fighting at all. I am a Christian and I like to think I come from a country which is still essentially Christian. In this region Islam lights the way of its peoples. You and I, Your Highness, are 'people of the book', doctrinally, theologically bound to respect each other's beliefs and cultures." He half-turned and pointed to the north. "Driving down from the mountains of Iran and Iraq is a Godless horde that respects neither Islam nor Christianity and is set upon condemning us all to the spiritual darkness of the atheistic Marxist-Leninist creed."

There was a delay as Thomas Barger translated every time Michael Carver halted. Both Saudi ministers listened respectfully.

"*We* shall fight," the Englishman said. "Alone if necessary but we *shall* fight; together, *we* the 'people of the book' may, with God's grace, turn back the Soviet monster from the Persian Gulf and some greater part of the lands to our north."

It was Yamani who spoke first.

"You speak well, General Carver. But what becomes of us *after* the battle?"

Michael Carver allowed himself a deathly smile.

"Ah. Surely that is a thing that is in God's hands, sir."

Chapter 39

Tuesday 26th May 1964
Camp David, Catoctin Mountains, Maryland

Captain Sir Peter Christopher, VC, ignored the pack of photographers and the long lenses of the television cameras. Having exited the United States Navy Sikorsky SH-3 Sea King ahead of 'the girls', as he and his friend Alan Hannay referred – with pride and affection - to their Maltese wives, he turned and reached up to *grab* Marija before she tried to bravely negotiate the steps down to the grassy landing field unassisted. It had been a long day and she had been on her feet constantly until they had boarded the helicopter for the one-hundred-and-twenty-mile, ninety minute 'hop' from Philadelphia to the Catoctin Mountains. Marija was weary, her bones were aching and she was – albeit as yet lightly – with child; so, before she could object Peter gently seized his wife under her arms and lifted her cautiously down to terra firma.

"I'm not ill," she muttered, her face still turned to his chest and therefore out of sight of the watchers. "I'm just..."

"Pregnant," he whispered, smiling.

"Yes, husband," she retorted, mildly accusative for the briefest of instants as behind the couple Alan Hannay helped Rosa – taking her hand rather than manhandling her in any way - out into the late afternoon sunshine.

Both wives were wearing new 'party frocks' ordered from Bloomingdales in New York – items from a trousseau specially procured by the agency of, and at the expense of Lady Patricia Harding-Grayson - for the 'at home' with the President and the First Lady. The husbands were in ceremonial uniforms, minus the customary swords, which was an immense relief to Peter Christopher because every time he had been out in public lately with that clanking, infernally awkward weapon hanging off his waistband he had been terrified he was going to trip over it, drop it, step on it, inadvertently stab somebody or otherwise disgrace himself at any moment.

For Peter Christopher this was to be his third encounter with the President of the United States of America; a month ago there had been that fraught meeting at the White House when the Prime Minister had torn the poor fellow off a frightful strip in front of his whole entourage, and another, less angst-ridden formal introduction at a somewhat ill-starred 'dinner' hosted by the House of Representatives the following evening.

President Kennedy looked old before his time but tanned, altogether healthier than a month ago as he stepped forward to greet his guests. The First Lady looked, well, like a movie star. The Marine Corps honour guard in their old-fashioned uniforms snapped impressively to attention, presenting arms immaculately. Behind them the band which had struck up 'Hail to the Chief' fell silent. At the edge of the landing field, a level square of grass trimmed like the green baize of a billiard table, surrounded by trees which concealed the chalets, barracks and bunkers glimpsed through the windows of the helicopter as it had swooped down to land, more soldiers and military policemen kept watch from the shadows.

Camp David was a heavily armed military camp. Such, it seemed, was the price of maintaining the sanctity of this Shangri La in the Catoctin Mountains, and keeping the First Family's guests safe in the modern age.

Lady Marija Christopher smiled and looked around at her surroundings, unconsciously smoothing down the folds of her expensive calf-length dress. She still felt a little uncomfortable accepting Pat Harding-Grayson's 'charity'. This even though her friend, and since the moment she arrived in England, her mentor, had assured her that 'I made a ridiculously large amount of money from my books in America before the war and if I tried to bring all those dollars home, they would be horribly taxed, and besides, you and Rosa are the very best of causes!' Marija and her sister had been measured up almost as soon as they arrived in Philadelphia; but the frocks and blouses and stockings and *lingerie* had been delivered the day after 'the shooting', and what with one thing and another neither woman had been in any mood to properly investigate their bounty until yesterday. Ever since 'the shooting' they had been far too busy trying to stop their respective husbands braining every American who crossed his path!

Men were so stupid sometimes!

Peter and Alan had been the guests of the US Navy that morning; shown around a big cruiser that was being, or had been – Marija could not remember which – converted to carry an array of space age guided missile systems. Meanwhile, she and Rosa had toured a local school. Actually, although she had enjoyed the school visit and the attention of the children – aged between five and ten - Marija would much rather have gone to the Navy Yard with 'the boys', then she could have written home to her Papa and her brother Joe, who had flown back to Malta from England a fortnight ago, about all sorts of 'Navy things' that they would have been really interested to hear. Never mind. Peter would tell her the 'interesting' stuff sooner or later.

He still had not wholly got used to the fact that she was interested, very interested, in every aspect of *his* professional world. She had after all grown up in a dockyard family and considered herself to be a font of knowledge on the subject of post-1945 British naval architecture, radar and electronic suites, engineering and weaponry. Peter, bless him, ought to have worked that out by now after all these years. Still, men were men!

Marija blinked, and tried very hard to concentrate on the here and the now.

However, this was much easier said than done when one was standing in front of the most powerful man in the World.

"I am delighted to meet you at last Lady Marija!"

The President of the United States of America's face was deeply lined and his faded green eyes were tired and faded. Not so his smile and the warmth behind his words of welcome.

"I am honoured, Mister President."

Marija looked into the man's eyes and was briefly transfixed; she blinked again, told herself that she was shaking the hand of a mere mortal, a man with the weight of history crushing down upon his shoulders and felt...*sad* for him.

It was the oddest moment of her life.

John Fitzgerald Kennedy's smile stalled, rekindled in an instant fired by the flicker of sympathy in the young Maltese woman's gaze. There was no awe in Marija's stare, just an absence of condemnation. She was not judging him; she was looking to him as if he was just another human being and that was so strange as to be...*comforting*.

Her hand was small in his.

And then he was greeting Rosa Hannay.

Rosa was so excited and embarrassed and out of her depth that Jack Kennedy was a little afraid she was going to swoon. That sort of thing had happened a lot before he blew up the World but lately, hardly at all.

The President's men had told him that Alan Hannay had been Admiral Sir Julian Christopher's flag lieutenant on Malta before he joined HMS Talavera. They had also informed him that he had won his Distinguished Service Order engaging 'a battleship with an anti-aircraft cannon' at 'point blank range' after everybody around him on the destroyer's aft deckhouse gun platform had been killed. Hannay just looked like an ordinary guy to Jack Kennedy; most real heroes did in his experience. There was respect and measured deference in the younger man's face but none of the awe which had rendered his wife incapable of speech moments ago.

The President and the First Lady formed up for the photo call with the Christopher's to the President's right and the Hannays to the First Lady's left. From behind a tautly held Marine Corps rope line the pressmen's cameras clicked and flashed. And then the party was walking into the woods, the British Naval officers flanking the President, their wives the First Lady.

Presently, alone at last in their allotted chalet Marija thankfully sat down on the corner of one of the two single beds, unashamedly sighing to be able to relax for a few minutes. Her husband carefully arranged his jacket over the back of a chair and came to join her on the bed.

She leaned against him.

Shortly before leaving the British Embassy, they had been informed that the Prime Minister's planned visit to Philadelphia had been delayed for several days. There was also a suggestion that Philadelphia would not be the venue for the scheduled 'summit'; although no alternative location had yet been promulgated. Their brief 'house call' at Camp David, where President Kennedy was recuperating after a 'minor operation', had therefore been extended some days, apparently at the suggestion of the First Lady. The message was that the President was taking a short break from the campaign trail to aid his recovery and he wanted 'to hear everything there was to hear' about the Battle of Malta' and 'Sir Peter's other adventures'.

"I think," Marija observed philosophically, "that if things carry on like this for a few more months we will both go mad, husband."

Peter opened his mouth to speak.

"No," his wife assured him immediately, "I am not unhappy. I am not complaining. This is, well, strange and very exciting and everybody else in the World would love to be living *this* life," she insisted, "it is just that I don't know what people expect of us. At home on Malta, I was just *Marija*, here you and I, we are something that we are not."

"I'm sorry."

"No, this is not a thing to be sorry about," Marija shot back, brooking no dissent. "This is what our life together is. We are *together*. If you had your own ship, we would be apart but I know you miss your Talaveras dreadfully. But this," she made a wiping away gesture with her right arm, "is not a thing *we* expected." She sighed, a little frustrated that she was not saying what she felt in a way that made sense of those feelings. "Oh, I don't know what I mean. Ignore what I say!"

The man kissed the top of her head, extended an arm about her shoulders.

"You know I'd never do anything *that* silly, wife."

Marija giggled.

"Men always ignore what their wives tell them to do!"

"How do you know they do?"

When she raised her face, he kissed her and after that nature swiftly took its inevitable course. Hot and bothered, half-dressed they lay together beneath the sheets until sometime later there was a knock at the door, which they ignored. The phone's insistent overloud clanging on the bedside table less than a minute later was impossible to wish away.

"Peter Christopher..."

He listened half-asleep.

"Very good," he muttered and put the handset back in its cradle.

Marija snuggled closer to her husband.

"We dine in the President's Reception Chalet at eight o'clock apparently."

"Eight o'clock, when's that?"

"Oh, er... In about an hour's time..."

"And hour!" Marija managed to half-shriek this in the middle of embarking upon a complacent yawn. "My hair must be a mess! I don't know what to wear!"

The dress she had been wearing that afternoon was creased and discarded on the floor and she almost tangled her feet in it as she struggled to her feet. This brought her back towards sanity in a hurry. The last time she had forgotten that she could not actually run she had fallen flat on her face; an hour before she 'dined' with the President of the United States of America it would be a very bad time to fall flat on her face again.

Alan and Rosa Hannay were not invited to join the Presidential family for dinner. Officially, they were attached to Peter Christopher's 'staff', and 'staff' did not get to sit at the top table. Notwithstanding, their friends saw them off on their short walk with two escorting Marines to attend the Chief Executive.

"There are some people here from NASA," Alan Hannay, acting in the capacity of a good flag lieutenant, warned his commanding officer, "visiting the President. A couple of them are going to be in on tonight's shindig."

As he spoke Rosa was checking out Maria's hair and making a series of encouraging noises about the dress that she had eventually selected.

"This is Wernher von Braun," the President declared, introducing Peter and Marija to the tall imposing man in his fifties who had stepped into their path. "Wernher is Director of the Marshall Space Flight Center down at Huntsville, Alabama."

The older man gave the tall young naval officer a hard, guardedly curious stare as the two men shook hands. Peter Christopher's scrutiny was of the shocked type, entirely explicable given he had just been introduced to the man who had designed and built the World's first ballistic missile. Notwithstanding the man's previous association with Hitler and his crowd, von Braun was his childhood hero. Given that these days he moved in the circles of Prime Ministers and Presidents, encountering the World's greatest rocket scientist ought not to have knocked him off his stride. But it did...completely knock him off his stride.

Before he was obliged to move on down the line he blurted: "My degree is in mechanical engineering and physics. I'd be honoured to visit your facility in Alabama, Mr von Braun!"

Dinner was a blur.

Peter Christopher had not expected to be seated at the President's right hand any more than Marija had anticipated being placed at Jackie's left hand.

"What did you talk to the President about?" Marija inquired later in a dreamy voice.

"I honestly can't remember," her husband confessed a little apologetically. "He spent most of the time quizzing Wernher von Braun," who had been directly opposite the Chief Executive, for the setting had been relatively intimate with only seven guests, "about the Mercury and the Gemini Programs. I was too interested in what the Director was saying most of the time to think of anything intelligent to say for myself. How about you and the First Lady?"

Marija and Jacqueline Kennedy had had a chat about children, Marija's career as a nurse and midwife on Malta and, extraordinarily, the life and accomplishments of her mentor and friend Margo Seiffert.

It seemed that the US Navy, into which Margo had been commissioned during and just after the Second World War had belatedly learned about her career and exploits in the Mediterranean and wanted to award Margo some kind of posthumous award. As if that was not revelatory enough, the First Lady had offered to take Marija riding in the morning; an offer Marija had turned down mainly because the idea of getting up on a horse seemed like an infallible way of making sure she fell on her face again. The First Lady had instantly apologised, thinking she had in some way offended the younger woman; giving the impression she had forgotten she had been briefed about her childhood injuries. Whereupon, Marija had sheepishly recounted her 'falling on my face' story about the day she had tried to run after Peter; and for several steps succeeded before her conscious mind had remembered she could not actually run, and thereafter, she had 'fallen on my face'.

The President's wife had laughed demurely.

"These people are not our enemies," Marija said eventually as she and her husband ambled unhurriedly back to their chalet accompanied by the ever-present Marines. "Everything looks different from where we are *now* but they are *not* our enemies, Peter."

"I know," her husband said. "I know. If *our* people back home were over here, they might understand our hosts a little better. Perhaps, you and I really can do something about building bridges while we're here?"

Marija nodded solemnly as they reached their chalet.

Inside the door the couple kissed.

"Your bones must ache?" He whispered gently.

"A little," she smiled shyly.

The man swept his wife up in his arms and carried her to the bed.

"No, no, no," Marija laughed. "This time I must fold up my dress before we..."

Her voice trailed away.

"Before we do what?" Peter teased.

Marija blushed and avoided his eye.

Suddenly she giggled girlishly.

"Before we do what we do!" She exclaimed happily, pulling him down on top of her.

Chapter 40

Wednesday 27th May 1964
RAF Brize Norton, Oxfordshire, England

Forty-five-year-old Alexander Nikolayevich Shelepin followed the others down the steps to the tarmac. There was no formal welcoming committee, no cameras, nor witnesses other than the detachment of British soldiers forming a cordon around the Tupolev Tu-114 airliner which had brought the 'delegation' directly from Sverdlovsk. The flight west across the Urals and the blasted wastelands of the Ukraine, White Russia, Central Europe, Germany, Holland and the North Sea had been uneventful, a sullen dispiriting affair. Even as the Red Army marched to new triumphs in Iraq the Soviet government had been forced to come, cap in hand, to its enemy. Alexander Nikolayevich Shelepin had sworn on the graves of his countless murdered countrymen that he would *never* forget this day.

Shelepin paused before clambering into the waiting car to look around at the great aircraft which had carried the delegation to England, sourly aware that only a handful of these magnificent machines had been completed before the Cuban Missiles War. Developed from the Tu-95 bomber, the Tu-114, with its swept back wings and a range of over ten thousand kilometres was the fastest propeller-driven aircraft in the World. Hundreds might have eventually been built to fill the skies had not Aviation Plant No. 18 at Kuybyshev – where the aircraft was built – not been obliterated in the war. The deafening roar of the Tu-114's four giant Kuznetsov NK-12 turbo-prop engines began to subside, and the huge, contra-rotating propellers slowed.

With a shake of the head Shelepin dropped into the luxurious back seat of the Bentley beside Alexei Nikolayevich Kosygin, the designated representative of the post-Cuban Missiles War 'collective leadership'. Neither man spoke as the car picked up speed across the airfield.

Kosygin was thinking about the last time he had been sent abroad to defuse another potentially disastrous situation. That mission had been to Bucharest back in February after Krasnaya Zarya zealots had launched a – thankfully, a largely botched – nuclear first strike at the British, the Royal Navy and anybody else they could think of in the Balkans and Egypt. Marshal of the Soviet Union Vasily Ivanovich Chuikov, Shelepin's deputy, Yuri Vladimirovich Andropov, Kosygin and his personal scientific advisor, the country's post-Cuban Missiles War premier surviving atomic physicist, Academician Andrei Dmitrievich Sakharov, had been seized by Nicolae Ceausescu's goons and thrown into a Securitate dungeon. He, Chuikov and Sakharov had survived shaken but otherwise in one piece, not so Andropov who had been beaten very nearly to death by his interrogators.

Andropov denied 'breaking' under the beatings; or more correctly, he claimed he remembered little or nothing of his experiences at the hands of Ceausescu's thugs. Nobody believed him, of course. After what he had gone through, he must have 'broken'. Fortunately, the Red Air Force had demolished Bucharest with a city killer bomb soon afterwards and the truth about Krasnaya Zarya and the smokescreen around Operation Nakazyvat had remained undiscovered until the first of Army Group South's T-62s rolled into Azerbaijani Iran.

The whole episode still gave Kosygin nightmares and now he could not help wondering if he was walking into another, even deadlier trap. This time Chuikov, the Minister of Defence in the three-man collective leadership had stayed behind, Party Secretary and Chairman of the Communist Party of the Union of Soviet Socialist Republics, Leonid Ilyich Brezhnev having decreed that after the 'Bucharest fuck up' at least two members of the 'troika' would always remain in the Mother country.

Kosygin turned to Shelepin.

"I do not think this is another trap, Comrade Director," he observed. "The British are a civilised people."

Alexander Nikolayevich Shelepin grunted his displeasure and scowled at Andrei Sakharov who had been nodding distractedly. The physicist's half-smile froze on his face. The man Sakharov worked for, Alexei Nikolayevich Kosygin, and Shelepin were the last two of 'Stalin's men' in the Politburo. The one, Kosygin had lived in terror at the end of the Man of Steel's reign, but not, he suspected, Shelepin and it was probably for this reason that Brezhnev, Marshal Chuikov and likely, Kosygin also, had excluded him thus far from the collective leadership.

Thus far being the key clause, because there was no more dangerous or secretive man in the reconstituted Union of Soviet Socialist Republics than Comrade Alexander Nikolayevich Shelepin.

Allegedly, Shelepin had been born the son of a railway official in Voronezh. Very little was known of his childhood or his youth. His surviving *official* biography stated that in his late teens and early twenties he had studied history and literature at the Moscow Institute of Philosophy and Literature; and that Shelepin had first come to Stalin's attention early in the great Patriotic War as the man who had recruited the legendary partisan fighter Zoya Kosmodemyanskaya, whose torture and execution by the Germans had made her a national hero. By 1943 Shelepin was a leading figure in the Communist Youth League; and after the war Stalin had appointed him head of the ill-named World Federation of Democratic Youth. Shelepin had been Director of the KGB between 1958 and 1961, when he became a First Deputy Prime Minister in Nikita Khrushchev's regime shortly before the Cuban Missiles War. In the aftermath of the war, he had been the obvious candidate to rebuild the KGB.

Within the Politburo, the senior echelons of the Communist Party and the wider apparatus of the Soviet state, dark rumours roiled around Shelepin like an impenetrable cloak wherein evil resided. Inevitably, not every rumour was true, or could in fact be true, but if not all the mud stuck then some of the blood could never be wiped away.

Every time Andrei Sakharov crossed the path of the First Secretary of the *Komitet Gosudarstvennoy Bezopasnosti* it felt as if the atmosphere around him had suddenly chilled by ten degrees.

It was said that Khrushchev had installed Shelepin at the Lubyanka – the former headquarters of the Rossiya Insurance Company building on Dzerzhinsky Square which had been taken over as the headquarters of the NKVD, or Narodnyi Komissariat Vnutrennikh Del – because only a man with his particular gifts could possibly 'clean out the stables'. Latterly, one whisper claimed that Shelepin had been the man who had 'cleaned out the stables' after German and Polish exiles in the West had started asking awkward questions about the twenty thousand Poles murdered in the Katyn Forest in April and May 1940, over a year *before* Hitler invaded and conquered *that* part of Russia in the Second World War. Originally, the outside World had assumed the atrocity was the doing of the Germans; but not even the NKVD could keep a thing like that secret, any more than Stalin could keep the monstrous archipelago of the Gulag secret. Once Stalin was dead people had *talked* and those who understood how the Soviet state worked had tacitly assumed that Khrushchev must have ordered Shelepin to make sure the truth about the massacre in the Katyn Forest never surfaced. It seemed outlandish, too obscene but like so many of the stories told about Shelepin it was only when one actually met the man that one began to give them credence.

It was a short car journey.

Within minutes the Russian delegation was led into what looked like a big shed. Inside the structure was like a windowless barn. Several chairs had been arranged for the 'visitors' to rest upon and a middle-aged man in a careworn pinstripe suit explained in faultless Russian that there would be a short *interregnum* before the *main plenary session* commenced.

"They want to talk to Waters," Shelepin said as he began to pace backwards and forwards like a caged Leopard.

Lieutenant-Colonel Francis Harold St John Water, VC, had been whisked away in a separate vehicle the moment his feet touched the tarmac.

The veteran SAS man had entertained hopes of a stiff drink and square meal when he got back home but this, it seemed, was to be delayed a little longer. He recognized Field Marshall Sir Richard Hull, whom he had met several times over the years.

The Russians had found him a badly fitting boiler suit that smelled of mothballs. Nevertheless, he threw the Chief of the Defence Staff a smart salute.

"At ease, Waters," the other man ordered. Hands were shaken. "You look all in?"

"The bastards haven't ground me down yet, sir," the younger man assured the professional head of the British Army.

Sir Richard Hull guffawed and introduced his companions.

Margaret Thatcher shook the ragged newcomer's hand daintily but looked at him with intelligent, decidedly mesmeric steely blue eyes that instantly tied the returning hero's tongue. That hardly ever happened the first time Frank Waters made a lady's acquaintance.

The Prime Minister smiled.

"Are you fit enough to act as our interpreter, Colonel Waters?"

"Absolutely, Ma'am," he retorted defiantly.

"That's marvellous. Just the spirit!"

Frank Waters shook the hand of the big, lugubrious man at the Prime Minister's shoulder. He did not usually have that much time for *lefties* like James Callaghan, the Leader of the Labour Party and Deputy Prime Minister in the Unity Administration of the United Kingdom.

"How do you do, sir," he grinned toothily at the taller man. It did not cost him anything to be polite and for all he knew Callaghan might be his boss in a month or two.

If war was a messy old business politics was positively *dirty*; a chap never knew where he stood with a bloody *politico*!

Chapter 41

Wednesday 27th May 1964
Advanced HQ 10th Guards Tank Division, south of Sadiyah, Iraq

Major General Vladimir Andreyevich Puchkov clambered up onto the broiling armoured carapace of the T-62 at the head of the column. The rounded steel of the dome-like turret was hot enough to sear human flesh or flash fry an egg in seconds. In the distance the haze shimmered off the arid, yellow grey floor of the plain where a ribbon of greenery traced the distant path of the Dyala River, and here and there small irrigated oases dotted the landscape. Otherwise, while the tanks of the column fanned out looking for depressions in the rocky escarpment in which to lie 'hull down' until the heat of the day had subsided, all he saw was empty countryside.

The smoke from the burning Iraqi M-48s which had attempted to ambush the column an hour ago still hung over the battlefield. The enemy had clumsily telegraphed his attentions, and charged in like idiots – albeit brave idiots – with minimal infantry support and an absence of anything a real soldier would recognise as co-ordination. Puchkov's veteran tankers had made short work of the attackers.

The commander of the 10th Guards Tank Division had ordered his boys to laager until nightfall and driven forward to confirm what the map told him about the ground ahead. The T-62s around him were low on fuel and if they were going to dash down the road towards Miqdadiyah at sunset they needed their tanks topping off first. Miqdadiyah was only thirty kilometres north-east of Baquba. From Baquba to Baghdad was just fifty kilometres – or as little as two days fighting further down the road.

Army Group South would reconsolidate at Baghdad, transferring every available Red Air Force aircraft south to forward bases around the city. Once Puchkov's tanks reached Baghdad, Iraq was at the Red Army's mercy. With just four under strength divisions – most of Army Group South was still snarled up in the Alborz and Zagros Mountains - Marshal of the Soviet Union Hamazasp Khachaturi Babadzhanian had conquered half of Iraq *and yet those useless bastards back in Chelyabinsk were still panicking like a lot of old women!*

Puchkov heard booted feet approaching, crunching across the stony ground, looked down.

A sweating KGB officer brandished a wad of charred papers.

"These people," he waved airily towards the nearest burned-out M-48 Patton tank, "were Shias. That's probably why they tried to make a stand here. There's nothing much between here and Miqdadiyah, sir. You see the local Shias believe *that* the place was named for Miqdad ibn Aswad Al-Kindi."

Vladimir Andreyevich Puchkov did not have much time for over-educated intelligence officers at the best of times; and even less for the KGB ones that shithead Andropov had foisted on his division, who spent more time writing down what *real soldiers* thought about politics than they did collecting *useful* combat intelligence. The scowl that creased his sunburnt, scarred face suddenly concentrated the KGB man's thoughts.

"Miqdad ibn Aswad Al-Kindi was one of the Sahabads of the Prophet Muhammad, Comrade General," the younger man went on hurriedly. "That is, one of the so-called *Four Companions*. Miqdad ibn Aswad Al-Kindi was said to be a perfect Shia..."

Puchkov shook his head.

Where did the KGB find these useless fuckers?

"Great. So everywhere we go we can expect to have a bunch of religious fanatics come at us in a fucking *banzai* charge like these comedians?" He gestured towards the scorched, smoking carcasses of the knocked-out M-48s.

"Er, I don't know, sir."

Puchkov told the officer to *fuck off* and not to come back until: "You've got something useful to tell me!"

He turned to get down from the turret.

A ninety-millimetre round from one of the M-48's had hit the cupola beneath his feet and bounced off, leaving a twenty-millimetre-deep boot-long gash in the armour. An armour-piercing round from a one hundred and five-millimetre fifty-two calibre rifled British L7 gun fitted in the Centurion Mark II, would have cleaved through the steel at his feet like a red-hot knife through butter. Puchkov hesitated, stared a while longer at the blackened M-48s, wondering privately how this little battle would have turned out if the Iraqis had been riding in British Centurions or the latest American M-60 main battle tanks.

Bloodily, he suspected...

However, he did not dwell on this thought overlong as he jumped down and trudged towards where he had ordered his communications truck to park up in dead ground below the ridgeline. A mine clearance detail halted in mid-stride and snapped to attention as he passed.

Nobody seriously believed that the suicidal zealots who had attacked a numerically superior force equipped with bigger, longer range ordnance in broad daylight had paused to lay mines under or alongside the road ahead. But it paid to be safe. Up until the last week the main enemy had been the terrain and the occasional interventions of high-altitude RAF bombers; whereas, the last few days had seen a number of sharp little actions like this afternoon's south of Sadiyah.

Troopers from the Divisional Headquarters Company were disembarking from half-tracks and ancient requisitioned Fords and Dodge six-wheelers when he arrived at the radio truck. His boys had been forced to seize and repair whatever vehicles they found on their way south.

By the time the Division got to the Persian Gulf it was going to resemble a bloody gypsy caravan at this rate!

Chapter 42

Wednesday 27th May 1964
Headquarters of the 3rd Imperial Armoured Division, Khorramshahr, Iran

Brigadier Mirza Hasan Mostofi al-Mamaleki was in sombre mood when Lieutenant General Sir Michael Carver arrived at his headquarters that afternoon. A week ago, the Provisional Government – an ad hoc collection of middle-ranking courtiers and survivors from the Shah's regime, and elderly Army officers based in a disused Royal Palace outside Isfahan – had appointed a new Military Governor of Khuzestan Province, which covered the Khorramshahr-Abadan Sector.

It seemed that General Jafar Sharif-Zahedi – members of whose family had literally been in bed with the Pahlavi dynasty ever since it came to power in the 1920s – a man who had little or no practical 'soldiering' experience who had based himself and his entourage in the town of Bandr Mahshahr some thirty miles to the east, was more preoccupied with recovering the 'jewel of Abadan' than he was securing the country's western borders.

Like other members of the Provisional Government, he viewed the war in Iraq as a sideshow; the main thing was to first, hold the Soviet invaders within the mountains of the north, and second, eventually expel them from the holy soil of Iran. Oh, and to gratuitously enrich oneself and one's family – and one's numerous retainers – in the process.

Bizarrely, it seemed that the Provisional Government had convinced itself that the Red Army's appetite for conquest would be wholly sated once it had consumed Iraq. The thinking went something like this: there was already a dysfunctional socialist regime in Iraq, therefore an Iraq ruled by the Soviet Union would in some way be a more stable, predictable neighbour and because it lay to the west of Abadan and the southern oilfields it was unlikely to impair Iran's ability to continue to export that oil via the Persian Gulf to the outside World...

It was the sort of complacent logic that made re-arranging the deck chairs on the deck of the Titanic look like a rational damage control strategy.

Al-Mamaleki had already made arrangements for his wife and children to travel south to stay with relations in Shiraz, hopefully beyond the reach of the idiots in Isfahan. His most recent meeting with General Jafar Sharif-Zahedi, a corpulent unimaginative man with no understanding of the realities of modern armoured warfare, had convinced him beyond any reasonable doubt that the inmates had seized control of the asylum. This he freely confessed to Michael Carver as they stood over the map table at his headquarters in the eastern quarter of Khorramshahr.

Picking up a pencil he prodded the line of the Alborz Mountains stretching across his country from the Caucasus in the northwest most of the way to Afghanistan in the east.

"A couple of squadrons of my Centurions could hold the passes through those mountains forever," he snorted derisively. "The Soviets know that. The key sector is down here opposite Basra. Abadan is the key."

"Is there anything to be gained by my travelling to Bandr Mahshahr to pay my respects to General Jafar Sharif-Zahedi?"

Al-Mamaleki shook his head.

"He would probably have you arrested, my friend." The Iranian officer sighed. "People like Zahedi care about nothing beyond their own little satrapy," he went on derisively. "He thinks that because he is the 'master' of Khuzestan Province that Abadan and the oilfields are his own personal *possessions*, to enjoy and to dispose of at his whim."

Michael Carver was silent for several seconds.

"What of *your* situation, Hasan?"

"My uncle is Governor in Shiraz. My family will be safe there." The Iranian shrugged, his lips formed into a grimly thin line on his still handsome now darkly bearded face. "My officers understand that this is the key front. This," he added resignedly, "is where the Russians will strike next when they have digested the *easy meat* of the Basra garrison."

The Englishman became aware that his friend's stare was suddenly hard, unrelenting.

"The fools in Isfahan and many of their *servants*, men like Zahedi in Bandr Mahshahr, imagined that *you* will meekly surrender Abadan to *me*. They don't believe me when I tell them that you would fight to the last tank and wreck the place from end to end to stop it falling into the hands of the Russians." He smiled roguishly. "Or *us*."

Michael Carver made no attempt to contradict the other man.

"This I know," al-Mamaleki guffawed. "Because you and I, we are soldiers. But those imbeciles in Isfahan? Even after what the Russians did to Tehran and the Shah," his momentary good humour died, "they still don't understand that unless we fight now, those bastards will enslave us for generations to come."

Not for the first time Michael Carver found himself admiring the poet that in troubled times invariably emerged from somewhere deep within the Persian soul.

"What of your officers, my friend?"

"Those who are still with me will fight when the time comes."

Al-Mamaleki's brigade had grown into an over-sized division boasting as many as two hundred armoured fighting vehicles of which over sixty were Centurions – a mixture of Mark Is and up-gunned Mark IIs - and over seventy American M-48 Pattons. Notwithstanding that the original 'brigade' had been re-designated a 'division', no battlefield or brevet promotion had been bestowed on its commanding officer; a thing which spoke volumes for the suspicion in which al-Mamaleki was obviously held by his new master in Bandr Mahshahr.

Before driving up to Khorramshahr from his headquarters in

Abadan – a journey of around seven miles – Michael Carver had summoned his staff to brief him on events in and around Abadan during his absence in Saudi Arabia.

His own smaller 'Abadan Garrison' force of some thirty tanks, several batteries of seventeen and twenty-five pounder anti-tank artillery, a total of six battalions of partially mechanised infantry, and around a thousand lines of communication troops supported by two squadrons of RAF Hawker Hunter interceptors, half-a-dozen helicopters of various descriptions and a flight of four Canberra jet bombers represented a formidable fighting unit but if the Red Army was to be struck a telling blow it would be by al-Mamaleki's massed armour, not by the British and Commonwealth forces defending Abadan Island.

In a perfect world Carver would have explored ways of extending Abadan's air defence umbrella – two batteries of long-range surface-to-air Bristol Bloodhound missiles – to cover the Iranian 3rd Imperial Armoured Division's over-extended northern front opposite Basra. The Bloodhounds covered the airspace over Khorramshahr, and two troops of Centurions were already imbedded with al-Mamaleki's garrison within the town. Sometime within the next ten days it was planned to bring HMAS Sydney up the Shat-al-Arab to offload several more Centurions, a squadron of Australian Navy Westland Wessex helicopters and to deliver an additional ANZAC rifle battalion to Abadan.

"I reported to Bandr Mahshahr that I 'demanded' fuel and lubricants from 'the British'," al-Mamaleki confessed, ruefully. "The idiots had no idea that the only thing which had been keeping the 3rd Division in the field was *your* supply organisation."

Michael Carver saw the funny side of this, and smiled.

Last night he had dined with the Foreign Secretary, Sir Thomas Harding-Grayson, a most erudite and perspicacious man with an apparently encyclopaedic knowledge of the history, religions and customs of the Middle East, and a profound understanding of the mindsets of principal members of each of the major governmental, religious and ethnic groupings.

Sir Thomas was deeply distrustful of Nasser even though he personally admired the man; 'fascinating, remarkable fellow' he had said ruminatively, 'but he will let us down in the end'. As for the Saudis 'they would blow up Abadan themselves if they could but without the Americans, they feel vulnerable, as much to an internal revolt as they do to external aggression.'

The Emir of Kuwait was pleading for his small country to be packed full of British and Commonwealth troops but shuddered at the idea of Egyptian tanks rumbling across his sands. Likewise, in the emirates along the southern shores of the Persian Gulf the local potentates, sheiks and despots felt both reassured and fearful watching the big grey allied warships out at sea, listening to the silvery jets noisily overflying their barren lands and by the ongoing 'pull out' of the American conglomerates prospecting for black gold in their fiefdoms.

The whole Middle East was ready to explode.

'Nasser won't send us more than a token brigade or maybe a couple of under-strength regiments from his 1st and 3rd Armoured Divisions,' the Foreign Secretary had explained. It was not said cynically, he was simply stating facts. 'Oh, he'll dress it up as a massive military commitment, a huge investment in pan-Arabism, or some such. But that's not the thing. The thing is that Egypt will be putting down a marker that the Soviets will not be able to ignore in years to come. It is pointless expending unlimited blood and treasure stopping the Red Army in its tracks if, when the shooting is over everybody looks to us to guarantee the peace because that is certainly *not* a burden we can carry *alone*.'

Michael Carver had quizzed the Foreign Secretary over the as yet unpublicised Anglo-Egyptian Mutual Defence Treaty.

'Will we actually go to war with Israel if the Israelis attack Egypt after this is over? Assuming we don't get thrown out of the Gulf, that is? Say, if there's a war between Egypt and Israel next year?'

'Probably not,' Sir Thomas had conceded. 'But Nasser knows that. In the long run he also knows that it will be in our interests to be his arms manufacturer and in the foreseeable future, his naval bulwark in the Eastern Mediterranean. The Israelis won't know what we and Nasser have cooked up; they'll have to assume, for a year or two at least, that if they make a wrong move that either the Ark Royal or the Eagle will come steaming into the Eastern Mediterranean. That wouldn't be good for anybody. In the meantime, Nasser knows he's got a free hand in Libya to secure his western borders against a possible insurgency and to start building his pan-Arab empire along the North African coast, safe in the knowledge the Royal Navy is guarding his seaward right flank. Diplomacy is like politics, and most things in life I suppose, it is the art of the possible. We have made a number of distasteful *compromises* and *accommodations* because at the end of the day *we* need a reliable constant supply of crude oil from this region.'

Hasan al-Mamaleki was watching Michael Carver with thoughtful eyes that threatened to read his friend's mind.

"General Zahedi doesn't understand," he said stepping back from the map table. "None of the people in Isfahan understand. If you and I were playing a staff college exercise, a *war game*, nine times out of ten the result would be the same. Whether we stand and fight or whether we run and hide the result would be the same." He nodded towards the map. "Abadan *will* be lost."

The Englishman nodded.

Chapter 43

Wednesday 27th May 1964
HMS Tiger, Tarout Bay, Dammam

Pipes twittered as the First Sea Lord, Admiral Sir Varyl Begg, marched down the gangway from HMS Triumph, the slab-sided former aircraft carrier which had been converted into a heavy repair ship, a floating dockyard by any other name. He blinked as he emerged from the shadows into the dazzling afternoon sunshine and stepped onto the deck of the cruiser.

The twelve-thousand-mile high-speed run from Malta, with a forty-eight-hour refuelling stopover at Simons Town at the Cape, had taken a heavy toll on HMS Tiger. The rigors of that twenty-three day passage had worn down both the ship and her crew and Rear Admiral Nicholas 'Nick' Davey, who had joined the ship in South Africa after flying down to Pretoria for meetings with the Republic's Prime Minister and other cabinet colleagues, to discuss a possible South African contribution to the assembling 'Middle East Task Force', had reluctantly shifted his flag ashore to permit the cruiser to come alongside the heavy repair ship HMS Triumph, to address her most pressing mechanical needs.

The First Sea Lord had determined that he wanted to see, and to be seen, on as many of the ships of the ABNZ Squadron assembled in the Persian Gulf as possible during his forty-eight-hour visit, and his host had been delighted to oblige him; hence the meeting on board the cruiser.

"Welcome aboard Tiger, sir," Rear Admiral Nick Davey declared proudly.

The other man looked around at the tangle of cables and the dismantled equipment in every conceivable state of repair strewn everywhere in a decidedly un-Navy like way.

"Good to be out here at last," Admiral Sir Varyl Begg retorted.

"Sorry about the mess, sir," Davey remarked. "I need Tiger back at sea in five days' time and there's rather a lot to do!"

"That's hardly surprising after her run around the Cape."

Dispatching at least one 'big ship' from the Mediterranean Fleet the 'long way around' the Cape of Good Hope to the Persian Gulf had been a largely symbolic gesture, a thing primarily designed for public consumption back home. Ideally, the 'big ship' would have been an aircraft carrier but unfortunately the Royal Navy had run out of seaworthy options in that regard; Ark Royal was in dockyard hands in Portsmouth, the Eagle could not be spared from the Mediterranean, Hermes was at Gibraltar undergoing major repairs to her starboard turbines, and repairs to HMS Victorious, currently being 'patched up' at Malta were anticipated – assuming she was not written off as being not worth repairing - to take a year to eighteen months once she was, most likely, *towed* either to Gibraltar or Portsmouth. The other 'carrier' in the Mediterranean, HMS Albion, was actually a 'commando' or 'helicopter carrier'; and although she looked good on the front pages of newspapers, she too was badly in need of time in dockyard hands, having been repaired in an unholy rush after her mining in Algeciras Bay back in December. Albion was currently unable to steam at more than twelve knots.

Albion's sister, Bulwark, similarly converted to the role of a 'commando' carrier, had remained in the Pacific when Centaur, the Navy's least modified 'aircraft' carrier, sporting an obsolete radar and electronics suite and incapable of operating the most modern fighter and strike fast jets had been, quite literally, the 'last carrier standing'. Basically, the Royal Navy's cupboard was somewhat *bare* and the only available 'big ships' left capable of a long, hard steam around the Cape had been one of the two big cats.

Tiger's surviving sister ship, the other 'big cat', the Lion had stayed in the Mediterranean, acting as the Eagle's guard ship. HMS Hampshire, the newly commissioned second ship of the new cruiser-sized County class of guided missile destroyers had been provisionally pencilled in to join Tiger; but then she had been requisitioned to transport big bombs conventional 'iron bombs' – Grand Slams and Tallboys - out to Cyprus for the RAF, and to carry away the nuclear warheads salvaged from the wreck of the big cats' sunken sister, HMS Blake in Limassol Harbour.

The Navy had run out of 'big' ships.

The South African government had offered to send the Type 12 frigate President Steyn, and the old 'W' Class former Royal Navy destroyer Jan van Riebeeck to the Persian Gulf but after much discussion it was decided that for purely logistical reasons, the Republic's contribution should be limited to sending as many as four battalluns of mechanised light infantry to the theatre utilising locally available shipping.

Davey's mission to the Cape after a brief stopover in Pretoria had been as much to co-ordinate the South African Navy's supporting role in the submarine blockade of the Falklands Archipelago and the islands of South Georgia, as it was to supplement the motley fleet coalescing in the Persian Gulf.

"When I was in South Africa the government there was mightily impressed with the line we're taking over the Falklands," the junior man remarked to the professional head of the Royal Navy. "I think they'd been beginning to ask themselves where it left them if and when we started retrenching, sir."

Sir Varyl Begg guffawed and shook his head.

"I think we're all asking ourselves that," he confided. "We might have lost David Luce and Julian Christopher but their spirit lives on. Dammit, after what Julian's boy did at Malta nobody in the Service would be able to look at themselves in the mirror if we started taking backward steps now."

Nick Davey nodded enthusiastically.

Deploying the Oberon and Porpoise class boats to the South

Atlantic had been a brave thing to do. Fortunately, they had a government that did nothing by halves.

Thank god!

The ongoing war operations in the South Atlantic came under the umbrella of *Operation Sturdee*, named in honour of the First World War victor of the Battle of the Falklands, Admiral of the Fleet Sir Frederick Charles Doveton Sturdee. The three two-hundred nautical mile Total Exclusion Zones – TEZs – had accordingly been named 'Invincible' (the Falklands Archipelago), 'Inflexible' (South Georgia), and 'Glasgow' (the South Sandwich Islands). At the Battle of the Falklands in December 1914 it had been the battlecruisers *Invincible* – Sturdee's flagship – and *Inflexible* which had battered the out-gunned armoured cruisers Scharnhorst and Gneisenau of Admiral Maximillian von Spee's German East Asia Squadron to pieces, in company with the light cruiser HMS *Glasgow*.

Nick Davey was less of a naval historian than many of his contemporaries; until his retirement from the service shortly before the October War, he had been much too busy living life to the full to bother overmuch with history books. Looking back, he had spent a large part of the first half of his career mucking about in racing yachts and chasing women with his greatly lamented recently deceased old friend, Julian Christopher.

Notwithstanding, he had once met an old salt from HMS Glasgow – the only British ship to have been present at the debacle of the Battle of Coronel in which von Spee's guns had demolished a much weaker Royal Navy Squadron off the Chilean coast on 1st November 1914 – and the Battle of the Falklands five-and-a-half weeks later. He could not remember the old salt's name, both men had been a little the worse for drink at the time, but he did remember that the man had told him that at one time during the Great War the Glasgow's mascot had been a pig called 'Tirpitz'...

All of which was incidental to current ongoing operations in the South Atlantic. As a result of his conversations with the Republic's Prime Minister, Hendrik Verwoerd, and several of his senior ministers, the South African Navy had taken responsibility for the protection of an oiler and a submarine support ship strategically positioned in mid-South Atlantic; floating depots for the submarines on station thousands of miles from the nearest friendly port.

Nick Davey had left Pretoria with mixed emotions. Having been forewarned that but for the October War Hendrik Verwoerd would gladly have severed all military ties with the United Kingdom, he had been surprised by the pragmatism of his mainly Afrikaner hosts. That said, their 'Apartheid' system of segregation had the look and the feel of a very dirty business. The Ambassador, John Maud, an old Etonian former Master of Birkbeck College, had warned him to steer well clear of 'local racial politics', and to forget anything he had heard about the Nationalist government having had Nazi sympathies 'during the forty-five war'. Not for the first time in his life Davey was glad he had never paid that much attention to politics. Politics was a decidedly filthy business at the best of times.

The South African contribution to Operation Sturdee meant that within the next few days three of the four larger Royal Navy ships based at Simons Town – the destroyer Cavendish, and the anti-submarine frigates Eskimo and Blackpool – would be steaming around the Cape to join Davey's squadron.

A man naturally given to optimism and good cheer he preferred not to dwell on the fact that the USS Kitty Hawk possessed several times the offensive punch of his entire rag tag Persian Gulf flotilla. The Americans were taking a backseat on this one; so be it. He would work with the tools he had been given by the Admiralty. Ideally, he would have liked a couple of big carriers – Ark Royal and Eagle would fit the bill nicely, thank you – and not one but both of the 'big cats' and lots of air defence destroyers like the modified 'Battles', not to mention a proper fleet train to keep his ships continuously at sea for weeks on end. But he did not have any of that. Thankfully, what he did have was a squadron made up of men and ships with plenty of recent experience who understood, as only men who have been in the heat of battle can understand, that the coming campaign was probably going to be a very close run-thing.

Nick Davey escorted the First Sea Lord down through the chaos of the stern to his day cabin where, without delay he called to his flag lieutenant to organise a 'brace of pink gins'.

Presently, the two men were alone, having dismissed their secretaries and flag lieutenants. They sat in chairs, eyed their surroundings for some moments as they cradled their glasses in steady hands. HMS Tiger was a wartime hull that had lain idle many years before she was completed with modern gunnery and electronics. Much of her below decks' layout was old-fashioned, albeit that there was more space for her crew because she mounted only two rather than the traditional World War II three or four main battery turrets. The day cabin was relatively spacious by contemporary standards for what was essentially, only a medium-sized cruiser. Light streamed in through several open scuttles and the ship had about her a hard driven but still new feel and smell.

"You and I have not always seen eye to eye, Nick," the First Sea Lord said. "That was a dreadful business on Malta," he added. "Julian was a damned fine officer and nothing that happened at Malta was in any way his fault. He was let down. We were all let down. I'd like to be able to say that we're better off without the Americans, except you and I both know that's not true."

Nick Davey said nothing. Varyl Begg had always been a man who looked for closer and better relations with the US Navy, for the greatest possible transfer of technology and ever more intimately compatible systems. He had been a missiles advocate who did not believe that the Navy needed or could afford more big carriers; but that had been in an age when every First Sea Lord had been able to count on the Royal Navy being in league with the United States Navy, operating in a tactical environment in which its ships *always* operated beneath the impenetrable shield of overwhelming American naval airpower. Nick Davey suspected that Begg, like so many sinners who genuinely repent of their former ways, was still a little uncomfortable with his former views. Recanting was one thing, atonement another.

"Julian Christopher and I had our differences," Begg admitted gruffly. "But that was all before the war. We exchanged friendly notes after his appointment to the Med, buried the hatchet, as it were. For the record I entirely endorsed your posting to the Persian Gulf Squadron. I think you are just the fellow for the job."

"That's jolly decent of you to say so, sir."

The men sipped their gins.

The First Sea Lord looked up.

"For your ears only at this stage, *Operation Cold Harbour* has been authorised at the highest level." He paused briefly. "Execution date and hour to be confirmed in due course, pending the finalisation of planning for Operation Lightfoot. Whatever happens in the coming weeks we will give the Soviets one heck of a bloody nose. You are the man on the spot. You have a completely free hand to liaise with C-in-C Middle East as to the implementation of Operation Cold Harbour. Your objective will be to inflict the maximum possible casualties on the enemy and to support Allied land forces to the absolute limit of your power."

Nick Davey contemplated his gin.

"Do you have any questions?" The Firs Sea Lord inquired quietly.

"No, sir."

"You should be ready to launch Operation Cold Harbour no later than the first week of July. The latest intelligence is that the Red Army will be in Baghdad by the weekend."

Nick Davey nodded, a rueful smile forming on his lips.

He raised his glass to the First Sea Lord.

"Confusion to our enemies!" He proposed.

"*Damnation* to our enemies!" The other man countered grimly.

Chapter 44

Wednesday 27th May 1964
RAF Brize Norton, Oxfordshire, England

"Comrade Alexander Nikolayevich," Lieutenant Colonel Francis Harold St John Waters, VC, translated, "maintains that we have to fight a war to justify our seats at the peace table, Prime Minister."

Margaret Thatcher raised a disdainful eyebrow, as did the Soviet delegation's female interpreter, a hard-faced, barrel-shaped woman of indeterminate middle years with piggy eyes and a fixed sneer on her lips.

This woman, dressed in a green uniform with KGB flashes on her jacket lapels rasped her own simultaneous translation of what the somewhat battered and hungry-looking SAS man had just said.

The Russians sat one side of a trestle table; Alexei Nikolayevich Kosygin flanked by Academician Andrei Dmitrievich Sakharov on his left and by First Secretary of the KGB, Alexander Shelepin to his right. Opposite sat Margaret Thatcher, with Deputy Prime Minister James Callaghan to her right, and the Chief of the Defence Staff, Field Marshall Sir Richard Hull to her left. Frank Waters sat at Sir Richard's elbow, and the Soviet Delegation's female interpreter at Shelepin's side.

There was nobody else in the draughty, cold hangar on the edge of the air base. Every few minutes the conversation ceased, drowned out by an aircraft landing or taking off.

The strained pleasantries and introductions had gone on interminably before Margaret Thatcher had cut to the heart of the matter and asked directly: 'Have you or have you not flown to England with a peace proposal?'

To say that this had perturbed the members of the Soviet delegation was an understatement on a par with a suggestion that the Cuban Missiles War had been an 'unfortunate misunderstanding'.

Kosygin and Shelepin had looked at her as if she had just disrobed and begun dancing on the table.

Alexander Shelepin's latest observation now went down like a lead balloon.

"That's the sort of nonsense that caused the war over Cuba," the Angry Widow retorted.

Margaret Thatcher had not expected this 'conference' to be a civil, or a necessarily productive encounter. She had demanded the Soviet authorities acknowledge her warning about the future use of nuclear weapons. A simple plain text radio transmission or a publicly broadcast unambiguous statement of policy would have sufficed; although she had secretly hoped for a renewal of face-to-face contact and, one last chance to defuse the escalating disaster in the Middle East before she once again sent British and Commonwealth troops into battle.

Alexei Kosygin cleared his throat, irritation written in his grey eyes.

"After the First War there was Versailles, after the Great Patriotic War there was Yalta and then the United Nations *experiment*." The sixty-year-old hero of the siege of Leningrad shrugged, as if he too was questioning whether there had been something lost in the translation of their previous remarks. "There will be a peace conference after this last war too. Or," he shrugged again, resignedly, "there will be more wars."

Margaret Thatcher shook her head.

"How can you talk about peace while the Red Army is invading two sovereign countries, Mr Kosygin?"

The Russian's eyes were bleak.

"You threaten us with nuclear weapons," he said. It was neither a question; nor an accusation. "You threaten us as if we are naughty children. This is no way to conduct international affairs."

"Neither is putting the Shah of Iran up against a wall with a group of semi-clothed young women and mowing them all down with machine guns!" Margaret Thatcher replied angrily. "Or destroying the capital city of a country with which you were *not* at war with a huge nuclear bomb!"

Kosygin waited for the translation.

He shrugged, spoke sadly.

"You destroyed my country. You killed one hundred million of my people."

"You need to tell President Kennedy that!" The Prime Minister snapped. "Not me!"

"Yet you still fight the Americans' war for them?" Kosygin said blandly.

James Callaghan stirred by his Margaret Thatcher's side.

He coughed.

"May I say something, Prime Minister?"

Margaret Thatcher nodded

"Of course, Jim." She sat back and made a conscious effort to relax her shoulders, swallowing a little of the rage that was threatening to consume her.

The eyes of the Soviet delegation switched to the large, clumsy-looking figure of the Deputy Prime Minister.

"The Cuban Missiles War happened because *you* and *our* allies, the Americans, made a series of terrible mistakes. We in the United Kingdom were just caught in the middle. In any event, recriminations belong to a World that no longer exists; the thing that we have to decide today is whether we want to live in peace in the World that we actually find ourselves in."

This prompted cold stares.

"May I ask a question?" Andrei Sakharov inquired, raising his right hand.

James Callaghan nodded ponderously.

"Why did you not retaliate when those *Krasnaya Zarya* zealots attacked you in the Mediterranean?"

The stillness was almost hurtful to the ear.

Margaret Thatcher did not trust herself to reply.

Jericho had blown away the last mysteries surrounding Red Dawn. Red Dawn had been a Stalinist legacy, a monster within the Soviet state but not, like the KGB had tried to convince the rest of the World, a *completely* rogue *apparat*. Red Dawn had been under the control – albeit flawed control - of the collective leadership of the new Soviet Union ever since the October War; a monstrous smokescreen for the Russians' long planned revenge on the West.

However, back at the beginning of February nobody had known that, and the 'not knowing' had been one of the reasons she had categorically refused to sanction an *Arc Light* thermonuclear counter-strike.

Every time the Prime Minister flicked a glance towards the glacially cold-eyed First Director of the KGB, Alexander Nikolayevich Shelepin, she had to suppress a shiver. Shelepin and his deputy, Yuri Andropov had been the puppet masters of the Red Dawn abomination. While Andropov had paid the price for losing control of the Krasnaya Zarya beast when he fell into the hands of Nicolae Ceausescu's secret police in Bucharest; the only reason Shelepin had not yet moved against the 'collective leadership' was that his own reputation, and to a degree the fear in which he was universally held in the Soviet Union, had been temporarily *tarnished* by *his* deputy's *shortcomings*. If the Rumanian Securitate had not beaten Andropov so badly that he almost died on the flight back to Sverdlovsk, it would have been Shelepin's head that was on the block.

Shelepin was the man who ran the Soviet *gulag*, the man who commanded the legions of penal battalions; the man who directed the slave labour camps scattered across the steppes providing the human fodder to run the new factories. Shelepin was the man who, in effect, oversaw the Soviet post-war 'dispersed command economy', the man who had been charged with 'enforcing' the Chelyabinsk-based collective leadership's first 'Five Year plan', the primary purpose of which was the rebuilding of the Soviet war economy.

It was all there, this and so much more, in the wealth of *Jericho* decrypts. GCHQ had been overwhelmed by the 'gold dust' which had fallen into its lap and every day piles of fresh intelligence piled up, mostly unread for want of qualified analysts. No matter, sooner or later the Prime Minister knew that she would need something with which to bargain, or if things went really badly, something she could *sell* to the Kennedy Administration. She had *Jericho* and Jack Kennedy had an election to win, *Jericho* might be an ace up her sleeve one day. Because of *Jericho* she had no need of existential psychic tricks, traps or powers to get inside the heads of the men sitting across the table from her because she knew *exactly* what they were thinking.

The Politburo, which held Kosygin, Brezhnev and the old soldier, Chuikov, in a loose but nevertheless threatening head lock; was getting cold feet about the war in Iran and Iraq and had ordered Kosygin to attempt to sow division in the 'capitalist camp' *and* to explore the possibility of persuading the 'Angry Widow' to step aside in the Persian Gulf.

The British threat to 'go nuclear' had grabbed the attention of the Soviet leadership but it had not panicked it; because the Soviets had never stopped fighting the October War.

"The Tehran strike was the first use of nuclear weapons by one sovereign nation against another since the October War," Margaret Thatcher said softly. "As you say, the strikes in February were the work of *zealots*."

Sakharov understood the distinction perfectly.

His companions regarded the distinction as being irrelevant.

"The Arabs will not fight against us," Shelepin announced disinterestedly. "Soon the Red Army will be in Baghdad," he clasped and unclasped his pale hands on the table. "And then, Basra. Do you really think you can stop us taking Abadan? Or anything else that we *choose* to take in the Arabian Gulf?"

Kosygin sniffed.

"Unless you want another nuclear war?"

"Nobody wants that," James Callaghan murmured.

Field Marshall Sir Richard Hull shook his head.

"Prime Minister," he prefaced respectfully. "I should be grateful to hear what *terms* these gentlemen have brought with them from Chelyabinsk? Before, that is, we send them on their way with a rather large flea in their ears."

The KGB woman interpreter very nearly choked on this.

Shelepin would have reached for his gun – had he had one – and both his comrades were very nearly as offended as the First Secretary of the KGB. However, Kosygin and Sakharov were disappointed for entirely separate reasons.

Kosygin had genuinely hoped for some kind of olive branch which might even now halt the war in Iraq; despite what Chuikov and Babadzhanian claimed, it was by no means a given that 'things would turn out all right in the end'. Operation Nakazyvat had been a reckless gamble from the outset albeit one that the collective leadership felt confident it could halt, rein in or abandon if things went wrong. In the event many things had gone wrong, yet the invasion had proceeded because the enemy had been unable, unwilling or simply oblivious to the things that had 'gone wrong' for Army Group South.

It was now clear that the British and their 'allies' – Kosygin shared the Red Army's contempt for the other 'armies' in the region – had no intention of coming to the rescue of Iraq, or of interposing themselves into the poisonous ongoing court infighting in Isfahan.

Worse, the British had formed some kind of local pact with the Iranian Army in the Abadan Sector opposite Basra, signifying that they intended to make a stand not on the plains of central Iraq but around what, by the time Babadzhanian got there, would be an isolated island citadel. Moreover, spies in England and elsewhere had reported a slow build-up of troops, light equipment and tactical aircraft based in Kuwait, Dammam in Saudi Arabia, the Gulf Emirates and in northern Oman within striking range of Basra and Abadan. As if this was not an ominous portent of things to come, major naval forces had recently appeared in the Persian Gulf including several small aircraft carriers and at least two cruisers. Recollecting how easily a British invasion force had eradicated Red Dawn from Cyprus in less than a fortnight, and how ferociously two small Royal Navy destroyers had thwarted greatly superior Red Navy forces off Malta, there was absolutely no cause to be complacent about the fighting capabilities of 'the British' in the Middle East.

Kosygin had come to England hoping for, if not a way out, then at least 'options' to take back home. While he had no doubt that Babadzhanian's tanks would get to the Persian Gulf, or that once dug in the Red Army would be immovable from large tracts of Mesopotamia; the problem was that a plan born out of a lust for revenge was threatening to embroil the Motherland in a never-ending war with an enemy ruled by an implacable mad woman!

Sakharov's angst was of an entirely more prosaic variety. He was a scientist who prided himself on his own personal rationalism; everybody else around the table seemed to be in the grip of some kind of dreadful 'war psychosis'. The father of the Soviet hydrogen bomb accepted that he was partly responsible for the tragedy of the Cuban Missiles War. Ever since he had been drawn into Kosygin's inner circle, he had tried to be a small voice of reason. Tragically, nobody was listening.

"For us," Kosygin explained wearily, "this war is a matter of survival. We lost so much in the Cuban Missiles War," he sighed, "and you so little. We too deserve our place in the sun. In the absence of a just settlement of our legitimate demands for reparations, we will win in battle new spheres of influence. You have no more 'right' to be in Iran or anywhere else in the Middle East than we do. You and the Americans killed a hundred million of *my* people; now we will take away your oil, your prestige and in time, North Africa and the Indian sub-continent will be *Russian* clients."

Margaret Thatcher listened to the waspish translation.

According to *Jericho* the Red Army's seizure of Basra would be the signal for Soviet agents in Egypt, the Lebanon, Syria, and throughout the Arabian Peninsula to commence campaigns of assassinations, and to foment violent civil unrest and mutinies in the armed forces. At that time the Red Air Force would launch hit and run bombing raids on shipping in the Persian Gulf, and targets along its southern shores including Kuwait City and possibly in the Dammam-Dhahran area. There were also some references to provoking civil unrest in the United Kingdom, Spain, Portugal and oddly, agents in France seemed to be planning some kind of 'action' against 'ports along the English Channel coast and '*targets of opportunity*' in the Mediterranean'.

Since many of the decrypts were only partial due to problems rebuilding the interception grid – there were no listening stations in Germany or Italy, for example – it was hard to know the context, or anything much in particular about the significance of the traffic directed at or emanating from south and central France. It was not that this material was unreadable simply that it was difficult to know what to prioritise.

GCHQ's Director of Cryptanalysis, Hugh Alexander, had told the Prime Minister only a day ago the '*really* interesting thing about the French traffic is that several operators in France are communicating using the codes we captured off Malta'.

Whatever was going on in France remained a bit of mystery...

The Prime Minister gathered her wits.

"What are your terms, Comrade Kosygin?"

"For peace?"

"For a peace? Or a ceasefire?"

The Russian thought about it for several seconds.

"Abadan," he said. "We demand the surrender of Abadan and the withdrawal of all British forces from Iraq and Iran. In those countries we demand a free hand."

Surrendering Abadan was out of the question and if the Russians had a 'free hand' in Iraq and Iran the United Kingdom's position in the Persian Gulf became untenable.

"And what do you promise in return?" She asked coldly.

"The Arabian Peninsula would become a British sphere of influence."

"And what of Syria, Lebanon, Egypt, and India?"

"Syria and the Lebanon will become Soviet spheres of influence sooner or later whatever we discuss here today. As to India and Egypt, that matter may be deferred for the consideration of a general peace conference once the dust has settled."

Less than half a century ago Margaret Thatcher's predecessor, David Lloyd George had sat down with the other victors of the Great War and carved up the Middle East and Eastern Europe in exactly this kind of cold-blooded, obscene fashion. From the abomination of the Versailles Treaty had sprung Fascism and the seeds of a yet more terrible global war. The post-Versailles Middle East had been a disaster, nothing short of an imperialistic land grab by the victors – America, Britain and France – designed to steal the region's oilfields. Versailles had not caused the October War, that had been Cold War psychosis, but its legacy still dominated practically all of the 'facts on the ground' in the Middle East. Thus, it was that she found herself defending the indefensible – that vile post-1918 land grab – against an enemy who made the monsters around the table at Versailles look like babes in the wood!

"No," Margaret Thatcher said.

Jericho had told her that the Soviets had no intention of making any kind of peace with *her* until they had subdued the entire Middle East and choked off the West's oil for a generation.

"No," she repeated.

Kosygin, Sakharov and even Shelepin frowned as if they did not believe their ears.

Had she really said that?

"No," the Angry Widow repeated. "While I live you will never get your hands on Abadan. *Never!*"

She pushed back her chair.

She stood up and the Deputy Prime Minister, the Chief of the Defence Staff and Frank Waters, the latter with a broad, admiring smile splitting his handsome, weather-beaten face struggled to their feet.

"Please escort these people back to their aeroplane." She ordered, sniffing the air like a Tigress searching for the scent of fresh prey. "They have a long flight back to Russia."

This said she turned on her heel and walked away, her heels clicking on the stone floor of the hangar.

Chapter 45

Sunday 31st May 1964
On board Victor 'The Angry Widow', approaching RAF Akrotiri, Cyprus

Of the three V-Bomber types the Vickers Valiant, the first of the three to see service was the workhorse, and the least radical in concept and design. The second *type,* the Avro Vulcan's great delta wing made it instantly recognisable miles away, like a menacing Hell-bound black bat. The third and the most advanced – it was revolutionary and ahead of anything that anybody in the World had had on the drawing boards at the time of its first flight in 1952 – V-Bomber, the Handley Page Victor simply looked and performed like something out of a Buck Rogers or Flash Gordon movie.

The Victor was bigger, stranger looking – even than the Vulcan – and it had the mother and father of all enormous bomb bays. To the crews of No 100 Squadron, the Victor was always 'the Beast'; because what other description would any sane aviator give to a flying machine that could haul and drop, with terrifying precision, up to thirty-nine general purpose (GP) one-thousand pounder bombs, or a pair of six-ton Tallboys, or a single ten-ton Grand Slam to a target three thousand miles away?

Last night Victor B.2 *'The Angry Widow'*, and four No. 9 Squadron English Electric Canberras had bombed Red Army concentration points and depots, two air bases close to Baghdad, and a water treatment plant and a power station within the city. Apart from being 'painted' by several enemy ground-based radar systems at long range and encountering minimal – negligible, actually – electronic jamming in the Baghdad area the five bombers had been allowed to get on with their business unmolested.

Now *The Angry Widow* was racing the dawn across the dark Eastern Mediterranean three miles below on final approach to RAF Akrotiri.

"You have the controls, Guy," the aircraft commander declared cheerfully.

"I have the controls," Squadron Leader Guy French acknowledged, trying very hard not to grin like a Baboon under his chaffing oxygen mask. His hands tightened involuntarily on the controls, even though the aircraft's automatic flight control system was still actually flying *The Angry Widow.*

Guy French had fallen in love with 'the Beast' the first time he had sat in the right-hand co-pilot's seat over a month ago. He and his fellow 'Vulcan boys' had regarded their immensely powerful and manoeuvrable steeds like giant Spitfires and revelled in the joy of flying an aircraft that – with its massive delta wing - was literally, unique.

And then he had been exposed to a Victor B.2. 'B.2' because it was the second main production variant of the bomber fitted with upgraded engines and avionics to permit it to operate at altitudes above fifty thousand feet carrying the latest nuclear bombs. External fuel tanks mounted on pylons beneath each wing excepted, a casual observer would have had trouble distinguishing the B.2 from its more numerous predecessors because practically all the other upgrades and 'improvements' had been accommodated in a virtually unchanged airframe.

That airframe was marvellously futuristic, superbly streamlined with four turbojet engines - Armstrong Siddeley Sapphires in the B.1, and Rolls-Royce Conway Mk201s in the B.2s like *The Angry Widow* – buried in the wing roots. The wings were swept back, as was the towering tail plane and beneath the nose, which came to a needle-sharp point was a 'chin' bulge containing the targeting radar and nose wheel assembly.

In common with earlier Handley Page bombers, a more than passing consideration had been given to the disposition of 'the Beast's' five-man crew. *The Angry Widow's* crew were accommodated on the same deck level in a single relatively large – positively 'roomy' by the standards of the Vulcan and the Valiant – pressurised compartment. The three 'backseat' crewmen - the navigator/plotter, the navigator/radar operator, and the air electronics officer – faced rearward. As was common in the V-Bomber fleet only the two pilots had ejection seats, although in the Victor the backseat crewmen sat on 'CO2-powered exploding' cushions, allegedly to 'assist in their escape from the aircraft in an emergency'.

Nobody in the RAF could actually remember *any* backseat crewman surviving a serious V-Bomber 'incident'; so most back-seaters did not spend a lot of time worrying about what to do if there was an 'emergency'.

Before the October War *The Angry Widow* would have been decked out in the white and silver 'flash' camouflage of all RAF nuclear bombers; now she wore a mottled dark and buff checkerboard scheme to break up her form from overhead, while being painted eggshell blue underneath to match with the sky above.

The V-Bomber force was equipped with a common *Navigation and Bombing System*, or NBS in short. This equipment used information from the aircraft's H2S, Green Satin and other radar systems to feed information into an electronic 'bomb sight'. H2S, albeit in a rough and ready primitive incarnation, had first seen service with Bomber Command two decades ago during the Second World War. Now, backed up with Green Satin, a Doppler system which monitored the aircraft's drift and direction, it was possible to feed very accurate wind speeds into the NBS thus utilising H2S's ground-scanning capability into a viable precision bombing tool.

At the time of the October War *The Angry Widow* had been in the process of being accepted into squadron service and had sat out the cataclysm in a hardened revetment at RAF Wyton. In fact, for want of trained air and ground crews the aircraft had only recently been 'activated'. She was therefore, a brand-new machine.

Whereas the Vulcan that Guy French had flown across the Baltic on the night of the war had been a typical 'Avro plane'; cramped, stinking of leather and hydraulic fluid, hot metal, sweat and now and then, vomit, The Angry Widow was an entirely different kettle of fish, as evilly business-like inside as she was outwardly, and everything was cleanly modern, even the control systems. The aircraft had duplicate powered controls which transmitted the pilot's movements through low-friction mechanical systems that artificially fed back 'feel' to the pilot.

Built with multiple flight surface redundancies the Victor incorporated eight separate hydraulic circuits, and the later B.2 variants were all fitted with a Blackburn Artouste airborne auxiliary power unit – effectively a small fifth engine – located in the right-wing root to provide emergency power in the event of an engine problem, and high-pressure air for rapid engine start-ups. The whole aircraft could be automatically 'fired up' ready for take-off in approximately two minutes at the press of a single button. The four main engines, Rolls-Royce Conway turbofans were so powerful that if a pilot inadvertently dropped the nose of the bomber – designed for sub-sonic flight - at high engine settings 'the Beast' would effortlessly blast through the sound barrier to well over Mach 1.1 within seconds.

This aircraft, The Angry Widow, equipped with the latest state of the art ECM – electronic counter measures – suite including the Red Steer fighter warning radar module, was probably the biggest and most modern 'beast' on Cyprus and Guy French could hardly believe his luck being assigned to her.

Notwithstanding that in terms of both dimensions and weight the Victor was the largest of the three V-Bombers – The Angry Widow's maximum certified operational take-off weight was around ninety tons – Guy French had once seen a Victor B.1 perform a series of loops and astonishingly, a barrel roll at the Farnborough Air Show of 1958. For such a big aircraft the lightness of her power-assisted controls and in extremis, the judicious employment of her main wing and tail plane mounted tail brakes gave 'the Beast' astonishing acrobatic agility.

Or at least that was what Guy had been told by the old hands on 100 Squadron, chaps who generally seemed to know exactly what they were talking about. He had been fascinated to learn through the 'squadron grapevine' that the earlier Victors had had a curious 'self-landing' capability; apparently once a fellow had lined a 'beast' up with the runway, as the airspeed bled away close to the tarmac during final approach the aircraft would spontaneously flare as the wing encountered some kind of mysterious 'ground effect', allowing the tail to go on gently sinking earthward resulting in a soft landing without the pilot having to do anything other than keep the kite on the straight and narrow.

Over the target last night, The Angry Widow had descended to twenty-eight thousand feet, approximately half her service ceiling to bomb. From over fifty thousand feet free fall bombs could go anywhere. The boffins said NDS would put a bomb load within four hundred yards – a tad under a quarter-of-a-mile - of a target from that altitude, which was fine for a three-and-a-half ton *Yellow Sun* bomb fitted with a four hundred kiloton yield *Green Grass* warhead that was going to knock down anything within several miles of ground zero, but not so good if you wanted to wipe out a communications centre, block a road or crater a large amount of turf that the enemy planned to, or was actually moving across at the time. Theoretically, the 'mean circular bombing error' from below thirty thousand feet might be as low as fifty yards; which, all things considered, was 'close enough' if one was in the business of unloading nearly forty thousand-pound general purpose high explosive free fall bombs; with the purpose of obliterating all sentient life inside a mile-square patch of somebody else's real estate.

Of course, down *that* low, one was in no man's land if the enemy had fast jet interceptors or any kind of properly configured surface-to-air missile capability in the vicinity of the target. The intelligence people said the Russians were in a mess; and not to worry about things like that for a while. This joyous situation was not going to last so the idea was to make hay while the sun shone because Guy French, for one, had no illusions about how well fitted *The Angry Widow* was for real low-level operations – down on the deck type sorties - against heavily defended targets.

Magnificent as she was, a 'beast' was not the airframe for that particular kind of dance. When it came to that sort of war things were liable to get very bloody very fast.

In the meantime, he would discover sometime in the next few minutes if he was going to have to land *The Angry Widow,* or if she would do it for herself.

Life was good on a morning like this.

Chapter 46

Sunday 31st May 1964
Al-Rasheed Air Base, South West Baghdad

The city had fallen without a fight. Or rather in a city which bore the unmistakable and widespread signs of the bitter battle between opposing factions of the Iraqi Army, the fighting had abruptly ceased, the combatants had thrown down their weapons, abandoned their tanks and melted away into the modern urban sprawl of the ancient capital of the Abbasids the moment the Red Army had appeared on the scene.

In the mid-1950s the West had viewed Iraq as a potential bulwark against Soviet aggression but Iraq had always been a weak link, a likely fracture point in any defensive regional alliance. It was a non-country, an artificial construct arbitrarily created at Versailles, distrusted by its neighbours and despised by the Iranians. Post-Versailles, the Hashemite monarchy inflicted on the so-called 'Iraqi' people in 1921 had been a truly dire foundation upon which to build a meaningful national identity. The only surprising thing was that it had taken until July 1958 for the Hashemite regime to be overthrown in a bloody coup d'état. And bloody it had been; with King Feisal II, Crown Prince Abd al-Ilah, and Prime Minister Nuri al-Said and numerous members of their families – literally - butchered during the coup.

The monarchy, having shrugged off several previous attempts to overthrow it –with British and American assistance – most notably during the Al Wathbah Uprising in 1948 and the Iraqi Intifada of 1952 had been swept away in an orgy of bloodletting and a revolutionary movement eventually led by Abd al-Karim Qasim had set about systematically purging 'imperialistic' and basically, foreign, influence from Iraq. Following years of Western sanctions, the regional economic collapse in the wake of the October War had kicked the ground from under the feet of the revolutionary government last year. After pursuing policies which deliberately exacerbated both religious and ethnic tensions, setting Kurds against Arabs, Sunni Muslims against Shia at the same time that non-Iraqi workers had been driven out of – and their absence had subsequently crippled - the oilfields, Abd al-Karim Qasim himself had been assassinated and the revolution overturned in a new coup mounted by a cadre of mainly Sunni Army officers. Thereafter the Army had cracked down hard on opposition, conducting a reign of terror against the Kurds of the north, while simultaneously making threatening moves against Abadan and the Emirate of Kuwait in the south, signalling its long-term intentions towards the latter by declaring it a 'Province of the State of Basra'.

Not surprisingly, as soon as it became known that the Red Army was on the move south the fragile Iraqi – 'nationalist' now rather than 'revolutionary' – government had shown all the resilience of a crystal decanter hurled against a brick wall. It had splintered and the resulting infighting had soon developed into a civil war, fought in the main in and around the capital, Baghdad. The fighting had continued right up until the moment the first T-62s of the 10th Guards Tank Division had rolled into the north eastern outskirts of the city.

Major General Vladimir Andreyevich Puchkov had already decided he hated Iraq by then. He hated Iraqis, he hated the deserts, the mountains, the shitty roads, the bad water, the way the food always seemed to have sand or grit in it, and most of all he hated an enemy who would not stand and fight!

Not that it was the Iraqis who were the real problem.

Standing on the roof of the house overlooking Al-Rasheed Air Base surveying the columns of smoke rising over the northern suburbs, and the charred, smouldering wreckage all around him, the last thing he was worrying about was the prospect of some belated Iraqi Army counter attack attempting to expel his exhausted tankers from the city. No, his problem was the British. Specifically, the British Royal Air Force, and to a lesser extent, the Red Air Force which thus far in *this* war had been as much use to the 10th Guards Tank Division as a eunuch in a whorehouse!

Presently, his tanks held the northern and eastern sides of Baghdad, basically, those areas west of the Tigris, the great river which meandered through the city like a giant python. Strictly speaking, any claim that he 'held' Baghdad was of dubious provenance, all his boys actually 'held' were several scattered enclaves, or 'bastions' ahead of the arrival of the 18th and 22nd Siberian Mechanised Divisions.

Unfortunately, the fragmentary information he was getting was beginning to suggest that the forward brigade of the 18th Siberian Mechanised Division no longer existed, courtesy of the RAF. Some idiot had halted the leading tank regiment on open ground north of the city to 'consolidate and to re-group' before entering Baghdad in daylight. Nobody yet had a count of how many tanks and other vehicles had been destroyed. Moreover, until somebody started counting body parts there would be no reliable head count either. What was already clear was that courtesy of the RAF the 18th Siberian Mechanised Division did not currently exist as a fighting unit; and that its wrecked tanks and the scorched and blasted bodies of as many as a thousand of its men now blocked the road into Baghdad from Baqubah.

Baqubah was another *problem*.

The centre of Baqubah was now in ruins and the road to the north and the south of the city cratered 'to Hell' according to the pilot of the helicopter he had sent up there to give him a reliable situation report. No traffic was going to be passing south through Baqubah for at least forty-eight hours.

There was something deeply disturbingly, and sickeningly *pragmatic* about the way the British waged war, Major General Vladimir Andreyevich Puchkov was realising. The British pretended to be gentlemen; and that the 'rules of war' were inviolable but when a thing needed to be done, they were utterly ruthless. If the only way they could block a road was to destroy the town around it then, so be it. When they needed a sledgehammer, they used it; when they needed to be more surgical, out came the precision tools kept at the bottom of their bombing toolbox. Shortly after the Siberians had been hit north of the city, there had been a series of smaller raids targeting oil storage tanks and the city's water treatment and pumping stations. Huge pillars of filthy grey black smoke now bubbled up from ruptured oil tanks and half the city had no clean water this morning. In addition, Al-Rasheed air base – even if the Red Air Force had had the balls to fly its precious aircraft this far south - was self-evidently out of commission, as was a second airfield on the western outskirts of the city.

Puchkov was asking himself: *When is the first big bomb going to drop on one of the key bridges across the Tigris?*

As a result of the bombing the next thing that was going to happen was that some of the Iraqi soldiers who had gone to ground a day or two ago would stop shitting themselves long enough to suddenly rediscover their courage.

It was still over six hundred kilometres from where he stood to the shores of the Persian Gulf. Puchkov had yet to fight a proper battle; and already he had lost half his T-62s. His boys badly needed to rest up, to repair and to overhaul equipment.

Most of all he needed air cover.

Puchkov looked towards the centre of Baghdad some ten or eleven kilometres to his north west. He had less than three thousand troops and somewhere between thirty and forty tanks – and perhaps as many other armoured vehicles - in a city with a population of perhaps one-and-a-half million people. There had to be twenty or thirty thousand Iraqi Army troops hiding, invisible in the backstreets. He had known Operation Nakazyvat was always going to be fraught with peril but right now, if the Iraqis rose up against the invaders the whole enterprise was going to end in humiliation and defeat.

Babadzhanian was right when he had told him that 'Baghdad is the key; seize Baghdad and we will have a lodgement in this country that nobody will ever kick us out of!' However, Puchkov did not believe that his commander had imagined for a moment, not even in his worst nightmares, that Army Group South would be this stretched out, disorganised and frankly, worn down at this stage of the invasion with the job less than half-done.

He took one last look around.

Puchkov sighed and then he wheeled around and began barking orders.

Chapter 47

Monday 1st June 1964
Flight UK1, Mid-Atlantic en route for New York

The RAF had re-arranged the seats in the mid-fuselage section of the modified long-range Comet 4 jetliner to facilitate mid-air conferences and meetings. Two groups of six previously forward-facing seats had been reduced to four seats each, with the two pairs of seats nearest the nose of the aircraft turned around. In the gap between the seats a table had been installed, likewise a direct telephone link to the cockpit, where cutting edge scrambler and secure communications kit had been installed enabling VIPs to continually be in contact with their offices and staff back in the United Kingdom, or wherever else they needed to be in contact with while they were in the air.

That afternoon Margaret Thatcher, her Chancellor of the Exchequer Peter Thorneycroft, Foreign Secretary Sir Thomas Harding-Grayson and Alison Munro, the Minister of Supply and Transportation in the UAUK had convened to discuss the latest news from the Middle East and the South Atlantic.

Peter Thorneycroft and Alison Munro's inclusion in the Prime Minister's delegation, and the absence of a representative of the Chiefs of Staff or of a senior officer of the Security Service was no accident. If the Kennedy Administration or any subsequent administration in Philadelphia wanted to have any meaningful long term 'alliance' or 'understanding' with the United Kingdom it was going to have to be one that was mutually beneficial to both parties *outside* of the sphere of military or security co-operation. In these last two respects the Prime Minister felt herself to have been personally 'let down' by her transatlantic 'friends'; in future Anglo-American relations would be placed on a firm 'financial' foundation, or not at all. She had, therefore, left her military advisors at home because they 'had little or no time to spare discussing hypothetical matters pertaining to the national security of the United Kingdom with Johnny-come-lately *friends* who could not be relied upon in a crisis!'

The ministers gathered around this small table high above the stormy North Atlantic understood that they had been invited on this 'mission' to the United States, to extract a *quid pro quo* that was to be measured in strictly monetary terms from the United States government, in exchange for the United Kingdom's continuing global 'co-operation and toleration of American commercial interests.'

Grand strategy had not worked out as planned; therefore, a different accommodation was to be sought. The time for fine sentiments was over.

Today, the first item on the agenda was a briefing on the current 'strategic situation' of British and Commonwealth forces; just so that everybody was on the same page when 'the Americans' started asking individual members of the delegation questions.

The news from the Middle East from Persian Gulf Command Headquarters at Dammam in Saudi Arabia was good, and bad. Rather like a proverbial curate's egg, it was very hard to know what to make of it.

An RAF photo-reconnaissance Canberra based on Cyprus had been attacked by two Soviet fast jets in the vicinity of Baghdad the previous day. The aircraft, flying at fifty-three thousand feet had successfully evaded the enemy fighters; but it was the first time the Red Air Force had appeared over central Iraq and it was a bad portent of what was to come as the enemy consolidated his territorial gains, developed forward air bases and missile defences and progressively impaired the bombing campaign's ability to blunt the Soviet drive south. In this connection the RAF had wisely 'drawn in its horns', mindful of the principle of conservation of resources. Every available aircraft would be needed in the battles to come, and in increasingly MiG-infested airspace risking the loss of a V-Bomber or a Canberra cratering a road or knocking down a bridge in the middle of nowhere was a mug's game.

Nobody yet really had a feel for whether the Soviet 'halt' in the Baghdad area was a good or a bad thing. While *Jericho* spoke to the mess the Soviets were in, it did not answer the main question.

Had the Red Army run out of steam?

Or was this simply a re-grouping 'pause' before it rolled south with ever greater and unstoppable momentum?

The Iraqi Army had melted away before the invaders abandoning large numbers of armoured and other vehicles to the Russians. Infuriatingly, this was going to make good some of the losses the invaders had incurred in the mountains, and mitigate the rigors of campaigning over ground inimical to tracked and untracked vehicles alike.

On the positive side *Jericho* was revealing that the first V-Bomber strikes had panicked the Soviet High Command to the extent that several senior officers had been peremptorily recalled, to 'account for their actions' back home. Moreover, all the indications were that the Soviet forces who had reached Baghdad thus far had only managed it by 'living off the countryside' and were short of everything from reloads for the 115-millimetre guns of its T-62s to spare parts for radio sets. Evidently, the system for supplying rations to the troops had completely collapsed long before the leading elements of the two Soviet Armies, 3rd Caucasus Tank Army and 2nd Siberian Mechanised Army had broken through the high passes in the Zagros Mountains into northern Iraq.

Meanwhile the plans for *Operation Cold Harbour*, the naval element of *Operation Lightfoot*, Lieutenant-General Michael Carver's plan to stop the Red Army in its tracks in Basra Province, were looking increasingly fanciful. As was the whole concept of *Operation Lightfoot* because it was anybody's guess whether the garrison at Abadan would soon be under attack from Iranian and or Iraqi forces, or caught in the middle of a regional Iranian civil war between the factions vying for hegemony now that the Shah was gone.

In either event Case Zero-One of *Operation Lightfoot* might have to be invoked at as little as twenty-four hours' notice; specifically, the controlled demolition of the main facilities on Abadan Island, and the commencement of an emergency evacuation of British and Commonwealth forces and all western civilian workers by sea and air.

Once invoked Case Zero-One would render the larger objectives of *Operation Lightfoot* null and void.; and 'Case Two' would be invoked. Powerful armoured forces and supporting arms would be built up in Kuwait ready to either hold static defence lines, or to mount a major 'spoiling' attack against the enemy with the purpose of making any immediate further invasion of Kuwaiti or Saudi territory impractical, hopefully for as long as possible. At that stage there might be a chance of some kind of 'peace conference' or, alternatively, the Kennedy Administration might by then have come to its senses; although nobody thought that was remotely likely.

In the South Atlantic things were getting grim.

The Argentine 'Army of Liberation' on East Falkland had threatened to take hostages from among the civilian population and shoot a dozen or so of them every time a British submarine attacked a 'vessel in the illegal *exclusion zone of death*'. After the sinking of the Argentine aircraft carrier *Indepencia* by HMS Oberon, apparently with the loss of as many as six hundred lives – the loss of life had been unnecessarily heavy because her escorting destroyers had steamed over the horizon at flank speed rather than standing by the stricken carrier – Brazil, Uruguay, Paraguay and Venezuela had all broken off diplomatic relations with the United Kingdom and closed their ports to British and Commonwealth, registered ships, impounding or interning several vessels at that time.

One submarine, HMS Orpheus, had succeeded in landing a small group of Royal Marine SBS – Special Boat Force – men on the south coast of East Falkland near a settlement called Fitzroy several days ago but no further word had yet been heard from it.

Worryingly, the Argentine authorities were still refusing to issue any information about the fate of the eighty-two-man strong Royal Marine garrison of the Falkland Islands. Also, missing and 'unaccounted for' was a Royal Navy detachment of seventeen men undertaking a hydrographical survey of Falkland Sound, the stretch of water separating East and West Falkland. Meanwhile, after being held incommunicado under what amounted to house arrest in the British Embassy in Buenos Aires for nearly two months the United Kingdom's diplomatic mission was only now being permitted to depart the city.

In an act of pure political pique, the Argentine government had declined to allow the fourteen men and three women of the pre-war, somewhat reduced diplomatic presence, to fly out of the country, forcing them to take the arduous overland route to the Chilean border.

Chile was another imponderable; a friendly neutral at the outset of the crisis Argentina had offered to end the long-standing dispute between the two neighbours over the sovereignty and navigational rights to the Beagle Channel – the stretch of water at the foot of the South American continent which permitted ships to transit from the Atlantic to the Pacific without having to brave the storm-wracked waters of Cape Horn – and the Chilean government, eager to avoid a shooting war with its neighbour had softened its former condemnation of 'the Malvinas aggression'. Worse, it had publicly withdrawn its invitation to 'offer sanctuary to damaged British warships'.

To the Argentine the Falkland Islands were 'Las Malvinas', cruelly stolen from the young republic in the 1830s by a rapacious John Bull at the point of a gun. Across the entire South American continent other 'oppressed and impoverished' former European colonies were jumping on the Buenos Aires bandwagon. This would never have happened if the United States, which had treated the Americas North, Central and South as its national 'sphere of influence' for much of the twentieth century, had not selectively abdicated its responsibilities since the October War. After decades of gerrymandering in the political and economic life of tens of millions of South Americans the Kennedy Administration had by default, disengaged from the fray leaving chaos and even greater instability in the wake of its withdrawal. J. William Fulbright, Dean Rusk's successor at the State Department had tried to put a brake on the process but much of the damage had already been done; which was precisely why the Falklands crisis had come as almost as big a shock to the Kennedy Administration as it had to the Unity Administration of the United Kingdom.

"I confess, Prime Minister," Alison Munro, Secretary of State for Supply, Transportation and Energy – the woman responsible for ensuring that the British people did not starve and that the sinews of war were kept as healthily robust as possible – retorted when Margaret Thatcher threw open the floor for discussion, "that I had not realised you planned to confront the Administration with the consequences of its foreign policy volte face in such uncompromising terms?"

Margaret Thatcher allowed herself a grim smile.

She had had her doubts about bringing the older woman into the Cabinet when she moved her old friend and mentor Airey Neave into the hot seat at the new Ministry of National Security. Although Alison Munro had not been an unknown quantity - she had had many dealings with her in her year at Supply in Edward Heath's immediate post-October War Interim Emergency Administration of the United Kingdom - she had worried that she was inviting a bull into a china shop. Airey's reassurances to the contrary had swayed her in the end and Alison Munro had stepped into the breach as if to the manner born, even if she and her Prime Minister were sometimes temperamentally and intellectually at cross-purposes.

The Chancellor of the Exchequer, Peter Thorneycroft, the one surviving grandee from Harold Macmillan's pre-October War government and very much the elder statesman and the keeper of the flame of what was left of the old Conservative and Unionist Party, chuckled almost but not quite under his breath.

"I think that Margaret was the first among us to embrace the fact that the time for half-measures was over, Alison," he observed dryly. "The reality of the matter is, as you know, that the United Kingdom is bankrupt and has been since the war. Our overseas treasure, meagre as it was in October 1962, is exhausted and practically everything in the country is now mortgaged to Wall Street. The pound sterling is worthless outside the Commonwealth, much of our gold and precious metal reserves are still buried in vaults beneath the rubble of Greater London, we have no real banking system and our civil and military economy is sustained solely by the fiction that 'notes' issued by the UAUK are actually worth something. In effect we have replaced a *money economy* with a *rights economy* in which work carried out, or services supplied to the state and humanitarian rights, such as the right of our citizens to be fed, have been converted into tokens exchangeable for vital commodities; food, fuel, medicines if they exist and so forth. Self-evidently, this is not any kind of long-term basis for running a viable economy or a sustainable financial system. As Margaret has remarked many times, this 'Soviet', or 'command' economy is intrinsically 'un-British' and sooner or later will collapse under the weight of its own contradictions."

The Prime Minister nodded, her face wearing a slightly vexed look.

"Whatever happens in the Middle East or in the South Atlantic," she declared, rather more trenchantly than she intended because the proximity of Alison Munro always made her oddly *competitive*. "It is imperative that we put the country on a sounder economic footing. The United States may not want to get involved in *somebody else's* 'foreign wars' but that does not mean it wants to stop trading with and attempting to harvest the wealth of other nations. We may not have much economic influence in the World anymore," she held up a hand knowing that Peter Thorneycroft was going to remind her of the links with the Commonwealth and other long standing mutual obligations around the globe, "in comparison with our former glory," she qualified, "but we have immense power, of the moral, political and in the final analysis military kind, with which to frustrate American economic ambitions. Moreover, if the worst happens, we reserve to ourselves the right to come to a separate accommodation with the new Soviet regime."

Tom Harding-Grayson, who had been silent for some minutes, was suddenly in the spotlight. He returned his colleagues' looks with sphinx like inscrutability. Back in the late 1950s his brilliant career in the Foreign and Colonial Office had faltered and then imploded because he had advocated – in a passable impersonation of King Canute attempting to turn back the incoming tide – a more pragmatic reconfiguration of the transatlantic relationship; essentially, one more closely aligned to a more Euro-centric accommodation with willing like-minded Commonwealth allies. His career in ruins, drinking heavily, his marriage on the rocks he had become a pariah in Whitehall for proposing a 'special relationship' with the United States that was not predicated by the transient political moods of American

Presidents and British Prime Ministers, but upon the firmer ground of what was actually in each country's long-term national interests. In other words, a relationship that recognised the military realities of the World but which also recognised that US global hegemony ought to come at a price; that British acquiescence should never be a given, and that no British government would ever again blindly follow wherever the American behemoth went. Before the October War such talk had been apostasy, heresy in the corridors of power in London and he had suffered the Whitehall equivalent of the fate of all heretics down the ages.

Even now, after all that had happened in the last nineteen months the Foreign Secretary was a little bit surprised that finally, in the wake of the cataclysm, a British government of which he was a senior member was actually about to take the first step towards establishing a 'new special relationship' with the World's last remaining superpower.

Between twelve and fifteen million Britons had died in, or as a direct result of, America's war of survival with the Soviet Union in late October 1962; now Margaret Thatcher was travelling to meet Jack Kennedy at Hyannis Port to demand the first down payment on the debt the United States owed its oldest ally.

Chapter 48

Monday 1st June 1964
Hall of the People, Chelyabinsk, Russia

This sort of thing might have happened once or twice in the old days just after the revolution, or been mimicked in the preliminaries which often preceded Stalin's show trials but Marshal of the Soviet Union Hamazasp Khachaturi Babadzhanian was under no illusion that not just his career, but his life rested in the hands of the lynch mob assembled in the inappropriately named 'Hall of the People'.

The 'Hall' was a former Red Army canteen, somewhat smartened up, serendipitously located adjacent to a deep fallout shelter on a heavily camouflaged military base abutting the eastern suburbs of Chelyabinsk. It was one of three regular venues for the monthly – or in times of emergency such as this, *weekly* conclaves - of the Politburo. Until the last couple of months, the collective leadership had employed the full Politburo as nothing more than a rubber stamp on the decisions it had already taken and put into effect. The ongoing, worsening delays and travails of Operation Nakazyvat had changed all that!

Another, ominous change was that Alexander Nikolayevich Shelepin, the ambitious Stalinist First Director of the KGB had used the gathering crisis to strengthen his own personal power base in the Party at home in exactly the same way that his embittered acolyte, Yuri Vladimirovich Andropov was insinuating himself into every aspect of the military campaign in Iran and Iraq.

"Operation Nakazyvat." Shelepin reminded Babadzhanian, "envisaged that Basra would be in our hands three days ago and that at this time our troops would be moving forward to seize the Faw Peninsula and into advanced positions from which to assault Abadan Island."

No man rose to the rank of Marshal of the Soviet Union who did not understand that to betray weakness in situations such as these was *fatal.*

Moreover, Hamazasp Khachaturi Babadzhanian's predominant emotion at this moment when his career and his life was balanced in the hands of the cold-eyed men sitting behind a half-circle of polished desks, was not one of fear but of anger. Anger that they understood *nothing*, anger that they had weakened his forces by deploying KGB battalions *behind* his fighting troops allegedly to *encourage* the others to fight harder, and anger because one of, if not his biggest headache, was the collapse of his Army Group's logistical organisation *within Russia.* Reinforcements, vital parts, and ammunition were not reaching 'the front'. All along the elongated, horribly stretched lines of communication back through northern Iraq, Iran and Soviet Azerbaijan the cronies of many of the men sitting in judgement of him this very day, were siphoning off *his* supplies to sell on the black market in the Motherland to feather their own nests!

Babadzhanian, who had been compelled to stand before the Politburo like a naughty schoolboy turned to face Shelepin.

"I have no need of non-combatant KGB supernumeraries in my Army, Comrade First Director," he said coolly. "Had the men currently inhibiting my operations in Iraq been deployed in Iran and at home safeguarding my supply lines and cracking down on theft and corruption at home, my tanks *would* have been in Basra by now."

Babadzhanian had always regarded the original timescale for Operation Nakazyvat as being ludicrously optimistic but this was not the time to concede ground to his enemies.

"In the matter of the KGB 'police' units operating within Army Group South," he continued, his tone unapologetically irritated, "they are consuming huge amounts of fuel, food and other war supplies needed by the men who are actually doing the fighting. This further drain on the pitiful level of supplies reaching my spearheads securing the north and currently 'pacifying' Baghdad means that I must shortly order a halt to *all* offensive operations in central Iraq."

Shelepin looked as if the top of his head was about to explode with rage.

"My troops are also taking part in those *pacification* operations, Comrade Marshal."

Babadzhanian snorted derisively.

"I don't need fucking policemen who've been sitting on their fat arses ever since they put on their uniforms intimidating old ladies and so-called 'enemies of the state', I need fucking soldiers, Comrade First Director! The first time *your* boys get into a serious fight they shit their pants and run away. It's like Budapest all over again; the Red Army always has to clean up *your* shit!"

The veteran of Kursk and a score of other battles turned his attention back to the three men seated to his front, curious to discover if they still ruled the new Union of Soviet Social Republics. If they did, he might get out of Chelyabinsk alive, if not, well so be it...

The silence that followed was of the icy, frightened kind.

While each member of the Politburo wordlessly considered his next move there were heavy sighs, shaken heads and hooded glances across the crescent of tables as the strength of untested alliances was gauged, and the risks of breaking cover to throw the first stone were meticulously calculated by men who had spent their whole adult lives plotting and counter-plotting to attain their current positions of power.

Eventually it was the oldest among them; the last 'Old Bolshevik' who broke the silence.

Sixty-eight-year-old Anastas Ivanovich Mikoyan, whom the collective leadership had elected Chairman of the Presidium of the Supreme Soviet – a largely honorific sinecure in the post-Cuban Missiles War governmental arrangements – was a grey, ashen shadow of his former self. He had almost died from radiation sickness sixteen months ago and had been an infrequent attendee at Politburo sessions. Infirm and without any kind of power base within the Party,

Brezhnev and Kosygin had kept him close; regarding him as a vote in their pocket and a tangible, albeit fading, link to a more glorious past.

"I am not long for this world," the old man said, his rheumy eyes fixed on the face of the soldier at the nexus of the firestorm. Like Babadzhanian, Mikoyan was an Armenian but nothing he planned to say had anything to do with any kindred spirit he might have felt for a fellow countryman; that was not the kind of man he was; he had never been in any way *sentimental* in his devotion to the Motherland and the Party and he was not about to change the habit of a lifetime at this late juncture.

Only Mikoyan had served in and survived the governments of Lenin, Stalin, Khrushchev and now that of the 'Troika', or as it was euphemistically known 'the collective leadership' of Brezhnev, Kosygin and Chuikov. No man had survived more purges and internecine Party wars than Anastas Ivanovich Mikoyan, and before he died – which would be soon now – he intended to make *his* voice heard.

Born to a father who was a carpenter and a mother who was a rug weaver, Mikoyan was the elder brother of Artem Ivanovich Mikoyan, who with Mikhail Iosifovich Gurevich had founded – and still at the age of fifty-eight remained with Gurevich the guiding light of - the MiG aircraft design bureau. The brothers had been educated in Tiflis in Georgia, and at the Georgian Seminary in Echmiadzin in their native Armenia. While Artem was too young to play a leading part in the Revolution, Anastas, aged twenty had formed a workers' soviet in Echmaidzin, enlisted in the Bolshevik wing of the Russian Social Democratic Labour Party – the forerunner of the Bolshevik Party – and become a leading figure in the revolutionary movement in the Caucasus. In Baku he had edited subversive newspapers, robbed a bank in Tiflis and brawled in the street like a 'good' revolutionary ought to!

In retrospect those were days of innocence.

The Revolution of 1917 was only the first of many terrible struggles. Bringing down the Tsar had been the easy part; the ensuing civil war against the anti-Bolshevik, 'White' Russians was a desperate and filthy business. It was in those days when he was a commissar in the newly formed Red Army that he met and saved the life of Grigol – generally known as 'Sergo' – Ordzhonikidze, a close associate of another Georgian Bolshevik, a certain Iosif Vissarionovich Dzhugashvili, now better known to history as Joseph Stalin. Together, the three men had become known as the dreaded 'Caucasian Clique'.

At the time of the Cuban Missiles War, Khrushchev had asked Mikoyan to go to Havana to talk sense into Fidel Castro. Ever the dutiful, utterly reliable staunch right hand of the Party's leader he had been preparing to leave on his mission – notwithstanding that his wife was dying at the time – when the crisis had exploded into the cataclysm of the war. He had been at his dacha north of Moscow when the first bomb went off; and stumbled into his shelter just before the next two strikes arrived. He had been sick, dying basically, ever since.

"I am not long for this world," Anastas Mikoyan repeated wearily, "so whatever I say probably has little or no weight in this forum. No matter. I will say what I must say and then I will have done my duty. In times such as this that is all a man, a true Party man faithful to the Revolution can do."

The Old Bolshevik paused to regain his breath.

Unconsciously he brushed his formerly boot black, now silver moustache before clasping his emaciated hands on the table before him.

"After we threw back the Fascists before Moscow in December 1941 it took us over three years to get to Berlin. If any one man in this Politburo actually honestly believed that the great work upon which the Red Army embarked a little less than two months ago could sweep all before it in sixty days then they were deluding themselves, Comrades."

Mikoyan coughed hurtfully, fought for breath.

"How would we have fared at Stalingrad if after a month or two we had thrown up our hands in horror and said 'the battle is lost because it is not yet won?' What would have been our fate if we had surrendered Leningrad to the Germans after only two months of siege?" The questions were asked with slow, excoriating sarcasm.

Presently, he nodded to Babadzhanian.

"Comrade Marshall Hamazasp Khachaturi is correct to demand that the KGB start shooting the counter-revolutionary traitors at home and behind the lines responsible for the failure to adequately support our armies in the field." He forced a cruel smile. "On that subject it seems to me that we could do worse than to shoot a few Red Air Force generals at the same time; if only to 'encourage the others' to get on with the job of supporting the courageous men on the ground in Iraq." He glanced at Shelepin as his exhaustion threatened to slur his words. "It doesn't matter which generals, the example is the thing, Comrade Alexander Nikolayevich."

Nobody spoke.

The last Old Bolshevik had not yet finished.

"There were those around this table who said we should hold our hand. Wait another year until we are stronger. That was a counsel of despair. Our enemies surround us and they will always be stronger..."

This time the coughing was agonising and the rag he held to his mouth came away bloody.

"Stronger, as they were in the recent war over Cuba. We must strike now and again and again while we still have the strength or we are finished..."

Chapter 49

Monday 1st June 1964
Kennedy Family Compound, Hyannis Port, Barnstable, Massachusetts

It was *not* going to be any kind of conventional summit. There would be no great fanfare, nor was there going to be an official, agreed communiqué at its conclusion. Nevertheless, ahead of the 'conference' the village of Hyannis and nearby Hyannis Port and from what Peter Christopher had seen, most of Cape Cod, had been transformed into an armed camp.

His and Marija's brief idyll at Camp David had been cut short two days ago with an urgent summons back to Philadelphia, where within an hour of reaching the British Embassy he and several members of the Ambassador's staff had boarded a US Air Force transport jet bound for Otis Air National Guard Base, located some fifteen miles from the Kennedy Family Compound at Hyannis Port. On arrival in Massachusetts, the Ambassador, Lord Franks had asked Peter to travel with him to 'have foresight of the summit venue' while the rest of the Embassy party went ahead to check the security of the small hotel in New Bedford where the Prime Ministerial mission would be staying.

The Ambassador wanted to talk to Peter about his 'conversations with the President' at Camp David.

Both Peter and Marija had been bewildered by the personal hospitality of the President and the First Lady. They had dined with the First family twice, albeit with other dignitaries present; Marija had been introduced to the Kennedy children at a 'coffee morning' with the First Lady while Peter had been called to a surprise late night chat beside a crackling log fire in the Presidential chalet on the couple's second night at Camp David.

The President had wanted to hear all about HMS Talavera's part in the Battle of Malta.

'That's a heck of thing!' He had sighed several times as Peter had self-effacingly recounted his tale. 'Heck of a thing!'

The younger man had summoned the temerity to ask his host about his own wartime exploits in the Pacific. Jack Kennedy had been reticent.

'We had some close shaves and I got my boat rammed by a Japanese destroyer,' he had drawled. 'I still don't know how we got ashore without being eaten by the sharks!'

Peter was at pains not to parry Lord Franks's earnest questions.

"To be honest I just think the President and the First Lady were grateful for the opportunity to spend a little time with people who aren't," he had shrugged, "*political.*"

"Don't under-estimate yourself or Lady Marija," the British Ambassador had countered ruefully. "If you stood for parliament you'd walk into any constituency in the land. As for your charming wife, Lady Marija is the nearest thing the Maltese people have to a princess!"

"Yes, but were not *political*," Peter had insisted. "We're patriotic, obviously and we both understand our duty, and so forth but we aren't *politicians* and we aren't about to start behaving like *politicians*."

Oliver Franks was too wise a man to believe that for a moment.

Photographs of Marija Christopher and Jackie Kennedy with the President's offspring were splashed across every newspaper. The Administration's publicity machine was churning out stories and by-lines about Jack Kennedy's "natural affinity" with the hero of the Battle of Malta, and the complimentary asides that Peter had voiced about the US Navy's part in the latter stages of that engagement had been seized on by every newsman in the country. Both husband and wife had offered humble and moving tributes to the 'brave American sailors' who had dived into the cold oily waters of the Mediterranean to save badly wounded *Talaveras* when the old destroyer's back had broken. After the President and his wife, the Christophers were the most famous and recognisable couple in the country at present, and it was only to be expected that the Administration would exploit their popular notoriety.

The fact that every time either Peter or Marija opened their mouths or smiled in public, American hearts melted a little towards the old country seemed to be a fair exchange for whatever credit the Kennedy Administration garnered from the exercise.

"The President invited me to go sailing with him during the conference," Peter explained. "I said I'd love to, exigencies of the Service permitting."

Their hosts had provided a plush limousine to carry them from Otis Air National Guard Base to Hyannis Port. The two men stared out at the verdant landscape slipping past the windows, every now and then glimpsing the sea. In this part of New England, one was never far from the sea or of reminders from whence the majority of its original settlers had hailed. They were being driven east along Falmouth Road and there were road signs pointing to Yarmouth, Barnstable and Chatham.

"I don't know much about the Summer White House," Peter admitted.

Oliver Franks chortled.

"As long ago as 1926 Joseph Kennedy, the President's late father, rented a place in Hyannis port for the summer. In the way of wealthy men from time immemorial, liking what he found he bought the biggest house in the street a couple of years later. These days the family compound comprises three houses set along six acres of seafront overlooking Nantucket Sound. Jack and Bobby Kennedy own the two adjacent properties to the original big house acquired in 1928. Given the wealth of the Kennedy family people are often a little surprised by how unremarkable the three houses are. They're all white-framed constructions in the clapboard style popular in these parts. The main house has splendid porches, a living, TV, sun room and dining room on the ground floor and a dozen or so bedrooms and suchlike on the first. Old Joe Kennedy installed a movie cinema in the basement, a wine cellar built to resemble the inside of a wooden ship's hull and a so-called "sipping" room. Basically, the compound must have been a pretty convivial place from which to organise a Presidential campaign back in 1960."

Peter Christopher was still digesting this when the Ambassador asked him a question that took him completely by surprise.

"What is your personal impression – man to man, I mean - of the President?"

The younger man still had not got used to the idea that people in authority actually gave a damn what he thought about such things, and therefore had no pre-prepared or remotely organised answer poised on the tip of his tongue.

He did not reply for some seconds.

"Honestly, I think he wishes he was still back on board PT107, sir."

"What about *America First?*"

"I don't know. I've never had to make the sort of terrible decisions he has had to take."

"No, what about taking on the whole Red Navy single handed?"

Peter felt the heat flush his face.

"That was different, sir."

"How so?"

"I was just doing my duty, sir."

"Okay, how do you think President Kennedy feels about letting us down in the Persian Gulf?"

"Isn't it the first duty of a politician in a democracy to get himself elected, sir?"

Oliver Franks smiled.

"I thought you said you weren't a politician, Sir Peter?"

The younger man brushed this aside.

"Once you get used to the idea that one has a duty to one's people, Queen or whatever, I suppose that makes the hard decisions easier. I think he knows that we're natural allies. He probably feels awful about standing aside in the Gulf but honestly, if he wants to be President in November what is the man supposed to do, sir?"

The Ambassador was silent.

"Every time," Peter went on lowly, "I pick up a paper or hear one or other of the men who want to be the next President, that dreadful man Wallace in Alabama, Cabot Lodge, or Nixon or Rockefeller, or even the other Democrats, I mean, apart from that Hubert Humphrey fellow they all seem horribly bigoted, anti-British, ineffectual, irrelevant or just plain barking. Honestly, sir," he sighed, "at least with President Kennedy we all know in our heart of hearts that he probably has *his* heart in the right place."

Oliver Franks shook his head.

"Now you're even talking like a politician, Peter."

Later the two men stood on the lawn in front of the "main house" with their backs to Nantucket Sound. Although it was a bright, balmy early summer day the wind was biting and both men were grateful for their coats. The President's Chief of Staff, Marvin Watson had sent ahead his own representative to liaise with the State Department's "protocol people" just to "smooth things out".

Marvin Watson's man, a crew cut Texan in his thirties with coat hanger shoulders and a military bearing had walked the two visitors through the house, explained the prospective layout of the "meeting rooms" and the "commissary arrangements" for the principals and their staffers.

There would be a photo call on the lawn tomorrow morning and then the press and the cameramen would be escorted outside the two mile "security zone" around the compound.

Oliver Franks had handed over a suggested draft agenda.

The US Navy had stationed a destroyer, the USS Southerland (DD-743) in Nantucket Sound. Her long low menacing silhouette visually augmented the impression conveyed by the constant thrumming of the rotors of the helicopter gunships patrolling the landward perimeter of the "secure zone". Closer inshore smaller patrol boats cruised beyond the surf line.

"The Secretary of State is due to be landing at Otis Air National Guard Base shortly, sir," the White House staffer had explained. "I'll make sure he has this *draft* document in good time for your scheduled meeting this evening."

"Are you able to confirm that the Treasury Secretary will be able to join our deliberations?"

"Yes, sir."

Oliver Franks checked his watch.

"We need to return to Otis in time to greet the Prime Minister's party," he decided. The Secret Service men kept a respectful distance, always watchful. Their nervousness, the destroyer patrolling out in Nantucket Sound and the constant distant thrumming of the rotors of the circling Bell UH-1 Iroquois Hueys spoke to the deeply trouble land in which the two Englishmen now walked. If even here in this relatively calm corner of the Atlantic north east nowhere was safe; where was any man safe in America?

"Diplomacy is a funny old thing, Peter," the older man observed professorially. "In the next few days, I rather fear we will be plumbing the depths, exploring as it were, the nadir of Anglo-American relations. In amongst all the recriminations it is likely that we will forget all the things that tie us together, the countless things large and small which make us more alike than unalike. We forget at our peril that we have many, many vital interests in common. Not to put too fine a point on it I believe that we and the United States are inestimably stronger together than we are apart."

That made a lot of sense to the younger man.

After the Battle of Malta, he would have drowned if the commanding officer of the USS Berkeley had not risked his ship by coming alongside Talavera when she was obviously sinking. That officer had known Talavera, already on fire could have turned turtle or even, blown up, at any moment and yet he had still unhesitatingly conned his ship alongside. Thereupon, crewmen from the Berkeley had jumped onto the decks of the sinking ship without a care for their own lives, and soon afterwards when Talavera went down other *Americans* had dived into the oily, flotsam-fouled waters to save badly wounded *British* seamen. Two of those brave *Americans* had died in the rescue but many of Talavera's badly injured survivors were alive today only because of the selfless bravery and sacrifice of those brave *Americans*. As long as he lived Peter Christopher would be in the debt of those courageous men from the *United States Navy*.

"I'd have drowned two months ago if an American captain had not put his ship in peril to come to Talavera's aid, sir."

Oliver Franks nodded.

He halted and met Peter Christopher's gaze.

"You were sent to America as a propaganda stunt," he said. "You and your lovely wife, Lady Marija, and the Hannays have done a marvellous job flying the flag and fighting the battle for hearts and minds; but it may be that the lasting fruits of your time in America will be in the contacts and friendships you are able to establish." He sighed. "To that end I have recommended, with the endorsement of the Foreign Secretary, to the Prime Minister that we give you a "proper job" and a "proper diplomatic role" for the rest of your "tour" in the United States."

Peter was not sure he was very keen on this development; although for the while he kept his reservations to himself.

"The reason *we* – as a nation – honestly and truly do not know where we stand with *America* anymore," Lord Franks explained, "is that the *United States* does not know where it stands in the World, or even whether it is still *united*. The Kennedy Administration, the House of Representatives, State Governors are at odds not just for the Hell of it but because everybody suddenly has their own idea of what the *Union* means to him. Before the October War the United States was a continental empire bound together by the Constitution and a sense of *oneness*; nowadays the Constitution has become a thing to beat one's foes over the head with, and an awful lot of people are looking for somebody to blame for everything which has gone wrong. Whoever wins the next Presidential election will inherit a Union that has probably never been more disunited since the Civil War. That said, it will still be in *our* British national interests to exert as much influence as possible on the new Administration employing every lever at our disposal. For that reason, we are currently investigating the practicalities of setting up diplomatic missions – officially somewhat beefed up "consular" establishments – in several of the most populous states. The most important of the first tranche of upgraded consular offices will be in California. We propose to style it "*the United Kingdom Consulate to the West Coast Federation of States*", covering California, Oregon and Washington State. Our mission, which will have offices in Los Angeles and San-Francisco or ideally Sacramento, and in Portland

Oregon, and Olympia Washington will require a high-profile Consul with proven leadership and public relations skills."

The younger man was fascinated by what he was being told.

Right up until, that was, he worked out why he was being told what he was being told; and then his troubled expression exactly mirrored the sudden alarmed perturbation of his thoughts.

"I'm just a junior naval officer, sir," he protested.

"No, you're not," Lord Franks reminded him. "You are the youngest Post Captain in the Navy and, notwithstanding your relatively tender age, pretty much the most highly decorated and by far and away the Royal Navy's most famous living hero."

The older man paused briefly to let this sink in.

"Coincidentally, you happened to be married to a highly intelligent, utterly charming, and highly photogenic young woman with equally, if not more, heroic credentials, who the American people are desperate to take to their hearts."

Peter could not take issue with any of that no matter how hard he tried.

"I'm awfully flattered and all that, but..."

"I envisage the West Coast Consulate to be, in effect, the West Coast *Embassy* second in precedence among our diplomatic missions in America only to the Embassy in Philadelphia." Lord Franks took pity on Peter. "Whatever happens in the Middle East in the next few days and weeks we need to make friends wherever we can, and to build bridges. Besides, once you get out to California it will be like having your own independent command again. Isn't that what you really want?"

Chapter 50

Tuesday 2nd June 1964
Khorramshahr, Iran

Lieutenant-General Michael Carver had driven up from his headquarters on Abadan Island that morning to establish if, and or what, assistance the British and Commonwealth garrison could offer his Iranian allies. Now and then a speculative long-range artillery shell smashed down into the desert to the east and in the distance columns of black smoke merged into a shimmering mirage-like haze in the blazing afternoon heat.

He had found Brigadier Mirza Hasan Mostofi al-Mamaleki covered in dust, having only recently returned from a flying visit to his forward units. His friend's dark eyes glowed with angry violence.

"That bastard Zahedi ordered me to report to him in Bandr Mahshahr this morning at about the time he began shelling my Divisional perimeter!" He reported disgustedly. "Then half-an-hour later the fucking idiot sent a couple of regiments of armour and mechanised infantry to probe my lines. My anti-tank gunners and a couple of hull-down Centurions turned the attacks back inside ten minutes. My boys probably brewed up a dozen M-48s and as many APCs; you'd have thought that would have been enough for that fat-headed imbecile! But, no! On the stroke of mid-day there was a general assault all long my north-eastern sector, M-48s and a handful of Mark I Centurions driving straight onto my guns!"

Michael Carver absorbed this, his emotions significantly less sanguine than his stern, stoical outer mask.

"I have two Hawker Hunters loitering at thirty thousand feet over Bandr Mahshahr," he informed the dusty Iranian officer, "and four other fighters and two Canberras on QRA. Before I left my HQ, I alerted 2nd Royal Tanks to fire up their Centurions, and 3 Para and two troops of twenty-five pounders are ready to move at one hour's notice."

Al-Mamaleki nodded, his breath slowing.

2nd Royal Tank Regiment's eighteen Centurion Mark IIs, the six hundred men of the 3rd Battalion of the Parachute Regiment, and the guns of the Royal Artillery constituted a substantial part of the 'mobile reserve' of the British and Commonwealth garrison of Abadan Island.

"That is good to know, my friend."

Although the two men had instructed their respective staffs to plan for the worst some days ago, neither man had actually expected the Provisional Government in Isfahan to move so precipitously against either al-Mamaleki's 3rd Imperial Armoured Division, or to directly threaten the defences of Abadan this early, or without at least some kind of warning preamble in the form of threats or demands for 'talks'.

It seemed that the Military Governor of Khuzestan Province,

General Jafar Sharif-Zahedi – an unimaginative, corpulent man who owed his rank to the unseated Pahlavi dynasty rather than any military credentials – was as stupid as he was greedy.

Michael Carver had feared the early morning attacks on al-Mamaleki's rearward-facing defences was the prelude, a diversion, presaging a major assault on Abadan across the desert south of the Shedegan Lake and the marshes which blocked any landward approach to the north eastern end of the Island. However, when no reports had come in from the SAS patrols operating on the eastern bank of the Bahmanshir River he had begun to suspect that whatever else he was up against, General Sharif-Zahedi was no second Napoleon. Any man who was so ill-advised as to send armour unsupported by infantry against prepared defences manned by men equipped with 120-millimetre recoilless ant-tank guns and the 84- and 105-millimetre precision rifles of hull-down Mk I and II Centurions, across country previously 'zeroed in' by al-Mamaleki's Divisional artillery was not so much incompetent, as he was criminally negligent.

The countless columns of smoke rising on the eastern horizon graphically illustrated the width of the killing ground now littered with the wrecks of burning tanks, shattered APCs and miscellaneous thin-skinned, unarmoured vehicles. Zahedi had obviously thrown a significant proportion of his entire mobile combat strength at al-Mamaleki's force. Clearly, after expending assets on such a profligate scale, it greatly reduced the fool's options when it came to mounting a similar attack on the formidable defences – augmented by the not inconsiderable eastern river barrier of the Bahmanshir – of Abadan Island.

What troubled the British general was not the ineptitude of the attack but that such an operation could be contemplated in the first place, let alone carried out. It was madness, sheer unadulterated madness! The Red Army occupied the mountains of Iran, there was little to stop its tanks motoring south from Baghdad to the Persian Gulf; within weeks there might be a Soviet tank army immediately to the west of Abadan Island, or coiled ready to surge across the Arvand River through the Khorramshahr gap into southern Iran. Yet it seemed General Jafar Sharif-Zahedi, the Military Governor of a large part of south western Iran, was preoccupied only with waging war on a formation of *his own* Iranian Army that would not bow to his personal will.

It all rather smacked of fiddling while Rome burned.

Al-Mamaleki was rightly disgusted and appalled by what had happened. Under the regime of the Shah career military officers got used to the idea that occasionally, one was liable to be ordered to shoot at fellow Iranians. That was the way of things, the natural order of affairs. However, slaughtering fellow soldiers for no better reason than that they had the misfortune to be commanded by an imbecile was another thing, a profoundly dirty and dishonourable affair.

He was about to vent a little more of his disgust when both men felt the ground twitching beneath their feet and a few seconds later, the very distant, drum roll of thunder from the west. It was like somebody was hitting the crust of the earth with a giant hammer many, many miles away. As one man they hurried into a nearby building and went up to the flat roof.

There was nothing to be seen.

Basra was over forty miles away as a crow would fly and the haze was too impenetrable. Nevertheless, both men guessed what was happening; the Russians were bombing the city. Not a hit and run raid. This was a sustained pounding by strategic bombers dropping hundreds of big bombs.

If anybody had doubted the enemy's intentions before there could be no doubt now.

The Russians were coming.

Chapter 51

Tuesday 2nd June 1964
HMS Hampshire, 27 miles North of Cap Matifou, Algiers, Algeria

A balmy Mediterranean afternoon had darkened into a warm summer night as HMS Hampshire cruised west at eighteen knots. She was returning from her second 'fast run' to Cyprus carrying an additional consignment of huge World War II vintage Grand Slam and Tallboy bombs to the military port at Limassol, and her officers and men were basking in the satisfaction of a job well done.

On the previous 'trip' the big guided missile destroyer had taken on board all thirty-eight nuclear warheads recovered from the wreck of HMS Blake and successfully conveyed them home, stopping off briefly at Malta and Gibraltar to offload respectively four and six devices. Back in Portsmouth a tanker had come alongside to refill her empty fuel bunkers and within an hour of unloading the last of the remaining 'warheads' she had been towed across the harbour to the ammunition wharf to take on a second load of monstrous conventional bombs.

A month ago, the Hampshire had been a brand-new ship with a green crew, that evening she was a fighting ship which had earned her first laurels, and her complement of nearly five hundred men was justifiably proud in the knowledge that their new ship had won her spurs.

However, that was not to say the cruiser-sized destroyer was as yet any kind of well-oiled fighting machine because she was anything but. The Hampshire had been rushed to sea because the cupboard was completely bare and eighty percent of her crew were still painfully raw recruits. Although superficially she looked a mean, lean fighting ship; presently her fighting capabilities *and* her capacity to defend herself from attack were negligible. She had been sent to sea too fast, too many compromises had been made in her design and construction, and few of her planned weapons systems, and hardly any part of her electronics suite – the big Type 965 air search bedstead apart – had actually been installed before she was commissioned.

Hampshire was the second ship in the first tranche of four County class guided missile destroyers scheduled to join the Fleet. The *Counties* had been designed and re-designed throughout the latter 1950s; their blueprints tugged this way and that by the old 'gunboat' adherents and the dangerously eccentric 'missile' men at the Admiralty. The *Counties* had eventually been laid down as hybrid cruiser-destroyers, nearly twice the size of the preceding Daring class and by the command of the then First Sea Lord, Admiral Lord Louis Mountbatten belatedly redesigned around the 'beam riding' GWS1 Sea Slug missile system. By then the role of the *Counties* had become the air defence of the Royal Navy's aircraft carriers, a task currently in the hands of the much smaller modified Weapon and Battle class vessels.

The story of the *Counties* was a sorry one; a cautionary tale which might have been a metaphor for the Royal Navy's broader struggle to come to terms with its post-empire role in the World.

After many delays and false starts it was envisaged that the first batch of at least eight *Counties* would be commissioned in 1962 and 1963 with a missile system, Sea Slug, that was *already obsolete* and the accommodation of which dangerously compromised the battle worthiness of every ship it carried, with an equally *obsolete* mid-1950s radar suite.

Not that HMS Hampshire, *had she been completed as specified* – even with her already old-fashioned Sea Slug system – was not a potentially formidable adversary. As designed with her advanced COSAG – combined steam and gas – turbines, her two twin Mk 6 4.5-inch turrets forward, GWS Sea Cat launchers, the much-derided Sea Slug launcher, and her anti-submarine helicopter she was hardly any kind of pushover. In fact, with her full armament set and competently handled by a well-trained and experienced crew her built-in obsolescence might have been greatly mitigated in any number of combat scenarios.

The problem was that within the Royal Navy everybody knew that too many compromises had been made to accommodate Sea Slug; and that practically none of those compromises *ought* to have been acceptable in any fighting navy in the 1960s. Basically, most of the aft third of the *Counties* above the waterline had had to be gerrymandered around the Sea Slug system and nobody thought that was in any way a very good idea.

If a future historian of post-1945 British naval architecture wanted a classic example of muddle-headed thinking, both in terms of what was required in a modern fighting ship and exactly what kind of enemy one thought one was fighting; the Armstrong Whitworth Mark I Sea Slug and its eventual deployment in the *Counties* was an object lesson.

The first problem with Sea Slug was its limited capability. It was a first generation surface-to-air 'beam-riding' missile installed in a ship expected to serve in an environment dominated by fast jets and hugely more capable second, third and fourth generation guided weapons. Even at the time of its operational trials in the mid-1950s high flying targets like the Soviet Tupolev Tu-95 which could fly at well over five hundred miles an hour was at the very ragged edge of Sea Slug's 'engagement envelope'. Basically, Sea Slug was subsonic and a target flying at high altitude at over five hundred miles an hour virtually had to fly – in a very straight line – right over the top of a *County* to be remotely 'engageable' let alone in any way 'endangered' by Sea Slug.

The second problem was that the Sea Slug missile was gigantic, twenty feet long and weighing in at around two tons, and not even the cruiser size *Counties* were anywhere big enough to *properly* accommodate a single double launcher. Worse, because the missile's propellant was inherently dangerous and unstable – a liquid oxygen petroleum Devil's brew – and it was impossible to locate the missile magazine below the waterline, in battle a single unlucky hit by a relatively small round could easily result in the whole ship blowing up.

Thirdly, because Sea Slug was a first-generation system it relied on big, heavy Type 901 fire control and Type 965 air search radars which needed to be mounted as high as possible in the ship, drastically reducing how much other vital war-fighting equipment could be installed in a superstructure that was of necessity, lighter in construction and therefore less resilient to than it otherwise would have been to battle damage.

In the event, HMS Hampshire had gone to sea with all the accumulated deficiencies and structural shortcomings caused by the need to accommodate Sea Slug; but without the questionable boon of actually having either a Sea Slug launcher installed in her stern, or any other missiles to shoot. Not only had she been commissioned in such an ungodly rush that she had no long-range air defence capability (Sea Slug); but there had not been time to wait for her short-range missile defence system (Sea Cat) to be delivered from Short's factory in Belfast either. In addition, the need to weld steel cradles for the RAF's super bombs – Grand Slams and Tallboys – on her helicopter platform had made it impossible for her to operate an anti-submarine and reconnaissance helicopter. Finally, her Type 901 fire control radar, although installed, was inoperable making it impossible to shoot her only 'live' weapons system – her 4.5-inch guns – in anything other than local line-of-sight mode.

Hampshire had left Malta thirty-nine hours ago, where every man on board had been given the option of an eight-hour run ashore. North of Bizerta, Tunisia, ground stations along the North African coast had begun to track the big destroyer's progress. The ship had followed the coast, careful to stay at least twenty miles from land. Tonight, the lights of Algiers glimmered distantly, their dim glow beneath the southern horizon illuminating the clouds. The weather was changing and Hampshire was running ahead of a sharp Mediterranean storm; on a smaller ship the crew would already have felt the gathering motion of the destroyer under their feet.

Although the US Sixth Fleet had buzzed Spanish destroyers in this region in recent weeks no allied vessel had been harassed in these waters. Many ships had reported distant 'radar shadows', contacts at the edge of their radar plots in these waters south and east of the Balearic Islands. It was known that several French and Italian warships had survived the October War, as had the entire, albeit antiquated Spanish Navy. The operational status of the surviving units of the French Fleet remained unknown; that fleet's affairs having been very low on the priority lists of British and Commonwealth forces in the theatre of operations. More recently, prompted by the sudden declaration of a 'no fly zone' over French airspace by the Provisional Government of South France, Malta-based submarines and aircraft had begun to show a little more interest in the doings of the French; but not that much more interest. What with one thing and another, the Mediterranean Fleet had been too busy lately to worry overly about what the French were up to.

In any event there was no particular nervousness, nor any heightened state of alert on board the Hampshire as she traversed the waters off the Algerian coast that night.

The inexperienced rating manning the big green Type 965 repeater screen in the CIC – Command Information Centre – situated directly beneath HMS Hampshire's bridge had been tracking the two contacts almost directly north of the destroyer. They had appeared late in the afternoon at extreme range and slowly closed to approximately nineteen nautical miles.

The Officer of the Watch had casually ordered him to 'keep an eye' on the anonymous 'friends out there...'

"Sir!" The man at the Type 965 repeater called in alarm. "Something's happening!"

Suddenly there were men at the operator's shoulder.

"What the Devil is that?" Somebody asked.

Where there had been two contacts now there were three.

The new contact was travelling impossibly fast...

"SOUND AIR DEFENCE CONDITION ONE!"

Klaxons began to screech.

"Label that incoming contact Bandit One. I want reports! Keep them coming. Bearing and range and speed. *Only* bearing and range and speed!"

"CONSTANT BEARING DECREASING RANGE!"

Collision course...

"RANGE ONE-FOUR MILES!

The ship began to heel into a turn to port, her engines racing. There was no need to ratchet up Hampshire's advanced combined gas and steam turbines, down in the bowels of the ship the engineers just 'turned on' the power at the press of a button. The destroyer picked up speed.

"BANDIT ONE ON CONSTANT BEARING!"

"RANGE ONE-ONE MILES!

"BANDIT ONE SPEED ESTIMATED AT SIX-ZERO-ZERO KNOTS!"

A fourth contact, moving as impossibly fast as Bandit One winked into life on the big green repeater screen.

"BANDIT TWO ON CONSTANT BEARING DECREASING RANGE!"

"RANGE ONE-EIGHT MILES!"

"SPEED FIVE HUNDRED KNOTS INCREASING THROUGH FIVE-FIVE ZERO KNOTS!"

In the Hampshire's CIC nobody was actually afraid.

Not yet.

The terror came a little later when the men in the room realised that the impossibly fast contacts barrelling towards the big destroyer at close to the speed of sound were missiles.

Missiles with HMS Hampshire's name written on them.

Chapter 52

Tuesday 2nd June 1964
Kennedy Family Compound, Hyannis Port, Barnstable, Massachusetts

The President of the United States of America had opened the first session of the 'informal' US-UK 'symposium' with the declaration that tomorrow he planned to 'go sailing'.

Margaret Thatcher had received this news stoically because she could hardly claim it was any kind of bombshell. Shortly before the parties convened in the hurriedly 'opened up' dining room of old Joseph Kennedy's summer home from home, Peter Christopher had passed her the President's hand-written note inviting him to join him 'on the waters' at 'eight sharp tomorrow AM'.

Sir Thomas Harding-Grayson, the Angry Widow's Foreign Secretary had chuckled out aloud, much to the Prime Minister's displeasure.

'Margaret,' he had soothed emolliently, 'if FDR could have his old English Navy chum Winston Churchill, JFK can have his surely?'

Peter Christopher had felt a little like the meat in a sandwich wedged between two rocks with a hammer. He had still not fully digested what the Ambassador, Lord Franks, had put to him the day before about his becoming, in effect, the United Kingdom's emissary to the West Coast Confederation of States. Notwithstanding that the last time any American 'state' had attempted to form any kind of 'confederation or *confederacy*' very bad things had happened, he really did not want to take his pregnant wife and his friends into the middle of somebody else's war, and besides, nothing in his life and career to date had remotely prepared him for such a 'diplomatic role'. He might have felt a little better about it if he had had the chance to talk to Marija, but all the phone lines in the British delegation's hotel in New Bedford had been humming with official business or been reserved exclusively for ministerial use last night.

Marija had already made light of having been whisked off to not one but two foreign lands almost immediately after their marriage; however, underneath her placid acceptance of being transplanted thousands of miles from her home in Malta, he suspected she was as disorientated by recent events as he was. And then there was the baby...

"May I join you?"

Peter had been staring out to sea to where the USS Southerland was slowly quartering the approaches to Hyannis Port. He was at a 'loose end' with no formal role in the proceedings other than to stand at the Prime Minister's shoulder as required. Officially, there was no 'military component' to the US-UK 'symposium'; and apart from the troops guarding the compound and the surrounding countryside, and the sailors out in Nantucket Sound nobody was in uniform.

Fifty-year-old General William Childs 'Westy' Westmoreland was attending the 'Cape Cod *Dance*' – as the event was derisively referred to in the new 'Philadelphia Pentagon' – as an observer on behalf of his boss, Secretary of Defence Robert McNamara. Like his political master Westmoreland was intrigued by how sure-footedly the British had played, and were continuing to play, their 'poor' military hand in the Middle East. The selective use of air power, the ongoing attempts to make new alliances and rebuild old ones, and the way a 'penny packet' formation of British armour had intervened decisively in the imbroglio to frustrate – frankly lunatic – Iraqi ambitions at Khorramshahr, was deeply impressive. It was something of an object lesson in the shrewd employment of limited resources.

The Pentagon had been closely monitoring the British and Commonwealth - mainly Australian but with significant contributions from both the New Zealand and South African governments, the latter in assuming Royal Navy duties in the South Atlantic in support of Operation Sturdee - build up in the Persian Gulf with mixed feelings.

Before the Soviet invasion of Iran and Iraq, J. William Fulbright had been talking about 'bottling up' the contradictions of the Middle East, and of moving towards a 'balance of power' that guaranteed the long-term security of American oil reserves in Saudi Arabia. All that had blown up in Fulbright's face when the Red Army had moved into Iran; suddenly the real consequences of 'America First' and the withdrawal of US ground, air and sea forces from the Arabian Peninsula had come home to roost...

Peter Christopher turned to face the shorter, stockier man.

"By all means join me, sir," he half-smiled, recognising Westmoreland.

"This is a heck of thing?" The older man remarked. The rumours about the British sending 'an ambassador' to the West Coast had been ripping up the corridors of the State Department for several days. With the Administration's attention focused inward on the forthcoming Presidential race and the current thrust of federal business flying in the face of two decades of State Department thinking and advice, somebody badly needed to get their eyes back on the ball.

"What's that, sir?"

"The damned fine mess we've both gotten ourselves into."

"Oh, that," Peter Christopher murmured. "At least this conference isn't about preventing our two countries from going to war, sir."

"That's something," Westmoreland grumped. The two men stared out to sea for several seconds. "The President can't give your boss any of the things she wants."

"That's all rather above my head, sir." He sighed. "But for what it's worth I think you're mistaken. In part, that is, sir."

"There's no way the President can sell a transatlantic 'free trade zone' to the American people in election year. As for loans and subsidies, that's a non-starter."

Peter did not think Westmoreland would have sought him out in the first place unless his masters had worked out that in an odd way, each man performed similar roles at the 'symposium'. They were undeclared, unacknowledged honest brokers.

"The Prime Minister can," the younger man suggested, "for example, unilaterally lift the sanctions against the Irish Republic at a time of the President's choosing. Say, to coincide with the Democratic convention next month?"

Westmoreland mulled this for a moment.

The 'blockade' on Irish ports imposed after the atrocities at Brize Norton and Cheltenham in early April, was like a knife in the side of the Kennedy re-election campaign.

"The Prime Minister is also prepared to give an undertaking that the United Kingdom will refrain from sending Ambassadors to individual states."

"We could veto that, anyway," Westmoreland pointed out.

"You could," the younger man acknowledged. "But that would look like weakness on your part."

The American grinned; the hero of the Battle of Malta had been well-briefed by his principals.

"We could give the Red Army a free hand in the Middle East and hold the Arabian Peninsula as a British *fiefdom*," Peter Christopher went on, playing Devil's advocate.

"You're talking about making a separate peace with the Soviets?" Westmoreland checked, not liking the idea one little bit.

"Perhaps, but only after *we* have fought them first, sir."

Westmoreland wanted to cut the young Englishman off at the knees, except he could not because he felt...guilty. Once again, his country had betrayed its oldest ally; and this time the Brits would never, ever forgive the United States of America.

"And we will fight them, sir," Peter Christopher promised. "Not at long-range with missiles and bombers but on the ground; with cold steel if it comes to it. On that you may depend."

Westmoreland nodded.

"Presumably, that's what you'll tell the President tomorrow?"

Peter met the older man's gaze.

Lord Franks and Sir Thomas Harding-Grayson had warned him that 'things are so bad that both sides will be looking to explore *back channels* at this symposium', and patiently walked him through his script.

The United Kingdom and the United States were no longer allies other than in respect of existing *military arrangements*; such as those currently in place in the Mediterranean under which the US Sixth Fleet 'co-operated' in 'theatre defence' measures with the British and Commonwealth forces in situ. It was anybody's guess how long those 'arrangements' would persist but in the present rapidly cooling climate none of them were likely to be renewed or redefined in the foreseeable future, and most, therefore would eventually wither on the vine. In the event of a change of US policy in years to come nobody in the United Kingdom took it for granted, or necessarily imagined it to be in any way desirable, that there would be a groundswell of opinion in the old country to restore the former, NATO – North Atlantic Treaty

Organisation – defence pact which had failed the country so badly in October 1962.

What was the point of signing a mutual defence treaty when you *knew*; you absolutely *knew* from very painful experience, that the other party could not be trusted to fulfil its side of the bargain?

It was better by far to place future relations on a new, firmer footing and to move on.

"If the President asks," Peter Christopher confirmed. "Yes, sir, that is exactly what I will tell him."

Chapter 53

Tuesday 2nd June 1964
French Navy Ship Cassard, North of Cap Matifou, Algiers, Algeria

The consignment of seven P-15 Termit anti-ship missiles had been flown into the Marseille–Marignane Air Base of the Provisional Government of Southern France five months ago. Initially intended to be just the first batch of a much larger arsenal of former Red Navy and Red Air Force guided munitions recovered by *Krasnaya Zarya* salvage teams operating in the 'dead zones' of the Crimea and the Ukraine, they had been transported in pieces by river and sea and then overland to territories under the control of Red Dawn insurgents before being dispatched, one missile per flight, to the movement's agents in France.

At first nobody in Marseille had had the first idea what to do with the disassembled missiles. Technicians were due to come from the east in February and March with other, equally lethal modern weapons systems but they never came and later when the Provisional Government learned of the fighting enveloping the Aegean, Cyprus, Turkey, Greece, the Balkans and Rumania they had realised that they were alone. Or rather, they had believed that they were alone for several weeks until commissars from Chelyabinsk had flown into Marseilles-Marignane to formally re-establish fraternal comradeship with their *Krasnaya Zarya* 'brothers'. Shortly afterwards a handful of the previously promised missile technicians, and a small detachment of KGB troopers had arrived at Marseille-Marignane, to assume 'guard duties' for the Soviet 'technical delegations' that were to be established at Marseille and Perpignan on the coast, and to the beleaguered Soviet 'diplomatic mission' in Clermont-Auvergne, the capital of the Revolutionary Provisional Government of South France.

Progress was painfully slow; while the French regarded Russian claims that there was a shortage of suitable transport aircraft, it was undeniable that there were very few 'secure' air bases in the territory under the direct control of the Provisional Government. That 'territory' although large geographically, was far from contiguous and the writ of the Central Committee based in the Auvergne, probably ran in less than half of the country they actually claimed to govern. Moreover, all the parties agreed that if the British or the Americans discovered that there was a Soviet presence on French territory 'too early', it would invite pre-emptive bombing raids or other 'problematic' consequences likely to spread alarm among 'the people'. In fact, the need to maintain secrecy was so paramount that it justified...exceptional measures.

Smoke and mirrors.

Over two-thirds of the French Mediterranean Fleet had been destroyed in port on the night of the October War, with only a few submarines and ships at sea, and the Ajaccio Squadron based in

Corsica having survived the cataclysm.

Nobody in Clermont really trusted the Navy.

In the bitter fighting that had eventually resulted in the formation of the Provisional Government in Clermont-Ferrand in the Auvergne the previous autumn, the Navy had remained aloof. In Brittany, navy men had stiffened the resolve of the North Atlantic 'communes' to resist the regime in the Auvergne. Even when the Ajaccio Squadron had accepted overtures from Clermont-Ferrand to return to the 'patriotic fold', and re-established relations with the Army Junta which had seized control of Corsica after the October War; doubts had remained.

Many Navy men had recoiled at serving the zealously Marxist-Leninist regime in Clermont; they had been purged. Those who had sworn loyalty to the new South France-Corsican Axis took comfort from the fact that on board their ships they were not at the mercy of the regime's secret police and regiments of 'citizen spies'. Besides, in a World so obviously devastated by the October War most men ached for the opportunity to belong again to something, anything that resembled *France* and the majority of the men manning the ships of the Ajaccio Squadron had no real conception of the magnitude of the disaster which had befallen their country.

In Corsica and throughout revolutionary France there was little news of the outside World, which most French men and women assumed to have been swept away by the war. The Provisional Government had made it a crime to possess a radio in the reconstituted prefectures under its writ, the Government dealt in printed proclamations and local rabble-rousing rallies, occasionally broadcasting exhortations and calls for national *fraternity* to the disease-ravaged population. It was believed that Paris and the cities of the north and the east had been consumed in the fires of the war, as had the great Atlantic ports. Across the English Channel the United Kingdom was a strange and alien place; an enemy to be feared, its every attempt at communication shunned. All that mattered was the ideological purity of the revolutionary republic, which henceforth would exist apart from the rest of Europe, safe in its own ideologically pure enclave.

The piecemeal domain of the Provisional Government stretched from the Côte d'Azur in the south east nearly to the Atlantic coast of the Pyrenean Basque country in the west, inland as far north as Orleans and as far east as Dijon. Regime propaganda claimed that the wrecked Atlantic ports of Bordeaux, Royan, La Rochelle and St Nazaire were all now within the grasp of the Provisional Government and that several expeditions had returned to the Auvergne after 'probing the radioactive ruins' of Versailles and Paris. However, there were also rumours of independent armed communes in and around Paris, in Brest, Normandy and around several northern cities, and of Provisional Government's 'expeditions' being bloodily repulsed; but loose talk was dangerous and nobody passed on gossip about contacts with British and German 'search parties' or more ominously, 'raiding parties' from the East.

The men on the destroyers Surcouf and Cassard, operated therefore, in a regime-managed bubble of ignorance, shielded from the ongoing torment of their countrymen and women at home. For the last eighteen months both ships had been based in the unbombed haven of Ajaccio, separated from the nightmare at home, and anybody openly displaying 'ideological unreliability' tended to be sent ashore, never to be seen again. On Corsica, notwithstanding that martial law prevailed, if a man kept his mouth shut and repeated the right mantras then life was, if not good then tolerable. Nobody had shut the whorehouses, drink was cheap and the Navy presence was largely self-contained, and most of the time, above politics. Out at sea it was almost possible to forget that in late October 1962 the old World had been blown away and that now the very air men breathed was invisibly poisoned.

Three nights ago, the Surcouf and the Cassard – two of the three surviving ships of the twelve vessel T-47 class of fleet destroyers built for the French Navy in the mid-1950s – had slipped their moorings and, darkened from stem to stern, made for the open sea.

The crews of both ships had assumed that this was just another exercise. The sudden appearance of the United States Sixth Fleet in the Mediterranean in recent weeks had kept both ships in harbour while the High Command decided what to do; most of the men on the Surcouf and the Cassard had assumed this mission would simply be to monitor ship movements between Gibraltar and Malta along the North African coast. It was a game they had played often, using their turn of speed – even with fouled bottoms from respectively two, and two-and-a-half years without being dry docked the Surcouf and the Cassard could sustain twenty-eight to thirty knots – to hold targets at arm's length on their radar plots. Their orders had always been to passively observe, and to immediately disengage if a target showed hostile intent. That was all the Ajaccio Squadron had done for most of the last year; watched, listened and collected intelligence on British shipping in the Western Mediterranean basin. Anything was better than swinging around anchor cables in port week after week, month after month, doing nothing.

It was four weeks since the Cassard's conversion had been completed and in the days since her crew had wondered if they were going to be allowed to 'play' with their new 'toys'. The destroyer's rear gun turrets had been removed and the decks plated over, and two bulky missile launching pylons and a new radar mast raised over the after superstructure. The two disassembled P-15 missiles had been stowed in the ungainly, ugly new deck house that now spoiled the ship's formerly elegant lines aft of the second funnel.

The missile launchers which had replaced two of the three twin five-inch turrets which had been sent ashore were bulky, top heavy-looking structures normally shrouded in grey tarpaulins. Within an hour of leaving Ajaccio the 'missile crews' – under the direction of Russian 'experts' - had been ordered to begin assembling the first P-

15.

It had taken nine hours to assemble and load the first missile onto its launcher; and another five to load the second. Then the system tests had begun before some thirty hours after departing Ajaccio, the missiles were fuelled and declared 'ready' for launch.

All the while the two destroyers had been forging south across a metre high cross swell into a fluky south westerly wind. As was customary the destroyers observed complete radio silence, communicating with each other only by signal lamp. At night they ran without lights, reducing speed to fourteen knots. On previous missions the ships of the Ajaccio Squadron had loitered south of the Balearic Islands, or ENE of the Straits of Gibraltar, or a hundred miles north of the Algerian coast and silently waited, often for as many as six or seven days. Traffic along the normal pre-war trade routes was sparse, advertised only by distant radar emissions. In past operations the Ajaccio Squadron had gathered intelligence about those radar 'signatures', tracked the air traffic east and west, never risking visual contact.

Two months ago, the Surcouf, in company with Duperre class destroyer La Bourdonnais, had inadvertently strayed into the 'engagement envelope' of the modern American warships escorting the old battleship USS Iowa; their radars suddenly blinded by a fog of jamming the French ships had turned away and run north at flank speed. This first encounter with modern American vessels had been a chastening experience; running through the night with no way of knowing if the enemy was in pursuit.

Last night the two warships had crept within twenty miles of Algiers before seeking sea room before dawn. The Cassard and the Surcouf had come to battle stations two hours before dusk and both ships had made revolutions for twenty-six knots.

The Cassard shuddered; the roar of the igniting rocket motor of the P-15 Termit ship-to-ship missile screamed into nearby compartments and filtered into every corner of the three-thousand-ton warship at 20:08 local time that evening. Many men braced for the half-expected premature detonation of the weapon.

But there was no massive secondary, ship-wrecking explosion.

Instead, the two-ton missile climbed into the night rapidly leaving the Cassard behind in the darkness.

NATO nomenclature for the P-15 ignored the Soviet 'Termit' – which translated as *Termite* – and used the reporting name of *Styx* or the designation SS-N-2. The P-15 had been developed by the Soviet Raduga Design Bureau in the 1950s as part of the Soviet Union's investment in ship-to-ship guided weapons as a quick fix to address the numerical and technical inferiority of the Red Navy's surface and submarine fleets. The Red Navy had been wiped out in the Second World War and even by the time of the Cuban Missiles War it remained tiny in comparison to the combined US and British armadas. Hard hitting ship-to-ship missiles like the P-15 were a pragmatic attempt to even up the odds.

The P-15's on board analogue based electronics were primitive by Western standards and its radar sensor a basic conical scanning device; but the object of the exercise was to produce a large number of practical, working missiles as soon as possible rather than to perfect technologically state of the art weaponry at some indeterminate future date. Early models had been powered by a turbojet – the Styx was, after all no more than a much enhanced, modified *homing* V-1 type system – made many times more lethal by a decade of advances in electronics and rocketry.

Fuelled with highly acidic liquid propellant which started aggressively corroding the missile fuselage the moment it was loaded, the P-15 had a launch weight of 2,340 kilograms, a maximum speed of just short of the speed of sound and an effective range of about forty kilometres. Because of the rudimentary nature of the mechanisms injecting propellant into the main rocket motor and the booster slung under the P-15's belly, even operating at extreme range there would always be a significant amount of unburned fuel in the missile when it reached its target. Taking advantage of this incendiary design by-product, the warhead, a half-ton hollow charge located *behind* the fuel tank in the weapon's nose, would *always* detonate with an enhanced fuel-air blast. Activated at approximately eleven kilometres from the target the P-15's homing system was programmed to descend at a terminal attack angle of between one and two degrees to the horizontal.

The P-15 was not infallible, quite the opposite in fact.

However, employed against a single target that had had no inkling of an imminent attack, that had no operative ECM – Electronic Counter Measures – on line, or working chaff launchers installed with which to fill the atmosphere with alternative radar noise and targets, the known fallibilities of the P-15 would be largely untested.

In the Operations Room of the Cassard the radar repeaters and the constantly updating gunnery director plot showed the two P-15s – launched within less than two minutes of each other – streaking unerringly towards the target.

High on the bridge of the destroyer lookouts saw the first flash of the huge fuel-air detonation on the southern horizon; counted the seconds to the second strike knowing that they had already hit their enemy.

The track of the following P-15 merged with that of the target and disappeared but there was no visible second explosion.

Following the letter of his orders the commander of the Cassard turned his ship's bow to the north and demanded full power. Within minutes the two French warships were creaming away into the night while far to the south their victim lay dead in the water.

Most likely sinking.

Chapter 54

Wednesday 3rd June 1964
Yacht Gretchen Louisa, Nantucket Sound

The mood overnight had been one of grim resolution. If the news from the Mediterranean that HMS Hampshire had been attacked without warning and seriously damaged with heavy loss of life was bad; the subsequent intelligence confirming that the attack had been carried out by a pair of French destroyers was of a wholly deeper shade of black.

It transpired that the activities of the 'Ajaccio Squadron' had been sporadically monitored by high-flying Canberra photo-reconnaissance aircraft operating from Malta, and occasional electronic eavesdropping flights by one of the two Avro Shackleton anti-submarine and maritime reconnaissance turboprop aircraft based at Gibraltar, since the Battle of Malta. These over flights had not been mandated because anybody seriously contemplated that the small French flotilla based on Corsica was any kind of threat; but in response to the Provisional Government of South France's surprise declaration of a no-fly zone over former French territory.

The Prime Minister had been informed that the 'A' class submarine HMS Alliance had actually been lurking submerged five miles off Ajaccio, when the Surcouf and the Cassard had slipped their moorings and gone to sea on 31st May. The submarine had been there by chance, her captain having determined to test his crew and his command by operating close inshore for three successive nights, before moving to a patrol area further up the Corsican coast. Although unable to identify either ship by name T-47 class destroyers had distinctive acoustic signatures, enabling Alliance to report that two of the three T-47s based at Ajaccio had put to sea and headed south east at fourteen knots. Alliance had made no attempt to shadow the destroyers; even running at her best speed on the surface she had no chance of keeping up with them, and had continued with her planned evolutions, maintaining a watching brief off Ajaccio Bay.

A hurried analysis of several of the most recent Canberra high-altitude photographs had revealed that at least one of the T-47s was undergoing, or had recently undergone, major modifications to her after superstructure; presumably only to her upper works because it was known that neither of the main dry docks in Ajaccio had been used since the October War. Until then nobody had attached priority to examining what *might* have been going on in Ajaccio. Expert photographic reconnaissance and naval intelligence analysts were in critically short supply and there was a host of other apparently more immediate 'threat vectors' demanding attention.

Or that at least was Peter Christopher's trenchant explanation as he was cast in the role of the Unity Administration of the United Kingdom's senior 'military expert' on the spot in New Bedford overnight.

The Prime Minister had been somewhat 'testy' about the 'Commander-in-Chief Mediterranean' having been caught by surprise by this 'latest this outrage'. It had fallen to the twenty-seven-year-old most junior Captain in the Royal Navy to have to remind Margaret Thatcher that Admiral Cleary, the commander of the United States Sixth Fleet had more 'electronic countermeasures and surveillance capability in a pair of the USS Independence's Northrop Grumman E-2 Hawkeye airborne early warning and command aircraft, than Air Marshall French at Malta possessed in the 'whole Mediterranean'. This was a slight exaggeration but he had already learned that half-measures were wasted on his political mistress. Margaret Thatcher had not been amused to be so rudely acquainted with reality; she had however, albeit with bad grace, bowed to it.

'Why on earth don't we have aircraft like those?' She had asked.

"I don't know,' Peter had confessed. 'Perhaps, it is because we spent the money on other things? Or we couldn't afford it?'

Afterwards, he could have sworn the Angry Widow quirked a momentary smile. It might have been his imagination because within minutes she was dictating vitriolic cables to Oxford demanding answers to questions to which Peter Christopher suspected there were no answers.

More information had trickled in during the small hours of the morning.

The Hampshire's captain had done the only thing he could have done in the circumstances. He had called for maximum revolutions and thrown the big guided missile destroyer into a violent figure 'eight' evasion pattern. That is, turned one circle with the wheel hard over to port and then reversed course to starboard to prescribe another circle, and so on.

It seemed that several men on the destroyer's upper deck had had the presence of mind to fire off every emergency and signal flare they could lay their hands on in an attempt to 'distract' the incoming missiles.

Of course, none of this had helped in the least.

'Styx,' he had concluded soon after reading the first reports. 'This thing was huge. Much bigger than anything we've got on the drawing boards or practically everything the Americans brought into service before the war.'

HMS Hampshire was only still afloat that morning; limping towards Gibraltar at eight knots because she had been outrageously lucky. The first missile had struck her aft, possibly exploding on contact with the metalwork welded to her helicopter platform to accommodate her cargos of Grand Slams and Tallboys. The missile's five-hundred-kilogram hollow charge, its detonation dreadfully enhanced by several gallons of unexpended liquid rocket fuel had gone off directly above the stern of the destroyer. Even though much of the energy of the blast had been expended – relatively harmlessly - above and beyond the Hampshire's hull the huge fireball must have briefly enveloped the aft half of the ship's five-hundred-and-twenty-foot length. Anybody on deck would have been killed instantly or blown over the side, likewise anybody in the helicopter hangar or in the mercifully empty Sea Slug magazine, or in any of the adjoining stern compartments would have stood no chance of survival.

The warhead of that first Styx would have ignited very much in the fashion of a giant Napalm bomb, showering the whole ship with a hideous modern version of *Greek fire*. An older ship with less sophisticated fire-fighting mains and kit – Hampshire had been designed for the nuclear age with the integral pipe work and powerful pumps necessary to wash 'down' the vessel after it had steamed through a fallout cloud – might have succumbed to those fires. As would the Hampshire if the second Styx had not over-flown her and blown up in the sea a hundred yards off her port bow as she reeled away from the first terrible blow.

HMS Hampshire had been lucky.

The Styx had gone off pretty much directly above where – had she been completed as designed with a full weapons set – her twin Sea Slug launcher was located; right on top of her lightly protected, horribly vulnerable Sea Slug magazine beneath the unarmoured helicopter deck. If Hampshire had had her complement of Sea Slugs on board she would probably have gone up like a massive Roman candle!

By the time the limousine arrived to pick up Peter to whisk him off the Hyannis Port to 'go sailing' with the President, the latest casualty list from the Hampshire reported forty-seven dead and thirty-one seriously wounded.

He had recounted everything he knew to the President of the United States, including his initial analysis of why the Hampshire had not actually been sunk. The destroyer's survival was both miraculous and a testimony to the inherent unreliability of pre-October War Soviet guided missiles technology.

That morning had been dreamlike, unreal.

Peter Christopher was going sailing with John Fitzgerald Kennedy!

And a coterie of stern-faced Secret Service men; that said, it was 'going sailing' only in the sense that he was on a yacht – a really big one owned by some Democratic Party bigwig; the name of *Claude Betancourt* was mentioned, the boat was apparently named for his daughter *Gretchen Louisa* – which happened to be 'sailing' in Nantucket Sound. He was a passenger, uninvolved in the business of hauling on sheets, ducking under swinging booms or running about the boat leaning over the side to make it sail closer to the wind. Notwithstanding, it was liberating to be on the water and to feel the sting of salt in the wind on his face.

The President, dressed in casual slacks and a Navy-style sea jacket, seemed younger and more at ease the farther the boat sailed from the shore. JFK had been looking forward to today for 'weeks' he confessed.

"I thought about inviting your Prime Minister onto the water," the most powerful man in the World guffawed to his 'special guest'. Peter Christopher was one of several, relatively youthful and junior staffers along for the ride. The others carefully kept their distance from their Commander-in-Chief. "But I guess she's not really a nautical lady!"

"No, sir," Peter had agreed.

Inshore the Gretchen Louisa had ridden the choppy seas easily. The sun had poked brightly through gaps in the clouds and the breeze had gusted off Cape Cod. Out in the deeper water the boat had skipped and plunged as she tacked across Nantucket Sound towards Martha's Vineyard before heading south for an hour prior to turning around for the long haul back to Hyannis Port. President Kennedy had talked of his admiration for Peter's father – the gallant but fated America's Cup contender of the 1930s rather than the fighting admiral who had been the bane of the US Navy in the aftermath of the October War – and how he personally missed being able to 'get out on the water these days'.

"I wasn't in command of HMS Talavera long enough to ever really feel the real weight of the pressure of the World on my shoulders, sir," Peter had confided to the older man.

Out on the water the careworn, greying man of the day before had shed ten years, there was a sparkle in his green eyes and a smile came easily to his prematurely lined face.

"I think sometimes of what it must have been like for my father when he realised everything had gone wrong that last day on Malta." Peter Christopher had opened his heart to Marija in the still of the night, but never to another living soul. "He knew he was going to die, that a lot of *his* people were going to die, that he had *failed*, and," he stared out across the grey waves, blinking the spray from his eyes, "and that he'd probably sent me and my Talaveras to our deaths. I can't imagine how awful he must have felt."

Jack Kennedy nodded.

The two men were 'alone' in a huddle of Secret Service men next to the skipper of the Gretchen Louisa.

"Forgive my impertinence, sir," Peter grimaced, "but I think that you are one of the few men alive who can understand what goes through a man's mind at a time like that."

Chapter 55

Wednesday 3rd June 1964
Abadan Island, Iran

The Red Air Force had bombed Basra again last night with a force of twelve bombers but this time targeting what Lieutenant General Michael Carver's GSO2 – General Staff Officer (Intelligence and Security) – believed to be elements of two under strength Iraqi Army armoured divisions attempting to hide in the southern suburbs of the city. In typical 'Russian style' the bombing had been fairly indiscriminate, and the navigation of at least three of the participating bombers so faulty as to bring them well within the outer engagement envelope of the Bristol Bloodhound long-range surface-to-air missiles guarding the airspace around Abadan Island.

It had been very tempting to put a shot across the bows of the Red Air Force but the Air Defence Controller, obeying Carver's dictum to 'keep our powder dry until we are directly attacked' had resisted the temptation. Every available Bloodhound in Christendom had been sent to Abadan and when those forty-one missiles were gone, that was that!

The Bloodhounds were only to be used as a last resort: specifically, in the event that Abadan was under immediate threat of attack, or at a moment of the C-in-C's choice.

The two Iraqi officers escorted into Michael Carver's office were dapper, assured, but very weary men who had had a sleepless night and been sent on a mission from which they probably did not anticipate returning. They snapped to attention before the Englishman.

Brigadier Ahmed Hassan al-Bakr and Major Abdul Salam Arif were the personal emissaries of the Military Governor of Basra Province. Al-Bakr was the Governor's Chief of Staff; Arif was the acting commander of the 9th Armoured Brigade. They had been selected to 'approach the British in Abadan' because they both spoke excellent English.

"Good morning, gentlemen," Carver drawled, returning his visitors' salutes with a cursory motion of his right hand. He left his uninvited 'guests' standing at attention. "You catch me at a busy time. I'd be obliged if you would state your business directly, please."

The abruptness of this clearly unnerved both the Iraqis.

By reputation the Military Governor of Basra, General Abd al-Rahman al-Bazzaz was, as political soldiers can sometimes be, actually a middlingly competent officer. The appearance of al-Bakr and Arif at his Headquarters now told Michael Carver that al-Bazzaz had finally seen the writing on the wall. Having had his curiosity whetted, he was interested to hear what the two visitors had to say for themselves.

"General al-Bazzaz offers an alliance with your forces, General

Carver," Brigadier al-Bakr asserted, hardly believing his master had had the bare-faced cheek to put the words in his mouth.

"An alliance?" The Englishman tried not to laugh.

"Yes, sir. Together we will halt the Russians north of Basra."

Michael Carver thought this was a particularly fatuous statement. Nevertheless, he was an innately courteous man and he had no intention of heaping gratuitous humiliation on the two officers before him.

"What is the current order of battle of General al-Bazzaz's forces?"

"In addition to the Basra garrison elements of the 2nd, 4th and 9th Armoured Divisions of the Iraqi National Army, in total roughly equivalent to four brigades of armour in the British Army, sir."

Carver did not believe for a moment that al-Bazzaz could field over three hundred tanks, let alone actually 'command' them to do anything except hunker down. Moreover, the one and only time he had seen Iraqi armour on the battlefield six of his Centurions had chased off a force of over fifty Iraqi tanks and enabled his friend, Hassan al-Mamaleki's then under-strength brigade to chase a numerically much superior invader all the way back across the Arvand River west of Khorramshahr.

Carver sighed.

"With such a force at his disposal General al-Bazzaz should be able to dig in north of Basra and hold back any number of T-62s," he observed mildly, neutrally. Wild horses would not drag him into the quagmire of Iraq's feuding ethnic and religious factions. One could not fight a war – especially one against a more powerful enemy - if one had to spend all one's time looking over one's shoulder, and that was exactly what campaigning in Iraq, would be like. Sooner or later, if they had not discovered it already, the Russians would understand that they had jumped barefoot into a horribly well-populated snake pit. Even with its great oilfields no western government had actually *wanted* to be in Iraq before the October War. The British situation on Abadan had been increasingly *marginal* and sooner or later, war or no war, the Iranians would have taken it back; that after all was the logic underpinning his decision *not* to base his current war plans on attempting to hold Abadan Island. The position was untenable, indefensible, like that of the mutinous, splintered garrison of Basra. The officers and men of the 2nd, 4th and 9th Armoured Divisions of the Iraqi National Army would much rather be fighting each other than the Russians, or even the Iranians or even the loathed former imperial overlords, the British.

Truth be told they would much rather not be fighting anybody at all; fighting interfered with the politicking and gave the general populous, upon which they were accustomed to prey, the courage to stand up to the sad excuse for a fighting force that was supposed, when all was said and done, to be protecting them.

When the Red Army drove into Basra it would be a close-run thing whether men like Brigadier Ahmed Hassan al-Bakr and Major Abdul Salam Arif were captured by the Russians, shot in the back by their own men, or lynched by a vengeful civilian mob.

"Or if not an alliance," al-Bakr went on, "then some mutually satisfactory arrangement under which senior officers, officials and their families might be allowed to pass through your lines and granted sanctuary, as it were?"

So many rats leaving a sinking ship.

"General al-Bazzaz is a very wealthy man. The treasury of the city of Basra and many ancient artefacts and..."

"Let me understand you correctly, Brigadier al-Bakr," Michael Carver retorted, his face stiff with disgust. *The bloody fools were trying to bribe him!* "You want me to risk my men's lives fighting to defend a city that General al-Bazzaz is not prepared to defend himself?"

Answer came there none.

"Or is it simply that you want to buy sanctuary for traitors?"

All the Red Army had to do was motor south from Baghdad and the whole rotten country would fall into its hands like a nightmarishly poisoned low-hanging fruit!

"Frankly, gentlemen, I'd rather sell my daughters into white slavery than get into bed with you." Michael Carver shook his head. "Not only do you not have the gumption or the wherewithal to mount any kind of coordinated defence against the invader; you expect me to take any number of useless mouths into my lines *because* you don't have the guts to fight."

The two Iraqi officers were shamefaced in an angry, blood feud sort of way as if it was Carver's fault that they were members of an army beaten before it had fired a single shot in anger against the invaders.

"Take this message back to General al-Bazzaz," Carver decided, bruoquely. "I will not permit a single Iraqi civilian or soldier into my lines. If necessary, I will fire on any such person who approaches my lines." He waved a dismissive hand. "Good day to you, our business is concluded."

Chapter 56

Thursday 4th June 1964
Ministry of National Security, Brasenose College, Oxford

Airey Neave had awakened that morning before dawn with an odd feeling of unease, as if he was sickening for something or had gone to bed the previous evening with pressing questions unanswered. His wife Diana had remarked upon his apparent *mal de mere* over breakfast but he had shrugged it off.

'I just need a breath of fresh air. The walk to my office will do me the world of good, my dear,' he had assured her.

His wife knew better than to press him further. For all that he had been the Member of Parliament for Abingdon – a seat he had won in a by-election – since 1953 he had never cut his personal Gordian knot with the security services. A part of his life was forever closed to her and to most of his closest friends. Some men needed their secrets and Diana had never begrudged her husband his; nor, in a strange way his *attachment* to the extraordinary force of nature that was Margaret Hilda Thatcher, the woman *he* had skilfully mentored and guided to the premiership.

Airey Neave found himself briefly pondering the conundrum of his wife's true feelings about his friendship with Margaret, as he walked from the lodgings at Magdalene College along the High Street. He had grown so accustomed to the presence of his two armed plain-clothed bodyguards that he sometimes forgot they were with him; in the past this had led to inadvertent collisions when he stopped to wave to an acquaintance, or to look in a bookshop window without warning. In another age, time, and place he would have been able to confess that he loved Margaret.

He did actually love her in some ways; but it was the strictly platonic fascination of an artist for a work he has been partly responsible for bringing to public attention, *not* a physical *or* visceral thing. It was the protective love of a brother for a sister or teacher for a particularly gifted student; except now the apprentice had outgrown and outdone them all. It must have been hard for Diana, he recognised, albeit in retrospect. Although she and Margaret were firm friends he did not know if that had helped, or made things harder.

It was a funny old World...

People told him that Margaret had changed since the death of Julian Christopher. Perhaps, only time would tell. The Battle of Malta was still just two months old and the Prime Minister was not the only one nursing very fresh, very painful scars. Nobody in the government had come out of the near fiasco in the Central Mediterranean looking very good; and but for *Jericho* falling unexpectedly in their laps, the dog's breakfast that had had the gall to call itself 'the security services' – MI5, MI6, GCHQ and all the other tin pot little army, navy and air force 'intelligence' empires – would have had nowhere to hide in the last few weeks. Once things had settled down a little Margaret's decision to bring everything under the same roof would probably bear dividends. Unfortunately, that 'settling down' period was not about to happen overnight and, in the meantime, he was very much cast in the role of the poor chump in charge of putting Humpty Dumpty back together again just after he had fallen off that apocryphal wall!

Nevertheless, as long as they had *Jericho* all the other problems in the new Ministry of National Security seemed relatively insignificant, of an order of magnitude that could be filed under 'to be sorted out when we have a spare minute'. Despite what had happened off Algiers on Tuesday evening only one theatre of operations really mattered at present; the Middle East. Yes, he would have liked to have had some sense, some feel for what the blasted French were up to; whether for example, the UAUK was dealing with some rogue element, or something more sinister, organised and ordered from and or by, the 'Provisional Government' in Clermont-Ferrand. But no, in the big picture they could 'deal with the French' later.

The *main thing* was what was going on in the Persian Gulf, not least because they knew exactly what the Soviets were up to right down to where the leading echelons of 3rd Caucasus Tank Army and 2nd Siberian Mechanised Army stopped each night, their declining combat strengths, wastage rates and the names of many of the senior commanders.

Because of *Jericho* he knew that two very senior Red Air Force general officers had been arrested and replaced with men who understood 'the urgency of the situation'. The Red Air Force had been ordered by Leonid Brezhnev to 'prepare the way ahead' regardless of casualties, fast jets were being moved to forward operating bases around Baghdad and long-range bombers based in the Soviet Union were now engaged on daily ground attack and strategic bombing missions, mainly south of Baghdad, and of course, on Basra. In northern Iraq, II Corps of 2nd Siberian Mechanised Army was closing in on Mosul having already subdued Kirkuk and Erbil. In central Iraq around Baghdad, I Corps of 3rd Caucasus Tank Army had already sent out probing columns south towards Hillah and Karbala and west towards Falluja and Ramadi, testing the ground aggressively and encountering relatively 'feeble' resistance melting away *everywhere.*

In Baghdad there had been a number of murderous attacks on Red Army soldiers, a litany of ongoing small isolated incidents of armed insurrection demonstrating that not every man in the defeated Iraqi National Army had thrown down his arms and gone home. There was also mounting evidence of civil disobedience and religiously inspired protests; and as yet the Russians were neither present in sufficient force nor well enough organised to crush such resistance. Nor were they likely to be for some time, if ever, because Marshal of the Soviet Union Hamazasp Khachaturi Babadzhanian – the 'Butcher of Bucharest' – simply did not have the 'boots on the ground' to fight his way south to the Persian Gulf, *and* to pacify the civilian population at the same time. *Pacification* was going to have to be done by the

KGB's Ministry of the Interior forces because at the moment the invaders' manpower resources were so badly stretched that the gaps in the ranks could only be filled with drafts from penal battalions.

Airey Neave could not conceive of any circumstance in which padding out under-strength infantry units with criminals, dissidents and troublemakers was a good idea, or in any way remotely conducive to the promotion of increased fighting efficiency.

Notwithstanding that Tom Harding-Grayson constantly reminded him that 'just because we are reading the enemy's radio traffic it doesn't mean we've already won the bloody war'; the very fact that they were 'reading the enemy's radio traffic' meant that sooner or later a window of opportunity might open which *might* enable British and Commonwealth forces in the Middle East to seriously inconvenience the *Butcher of Bucharest*!

These days a wise man in England was *always* thankful for small mercies.

Airey Neave marched purposefully across Radcliffe Square into the main entrance to Brasenose College. Brasenose was one of the 'younger' Oxford Colleges, having been founded as late as 1509 by Sir Richard Sutton and William Smyth, the Bishop of Lincoln. The College had inherited its name – allegedly – from the bronze knocker that had been mounted on the door of the hall which had stood on the site in earlier times.

Rocky times were no stranger to Brasenose. It had remained a stronghold of Catholicism in the sixteenth century, a Royalist redoubt during the Civil War period and in more peaceful eras fallen behind many of the neighbouring colleges in its scholastic achievements and rigor, failings only belatedly rectified in the latter nineteenth century. Nevertheless, over the centuries the college had expanded slowly, surely, adding a library and a new chapel in the mid-seventeenth century and three quadrangles, the latest and largest 'New Quad' being completed just before the First World War. Brasenose's sprawling undergraduate annexe, Frewin Hall on St Michael's Street, a recent development completed in the 1940s had been taken over by the Security Service (MI5) and the Secret Intelligence Service (MI6) in recent weeks.

A courier had brought the Secretary of State for National Security the latest cables while he was still breakfasting that morning. Airey Neave insisted on that. There was nothing worse than walking into one's office of a morning to be greeted with a new disaster. It was better by far to have some warning of whatever debacle awaited one at the earliest possible moment.

HMS Hampshire was limping towards Gibraltar with a US Navy destroyer, the USS Berkeley – of Battle of Malta renown – keeping her company. The Berkeley was homeward bound for a refit and had been some eighty miles to the east of the Hampshire when the County class destroyer was attacked. Hearing the Hampshire's distress signal, she had raced to her aid at flank speed, catching up with the crippled ship in less than three hours.

Meanwhile, HMS Alliance had been ordered to 'loiter' in Corsican waters off Ajaccio. Another submarine, HMS Grampus, a more modern vessel working up to full combat efficiency after an overhaul in preparation for a possible deployment to the South Atlantic, had been ordered to patrol fifty miles west of the Sardinia. Both submarines had been authorised to attack any French T-47 class destroyers they encountered 'on sight'. A Canberra from Malta and a Shackleton from Gibraltar were currently searching the sea between Sardinia and the Balearic Islands for the ships which had attacked the Hampshire.

If humanly possible, revenge would be swift and final!

The Prime Minister had already personally approved an RAF plan to bomb the French Squadron in Ajaccio if the 'culprits were not sunk at sea first'. This had prompted a heated debate about the specifics of this prospective 'raid'; one camp wanted to involve Tallboy-carrying Victors from Cyprus, another wanted Vulcans from Malta to drop a very large number of thousand-pound general purpose munitions to sink *everything* in the harbour and to reduce most of the port area to rubble.

Nobody had attempted to talk Margaret out of hitting back at the earliest possible opportunity. Such an attempt would have been futile.

"Sir Richard is waiting for you in your office, Minister," Airey Neave was informed by his private secretary.

Sir Richard Goldsmith 'Dick' White, the Director General of the Security Services, was standing in the window looking down into the New Quad of Brasenose College. He turned and smiled a tight-lipped very grim smile.

"I've got some bad news, Airey."

The two men had known each other since the 1940s and trusted each other too well to beat about the bush.

"The Soviets have discontinued the use of two of the four *Jericho* ciphers we captured after the Battle of Malta," Dick White explained. "The naval code which is probably neither here nor there," he sighed, "and unfortunately, the *Command Jericho*."

"When?" Airey Neave demanded quietly.

"About thirty hours ago. We're still managing to decrypt traffic despatched before twenty-four hundred hours Chelyabinsk local time on Tuesday."

The Minister of National Security cut directly to the chase.

"We're still reading the *Routine Jericho*?" In this context 'routine' referred to the coding used by units below Divisional Command level. *Command Jericho* was the cipher employed by Divisional Command all the way up to Army Group Command.

"Yes. We've also still got our hooks into the *Diplomatic Jericho*. Hopefully, that will stay up long enough for us to find out what the French are up to."

Airey Neave did not think they were going to get that lucky.

The rule was: change one code – change the lot!

The UAUK's brief window into the mind, the thinking and the

minutiae of their Soviet enemy's campaigning, and an invaluable insight into the tensions within the Soviet regime behind the front, was about to be slammed shut.

They might have just lost the war in the Gulf before it had even begun.

The two old friends looked at each other resignedly.

Airey Neave groaned softly.

"Bugger!"

Chapter 57

Thursday 4th June 1964
Kennedy Family Compound, Hyannis Port, Barnstable, Massachusetts

The two leaders sat alone on the porch in two old rocking chairs shaded by the overhanging first floor balcony. There was nobody within earshot; the nearest Royal Marine bodyguard – dressed in mufti – and Secret Service Man patrolled twenty to thirty feet away and the leaders were speaking in low tones. The President was at ease in his chair, Margaret Thatcher less so; he let the chair 'rock' she sat forward, balancing it steadily. Their respective postures might have been metaphors for their underlying, contrasting personalities. The man had once upon a time been content within his skin; the woman would never be that.

Jack Kennedy's green-grey eyes viewed the woman thoughtfully. While their ministers and officials were scattered around the compound conducting 'bi-lateral' and other ad hoc meetings, that morning the British Prime Minister and he had both received briefings and had long conversations with their advisors on the phone.

He had spent over an hour talking with the Vice-President. Lyndon Johnson had already talked to the Secretary of State and other members of the Administration; but nevertheless, they had talked for over an hour. It was good to replay other conversations, to check that one had actually heard what one thought one had heard.

The President recognised that Margaret Thatcher's 'conversations' would have been of a different nature. Although the National Security Agency had not known what *Jericho* was until a few days ago, they had not needed to *know* because they had *guessed*. The way things had been lately he did not blame the British for keeping it to themselves; but now that the walls of *Jericho* had come tumbling down there was no reason not to share the secret. If the British *shared* the CIA, the NSA and every branch of the US intelligence community would be all over it; the possibility of breaking several months of previously incomprehensible traffic was a prize of incalculable value. Who knew what impossible nuggets of intelligence lay buried in the tens of thousands of intercepts logged just in the last few weeks?

"You came here with a shopping list," the man said. "I was prepared to step out of the election race for two or three days because you had, and still have, something I want. Now," he half-smiled that beguiling smile of old, "that *Jericho* is *devalued*, perhaps we can do business."

Margaret Thatcher's blue eyes widened for a moment even though she had hoped that they would reach this point sooner or later.

"I would have given you *Jericho* for nothing if Congress had ratified the US-UK Mutual Defense Treaty that you and I signed in January, Jack," she informed him primly. "I will give you *Jericho* now, if you join us in fighting the war that must soon be fought for control of the Persian Gulf and Arabia."

Jack Kennedy shook his head.

"I can't do that, Margaret. I'm shooting myself in the foot leaving the Sixth Fleet in the Mediterranean. Especially with this French thing going on, whatever it is. You know that. Things are what they are. Either I get re-elected any way I can or come January next year you'll be trying to do business with George Wallace or some other 'America First', isolationist bigot or Wall Street's man, or maybe some guy who suddenly emerges from nowhere. Between now and the election in November I've got to keep the South quiet, honour my pledge to stand beside Dr King one month from now on the steps of City Hall in Philadelphia, somehow buy off the secessionist movements in half-a-dozen states in the south and the west, and *not* get this country involved in any kind of foreign war. I know as well as you do that if Arabian oil isn't on tap in five years' time that this country will grind to a standstill. But that doesn't matter – what matters is for America to get through the next five weeks, then the next five months and *then*, and only then, the next five years and still be the United States at the end of it. You tell me about Middle East, I tell you about Chicago, Illinois and the Midwest, and the West Coast States. We've both got problems we can't make go away. That's the way it is." He vented a long, weary breath. "There is no *special relationship* between the old country and the United States. There might have been years ago, and now and then since the Second War but October 27th put an end to all that. You and I know that. Maybe we can trust each other enough in the future to avoid a shooting war. Maybe we ought to settle for that and build other bridges. I figured that you understood that. Isn't that why you wanted this conference?"

Margaret Thatcher nodded, remained silent.

"You *say* I owe you something," the President announced. "But that's not how this works. I think you understand that, too. What does that leave us? What it leaves us, is what do we have to trade because you and I badly need to sell whatever we do next to our own people?"

The woman got to her feet, crossed her arms across her chest and stood staring out to sea. Jack Kennedy joined her and the two leaders ruminated awhile.

"I stopped being *really* angry some months ago, Jack," Margaret Thatcher told her host. "The way things are there are far too many things to be angry about, and if one spent all one's time being angry one would never get anything important done." She hesitated. "Walter Brenckmann tells me that the Warren Commission is unlikely to 'get its act together' before the autumn?"

Jack Kennedy was not caught in any way unprepared by the woman's oblique question.

"Congress and the Senate are still wrangling over its terms of reference," the man said a little wryly.

"I'm reliably informed that Chief Justice Warren will be obliged to attempt to call witnesses from the United Kingdom? In the interests of *balance?*"

"You are well informed, Margaret."

The man and the woman gazed south to where the USS Southerland was slowly turning onto an easterly leg of its patrol. Onshore it remained balmy, out at sea white horses danced across the iron grey waters.

"My team," she continued, "and your people have been talking, in the main, about the economic and fiscal realities of the post-October War World. The United States, the United Kingdom and the wider Commonwealth are natural trading partners and the re-establishment of 'normal' commercial and industrial relations between us all as soon as possible is in everybody's best interests. However, the global financial system remains at death's door; American banks are virtually bankrupt, the American economy is in the process of falling off the edge of a cliff and the lack of liquidity – of any liquidity – means nobody can possibly get back to *business as normal*. Even the most diehard 'America Firster' understands that it is in his or her best interest to sell things to the greater part of humanity; including that part of humanity that resides outside the continental borders of the United States. Our treasury people have been talking about how that might be achieved. Our foreign affairs people have been talking about the framework of World diplomacy in the years to come in the absence of re-constituting the United Nations. Our transportation people have been talking about re-connecting the World. But none of that happens without a second Marshall Plan, hard cash and lots of it to enable *me* to begin the reconstruction work at home."

Jack Kennedy nodded, looked to the woman with smiling eyes.

"My people don't understand how you can be so focused on economic, monetary and *reconstruction* matters at a time like this, Margaret?"

The woman shrugged.

Then met his look with unblinking intensity.

"I will draw a line in the sand, Jack," she said very quietly. "*We* will at the very least halt the Soviets at the Saudi Arabian border. Hopefully, we and our *other* allies, a coalition of the willing as it were, will hold that line in the sand until America comes to its senses."

"What if America doesn't come to its senses?"

Margaret Thatcher's expression became a little vexed.

"I will hold that line in the sand and someday America *will* come to its senses; or you and your successors will regret it for all time, Jack."

Her conviction stopped him dead in his tracks.

There was no flexibility, no possibility of taking a step back. The line in the sand had been drawn and that was where she planned to stand regardless of the cost.

"Okay, you want a new Marshall Plan?"

"I thought we'd call it the *Fulbright Plan*."

"Okay..."

"We get the *Fulbright Plan*, American companies are allowed back into the United Kingdom and eventually, as the continent begins to recover, Western Europe," she frowned, "although not France, the way things are at the moment. We will put aside all discussions relating to our future military *alignment*. Providing, that is, the *Fulbright Plan* is launched in the next few weeks..."

Jack Kennedy held up a hand, which she ignored.

"The US Treasury can underwrite long-term loans from American banks to the UAUK which will, in turn, be converted into joint UK-US Government bonds, gilts, at the end of their term. In accounting terms this will equate to a massive asset injection into the vulnerable balance sheets of America's largest financial institutions; which in turn should allow them to begin to start lending again to customers in the United States. The Fulbright Plan will begin to pump hundreds of millions of dollars back into the US economy, and coincidentally, American consumer's pockets in time for the November Presidential election. I am reliably informed that you can instruct your Treasury to make the necessary executive orders to certain key 'strategic financial institutions' under the existing 'War Emergency Powers' vested in your person. I'm sure that Congress will object but there isn't enough time between now and November left for them to impeach you. And besides, there are several things that I can do which will greatly strengthen your re-election campaign."

"*Jericho* won't get me re-elected, Margaret."

To the man's astonishment Margaret Thatcher smiled. Instantly, she shed half-a-dozen years, and her eyes shone with the light of battle.

"Don't be so sure about that, Jack," she retorted. GCHQ had only been able to decipher a tiny proportion of historic intercepts and other traffic collected in the last two months; it simply did not have the capacity to handle the great mass of signals. The National Security Agency in Maryland possessed exponentially greater resources, when it got its hands on *Jericho* it would be *amazed*. "In any event, I am *giving* you *Jericho* as a token of good will to do with as you please. Give me the Fulbright Plan and I'll give you some other things you can use to beat your opponents over the head with!"

Jack Kennedy raised an eyebrow, his heart pounding.

"It goes against the grain," the woman went on, "but I can *normalise* the UAUK's relations with the Irish Republic with a stroke of the pen. It goes without saying that I would expect authorities on this side of the Atlantic to actively combat the smuggling of weapons and other contraband to Ireland."

The man waited, for the first time realising that the British Prime Minister was about to work her way down his own wish list.

"The proposed diplomatic mission to the West Coast Confederation will be the *only* high profile UAUK *mission* in the United States apart from the Embassy in Philadelphia. The UAUK will undertake not to entertain diplomatic representatives from any individual State in the Union, or enter into any state-specific trade or other agreement."

"I can announce that?"

"Yes. Moreover, at a time of your choice my government will welcome *your* statesmanlike intervention to act as an honest broker between the Argentine Republic and the United Kingdom over the war in the South Atlantic."

"Are you actually prepared to negotiate over the status of the Falklands?"

"No. But if the Argentine withdraws its forces without harming British citizens and provides full information as to the fate of members of the garrison, the war may end in due course."

"What else are you *offering* me, Margaret?"

"When Chief Justice Warren applies to the UAUK for British witnesses to testify before his Commission into the Causes and the Conduct of the Cuban Missiles War, I will veto those requests on the basis that it would be inappropriate for British officials to be in the limelight in the middle of an election."

The President thought about it.

"The affair of the USS Scorpion is still unresolved," he said, thinking aloud.

The Prime Minister nodded.

"The log of HMS Dreadnought and all relevant sonar and operational data will be made available to the Joint House Committee investigating the sad loss of the Scorpion. Royal Navy officers will make themselves available for interview under oath by members of that Committee *in England* at the Committee's convenience."

"This is going to get brutal, Margaret," Jack Kennedy declared, his drawl a friendly, pleasant contrast to the starkness of the political consequences of this 'private chat' on the porch of his father's old summer house.

"Give me the Fulbright Plan and you can tear me to shreds in public, Jack. Paint me as 'angry' and 'unreasonable', or just plain 'pig-headed'. If the worst comes to the worst, we can conduct bad-tempered transatlantic megaphone diplomacy. I don't care. Just give me the Fulbright Plan and I'll fight *our* war in the Middle East."

The President of the United States of America sucked his teeth.

Nobody would believe a word of this if he recounted this conversation in his memoires. Heck, he would not believe it himself!

The Angry Widow had just given him a shot at getting re-elected in the fall. Honest to God; he had not seen that coming.

Jack Kennedy offered his right hand; Margaret Thatcher shook it.

The man and the woman viewed each other warily.

Each asking themselves if they had just made some kind of Faustian pact which would later be their undoing...

Chapter 58

Friday 5th June 1964
HMS Alliance, 14 miles WSW of Ajaccio, Corsica

The two French destroyers had slowed, like two thoroughbreds after a long gallop, to a relative canter as they neared the Bay of Ajaccio. Clearly, they were timing their arrival in their home port for the middle of the day; no doubt expecting a heroes' welcome. The two approaching warships, identified as the Surcouf and the Cassard, had been sighted by a Royal Air Force Canberra flying out of Malta around sunset last night. HMS Alliance had been ordered to close in to the coast to maximise the chance of intercepting the murderers.

Lieutenant-Commander Francis Barrington stepped across the control room to study the slowly developing attack plot. If the enemy held their present course and speed, it would be less than an hour before they were in range of the four heavyweight Mark VIII torpedoes loaded in Alliance's forward torpedo tubes, or the Mark VIII and the single Mark XX passive-seeker acoustic homing torpedoes ready and primed in the boat's two stern tubes.

Having only 'dropped' the snorkelling tube and switched to battery power less than an hour ago the atmosphere in the boat was still fresh, albeit tainted with the dubious aromas of hydraulic oil, other lubricants and the as yet only vague hint of rotting vegetables and perspiration.

Alliance had actually been submerged for seven straight days, closed up on electric motors during daylight and running with the snorkelling tube – or 'snork' – raised to run on her diesels and to re-charge her electric batteries at night. Insofar as anybody on board knew, she had not been sighted and her presence remained unsuspected by the small French squadron based in Ajaccio. The night before last Alliance had crept to within two miles of the entrance to the harbour; the locals had been having some kind of firework display. Possibly, they had been celebrating their 'victory' off Algiers.

Francis Barrington did not have a lot of time for an enemy with whom one was not actually at war who launched a sneak attack, and neither did any other man on board the old, albeit somewhat modernised, Amphion class submarine.

The Amphions had been the last class of Royal Navy submarines laid down during the Second World War, although only two of the sixteen boats eventually commissioned – Amphion and Astute – had actually been launched before the end of hostilities. They were designed as long-range versions of the previous 'V' class, ostensibly intended to fight in the Pacific. After 1945, thirty of the forty-six boats ordered were cancelled and the remainder variously modified in one or two, sometimes three phases over the years to incorporate World War II lessons, new equipment based on captured advanced German U-boat plans and hulls, and the great strides which had been made in electronics and sonar technology since the end of Hitler's war. The Amphions were the Royal Navy's last class of 'submersibles' – vessels that operated best on the surface but which could also operate beneath the surface – rather than true 'submarines' like the boats of the later Porpoise and Oberon classes which could stay submerged with relative ease for long periods, and operate almost as effectively underwater as above.

Therefore, even with the 'snork' up Alliance was of that generation of Royal Navy submarines that became ranker and her combat efficiency progressively compromised, the longer she was on 'war' patrol.

For all that, with her modern sonar and a ninety percent charge in her batteries HMS Alliance was nobody's pushover.

"We will hold at six-zero feet for another thirty minutes before we come up for a quick look around, Number One," Francis Barrington informed his executive officer, twenty-four-year-old Lieutenant Michael Philpott.

The younger man repeated back the instructions.

"We seem to have a knack of being in the right place at the right time," Alliance's Commanding Officer observed ruefully.

Philpott chuckled.

Two months ago, Alliance had accepted the surrender of a Turkish destroyer off Malta and inadvertently captured a pile of Soviet code books and cipher machines. For her temerity Alliance had been quarantined in Lazaretto Creek at Malta for nearly three weeks before re-provisioning and oiling for the current war cruise.

If Michael Philpott had had any lingering misgivings about 'the skipper' before the Battle of Malta, they had been swept away in the last couple of months; the man had an uncanny unflappability and a grace under pressure that rubbed off on everybody around him. Nothing got under his skin, he never raised his voice; he was the crew's 'skipper' and father figure.

"There's time for everybody to have a hot drink and a sandwich before we start hunting in earnest," Barrington decided, pushing back his cap on his balding pate.

Life was full of surprises. Yesterday was his forty-third birthday. He had been a reservist – a solicitor's clerk in an English county town, Winchester in Hampshire - for over fourteen years by the time of the October War and had only been called back to the colours as late as last autumn. The last time he had been in Mediterranean waters it had been as a terrified sub-lieutenant on an old U-class boat – the Unbroken – but at least he had known who was trying to kill him in those days. These days, who knew? Red Dawn? The old Soviet Union? The Turks? *The Americans*? Sicilian and Algerian pirates and smugglers? And now the French!

Alliance had been operating in the waters west of Corsica for the last seventeen days. Barrington had used this time to methodically observe the habits and the courses steered by the sporadic traffic entering and leaving Ajaccio, and clinging close to the western coast of the big island. It was the knowledge he had gleaned that gave him a high degree of confidence that he had placed Alliance in the optimum position to intercept the two returning destroyers. It was a confidence buoyed by the fact that while he had been in these waters, he had detected only negligible sonar activity, and no indication whatsoever that the French Squadron bottled up in Ajaccio had any notion that it was under surveillance.

Ever since the 'Provisional Government' somewhere in southern France had broadcast a warning for aircraft not to overfly its territory – back around the time of the Battle of Malta – the boats of the 1st Submarine Squadron based in Lazaretto and Msida Creeks at Malta had been re-tasked to patrol in the Western rather than the Eastern Mediterranean. The US Navy had a pair of nuclear attack submarines somewhere at large in the east and the bellicose noises coming out of Clermont-Ferrand had found new work for the otherwise idle Amphions. Alliance's sisters Alderney and Auriga, both recently arrived in theatre from England, were loitering respectively in the Gulf of Lions watching over Marseilles and Toulon, and patrolling the waters off the Côte d'Azur.

The general intelligence picture in the north western Mediterranean Basin prior to the arrival of the Amphions had been distinctly 'spotty'. For example, although it was known that there was trade between Corsica, Sardinia and the Balearic Islands to the east, it was not known if this went on with or without the sanction of Franco's government in Madrid, or whether there was any contact or co-operation between Spanish and former French, or Italian naval units based at ports like Ajaccio on Corsica, or Cagliari on Sardinia.

RAF photo-reconnaissance flights and the activities of the 1st Submarine Squadron were slowly filling in some of the gaps in the picture, establishing that parts of the Mediterranean coast of France had been completely devastated, while others, like St Tropez and Nice in the east and Perpignan in the west were undamaged. The Alderney and the Auriga had recently confirmed that the ports of Marseilles and Toulon, both hard hit during the war were partially navigable, and that several as yet unidentified 'large' surface warships were anchored in the inner harbour of the latter.

As always, the Senior Service was running to keep up!

Francis Barrington assumed similar 'watches' to those which had been instituted in recent weeks by the Amphions in the Western Mediterranean would have been urgently commenced on the supposedly devastated Atlantic Brittany and Biscay ports of France, and now and then, high altitude photo and ELINT – electronic intelligence – sorties were being flown over or in the vicinity of other similar previously neglected 'places of interest' on the French mainland.

"SUBMERGED CONTACT BEARING ZERO-THREE-FIVE!"

Barrington's thoughts crystallised in an instant.

"Stop both! Pass the word for silent routine!"

Chapter 59

Friday 5th June 1964
RAF Brize Norton, Oxfordshire, England

Airey Neave took the Prime Minister's arm and leaned close to speak confidentially into her ear the moment he greeted her at the foot of the steps as she disembarked from the RAF Comet 4. His friend looked tired after her overnight flight back to England, and he completely understood how she must be dreading the reception that awaited her in Oxford where the Commons was already gathering to unleash its inchoate anger and scorn upon her head.

"I'm sorry, Margaret," he whispered, "but I have some very bad news. Normally, I'd have given you a chance to catch your breath but this won't wait."

The Prime Minister's stride faltered.

"Who have we lost?" She asked simply in the manner of one who has already been robbed of too many loved ones, friends and close colleagues by the cruel fates of this brave new post-cataclysm world.

"Iain," Airey Neave said. "Iain Macleod died last night. We all knew he was unwell. He was at his desk around midnight. They think he had a massive heart attack or perhaps, a stroke. There was nothing anybody could do for him. I'm sorry..."

Momentarily, Margaret Thatcher was afraid she was going to faint. The moment passed, leaving her feeling a little sick and nauseas and oddly...*afraid.*

Iain Macleod had been the living embodiment of one nation Conservatism before the October War, and after it the intellectual wellspring of both Edward Heath's and her own administrations. With Airey Neave, Iain Macleod had been her rock. He had been Leader of the House of Commons, the Chairman of the Conservative and Unionist Party and the government's tireless propagandist and apologist as her Secretary of State for Information. It had been Iain Macleod's behind the scenes manoeuvring that had handed her the premiership, and without his advice, support and patience she would have fallen flat on her face a score of times in the last six months.

How can I carry on?

Instantly, the Prime Minister picked up her pace and hardened her face.

"Poor Evelyn," she murmured. "Is somebody with her?"

Iain Macleod had met Evelyn Hester Mason, *née* Blois in September 1939 while he was awaiting his call up when Evelyn had interviewed him for a job as a volunteer ambulance driver. Later, after her first husband had been killed in the war they had married in January 1941. Neither of the Macleod's children, a son and a daughter, had survived the October War and its immediate aftermath; twenty-year-old Torquil having disappeared on the night of the war and Diana, having died aged eighteen – probably from cholera - the following February. It was a miracle that in this unkind age Evelyn, who had been afflicted by meningitis and polio at the age of thirty-three in 1952, had survived to outlive her husband.

"Pat Harding-Grayson has been with Evelyn since Iain's body was discovered."

"Good. What else has gone wrong since yesterday?"

"The Chiefs of Staff are up in arms over 'surrendering' *Jericho*," her friend reported grimly. "That's par for the course, I suppose. I think President Kennedy's address to the American people announcing that we'd quote 'backed down over Ireland and invited the US to broker a peace deal in the South Atlantic', and the inference that JFK had basically wiped the floor with us, well, *you* specifically, at Hyannis Port came too late for most of the papers, thank God! It goes without saying that we're being accused of being the greatest traitors since dear old Neville Chamberlain. Enoch Powell and that blighter Michael Foot have already been on the radio this morning talking about Munich, appeasement and 'peace in our time'. As we anticipated there is an EDM," in Parliamentary parlance an *Early Day Motion*, "before the House calling for another Vote of Confidence." The man groaned out aloud. "It's much worse than any of us imagined it would be, Margaret. And now poor Iain's gone..."

Airey Neave had walked on a further two paces before he realised he was alone. He looked around.

"No, Airey," Margaret Thatcher said with a school mistress like note of censure in her voice, "it is *exactly* as bad as *I knew it was going to be*. No, I did not anticipate that we would be at war with the bloody French when I left for America a few days ago, or that we'd lose Iain last night. But I did anticipate that things would be unbelievably bloody this morning. We're about to fight a war in the Middle East we cannot win. The country is bankrupt. We cannot afford to feed our people next winter and the Red Army is about to turn off our oil supplies. Things simply cannot be allowed to go on the way they have been going ever since the night of the October War. Either we make a break from that past or we are doomed. As we discussed before I went to Cape Cod, if the price of doing the right thing and getting the best possible deal for our children is *my* head, then that is a price well worth paying!"

Airey Neave stared at his protégé, peripherally aware that the other members of the 'Hyannis Port' delegation were disembarking from the Comet and giving both him and the Prime Minister very strange looks.

Margaret Thatcher swept past her friend and he scurried to catch up with her before she got to the first of the two armoured Rolls-Royce's waiting on the tarmac to carry the senior members of the returning transatlantic mission back to Oxford.

The Prime Minister's Royal Marine bodyguard had formed a broad tunnel directing the two politicians towards the cars. The Angry Widow's Praetorians were particularly grim-faced this morning, as if they were looking for somebody to shoot.

If anybody in Oxford was stupid enough to think that Margaret Thatcher was about to bow to pressure and quit, or in any way go *quietly*, they had another thing coming to them!

Chapter 60

Friday 5th June 1964
The British Embassy, Wister Park, Philadelphia

Lady Marija Christopher dispensed with any pretence at decorum instantly she spied her husband at the foot of the stairs in the lobby of the Embassy. She could hear the jeering and chanting of the big crowd outside the high, razor-wire topped wall of the Embassy and had watched the bottles and bricks flying through the air, crashing onto the roofs and the bullet-proof windows of the battered cavalcade returning from the airport.

"Peter!" She screeched ecstatically and flew down the stairs. Given her propensity to lose her balance and fall flat on her face when she tried to hurry, let alone run, this was an insanely reckless thing for a woman in her condition to do. Or it would have been had she not been absolutely convinced that if she fell her husband would surely catch her. This was pretty much what happened.

"Careful! Careful!" Her husband pleaded, but only after he had wrapped his wife in his arms. He would have made a much bigger thing of 'being careful' had he not been too busy hugging and kissing the woman who was the love of his life. Presently, he became aware that he and Marija were blocking the stairs.

"Oh, dear," he sighed, leading Marija BACK upstairs. "The natives outside seem to be unusually restive today!"

That morning's 'demonstration' seemed angrier and hugely better attended than the usual 'rent a mob' affairs that increasingly greeted official events and meetings attended by senior embassy staff in and around Philadelphia. The surging crowds along the road in front of the compound were waving particularly offensive placards, mainly on the themes of 'GO HOME BRITS!', demands to cease 'the Irish genocide', and various invitations to 'get your hands off our oil'. Peter had thought this last was a bit rich coming from citizens of this particular gas-guzzling land. The chanting had been vitriolic and apparently, organised, as had the hurling of missiles at the vehicles in the convoy from the airport.

"I think they are all crazy in this city," his wife concurred but as always, without malice. "Well, some of the people. Tell me everything!"

This had to wait a few minutes because Rosa Hannay tripped down the first-floor corridor to peck the homecoming hero's cheek – a feat only made practical because Peter Christopher bent his head down and Rosa literally jumped up on the tips of her toes. Alan Hannay, more prosaically, shook his friend's hand. Together the two couples retired to a day room overlooking parkland to the rear of the Embassy.

"I went sailing with President Kennedy," Peter announced. "We talked about the Navy, his and ours. Oh, and we're all going to

California. I'm to be some kind of special 'Consul' to the West Coast Confederation."

"California?" Marija laughed. She was suddenly delving into the folds of her frock. She produced an official looking envelope and brandished the letter within. "Margo left me a big house in San Francisco! This is a letter from her lawyers in New York. She left everything she owned on Malta and some stocks and War Bonds she'd left with a bank in Boston to the St Catherine's Hospital for Women, but according to her will she left me her old house at 1217 Haight Street, San Francisco because 'Marija will enjoy travelling'.

Peter blinked thoughtfully as he took this in. He and Marija had settled close together on a sofa while the Hannays had pulled up two padded chairs to face them across a low coffee table. He unconsciously patted his wife's left knee and she instantly took the opportunity to seize his right hand and clasp it to herself.

"So," the man checked, "it now transpires that I'm married to a woman of property?"

"The lawyers say Margo's younger brother, John, has been living at the house but he seems to have disappeared. It sounds a little mysterious to me. Anyway, if we're going to California we can visit," she checked the address again, "1217 Haight Street. It'll be fun!"

Peter nodded absent-mindedly. He was struggling to adjust to 'normality'. He had spent much of the last three days watching a British Prime Minister writing the longest and most comprehensive political suicide note in history. She had been doing the right thing for all the right reasons and yet, her own people would almost certainly crucify her when she got home.

Less than a hundred yards away in the road in front of the Embassy there was a baying mob, gloating over Jack Kennedy's self-proclaimed humiliation of the 'old country'; and back in England Margaret Thatcher would shortly be confronting another, possibly crueller and even more unforgiving *Parliamentary* mob, baying for her blood. And yet here he was, reunited with his wife and his friends contemplating, quite literally, several balmy seasons in the sun in distant California.

It was as if the war in the Middle East was nothing to do with him; or as if the fall of the shooting star which had been Margaret Thatcher's premiership was happening in another, disconnected world. A small voice in the back of his mind warned him against writing off the Angry Widow. Nothing in her demeanour last night at Otis Air National Guard Base had given him any inkling that *she* planned to meekly accept her supposedly *inevitable* downfall back in England. If he had learned anything from the whirlwind rollercoaster ride of the last few months it was that when all was said and done, they lived in a funny old World.

He glanced ruefully to his wife and his friends.

"Yes, it will be fun," he agreed. "I think we all deserve a little of that."

Chapter 61

Friday 5th June 1964
HMS Alliance, 5 miles west of Capu di Muru, Corsica

The French submarine had clattered across the Alliance's bow at a distance of about a mile-and-a-half, surfacing twenty minutes later as it entered the southern reach of the Gulf of Ajaccio.

Lieutenant-Commander Francis Barrington had let the noisy gate crasher go on her way unmolested; he had other, bigger fish to fry. Creeping along at barely four knots, he had worked Alliance closer to the coast guessing that the two T-47 class destroyers approaching from the south west would steer almost directly towards Capu di Muru and then use it as a navigational way point to enter the broad sweep of the great natural harbour to the north.

Unlike the French submarine which had announced its presence from afar, Alliance's most recent refit and modernisation had streamlined her hull and significantly quietened her machinery. Already a quiet boat when she was running on electric motors with all inessential equipment turned off, she could be, given helpful sea conditions – today there was a light chop running on the surface – like a wraith, deathly quiet at low speeds.

Neither of the oncoming French destroyers was using active sonar.

And helpfully, they were steaming very nearly in line ahead.

If Barrington had been in command of either of those ships – given that they had committed an act of war against a powerful foe with a long and vengeful sword arm – *he* would have been zigzagging as if his life depended upon it right now. The Mediterranean was a big sea and it was axiomatic to Barrington that the place one's new enemies would come to look for one was at one's home port; therefore, until he was safe inside the anti-torpedo booms which he presumed protected the inner harbour of Ajaccio, he would have been pinging his active sonar like mad and manoeuvring erratically so as to make it as hard as possible for anybody to compute a firing solution.

However, this was not apparently how the modern French Navy comported itself.

"RANGE TO FIRST TARGET TWO THOUSAND FIVE HUNDRED YARDS. MARK THIS BEARING!"

The plot confirmed the angle on the bow and fed the information into the torpedo director.

"RANGE TO TARGET NUMBER TWO THREE THOUSAND YARDS. MARK THIS BEARING!"

The periscope slid down into its well.

Lieutenant Michael Philpott updated the plot.

"They've come up to fourteen knots, sir."

Francis Barrington nodded.

The bastards wanted to cut a dash when they steamed into the Gulf of Ajaccio!

"UP PERISCOPE!"

Again, Barrington took a range and bearing for each target and dipped the periscope head beneath the waves.

"Targets have steadied at fourteen knots, sir."

"Very good. Open tubes one to four. I plan to 'air' the attack periscope again in," he checked his watch, "thirty seconds. We'll take final ranges and bearings and shoot as soon as the torpedo director calculates a firing solution. Your target will be the leading ship, Number One. Minimum spread."

Once Alliance's Mark VIIIs were on their way, he would reverse course and bring the boat's stern tubes to bear on the second destroyer. Hopefully, by the time the stern fish were away the crew in the forward torpedo room would have had time to reload one, perhaps two of the bow tubes.

Periscope up.

"RANGE!"

"BEARING!"

The targets' course and speed were unchanged.

The firing solution was computed.

There was a short, breathless delay.

'Firing solution confirmed, skipper," Michael Philpott reported.

"FIRE ONE!"

"FIRE TWO!"

"FIRE THREE!"

"FIRE FOUR!"

"Helm. Ten degrees left rudder, if you please!

"ALL FISH ARE RUNNING TRUE, SIR!"

The Mark VIIIs were in the water; there was nothing more that Francis Barrington or anybody else on the Alliance could do about them, other than wait for the first detonations.

The control room talker was counting down the time to impact as the submarine turned to present her two loaded stern tubes to the still, as yet, unsuspecting targets.

"Steady on two-seven-zero degrees," Barrington ordered the helmsman, his tone calmly conversational. "Wheel amidships." Then quietly to Michael Philpott. "Tell me when were level at sixty feet please."

As soon as the sound of underwater explosions rumbled across the mile of sea between the T-47s and the Alliance, Barrington planned to 'air' the attack periscope to take another periscope range and bearing to reset the torpedo director.

Francis Barrington waited patiently.

A Mark VIII torpedo was a beast of a weapon. Weighing in at over a ton-and-a-half, with a speed of over forty knots and tipped with an eight-hundred-pound Torpex warhead it was a proven ship-killer. Two of the four fish in the first salvo had been set to run at ten feet with contact detonators, two were set to run at twenty feet with magnetic exploders. The shallow running fish would hit a thin-skinned target like a destroyer like an express train, probably bursting into and exploding deep within the hull. The deeper running magnetic-fused fish would, if they exploded beneath a ship's hull, break its back.

"Level at sixty feet, skipper!"

The sound of a single heavy explosion pulsed through the water.

Francis Barrington resisted the urge to punch the air with elation; he waited for a second detonation. When it did not come, he stepped to the periscope.

"UP PERISCOPE!"

Chapter 62

Friday 5th June 1964
The House of Commons, King's College, Oxford

Enoch John Powell, the Honourable Member for Wolverhampton South West was no more than a shadow of his former self. With his ruined face atop an emaciated, pain-wracked body he cut an increasingly sad, outcast figure. He had waited patiently, like a horribly mauled big cat gathering his strength to lash out one last time at his tormentors.

He had listened with disinterest to the leader of the putative *Independent Labour Party's* excoriating condemnation of the Unity Administration of the United Kingdom's record. Michael Foot, the wild-haired, passionate, well-meaning and profoundly decent man around whom the disaffected rump of the old Labour and Co-operative Party had coalesced in the spring, was, in Powell's view not so much an idealist or a national leader in waiting but a dangerously naive fool. An idealistic innocent who did not understand that the real danger to the UAUK and to Margaret Thatcher lay not on the opposition benches in the House of Commons, but from within the body of her own supporters. In years past he would have had a better feel for which of the Prime Ministers 'loyal' colleagues and key 'parliamentary friends' was – like Brutus - planning to strike the first blow.

"Mister Powell!" The Speaker called.

The chamber fell silent as the terribly wounded parliamentary beast slowly rose to his feet and his good eye fell upon the faces of men who had once been his friends and allies, who were watching him now with mistrust and no little despite. That was to be expected, even in times such as these the Conservative Party honestly believed it had a right to govern.

Why then would it forgive a turncoat such as he?

"Tributes," Enoch Powell declared, his voice afflicted these days by a hoarseness that added a desperate gravitas to his words, "tributes have been paid to my old friend Iain Macleod. That he and I became adversaries will be a great sadness to me the rest of my days. Those days will be short, I am sure, but I sincerely grieve for my old friend nonetheless. This House has lost one of its greatest sons and I know not when we will see his like again."

For the first time he fixed his stare on the prim, tight-lipped face of the Prime Minister. Enoch Powell had noted how tired and thin the lady seemed; unlike others on his side of the House he had not made the mistake of thinking, for a single moment, that the Angry Widow was in any way a spent force. However, it would have been unnatural had she not been reflecting upon the disasters of recent months.

"I shall not attend this House again," Powell stated. "My time has come and gone, like that of other members of this House."

Behind him men jeered at the government benches across the

chamber.

Enoch Powell slowly rounded on the noisiest of the hecklers. "Have you no pride?" He asked angrily, bitterly. His disdain was professorially scathing, his contempt for the dour men and women clustered around Michael Foot and his acolytes icy. "What manner of fool seeks to take Party advantage of a nation's catastrophes?"

When there was a muttering of support from the government benches his manner was, if possible, even more contemptuous.

"In May 1940 this House met to debate the fiasco of the Norwegian Campaign. That debate, sometimes called the 'Narvik Debate', led to the fall of one Prime Minister and the elevation of the man who eventually led this nation out of the slough of despond to victory."

In April 1940 the 'Phoney War' in Europe had ended when German troops had conquered Norway; the British government's attempts to hold back the German tide had been – a particularly bloody naval victory at the port of Narvik apart – shambolic and ended in humiliating withdrawal. Two days after the 'Narvik Debate', Hitler had invaded France and the Low Countries, and within weeks only the 'miracle of Dunkirk' had prevented the United Kingdom from losing the war. Every member of the House of Commons had lived through that war, and some had actually been in the House during the two days of that debate. The Conservative government of Neville Chamberlain had, in parliamentary terms, prevailed in the end with its majority of two hundred cut to eighty-one but thirty-nine Conservatives had voted against their own ministers. There had been no subsequent vote of confidence in the government; everybody had simply understood that things could not be allowed to go on the way they had been 'going on' since the outbreak of war in September 1939. Chamberlain, the man who had proclaimed 'peace in our time' less than two years before, had had to go.

"I believe that we have reached a latter day 'Narvik' moment," Enoch Powell said. He knew his strength was failing him, as did everybody in the House of Commons. The quietness had settled around the man whom admirers and detractors alike regarded as one of the last of the great, pre-October War parliamentarians. It was as if everybody recognised that now was a time of listening before the failing of the light. "I do not believe, in my heart," the dying man continued, "that this is a time for grandiloquent rhetorical excess. I think that this is a time for us to look into our hearts and to speak plainly to each other."

The man's laboured breath was audible in every corner of the great Hall of King's College.

"Our armed forces are fighting three wars; in the Mediterranean, in the South Atlantic, and if not already, then soon, in the Persian Gulf. We are strong nowhere; in the Mediterranean we may, or may not be able to rely on the United States for support and succour, and in the Gulf the brave men from distant lands of the Commonwealth. But make no mistake, we are very nearly alone. We are at the limits of our endurance. Now we find ourselves the object of the scorn of the

President of the United States of America; forced to go cap in hand to the global bullyboy to ask for charity, crumbs from Jack Kennedy's table, a beggar's dole and like Oliver Twist, we are chastised for asking for 'more'! Are we not entitled to ask how our great nation has stumbled into this mess?"

Margaret Thatcher was buffeted by a rising groundswell of muttered, rumbling discontent that seemed to swirl around her as if she was in the eye of a vortex of rage pent up too long to be safely defused.

"In the course of the Narvik Debate my late colleague in this House, Leo Amery," Enoch Powell continued, struggling to be heard, "spoke of Oliver Cromwell's words to that renowned parliamentarian and roundhead captain John Hampden, of the need to find new men to confound their foes. *The fault is not in our people or in our way of life, there is nothing written in our stars that inevitably infers our downfall.* As Cromwell said to Hampden, *'we are fighting to-day for our life, for our liberty, for our all; we cannot go on being led as we are'*."

Margaret Thatcher sat rigidly still on the hard front bench pew.

She knew what was coming and there was nothing she could do about it.

"It is with sadness that I must repeat what Cromwell said to the Long Parliament," Enoch Powell hissed, his ruined voice betraying him, "when he decided that it had outlived its usefulness."

Margaret Thatcher looked up, braving the gaze of her nemesis.

Enoch Powell returned her gaze; but without triumphalism, only regret.

"*You have sat too long here for any good you have been doing, madam.*" He sighed hurtfully, swayed unsteadily prompting several members nearby to flinch towards him lest he fell before he straightened, brokenly to deliver the coup de grace. "*Depart,*" he whispered, exhausted now, "*depart I say, and let us have done with you. In the name of God, go...*"

Chapter 63

Friday 5th June 1964
Dammam, Saudi Arabia

It was as if the air itself was being torn apart. The livid flash of the great explosion lit up the night beyond the port. There was one great explosion and then a roiling, rolling expanding accompaniment of smaller, secondary detonations spreading out across the desert and into the suburbs of the Dammam-Dhahran port conurbation stretching along the shore of the Persian Gulf.

Rear Admiral Nicholas Davey had been enjoying a cigarette at the stern rail of his flagship, HMS Tiger as the cruiser prepared to anchor in the shallow waters off Ras Tanura beach. The presence of so many 'foreigners' in Dammam had been causing friction with the locals and two days ago he had taken every seaworthy vessel under his command to sea. Most of the flotilla was still some way off shore, learning to work as 'a flotilla'; Tiger had brought him back towards Dammam as evening fell.

In the morning the flagship was entertaining dignitaries from the Saudi government on board and the plan was for the cruiser to sail into port with flags flying, and her decks dressed fit for a Royal Review. However, as he looked landward the Flag Officer ABNZ – Australian, British and New Zealand – Squadron, Persian Gulf, suspected that the plans for tomorrow morning had just been torn up.

His first thought was that it had been a tactical, Hiroshima-scale nuclear strike. But that was wrong; he would have been blind by now if it had been.

What had happened was that the US War Stores Depot in the dessert west of Dammam had blown up; and was continuing to blow up as the flashover of big explosions set in motion a chain reaction in adjacent stores.

Nick Davey threw his half-smoked cigarette over the side as the cruiser's klaxons blared; ordering the crew to battle stations.

Suddenly men were running everywhere and the ship was alive like a hornets' nest inadvisably prodded with a stick. Under his feet he felt the screws bite the water and the deck heel one, two, three degrees as Tiger's rudder went hard over.

Sea room!

Until it was established what was going on the priorities were to find sea room; and to clear the main battery 'A' arcs so that Tiger's whole broadside could be brought to bear on a potential threat. Farther out to sea the ship's radars would be uncluttered with ground returns from the nearby shore; better able to identify and track potential threats and to direct Tiger's automatic quick firing six-inch and three-inch guns.

By the time Nick Davey climbed up to the bridge most of the windows had been covered with steel shutters; standard drill to prevent nuclear strikes blinding the ship's command team.

Assuming that the air base at Dhahran remained operational the aircraft kept on permanent QRA ought to be airborne by now. The big explosions might be the result of sloppy munitions handling or storage, sabotage or direct enemy action.

"RAF Dhahran has *activated* emergency response Alpha-Alpha, sir," Nick Davey was informed calmly.

That meant a Gloster Meteor night fighter, one of the two Avro Vulcans – each armed with a four hundred kiloton Yellow Sun bomb – and two Hawker Hunter interceptors had been scrambled and the four Bristol Bloodhound long-range surface-to-air missiles sited on the air base had been spooled up ready for launch.

"CIC reports the threat board is clear, sir."

"The Centaur Battle Group is maintaining Air Defence Condition One, sir." Forty miles away the bulk of the ABNZ fleet was exercising as a battle, or support group for the aircraft carrier Centaur. Tiger's heightened state of alert had automatically been signalled to the carrier's CIC, mandating the upgrading of the whole Battle Group's state of readiness.

By now the alarms would have sounded in Abadan and in other headquarters in the region from Oman to Aden.

"Tell everybody that the Dammam War Stores Depot has blown up. Categorise the event as sabotage-related. Broadcast that now please," Nick Davey instructed the cruisers communications officer.

Tiger's Captain, forty-six-year-old Hardress Llewellyn 'Harpy' Lloyd, a cheerful, solidly professional officer who had earned a Distinguished Service Cross commanding MTB 34 in a fight with German E-Boats in the North Sea in August 1942, joined Davey as he studied the navigation plot.

The two men had got on famously from the moment Nick Davey had hoisted his flag on Tiger.

"Ten miles out should be enough to give us unrestricted all-round eyes on the sky and surrounding seas, sir," the younger man suggested quietly.

"Very good."

The two men regularly dined together and yarned about past battles, the idiocies of the peace time Royal Navy and any number of mutual friends and acquaintances, living and dead.

"It'll give us time to start detailing off parties to go on shore to assist the civilian authorities," Nick Davey thought out aloud. "Assuming the locals don't start blaming us for their misfortunes, that is."

"Triumph is reporting minor topside damage, sir!"

The old aircraft carrier, converted to the role of heavy repair ship – a mobile workshop in lieu of ports with suitable dry-docking or maintenance yards – was tied up alongside at Dammam.

"What about Retainer?"

The fourteen-thousand-ton Royal Fleet Auxiliary armament support ship the Retainer had offloaded munitions for ABNZ ground forces and set up a naval ordnance dump outside Kuwait City at the head of the Gulf, delivered ammunition for the guns of the Centurions and the Royal Artillery units guarding Abadan, and returned to Dammam only two days ago. In the coming week the ships of the ABNZ Squadron would come alongside the Retainer to top off their magazines depleted in the last fortnight's 'battle exercises'.

RFA Retainer was presently moored Tarout Bay.

"No word yet from Retainer, sir."

Nick Davey shrugged.

"She'd have been several hundred yards further from the big bang than Triumph," he observed.

That was when the flash from the second huge explosion lit up the entire bridge despite the fact that practically every window was blanked by a steel scuttle.

Chapter 64

Friday 5th June 1964
Blenheim Palace, Woodstock, Oxfordshire

Parliament had spoken. It had not spoken with a united voice but its mood had been unambiguously expressed in the tally of the votes.

Immediately after the vote her friends and colleagues had advised Margaret Thatcher to delay her visit to the Palace until the morning, to reflect overnight on the 'possibilities' of the situation and to consider her 'options' with a refreshed mind after having 'slept on matters'. However, as the armoured Prime Ministerial Bentley cruised through the darkened country lanes, the Prime Minister understood that nothing would change overnight; and that the brutal arithmetic of the House of Commons permitted her no leeway.

Lady Patricia Harding-Grayson had offered her a stiff drink before they set out on the short drive to Blenheim Palace; Margaret Thatcher had declined it. Her thoughts were hamstrung by weariness and despair; alcohol would have further blurred her perspectives and that risked doing Her Majesty a disservice in their forthcoming interview.

The House had divided two hundred and seventy-four against two hundred and six; voting by a majority of sixty-eight that it had lost confidence in her Unity Administration of the United Kingdom. She had survived three previous votes of confidence; today's battle had been a battle too far.

All political careers end in failure; everybody knew that.

In the next hour she would be presenting her resignation to the Queen.

"Thank you for coming with me at such short notice, Pat."

The older woman forced a smile. Normally a Prime Minister might expect to be accompanied on such desultory journeys by a spouse, or a partner; Margaret Thatcher had lost both, her husband on the night of the October War and a man who could have been her soul mate, Julian Christopher, in the Battle of Malta.

Both women knew that in the coming hours and days the UAUK was likely to tear itself to pieces, as Tory grandees who had never really been comfortable having to account for their actions to a mere woman, manoeuvred and connived - cheered on by Michael Foot's irresponsible, pacifist and defeatist *Independent* Labour Party - to replace her as first among equals.

Had there ever been a more unholy alliance in British politics than that of the country 'gentlemen' faction of the Tory Party and the socialist hardcore of the Labour Party?

"I wouldn't have missed it for the world, Margaret," Pat Harding-Grayson assured her friend.

The Prime Minister shook her head, and smiled a rueful smile. Earlier in the year re-calling Parliament had been her idea. Her friends and ministers had thought she was mad and who was to say that in strictly political parlance, they were wrong? But *she* had followed *her* instincts, done what *she* thought was right. If they wrote that on her gravestone, she could have no complaints.

Yes, it was a little galling to be hoist by one's own petard.

But no, actually she would not have changed a single thing.

"No," she concurred, "neither would I..."

[The End]

Author's Endnote

Thank you for reading this book; and secondly, please remember that this is a work of fiction. I made it up in my own head. None of the fictional characters in 'A Line in the Sand: The Gulf War of 1964 – Part 1' – Book 7 of the 'Timeline 10/27/62 Series' - is based on real people I know of, or have ever met. Nor do the specific events described in 'A Line in the Sand: The Gulf War of 1964: Part 1' – Book 7 of the 'Timeline 10/27/62 Series' - have, to my knowledge, any basis in real events I know to have taken place. Any resemblance to real life people or events is, therefore, unintended and entirely coincidental.

The *'Timeline 10/27/62 Series'* is an alternative history of the modern World and because of this, real historical characters are referenced and in many cases their words and actions form significant parts of the narrative. I have no way of knowing if these real, historical figures would have spoken thus, or acted in the ways I depict them acting. Any word I place in the mouth of a real historical figure, and any action which I attribute to them *after* 27th October 1962 *never* actually happened. As I always state – unequivocally - in my Author's Notes to my readers, *I made it all up in my own head.*

The books of the *Timeline 10/27/62 series* are written as episodes; they are instalments in a contiguous narrative arc. The individual 'episodes' each explore a number of plot branches while developing themes continuously from book to book. Inevitably, in any series some exposition and extemporization are unavoidable but I try – honestly, I do – to keep this to a minimum as it tends to slow down the flow of the stories I am telling.

In writing each successive addition to the *Timeline 10/27/62 'verse'* it is my implicit assumption that my readers will have read the previous books in the series, and that my readers do not want their reading experience to be overly impacted by excessive re-hashing of the events in those previous books.

Humbly, I suggest that if you are 'hooked' by the *Timeline 10/27/62 Series* that reading the books in sequence will – most likely - enhance your enjoyment of the experience.

———

As a rule, I let my books speak for themselves. I hope it does not sound fuddy-duddy or old-fashioned, but broadly speaking I tend towards the view that a book *should* speak for itself.

However, with your indulgence I would like briefly – well, as briefly as is possible without being overly terse – to share a few personal thoughts with you, the reader about *the Timeline 10/27/62 World*.

I was not yet seven-and-a-half years old in October 1962 when I realised my parents were paying an awful lot of attention to the radio, devouring every line of print in the daily newspaper and were not quite themselves, a little distracted in fact, now that I think about it. I heard the word 'Cuba' bandied about but did not know until much later that the most dangerous moment of my life had come and gone without my ever, as a child, knowing it.

I was not yet eight-and-a-half years old when one day in November 1963 the World around me came, momentarily, to a juddering halt. I had heard the name of John Fitzgerald Kennedy, and I even knew that he was the President of something called the United States of America. I did not know then that he was a womanising, drug addicted and deeply conflicted man who had lied to the American people about his chronic, periodically disabling illness which in any rational age ought to have disqualified him from the Presidency; *but I did know that he was a charismatic, talismanic figure in whom even I, as a child more interested in soccer, model trains and riding my new bicycle, had invested a nameless hope for the future.* And then one day he was gone and I shared my parents' shock and horror. It was not as if a mortal man had been murdered; JFK had become a mythic figure long before then. It was as if the modern-day analogue of King Menelaus of Sparta - hero of the Trojan Wars and the husband of Helen, she of the legendary face that launched a thousand ships - had been gunned down that day in Dallas.

The Cuban Missiles crisis and the death of a President taught a young boy in England in 1962 and 1963 that the World is a very dangerous place.

Many years later we learned how close we all came to the abyss in October 1962. Often, we look back on how deeply Jack Kennedy's death scarred hearts and minds in the years after his assassination.

There is no certainty, no one profound insight into what 'might have happened' had the Cold War turned *Hot* in the fall of 1962, or if JFK had survived that day in Dallas. History is not a systematic, explicable march from one event to another that inevitably reaches some readily predictable outcome. History only works that way in hindsight; very little is *obvious* either to the major or the minor players at the time history is actually being made. One does not have to be a fully paid-up chaos theoretician to know that apparently inconsequential small events can have massive unforeseen and unforeseeable impacts in subsequent historical developments.

I do not pretend to *know* what would have happened if the USA and the USSR had gone to war over Cuba in October 1962. One imagines this scenario has been the object of countless staff college war games in America and elsewhere in the intervening fifty-three years; I suspect that few of those war games would have played out the way the participants expected, and that no two *games* would have resolved themselves in exactly the same way as any other. That is the beauty and the fascination of historical counterfactuals, or as those of us who make no pretence at being emeritus professors of history say, *alternative history*.

Nobody can claim 'this is the way it would have been' after the Cuban Missiles Crisis 'went wrong'. This author only *speculates* that the Timeline 10/27/62 Series reflects one of the many ways 'things might have gone' in the aftermath of Armageddon.

The thing one can be reasonably confident about is that if the Cuban Missiles Crisis had turned into a shooting war the World in which we live today would, *probably*, not be the one with which we are familiar.

A work of fiction is a journey of imagination. I hope it does not sound corny but I am genuinely a little humbled by the number of people who have already bought into what I am trying to do with *Timeline 10/27/62*.

Like any author, this author would prefer everybody to enjoy his books – if I disappoint, I am truly sorry – but either way, thank you for reading and helping to keep the printed word alive. I really do believe that civilization depends on people like *you*.

Other Books by James Philip

Europa Reich

Book 1: Moonshot
Book 2: Olympiad

The New England Series

Book 1: Empire Day
Book 2: Two Hundred Lost Years
Book 3: Travels Through the Wind
Book 4: Remember Brave Achilles
Book 5: George Washington's Ghost
Book 6: Imperial Crisis
Book 7: The Lines of Laredo
Book 8: The Halls of Montezuma

Coming in 2022

Book 9: Islands in the Stream
Book 10: The Gathering Place

The Guy Winter Mysteries

Prologue: Winter's Pearl
Book 1: Winter's War
Book 2: Winter's Revenge
Book 3: Winter's Exile
Book 4: Winter's Return
Book 5: Winter's Spy
Book 6: Winter's Nemesis

The Bomber War Series

Book 1: Until the Night
Book 2: The Painter
Book 3: The Cloud Walkers

Until the Night Series

Part 1: Main Force Country – September 1943
Part 2: The Road to Berlin – October 1943
Part 3: The Big City – November 1943
Part 4: When Winter Comes – December 1943
Part 5: After Midnight – January 1944

The Harry Waters Series

Book 1: Islands of No Return
Book 2: Heroes
Book 3: Brothers in Arms

The Frankie Ransom Series

Book 1: A Ransom for Two Roses
Book 2: The Plains of Waterloo
Book 3: The Nantucket Sleighride

The Strangers Bureau Series

Book 1: Interlopers
Book 2: Pictures of Lily

The River House Chronicles Series

Book 1: Things Can Only Get better
Book 2: Consenting Adults
Book 3: All Swing Together
Book 4: The Honourable Member

NON-FICTION CRICKET BOOKS

FS Jackson
Lord Hawke

Cricket Books edited by James Philip

The James D. Coldham Series
[Edited by James Philip]

Books

Northamptonshire Cricket: A History [1741-1958]
Lord Harris

Anthologies

Volume 1: Notes & Articles
Volume 2: Monographs No. 1 to 8

Monographs

No. 1 - William Brockwell
No. 2 - German Cricket
No. 3 - Devon Cricket
No. 4 - R.S. Holmes
No. 5 - Collectors & Collecting
No. 6 - Early Cricket Reporters
No. 7 – Northamptonshire
No. 8 - Cricket & Authors

———————

Details of all James Philip's published books and
forthcoming publications can be found on his website www.jamesphilip.co.uk

———————

Cover artwork concepts by James Philip
Graphic Design by Beastleigh Web Design

Printed in Great Britain
by Amazon